The McDonald Saga
Book 1

Banners of Honor

By
Keith E. Stuart
Barbara Phillips Stuart

airleaf.com

This book is a work of fiction. Any resemblance to persons, living or dead, is coincidental.

© Copyright 2005, Barbara Stuart

All Rights Reserved.

No part of this book may be reproduced, stored in a retrieval system, or transmitted by any means, electronic, mechanical, photocopying, recording, or otherwise, without written permission from the author.

ISBN: 1-59453-659-7

PROLOGUE

THE GLEN OF WEEPING

In 1688, William took the throne of England and Scotland from James the Second. One year later, the Scottish Highlanders fought in an uprising in an attempt to return the throne to King James. The effort failed and once again, James was defeated.

In August 1691, King William, who was now well entrenched on the throne, was feeling very generous. He offered amnesty to the Highlanders who had participated in the uprising on the condition that they swore written allegiance to him by January 1, 1692. Nearly all did. Except for the MacDonalds.

The MacDonald clan was situated in the spectacular and haunting valley of Glencoe. They were a small clan, numbering about 150 strong.

Their chief, Alastair MacIain, wrestled with his conscience about whether or not to pledge allegiance to King William. He had secretly hoped the struggle to return James to the throne would continue. But James, now in exile in France, sent messengers to the loyal Highlanders absolving them of their allegiance to him.

As a final act of defiance to King William, MacIain waited until the very last day to comply. On December 31, he traveled to Fort William. There he was told he had to give the oath at Inverary, which was 74 miles away. The winter weather was treacherous and the journey took two days. The fates were against him because when he arrived, the magistrate was not there. The chief waited and waited. On January 6, Sir Colin Campbell returned. The magistrate was reluctant to take MacIain's oath of allegiance since he had missed the deadline by five days. The magistrate finally relented and accepted the sworn and written oath. They both believed there would be no consequences over what was really a minor legal technicality. Chief MacIain returned to snowy Glencoe, secure that all was well.

It was not.

Political plots were brewing. Sir John Dalrymple, the Secretary of State for Scotland, took full advantage of MacIain's tardiness. He had great contempt for the Highlanders and openly hated the MacDonalds. In addition, he had a quest for power and influence. He saw that in one quick blow, he could make an example of the MacDonalds and eliminate some enemies as well. Dalrymple went to King William and swore that the MacDonald chief had not only refused to take the oath but was openly defying his rightful king.

King William was furious and agreed that punishment of the MacDonalds should be harsh and swift.

A letter, signed and countersigned by the king, stated:

> "...that troops be sent to destroy entirely the country of Glencoe. Your power shall be full enough and I hope the soldiers will not trouble the Government with prisoners."

Events moved quickly and a plot hatched to destroy the innocent clan using their old enemies, the Campbells.

On February 1, 1692, Captain Robert Campbell was sent to Glencoe with a company of 120 men. When he arrived, he told clan chief MacIain that there was overcrowding at Fort William and that the troops would be quartered there for a time.

For two weeks, the troops were shown good graces and hospitality, as was common practice throughout the Highlands. The people of Glencoe welcomed the soldiers into their homes and entertained them according to Highland tradition.

On February 12, Captain Campbell received the order of genocide:

> "Sir, you are hereby ordered to fall upon the rebels, the M'Donalds of Glencoe, and putt all to the sword under seventy...You are to secure all avenues, that no man may escape. This you are to putt in execution at five o'clock in the morning precisely...This is by the King's special command, for the good of the country, that these miscreants be cutt off root and branch..."
>
> John Dalyrmple

The murders began at 5 a.m. on February 13, 1692. Caught unaware, the old chief MacIain was shot in the head as he tried to rise from his bed. His elderly wife was stripped of her clothing and cast out into the raging blizzard.

In MacDonald villages throughout the glen, the brutality had begun. Children were run through. Men were tied, and then shot in cold blood. A woman and her young son were shot as they begged for their lives. Old women and young women with children and babies were stripped of their clothing and driven into the freezing storm where they soon perished. Homes were burned, possessions were stolen and livestock taken as booty by the soldiers. However, a few of the MacDonald clan managed to escape into the mountains to the safety of the Stewarts, who were bitter enemies of the Campbells.

When word of the massacre spread, the country became outraged and there was an outcry for those responsible to be punished. No one accepted responsibility. Dalrymple's only comment was that it was unfortunate that some of the MacDonalds had survived. King William pleaded ignorance, even though he had signed and countersigned the genocide order. The Campbells stated they were only following orders.

Nothing was done and so the uproar soon quieted. Nevertheless, the haunting and breathtakingly beautiful land of Glencoe will forever be known as the Glen of Weeping.

-o-

CHAPTER 1

In the early morning hours of February 12, 1692, Captain Robert Campbell selected several of his men to guard the head and foot of the glen and issued an order that would have an impact on the history of the Scottish Highlands forever.

~~~

Betsy Stewart pulled the curtain aside and peeked through the kitchen window. The yard was filled with soldiers.

"How much longer are they going to stay?" she wondered aloud.

Sheila MacDonald came up behind her niece and looked out at the soldiers, too. "Well, they've been here for two weeks and," she said rather flippantly, "I suppose they'll stay until they leave! You know, my dear, we Scots are very hospitable. We always have been and we probably always will be."

She took Betsy's hand and led her to the kitchen table. "Sit down, child. I have a very big favor to ask of you. I received a note this morning from Ian MacTavish. His wife has been poorly for several days and he has asked me to come and give them a hand. But I have my hands full here with my own family and the soldiers who parade in and out of here every day. And they are always hungry! Seems like all I do is cook all day. Your uncle and I have discussed it and hope you will consider going in my place?"

Betsy seemed almost relieved. "Aunt Sheila, I'd be happy to help. I've really enjoyed my long visit with you and Uncle Dougal and the boys, but to tell the truth, the soldiers are hard for me to deal with. They are everywhere! They are loud and crude and I hate the way they leer at me whenever I have to go outside."

"Well, you're a pretty little thing, Betsy. You better get used to men looking at you because it isn't going to stop any time soon."

"The MacTavish place isn't too far. I can probably get there by early evening, if I leave soon," Betsy said.

She liked the MacTavish family and so did her parents. Ian MacTavish was a pleasant man who struggled to raise sheep in this barren area of the Scottish Highlands. He had made good and now boasted forty head of sheep, a milk cow, and two horses on his parcel of land.

She hadn't seen the family since late fall when she first arrived. The winter had been long and cold and didn't allow much opportunity to visit neighbors, even if they were only a few miles away.

Yes, she thought, *it will be good to see the MacTavishes again.*

Aunt Sheila helped Betsy gather her things together and made sure she had ample food and drink for her journey.

"Here, Betsy. Take this." Sheila handed her a small loaded pistol with some extra powder. "You probably won't need this, but I'll feel better knowing you have it."

Betsy took the pistol and put it in her deep skirt pocket. She lifted one leg of her split skirt. "Look!"

Sheila could see the bulge of a scabbard tucked safely in the top of Betsy's woolen stocking.

"I know how to use this, too," Betsy said. "My father taught me well." She smiled. "I'm his only child, you know, and he wants me to live a long and healthy life!"

Uncle Dougal came in rubbing his hands together. "It certainly is a cold day. And it looks as though we might have some more snow today." He saw Betsy's valise. "Aye. I can see you have agreed to go to the MacTavishes in Aunt Sheila's place. Now, you'd better leave as soon as you can, lass, in case the weather takes a real bad turn."

"Yes, Uncle. I'm ready to leave now." Betsy kissed her aunt's cheek. "Tell the boys I said goodbye. I'll send word when I arrive and will let you know how long I expect to stay."

"I'll walk you to your horse, young lady, and make sure he's saddled and cinched properly." He took her arm and walked her outside.

Betsy could feel the bitter cold and already dreaded the long ride ahead of her. Dougal prepared her horse and loaded her saddlebags for her. He took a moment and held his niece at arm's length.

"I know your name is Stewart, lass, but you look like a MacDonald, you know. You look a lot like your mother."

Betsy laughed. "And I look a lot like you, too. That's understandable since you and my mother look enough alike to be twins! I'm proud to be a Stewart but I'm also proud of my MacDonald heritage."

"Wait a moment." Dougal pulled a tartan scarf from around his own neck and placed it around Betsy's neck. "Just a little added warmth for you." He kissed her forehead and helped her mount her horse. "God speed, my child," he said as she left the yard and headed out of town away from the village.

She saw very few soldiers. They were standing in small groups laughing and talking. No one saw her leave.

When the town was behind her, she slowed her horse to a walk because she knew that if she continued to trot, she would get much colder. A light snow was beginning to fall as she reached the main road and turned up toward the glen. She pulled the neck scarf up around her face to shield her nose and lips from the biting cold. It helped. *Thanks, Uncle Dougal,* she said silently.

All was quiet except for the muffled sound of the horse's hooves and the rustle of her outer clothes as gusts of wind caught them.

Betsy pushed ahead through the falling snow and tried to keep her mind off of how cold she was. She thought about her parents.

She had been blessed with good parents. Heather MacDonald Stewart was a cheerful woman who always seemed happy. Each morning when Betsy awoke, she could hear her mother humming or singing while doing her chores. They had a good mother and daughter relationship and Betsy couldn't remember ever having an argument with her mother. Now that she was older, Betsy considered her mother her best friend.

She did have one regret. Betsy was always sorry she was an only child. She would love to have a brother or sister. But she really couldn't complain too much. She was her mother's darling and her father's pride and joy. She got all of their attention. There was always so much work to do that she never had time to get bored or worry about what might have been.

Betsy's father, Ewin Stewart, was a good, hardworking man. He was a fisherman by trade and spent three seasons fishing. During the winter, he took time to mend nets, repair his boat, and tend to maintenance on his home. Betsy loved to spend time with her father. Sometimes she wondered if her father would have preferred a son because he taught her how to fish, how to hunt, how to use weapons, and how to keep out of trouble. Neighbor boys thought she was a very strange girl since she could do all the things they could do. No one dared to take advantage of Betsy Stewart!

She had been surprised when her parents told her she would be spending the winter with her aunt and uncle in Glencoe. They thought it would be a good opportunity for her to get to know the MacDonald side of the family.

Betsy was delighted! Traveling to Glencoe would be a great adventure for a fifteen year-old girl.

As she looked around at the frozen, snow-covered land, she realized how much she missed her parents. *I'll be glad when spring comes and I can return home to Banff,* she thought.

Shadows began to lengthen as the afternoon quickly gave way to dusk. It was still bitterly cold but at least the snowfall was lighter now. Up ahead she could see the glow of a fire. She still had several miles to go and she wondered who had started the fire out in the middle of nowhere, and why.

As she approached the campsite, she saw two men sitting in the shelter of a huge rock. One of the men stood up and approached her.

Betsy could see he was a soldier. *Probably a Campbell,* she thought. *Lord in Heaven, there are Campbells everywhere!*

"Now where are you off to, lassie, on such a cold night?" he asked.

Betsy hesitated. She wasn't sure she trusted these men. *What are they up to? Why are they out here?*

She decided the soldier seemed friendly enough. "I'm on my way to help the MacTavishes. They live beyond the head of the glen."

"Well, why don't you come to the fire and get warm," he said, then turned to his companion and winked.

The other soldier looked at Betsy as she dismounted and came to stand by the fire.

"Don't I know you?" he asked. "Aren't you one of the MacDonald girls? Your name is Betsy. Am I right?"

"Yes, my name is Betsy," she answered, not bothering to explain that her last name was Stewart.

Even standing in the snow by the fire, Betsy was a beautiful young girl. Her hair was a rich auburn color and luminous gray eyes set off her well-structured face. Although she was not quite sixteen, she was quickly growing into womanhood. She was tall for her age and had the natural grace of an elegant lady.

"Well," the soldier bowed ceremoniously, "I am Quinn Campbell and my cousin here is Sean Campbell. Now that we have been officially introduced, why don't you come over here and sit by me? I've just made some coffee and I imagine you might enjoy a cup."

Betsy nodded. "That I would, sir! I'm nearly frozen!"

"My cousin and I will do everything we can to make you warm," Quinn said as he poured some of the hot beverage into a tin cup and offered it to her.

Betsy savored the hot drink. It warmed her insides as the fire was warming her outside. She turned to Quinn. "May I ask why you soldiers are camping out on such a cold night?"

Quinn looked at his cousin and grinned. "Just helping to rid the world of rats."

A chill ran through Betsy and her heart started beating faster. "Rats!" she exclaimed incredulously. "There are no rats out here in the mountains. Even if there were, they would be burrowed in."

"Oh, no!" Quinn answered. "Not house rats. MacDonald rats... like you. In fact, I think you have the honor of being the first one in our trap."

Betsy's heart raced. She jumped up but was quickly pinioned by Sean Campbell who held her tightly. Quinn got up and looked in her horse's saddlebags, then inspected her other belongings in the bag hanging from the pommel of the saddle. He cut the bag loose, lifted the meat that was fastened behind the saddle, and then untied her horse. He smacked its rump and drove it off into the snow.

Quinn turned and looked at Betsy. "Did you notice that Sean put sugar in your toddy? We gave you something sweet, now we expect you to give something sweet back to us."

Just as Sean tightened his hold on Betsy, she twisted hard and momentarily broke his hold on her. She spun around and kneed him in the groin. Sean doubled over and groaned. Quinn grabbed her from behind and threw her to the ground.

"I'll go first," he said as he unbuckled his belt.

Betsy knew she had only a few seconds to act. Quickly, she reached into her stocking and pulled out the small dagger. As Quinn dropped to his knees and began to lower himself, Betsy raised the knife. Quinn saw the flash of the blade before he felt it go deep into his gut. Betsy's father had indeed taught her well! She twisted the dagger and then angrily rotated the blade.

Quinn's expression was one of surprise followed by feelings of great pain. He grabbed the handle of the dagger as if to pull it free, and then sat back on his haunches. Blood spread across the front of his uniform. "Sean!" he gasped. "She's killed me!"

Betsy turned to her side just as the dead man fell forward with a frozen look of surprise still on his face. Sean rushed at Betsy as she pushed Quinn's arm off her body. As she pulled away, she reached her pocketed pistol just before her attacker reached her with his Claymore sword drawn. Betsy took aim at his heart and fired her weapon. Her quick shot hit its mark. Sean Campbell took a few steps backward, dropped his sword, and fell onto his back. Betsy grabbed the sword and stood up. She straddled the dying man and placed the point of the Claymore on his throat.

"What did you mean about killing rats?" she demanded.

He opened his mouth to speak. Blood poured out and ran down his chin. He raised his head slightly and opened his eyes. A wicked smile curled his lips. "It's too late...your clan, the MacDonalds will all die."

"WHY?" Betsy screamed. "WHY would you do that?"

He lowered his head and closed his eyes.

"TELL ME! Don't you dare die until you tell me!"

"King...William." Every word was an effort for the dying man. "He ordered us...to do it. They'll all...be dead...this very night."

Suddenly she realized the full impact of what he had said. Her aunt and uncle and her cousins would be murdered too! Without hesitation, she leaned heavily on the sword and drove it through the man's throat. He gurgled as a burst of blood gushed from his mouth. He gave one last gasp as life left his body.

'CAMPBELL BASTARD!" she shouted into the cold, uncaring night air.

Except for the crackling fire, the night was silent. Betsy fell to her knees and sobbed.

"Oh, dear God!" she cried. "What have I done! Forgive me! I've killed two men!"

She looked at her hands. They were shaking and covered in blood. She used a canteen to wash them as best she could. *What do I do now?* she wondered, *I have to think.* Her heart was racing and her whole body was shaking. Her first impulse was to ride back and warn everyone, but she knew in her heart she couldn't save them. And, they would kill her as well. It didn't take her long to realize that her only hope was to get to the MacTavishes as fast as she could. She withdrew the Claymore from the throat of the dead soldier and looked around. Her horse was nowhere to be seen but she could see the soldiers' horses tethered a short distance away. She brought one of the horses to the fire and reloaded the supplies that were scattered around in the snow. She mounted the horse and rode over and untied the second, then started up the road toward the MacTavish farm.

She failed to see the MacDonald tartan plaid scarf that had been pulled from her neck and lay half buried in the snow.

It had completely stopped snowing. A pale moon gave light through the filtered clouds and Betsy could clearly see the road up ahead. Forgetting the cold, her mind and body numb from her horrible experience, she spurred the horse to a gallop.

After what seemed like hours, she rode into the MacTavish yard. She quickly dismounted and tied both horses to a rail. Exhausted, she staggered toward the front door.

Ian MacTavish, thinking it was Sheila MacDonald, met her at the door. His smile quickly vanished when he saw Betsy's condition. In spite of the cold, her face was ashen and her clothes were covered in blood. She stood there and looked at him as though in a daze.

"Oh, my dear child! What has happened to you?"

Betsy collapsed into his arms and started crying. Ian just held her for a while and patted her back while she cried. Then, when he felt she was ready, he led her to a stool by the fire.

Betsy rubbed her hands together, and then started shaking again. Tears were running down her cheeks. "I killed them!" she sobbed. "I killed them!"

"Who, child? Who did you kill? Tell me what happened, Betsy. It's all right now. You're safe here."

She blurted out the story as he listened intently.

MacTavish was outraged. "You mean the Campbells are going to kill all the MacDonalds? Tonight? Why would they do that? I can't believe it!"

"They were going to kill me, too, Mr. MacTavish. That's why I did what I did. I didn't have time to think. It all happened so fast. I just took both their horses and left as fast as I could. Now I don't know what to do. Is there anything we can do to save them?"

Sadly, MacTavish shook his head. "No, lass. There isn't time. If we tried to warn them we would all be killed as well. Don't blame yourself for what you did. You absolutely did the right thing. But now we must think about you. When the Campbells realize two of their soldiers have been killed, they won't rest until they find out who did it."

"Ian! Ian! What's going on?"

MacTavish heard his wife call from her bedroom. He hurried over to the doorway. "Tis Betsy Stewart, my love. She's come to help out but I fear she's in a wee bit of trouble. I'll take care of it. You stay in bed and rest and I'll tell you all about it later." He softly closed the bedroom door and returned to Betsy. "I'm afraid Mary is still very ill. She needs her rest."

Just then, Bruce and Donald MacTavish came through the back door, stomping their feet. "Whew! The storm has started up again. I fear it's a full blown blizzard," Bruce said to his father. "We brought in enough wood to keep us warm for a day or two."

"Boys," MacTavish called, "take off your wet clothes and come in here. We need to talk."

After the young men entered the room and greeted Betsy, MacTavish told them every detail of Betsy's dreadful story. They shook their heads in disbelief.

"Now we have to make a plan to get Betsy home as soon as possible. Back to her parents." He turned to the young girl. "Did anyone see you tonight, lass, aside from the two Campbell soldiers?"

"No, I saw no one else. And I don't think any of the soldiers saw me leave Glencoe. They were too busy being loud and noisy."

"Good! Then we must get you away from here and back to your family as soon as possible." He turned to his older son. "Donald, I want you to accompany Betsy. She can take the two horses she brought here and you can ride your own horse. Both of you must be very careful because by tomorrow afternoon, all the King's men will be scouring the country for any MacDonald survivor."

"I should be safe then," Betsy said. "I'm a Stewart, so after I am away from here I shouldn't be questioned. Unless one of the Campbell men should recognize me or my horses."

"That probably won't happen because you and Donald will have a big head start. It will take time for the news of the killings to spread to all the villages. Tell me, lass, do you have any money?"

"Yes," Betsy answered. "I have enough to pay for my expenses and Donald's as well."

"No, lassie. You can pay for yourself, but Donald goes as your protector and friend. It is our duty to see you home. And see you home we will! Now let's get you out of those clothes and get you some hot food!"

MacTavish went to the window and looked out. "Yes indeed. It's a blizzard all right! No one, not even the Campbells will venture very far until it subsides." He headed toward the kitchen. "Betsy, Donald, after you eat, I want you both to get some sleep. Bruce and I will pack your horses. As soon as the storm lets up, we'll wake you and you can be on your way."

Betsy nodded her agreement. She changed out of her wet, bloody clothing and was soon eating a large bowl of lamb stew and drinking a large cup of warm sweetened milk. When she finished, she lay down by the fire and was soon fast asleep.

Betsy's sleep was frequently interrupted with dreams of screams as women and children were brutally murdered. She watched helplessly as her aunt and uncle tried to run but were caught, then shot in cold blood. She saw the faces of Sean and Quinn Campbell laughing as they chased her through the snow. She ran but her feet wouldn't move fast enough. They caught her and threw her to the ground. Her heart raced and she screamed. Betsy woke with a start. Her heart was pounding as she realized she had been dreaming. Now fully awake, she could hear the wind howling outside.

Ian MacTavish kneeled beside her and brushed her hair from her face.

"Sleep, child," he whispered, "You're safe now. Morning will be here soon enough."

Betsy closed her eyes and, this time, drifted into a dreamless sleep.

At dawn's first light, MacTavish woke Betsy and Donald. It was still snowing but the fierce winds had died down and travel would be possible.

Betsy felt strangely refreshed. She quickly arranged her clothes and put the dagger back inside her hose and reloaded the pistol. She thought about her aunt, uncle, cousins, and all the MacDonalds in Glencoe and silently prayed they were all safe in Heaven. A sob caught in her throat but she quickly gained control of herself. There was no time to mourn. That would come when she was safe at home with her parents.

She and Donald ate a hearty breakfast and then went outside where MacTavish and Bruce were waiting with their horses.

"God speed, my son. God speed, Betsy," MacTavish said and embraced them both.

-o-

CHAPTER 2

It had stopped snowing, but it was a cold, miserable day. The only blessing was that the blowing snow covered their tracks almost as soon as the hoof prints were formed.

Donald led the way and Betsy followed close behind. By late morning, the pair stopped to rest. Donald built a small fire in a sheltered area and they ate a meager lunch.

Betsy was exhausted.

Donald was sympathetic. "I know how tired you must be, lass, and what you've experienced is almost too much to comprehend. But we must keep going. We should come to the village of Dalwhinnie about dusk. We'll stay there for the night."

Betsy looked as though she was going to cry.

"Can you hold on for a while longer?" Donald asked.

Betsy nodded. "I know what I have to do, Donald."

"Good girl," he said. "Rest a while longer and then we'll be on our way."

The afternoon seemed endless but after the clouds thinned and the sun came out, Betsy's energy was renewed. She spurred her horse to a canter and passed Donald. "C'mon, Donald, let's move a little faster!"

Donald laughed. "That's more like it, lass. But let's not wear out our horses before we get there. I'll lead and you follow." He pulled ahead of her once more.

When they finally reached the village, the sun was setting. Donald slowed to let Betsy catch up. "We've made it. Just as I said we would. I know there's an inn up ahead. We'll stop there."

Betsy and Donald enjoyed a hearty, warm dinner by the fireplace. They didn't talk, but eavesdropped on the conversation of those around them. There was no talk of the massacre. The only talk among the townspeople was concerning the blizzard, which had raged the day before.

Donald leaned close to Betsy. "So far so good. There's no talk of Glencoe. We're safe here."

Betsy was relieved. "I'll sleep better tonight knowing that the Campbells aren't chasing me. At least not yet!"

Donald awakened Betsy just before dawn. They ate a quick breakfast and headed north. The day was clear but cold.

"It's so much easier to travel with the sun overhead," Betsy said.

The steady travel took its toll on Betsy and when they stopped for the night, she ate a quick meal and went right to sleep. Again, there was no talk of the massacre.

Betsy wondered if the bodies of the Campbells had been found. She knew that once they were discovered, there would be soldiers scouring the country in search of the murderer.

All too soon, the news of the massacre spread like wildfire across the Highlands. By this time, Betsy and Donald were almost across Scotland and near her home in the small fishing village of Banff, located at the mouth of the Deveron River on the North Sea.

They arrived in Banff about noon. Betsy quickly dismounted and ran toward her front door. Her mother threw open the door.

"Betsy! Oh, Betsy, my darlin' daughter!" She embraced Betsy and together they rocked side to side. "You're alive! I can't believe it!" Betsy's mother started crying. "Dear child, we heard what happened in Glencoe. We thought you were dead, too! Oh praise God!" She held Betsy at arm's length and looked at her carefully. "Are you all right? Are you hurt?"

Betsy wiped away her own tears. "I'm fine, Mother. I'm fine."

Heather Stewart turned to Donald. "Thank you, son, for bringing my daughter home. As soon as you finish with the horses, please find Mr. Stewart. I think he's down at the pub. Then come in and I'll bring you some hot food."

Betsy could hear her father as he ran up the steps and burst through the door. He ran to Betsy and hugged her so tightly she could barely breathe.

"It's true!" he cried. "You're alive!" Like his wife, he held his daughter at arm's length. "Let me look at you! You've turned my day to sunshine!"

Mrs. Stewart served them all a hearty lunch. Donald ate seconds of everything.

When they were finished, they took hot drinks and sat by the fire.

Ewin Stewart couldn't take his eyes off his daughter. He sat close to her and held her hand. "Now tell me, my child, if you can. Tell me what happened."

As she told her story, Betsy's parents listened in silence, their faces wet with tears.

"I killed two people! I have to live with that for the rest of my life!" Betsy couldn't stop her own tears. "And even though I knew they were going to kill everyone in Glencoe, I could do nothing to stop them! I couldn't save Aunt Sheila or Uncle Dougal, or the children. Mother, I couldn't save your brother!" she sobbed.

Ewin gently pulled his daughter against his shoulder and cupped her head in his hand. "Shh, my darlin'! Hush now. No one could have saved them. Not even God himself!"

Heather dried her eyes, and then blew her nose. "I can't believe any Highlander would violate the Rules of Hospitality. They betrayed their benefactors and massacred an entire clan. This day shall never be forgotten!"

Ewin, too, was outraged. "As angry and bereaved as we are, we must think clearly. Betsy, you must not tell anyone where you have been or what you know. You may already be in danger. I need time to think." He paused, and then turned to Donald. "Son, I know you are anxious to get back home but you must stay here for a few days until you are well rested."

"My mother has been very ill and I am anxious to get back home to her. Thank you for your hospitality. I would like a few days to rest and catch up on some undisturbed sleep."

"One more thing," Ewin continued. "In order for you to have a safe journey with no one questioning where you have been or what you have been doing, I plan to give you a bill of sale for those two Campbell horses. That way you can sell them along the way for some sheep and everyone will think you were out buying more animals for your father's farm."

Donald laughed. "I like your idea, Mr. Stewart. Besides, it will be a good joke on the Campbells. But then, they'll never find out, will they now?"

During the next two days, Betsy's parents decided how they could best protect their daughter.

Ewin talked to Betsy. "As much as we would like you to stay here with us, lass - oh, we missed you so much! - your mother and I know you should leave once again until we feel it will be safe for you to return."

Betsy understood. "But where shall I go, Father?"

"It's all been decided. Your Uncle Roy and I will take you to Kirkwall in the Orkney Islands. We have family there and you'll be safe."

"Father," Betsy replied. "That's so far away!"

"I know, lass," her father agreed, "but it will only be through the spring and possibly the summer. When the time is right, we'll bring you home again."

Several days later, Ewin gathered food and supplies for Donald's trip back to Glencoe.

Betsy rose early the morning Donald left. She wanted to be there to say goodbye. The two had become very good friends since they began their journey.

"Donald, you're like a big brother to me. Thank you for everything. I'll really miss you," she said.

"You're a very brave girl," Donald told her. "I hope we meet again someday. I'll miss you too."

The family stood and watched as Donald and his two extra horses headed out of town.

Ewin had a strong boat that he could use to take his daughter to Kirkwall. It would be another long journey for the travel-weary girl but one that had to be taken. He refused to take any chances with his only child's welfare.

Both parents had decided that the only person who would know of Betsy's whereabouts would be Ewin's younger brother, Roy, who had already agreed to sail with them.

While Heather helped her daughter pack for the journey, Ewin left to find his brother and to prepare the boat for sea. They checked the tides and found that the ebb would begin at three in the morning. They agreed to leave then.

It was pitch black outside as the four members of the Stewart family finished their breakfast and then made a last minute check for their supplies.

Heather took Betsy in her arms and held her for a long time. "I just got you back and now you must leave again. Be safe, my dearest. Be safe."

Then Betsy, her father, and uncle made their way through the village of Banff to the waterfront.

Ewin was very proud of his boat. It was a stout little vessel about forty feet long with a strong hull and a high bow. He had named her *The Cormorant* because she could handle about any storms the North Sea could send her way. She was fitted with a small, snug cabin with a fire pot that would hold enough dried peat to warm the cabin and cook food. It was located under a metal hood that vented up above the deck through a pipe to allow smoke to escape. It worked very well.

When the trio reached the boat, they stored their belongings below in the cabin. Betsy started a small fire and heated some water that they could lace with a dram of whiskey to help keep the chill off. They drifted out into the river current until their sails could catch the wind.

They had traveled several hours before it began to get light. The wind, which had been erratic, settled into a steady westerly and the vessel was able to begin its first tack into the North Sea running east and north away from the coast. They ran on this tack for several hours and then turned about and ran steadily on a northwest tack. They held to this course all the next day and into the mid-morning of the third day. They approached the coast again in the vicinity of the mouth of the Brora River. Here they anchored alongside a small village. They went ashore to buy cloth, needles and thread so Betsy could make new clothes for herself. She was a very fine seamstress and enjoyed taking a fabric and fashioning it into a warm piece of clothing. She also bought two pairs of shoes and woolen stockings. Ewin bought food supplies that included hard bread, salted herring, salt pork, and potatoes.

Using the fresh breeze, they set out again as soon as possible. Their goal was to put distance between Betsy and any and all Campbells.

For the next five days, they tacked back and forth off the east coast of Scotland. Then they made another wide tack to the northeast out into the open North Sea before they changed course once again to find Burray Island and the east entrance to the Scappa Flow.

After two more days, *The Cormorant* sailed up to the quayside at Kirkwall.

Betsy and Uncle Roy stayed on board while Ewin went ashore to find transportation for them. Ewin soon returned with a carriage pulled by four horses. The driver assisted in loading Betsy's belongings onto the carriage.

After all were aboard, Ewin spoke to the driver and the carriage rumbled away. Betsy had never been to the Orkney Islands before and was enjoying her first view of Kirkwall.

Kirkwall was a very pretty town. The mainland island had been inhabited for as long as anyone could remember. There were groups of stone circles, indicating ancient Druids had lived here.

Betsy was excited when she caught a glimpse of the Cathedral of St. Magnus built sometime in the twelfth century. It was built on a hill and could be seen from miles around. Betsy also saw some new houses built so the gabled ends adjoined the relatively narrow street.

Betsy pointed to a large imposing structure. "What's that, Father?"

Ewin looked out the carriage window. "I think that's a palace that probably belonged to a Scottish Earl.

Roy looked too. "It's looking kind of shabby, isn't it? I wonder if the family ran out of money."

"Or maybe they were killed," Ewin suggested.

Betsy could see that most of the land was covered with grasses and peat bogs. The winds in the islands could be very violent so there were few trees except in sheltered areas.

They left the village and followed a main road for several miles before they turned off onto a side road. After traveling another half hour, the carriage came to an abrupt stop in front of a large peat house. The driver jumped down and carried Betsy's luggage up to the house.

Ewin went to the front door and knocked.

A pleasant looking, middle-aged woman opened the door. She broke into a wide smile and opened her arms. "Glory be!" she said excitedly. "Ewin! Roy! Come in! Please come in!"

"Hello, Aunt Dora," Ewin and Roy said in unison.

"Goodness gracious. I'm in shock" Aunt Dora said and gave a quick hug to each of her nephews. "What in the world brings you here to Kirkwall at this time of year? You usually come in the summer months."

"We'll tell you all about it, but first may I introduce my daughter, Betsy." He took his daughter's arm and led her into the house. "This is your Great Aunt Dora. She's my father's youngest sister, although she's not much older than I am."

Betsy walked toward her aunt, took her hand and dropped a curtsy.

"It's a pleasure, Mum," she said and suddenly found herself in the strong embrace of the older woman. She knew immediately that she would be loved and kept safe in this house.

Dora heard her husband come in. "Andrew, come and give our young niece a big hug and welcome her to our home."

Betsy's uncle, who was probably not much older than her father, looked old and weathered. He came over and embraced her. He smelled of tobacco, horses, and there was also a faint hint of fish on his heavy coat as he lifted her up and swung her around. He had a twinkle in his eye as he said, "You Stewart women will be the death of me, I'll wager! You have the look of a strong-willed girl to me."

Andrew Jones set her down again and said to his nephews. "Welcome back to our home. You have come a long way. Come! Sit! We'll all have something to eat and drink and then we'll talk for a while."

Four youngsters seemed to appear out of nowhere.

"Children!" Dora said cheerfully. "Come and meet your new cousin." She smiled at Betsy. "This is Tim…and this is Egan. The girls are Pearl and Mavis."

"Hello," Betsy said.

The boys seemed awkward and just nodded. They asked to be excused, then went outside. The girls quickly warmed up to their new cousin and took Betsy toward their room.

"Now!" Dora said. "Andrew, take our guests close to the fire so they can warm themselves. I'll fetch some hot drinks and some scones and jam. It'll just take a few minutes, then, Ewin, you can tell us why you are really here."

Andrew stood close to Ewin and Roy. "I didn't expect you to come until late spring. But since you are here, do you want to take some of our fine bounty with you?"

Roy looked at his brother. 'What do you think, Ewin?"

Ewin didn't hesitate. "We'll take a dozen, Andrew." He pulled some coins from his pocket and counted them out. "Here's payment in advance."

Dora walked in with a tray full of refreshments. When everyone was served, Dora sat down next to Ewin.

"Now, nephew. Tell us everything."

Ewin quietly told his aunt and uncle what had happened at Glencoe and how Betsy had to fight for her life.

Dora just shook her head. "Dear Lord in Heaven! That poor child!" She turned to her husband, "We have not heard about the massacre, have we Andrew? News takes a long time to get to us from the mainland."

Andrew was quick to assure Ewin. "Betsy is safe here with us for as long as necessary."

Aunt Dora broke in, "And don't worry. We will not tell a living soul what you have told us."

Ewin was grateful. "I hope I can send for her by mid-summer. Thank you, Aunt Dora. I will rest easier knowing she is in your safe care."

Roy stood up. "Ewin, we should say a farewell to Betsy now. We need to get supplies and ready the ship if we are to leave on the morning tide."

Ewin agreed. He went to find his daughter and took her to a quiet corner. "Your Aunt and Uncle are eager for you to stay here as long as necessary. They have assured me of your safety."

"Don't worry, Father," Betsy said. "I like these people. The girls and I will get along fine."

"God bless you, child. I'm glad you understand this situation. There may be hell to pay for the massacre and I want you out of it. As soon as I return home, I plan to take your mother to France to be with your grandparents. If this all blows over, I will bring her home probably in late summer. Should the Campbell dogs dare to do this sort of thing again, all the other clans will be against them. God forbid, for if it comes to that, all Scotland will be bathed in blood!"

Betsy's face flushed. "I will NEVER forget what the Campbells did. I know that I am ready to take retribution against them any time and any place I can."

"No, child! Don't let me hear you talk like that! Revenge is never a solution. It would only bring you misery. Defending yourself is one thing. Seeking to attack and destroy is another. I want you to put all of this behind you as quickly as you can and allow God to have his revenge."

"I'll try, Father. Really I will." In her heart Betsy knew this would be impossible. Her father didn't really understand. No one could. Every day she thought about her own personal ordeal as well as the massacre. It was the last thing on her mind when she went to bed and it was one of her first thoughts every morning. She hated the Campbells! She hated King William for his smugness and arrogance that taught him he could play God and order the murders of innocent women and children. She had sworn an oath that day that she would seek revenge on any Campbell she met who had been at Glencoe. She knew that she could never forgive! It just wasn't possible.

Ewin kissed his daughter, "It's time for us to go, lass."

After all of the goodbyes, Betsy stood at the doorway and watched as her father and Uncle Roy rode away.

Aunt Dora came up behind her and put her arms around Betsy's waist. She spoke softly. "Spring will soon be here. This late winter snow will soon melt and the land will once again spring forth with new life. I pray that you can do the same, child."

When news of the massacre finally reached Kirkwall, Betsy cried all over again. She learned that all of Scotland was horrified by what had happened and that King William was trying very hard to place the blame elsewhere. Although he had been successful in creating scapegoats, everyone knew that he was behind the slaughter.

Later that night, Aunt Dora heard her crying. She went into Betsy's room and gathered her into her arms and held her until she finally cried herself to sleep.

-o-

CHAPTER 3

Lieutenant Dirk Campbell sat at his desk in the Officers' Barracks at Fort William. He picked up a sheath of papers and, once again, read over the details of the infamous raid on Glencoe. As if he could forget! The memories were burned into his mind. He had been there that fateful day and knew that he would never forget. He certainly hadn't approved of the King's order nor did he understand why everyone had to be murdered. But he was a King's officer and he would always follow orders no matter how distasteful.

He leaned back in his chair, propped his feet on the desk, and closed his eyes. He tried not to think about the morning of February 13. After all, it was over and done with. He took some comfort in the fact that the people he had personally killed died quickly and didn't suffer. He had been merciful. As though that made much difference! Being a soldier, a good soldier, was hard work. He believed in a strong military and knew there would be times when he had to do things that seemed wrong. The massacre at Glencoe was certainly one of those.

Along with two dozen soldiers, Dirk had arrived in Glencoe the morning of February 12 to reinforce the troops already there. He was assigned to spend the night with the Dougal MacDonald family. His additional assignment was to kill them all early the next morning.

It had snowed off and on for the entire day. He spent most of the day talking to other soldiers who had been quartered in Glencoe for the past twelve days. They all had agreed that the MacDonalds were a most hospitable clan. Most of the residents stayed indoors that day. Dirk himself noted that those who did venture outside were polite and tried to make sure that the soldiers were well taken care of. By evening, snowfall increased and the winds picked up, so most everyone in town retired early that night. By midnight a blizzard was raging.

Promptly at 5 a.m., Dirk crept into the MacDonalds bedroom and walked over to the bed. Sheila stirred. He placed a pistol close to her head and pulled the trigger. Dougal woke up and cried out. Dirk raised his other pistol and fired point blank.

"Forgive me," Dirk whispered. He quickly reloaded his pistols and hurried to the children's bedroom. All hell was breaking loose. He could hear gunfire exploding. He wasn't sure if it was his weapons he heard as he fired at the children or if it was other soldiers carrying out their deadly orders.

Women screamed. Children cried. Dirk ran outside. The blowing snow blinded him. The fierce wind forced him forward and he stumbled across countless victims, some still moaning. One grabbed his ankle and pulled him down. Dirk scrambled to his feet and tried to get his bearings. Within minutes the gunfire ended. The slaughter was over. The only sound was the roar of the wind as it blew relentlessly across the bodies of the fallen MacDonald clan.

Dirk opened his eyes and sat upright. "I must stop thinking about it!" he said loudly. "There are other matters I must deal with now."

He continued reading the report of Captain Robert Campbell that detailed the events of that day and the days following. He reported that two days later, the two soldiers stationed at the foot of the glen returned to the village claiming they had seen no MacDonald try to escape. The two soldiers from the head of the glen had not been accounted for, so Campbell sent several soldiers to locate them. It was the following day when they returned with the bodies of the two soldiers who were identified as Quinn and Sean Campbell. One had been stabbed; his trousers were down around his knees. The second had been shot in the chest but also had a sword wound in his throat. Both of the soldiers' horses were missing. The only clue was a MacDonald tartan plaid neck scarf lying close to the body of one of the soldiers.

"Well, I'll be damned!" Dirk said aloud. "It looks like at least one MacDonald not only managed to escape but killed two of the King's men as well!"

He thought about who it might have been. He was sure everyone in the Dougal MacDonald household was killed. *No one could have escaped through that blasted blizzard,* he thought. *Even if he did, he couldn't have made it to the head of the glen on foot. But, let's presume he did. He would have been half frozen! Would he have had the strength to kill the two soldiers?*

Dirk thought of another more plausible scenario. It was a horse thief who killed the soldiers. Someone came through the glen the day before the massacre when the weather was still tolerable, killed the two soldiers, and stole the horses. *That's probably what happened,* he concluded. *The killer had to be found and tried for murder. No one can be allowed to kill the King's men and go unpunished!*

Dirk carefully wrote down his suspicions and walked to the office of the Commanding Officer. As he knocked on the door, he heard a deep voice.

"Come in!"

A heavy-set balding man in his mid-forties was looking through some papers on his desk. He was dressed in the uniform of a colonel in the British regulars.

"Ah, Lieutenant! What can I do for you today?" the Colonel asked.

Dirk handed the colonel his findings. "Sir, I have been studying Captain Campbell's report of the events at Glencoe. We lost no soldiers that morning, but two days later, two soldiers who had been on patrol in the area were found murdered. I don't see how it could have been a MacDonald who escaped. It just wasn't possible. I believe it was a horse thief."

"Probably some damned Highlander!" the Colonel said with disgust. "When will they stop being an annoyance?" He paused. "Well, what do you want me to do about it?"

Dirk had it all figured out. "Give me two mounted men and I will run this horse thief to the ground and bring him back here to stand trial."

The Colonel thought for a moment and stroked his balding head. "Hmm, I don't know, Dirk. All the Highlanders are in turmoil right now. If I do allow you to go in search of this man, or men, I want you to promise not to create any incidents that could set off a rebellion."

Dirk nodded his understanding. "You have my assurance. I just want to close this chapter as quickly as possible."

"Good! I'll give you the order in the morning."

Dirk saluted and left the C.O. to his papers.

The next morning, with orders to pursue and capture the horse thief, Dirk Campbell departed Fort William with two cavalrymen who had been assigned to him. The trio headed south toward Glencoe. The weather was still cold but the sky was fair and so the ride was not unpleasant. The three men trotted along at a good pace and, after crossing a ferry, came to the town of Ballachulish on the south side of Loch Leven. As they rode down the street, they passed a public house bearing an obviously new and very large sign that read, *Campbells are not welcome here!*

They continued on to a lodging house where they dismounted and walked in. When the customers seated inside saw the three soldiers, they stood up and walked out.

"What's going on here?" Dirk asked.

The innkeeper's eyes narrowed. He walked up to Dirk and looked him straight in the eye.

"I swore allegiance to the King, but I don't hold with cold-blooded murder. I don't know of any Christian soul who does! You are not welcome here. And if your name is Campbell as well, you are doubly not welcome here! No one in Ballachulish will offer you hospitality. Perhaps you can stay in one of the barns in the area. I don't think the sheep will mind."

Dirk held his anger as he remembered his C.O.'s warning and turned on his heel and left the inn. The two soldiers with him were bewildered.

"We were just following orders, sir. Don't they understand that? It wasn't anything personal."

Dirk jumped up on his horse. "I don't think that makes any difference to these people. We probably killed some of their friends. C'mon. Let's get out of here." Dirk spurred his horse and the others quickly followed.

Dirk felt sick at his stomach whenever he thought about the morning of the slaughter. He had killed a family who had given him food and shelter. All of the soldiers at Glencoe had violated the sacred rules of hospitality and destroyed one of the best unwritten laws of the highlands. Although he knew that sometimes soldiers must do terrible things, this knowledge did not seem to help him now. He was going to struggle with the events at Glencoe for many years to come.

As they rode out of Ballachulish late that afternoon, they saw disgust in the eyes of every man, woman, and child they met.

Several hours later, they located a place where they could make camp. It was in a rock overhang up from the shore of Loch Leven. They cooked some of their rations and while they ate, their conversation centered on the unimportant and mundane. No one wanted to talk about Glencoe.

Dawn brought a cold rain as they continued along Loch Leven until they reached the bottom of the glen. By this time the wind was blowing down the glen and straight into their faces. When they reached what was left of the village of Glencoe, all three men were soaked. Captain Edward Collins who had been in Glencoe since the troops first moved in commanded a contingent of soldiers still quartered there.

"Damn, man, you're a sight for sore eyes!" Collins was surprised to see his old friend.

Dirk smiled as he dismounted, "It's good to see you too, Edward."

Collins seemed anxious. "Have you heard of any uprisings?"

"What do you mean?" Dirk knew full well what Collins meant.

"You know very well what I mean, Dirk. Damn, I thought all the Highlanders would be out for revenge by now. The MacDonalds had many friends. The people in this valley won't even talk to us now. Truthfully, I can't say that I blame them much."

"Have they shown any signs of acting against you?" Dirk asked.

"Not to this point," Collins continued. "I think they are all expecting the government to do something."

Dirk laughed. "You and I both know THAT won't happen. No one is accepting responsibility so no one can be held accountable. Not even the King!"

Edward shook his head sadly. "It's tragic. After we killed those poor people, we had to create a cemetery and bury them. I almost cried when we found women and children in the snow. God almighty, Dirk, they were frozen to death! I knew so many of them, too, from the twelve days we spent with them until the order came down to kill them. Can you believe it? They fed us and entertained us. Some of them even kept us overnight. History will not remember us well for what we did here. The memories are still so fresh..." Collins swallowed hard then quickly changed the subject.

"Come into my quarters, Dirk, and get out of those wet clothes. I'll have someone fix us a pitcher of rum punch and then maybe we both will feel better."

The other two soldiers left with a corporal to put up the horses.

Dirk changed clothes, and then eagerly accepted a cup of hot rum punch from his friend.

"Now it's time to tell you why I'm here," he said. Dirk sat in front of the fireplace, sipped his drink and related the details of Captain Campbell's report.

"What do you think, Dirk?" Edward asked.

"Well, it's pretty obvious that Quinn and Sean Campbell were murdered. Probably for their horses," Dirk said. "And that's why I'm here. I'm on a fact-finding mission and I hope you can help me."

Collins quickly agreed. "I'll help you in any way I can."

"Did you know Quinn and Sean Campbell personally?"

"Oh, aye, I did. They were both drunken louts, I'm afraid. As I remember, they couldn't earn their livings so the clan chief sent them away to the army. I guess every clan has its ne'r-do-wells."

"I'm sure of that, my friend. Happens in every family," Dirk agreed.

"It makes no difference, though," he continued. We can't have people going around killing the King's soldiers." Dirk refilled his cup with hot punch. "Edward, do you know of anyone who lives in the vicinity of where the soldiers were killed?"

Edward nodded. "The only one I know for sure is a sheep farmer by the name of MacTavish. He lives several miles beyond the head of the glen. Would you like me to make some inquiries?"

"No, I don't think so. It's my responsibility. I'll see to it. But thanks for your help."

The next morning, Dirk and his two companion soldiers left Glencoe and headed north toward Ian MacTavish's farm.

-o-

CHAPTER 4

Betsy was surprised to learn the weather in the Orkney Islands is not what she would have expected. Warm gulf waters keep the year-round temperatures between 35-65 degrees. It seldom snows, but high winds and fog are common to the area.

She adapted easily to the weather and to her new family as well. She, Pearl, and Mavis were almost inseparable. After their daily household chores, the three girls took long walks through the town and down to the sea.

Her male cousins, who were a little older than she, paid little attention to their sisters and Betsy. Their chores were performed outside under the watchful eye of their father. There seemed to be an endless amount of chores for the entire family.

Uncle Andrew raised sheep and maintained paddocks for his animals that ranged over his extensive property. There was a hired man named Abel. He spent a lot of time watching Betsy. It made her uncomfortable and reminded her of the soldiers in Glencoe who leered at her and whispered things under their breath whenever she walked past them.

Andrew trusted Abel. He depended on him even more than he did his sons. Abel was older and stronger than the boys. He spent time teaching them how to shoot. Sometimes in the later afternoon when the chores were finished, the three would run foot races. Abel always won.

One night Betsy couldn't sleep. She heard the squeaking of wagon wheels out by the barns. She had heard the sound before but tonight she decided to investigate. She wrapped a cape around her shoulders and quietly left the house through the back door, and then followed the squeaking sound. It led her toward one of the sheep barns. She could see the silhouettes of two men and could hear their voices although she couldn't understand what they were saying. It was her Uncle Andrew and Abel.

Betsy tiptoed to the barn and peeked in, taking care not to be seen. She saw a large metal container cooking over a fire. There were a large number of jugs sitting on shelves against the walls. It took her a few minutes to realize that they were in the process of making whiskey.

Oh, my God!, she thought. *My Uncle Andrew is a bootlegger!* She wanted to laugh but knew she'd be in trouble if she were caught spying. She covered her mouth and quickly retreated. Betsy re-entered the house, hung up her cape, and crawled back into her bed. She thought that Aunt Dora probably knew about the illegal still but doubted that Pearl and Mavis did. Tim and Egan probably didn't know about it either. She couldn't wait until morning. She was going to have fun asking questions and playing dumb. She laughed to herself. *This is going to be fun!*

It was some time before she finally fell asleep.

The next morning at breakfast, Betsy watched Aunt Dora as she prepared breakfast.

"I know the boys are already doing chores, but where's Uncle Andrew this morning?" Betsy asked innocently.

"Oh, he worked late last night. He's sleeping a little later than usual."

"What work does he do late at night?" Betsy continued.

"Oh, my child. On a farm this big, there's work enough to keep a man busy for twenty-four hours a day!" Aunt Dora served Betsy a bowl of porridge.

"Aunt Dora," Betsy asked rather quietly, "Is Uncle Andrew a drinking man?"

Dora stopped what she was doing and frowned at Betsy. "What a question!" she said. "Why do you ask?"

Betsy acted nonchalant. "No reason, really. It's just that I've never seen him with a dram. My father likes a dram once in a while. So does Uncle Roy."

"Well," Dora said, 'He doesn't make a habit of it, if that's what you mean."

"No, that's not what I mean. What I mean is…Oh, never mind… I'm sorry I said anything."

Betsy looked at Pearl and Mavis. They seemed completely uninterested in the conversation.

Banners of Honor

After morning chores, Betsy went outside and saw Abel standing by the well.

"Good morning, Abel," she said cheerfully.

He looked at her and smiled. "Good morning, colleen. I didn't think you were ever going to talk to me."

"Well, you're wrong," she said.

"Have you time to take a short walk?" Abel asked. "Maybe I can get to know you a little bit better."

"I have time," Betsy said. "Let's walk over there." She pointed to one of the barns.

He blocked her way. "Why do you want to go over there?"

"Well, it's spring now. Maybe there are some baby lambs I could look at."

Abel took her arm and led her in a different direction. "Sorry, colleen. There aren't any baby lambs in that barn."

Betsy didn't argue. She just followed along with him. "Why do you call me 'colleen?' Don't you know my name is Betsy?"

"Aye, I do. I come from Ireland, Miss Betsy Stewart. There we call a young girl colleen. It's the same as lassie. I've heard Andrew call you lassie. Do you mind if I call you colleen?"

"I'd rather you called me Betsy." She said.

"And you can call me Abel." He smiled and there was a twinkle in his eyes.

Betsy looked at this young man. He was about her height and had very dark hair. His eyes were surprisingly blue, a bright blue like the sky on a summer day.

I like him, Betsy thought. *I think we can be friends.*

The two spent more time together. So much time, that Mavis and Pearl became a little jealous.

"You're never with us anymore," Mavis complained.

Pearl agreed. "Now that you have a boy friend, we don't matter anymore."

Betsy assured her cousins that Abel wasn't her boy friend and promised she would spend more time with them. She was as good as her word.

29

She watched and she listened and became familiar with the late night work that kept Andrew and Abel so busy. She waited for an opportunity to learn more.

There was a pattern to her uncle's whiskey making and Betsy caught on quick. The portable still was moved from sheep barn to sheep barn on a small wagon usually used to haul fodder. The still was moved only at night and in the dark of the moon or on foggy nights. She decided to find out more.

One afternoon she followed Abel to one of the sheep barns.

"Abel!" she called.

Startled, Abel turned around. "Betsy! You surprised me!"

"I didn't mean to startle you, but I need to ask you something." Betsy looked around the barn but saw no telltale signs of whiskey making. "Do you and Uncle Andrew have a lot of customers for your whiskey?"

Abel was taken off guard. "What kind of a question is that?" He quickly looked around to see if there was any evidence lying around in plain sight. "What are you talking about?"

"Don't play games with me, Abel. I know all about your bootlegging operation! I find it fascinating. I want to know more about it."

Abel became angry. "I don't know what you are talking about, but I'll give you a piece of advice. Don't say anything to anybody about such nonsense. It's not a good idea to make trouble for yourself or for others."

He turned on his heel and left her standing in the barn.

She chuckled, "Guess that didn't go over so well. I should have been a little more subtle!"

Betsy continued watching and listening and learning. She learned that Abel would often go to town, probably to make contacts with middlemen who would distribute the whiskey to mainland Scotland.

She asked Aunt Dora lots of questions and found out her father made several trips a year to Kirkwall. Now the pieces of the puzzle were falling into place. It was true her father and Uncle Roy were fishermen but it was also true that bootlegging was a big part of their lives as well. She didn't understand why some people could make whiskey and it was legal while others made it and it was illegal. It pleased her to know that all bootleggers, not just her father and uncle, were actually cheating the King. Revenge for Glencoe was still on her mind.

Spring was a busy time on the farm. Crops had to be planted and there were hundreds of sheep to be sheared. Good and fast sheep shearers were a rarity. Betsy was fascinated with the process and asked for permission to help.

Uncle Andrew seemed surprised. "That's a man's work, lassie. Are you sure you want to learn?"

"I'm sure," Betsy answered. "Aunt Dora said that after I finish the inside chores, I can be free to help you."

Andrew laughed. "You constantly surprise me, child. If you really want to learn I'll see what I can do." He looked at Betsy's clothing. "You'll need some proper clothing and a good teacher. I'll talk to Abel about both."

Abel had stayed away from Betsy since her inappropriate questions about the whiskey still. Now he had to teach her how to shear sheep! He told Andrew he'd rather not.

"What about Tim or Egan? They could teach her."

Andrew laughed heartily. "No, Abel! You're the man for the job. Tim and Egan have their hands full right now. Besides, you're a better teacher."

Reluctantly, Abel approached Betsy. "Now listen to me, young lady. I'll teach you to shear sheep, but I don't want you asking me any more foolish questions. Is that clear?"

"Yes, Abel," she agreed. "It's clear. Besides, I don't need to ask you any more foolish questions because I have it all figured out!"

Betsy was a good pupil and became adept at handling sheep. As she gained strength, she could lift and turn the sheep onto their backs so they could be held from behind while they were being sheared. Her hands developed strength from using the clippers. Since she was more agile than the boys, she could herd sheep into the shearing chutes almost as efficiently as Abel. By the time spring ended, she was proud that she could shear almost as well as Tim and Egan.

Abel liked to spend time with Tim and Egan. When they weren't shearing sheep, they were either running races for fun or taking turns at target practice. Lately, Abel and the boys were practicing with cutlasses.

Betsy liked to sit on the sidelines and watch them. Abel noticed that Betsy was there.

The boys decided they wanted to learn to use the Claymore, which was, at best, a clumsy weapon. Even though he used a cutlass, Abel let the boys take turns using the Claymore against him. He would fend off their blows, charge in after one of their clumsy swings, and laugh as he either knocked them down with the cutlass hilt or feigned slashing their stomachs open.

One day he teased the boys. "You know what, boys? I think I can teach Betsy to beat you!"

Tim shook his head. "That won't happen, Abel."

Egan laughed at the idea of a girl beating him.

"Then you accept the challenge?" Abel asked.

"Yes, we accept." Tim said. "Don't we Egan?"

Egan was still laughing, but he nodded his head in agreement.

That very afternoon, Abel started teaching Betsy the proper use of a navy cutlass, which was considerably lighter to handle than the Claymore sword. It took a while but she was a fast learner. After about a month of intense training, she was almost up to task.

"All right, my little colleen. I think you are ready," Abel announced.

Betsy wasn't so sure. "I think I'm about as good as I'm going to get. But wait until tomorrow. I need a good night's sleep first!" Then she became very dramatic. "We'll have our duel at dawn!" She turned to leave. "Good night, gentlemen!"

The next morning, Tim and Egan drew sticks to see who would humiliate Betsy on the field of honor. Tim drew the short stick and the combat began.

Betsy deftly warded off his blows. Tim was no taller than Betsy and not as quick. She never fooled herself into thinking she could defeat a strong, well-trained man but she was holding her own with

Tim. She could see that Tim was deliberately holding back. *He doesn't want to hurt me,* she thought.

As her strength began to wane, she moved back, away from Tim. At the same moment, he advanced toward her. Betsy waited a moment longer, then deftly dodged his attack. She turned and quickly drew out her pistol and fired a blank charge directly at him. Tim stopped in confusion.

Abel shouted, "Too bad, my brave, Scottish lad. You are now officially dead!"

Stunned, Tim stood silent for a moment holding his Claymore at his side. Then he found his voice. "Wait! That's not fair!"

Abel and Egan laughed loudly.

"Fair?" Abel said, "Did you say fair, Timmy boy? If an opponent kills you it is inevitably fair as far as he is concerned. Perhaps you learned something today."

Tim looked at Betsy. He was embarrassed but tried to save face. "Your trick took me by surprise. But the truth is that a lassie could never kill a man in real combat. I dare say you know that as well as I do."

Egan stood by his brother. "You were just lucky, Betsy. We all know that, don't we Abel?"

Abel patted Betsy on the head in a condescending manner. "Luck always plays a part in things, Egan. And we all know what Tim said is right. No woman could kill a man in real combat."

Tim was relieved when they both agreed with him, but he admitted to Betsy, "You got the best of me this time. I'll tell you now, though, it would never happen again."

Abel was proud of his pupil. "Colleen, you did well with the cutlass. I want you to remember this day," he handed her the cutlass. "Wear it well. You'll probably never need such a weapon, but if you do, you'll know how to use it."

Betsy accepted the cutlass. She smiled courteously and said, "Thank you." To herself she thought, *I wonder what you smug men would think if you knew I have already killed two of the King's soldiers. Yes, Abel, you taught me to use the cutlass but the best lesson you taught me is that men never consider women as being* worthy opponents. I will always remember that. It will give me a definite advantage.

In late summer, Betsy received a letter from her father.

> *My Dearest Daughter,*
>
> *I believe it is safe for you to return home. Although there is still a great sadness over what happened, there are no uprisings. No one will pay for the terrible events of Glencoe but life moves on.*
>
> *Uncle Andrew will make arrangements for you to cross to the mainland to the village of Wick. From there you will take the Royal Mail Coach to Inverness and return home from there. With God's speed, you will be home in a fortnight.*
>
> *I can't wait to see you!*
>
> *Your Loving Father*

"Oh, I'm going home," Betsy said. She was elated at the thought. "I have been gone for so long. When I get home, I'll never want to leave again!"

Betsy had enjoyed being in Kirkwall with her aunt and uncle and cousins. She had learned a great deal but she knew it was time for her to go home.

Pearl and Mavis didn't want her to go.

"We'll never see you again!" Pearl cried.

Mavis hugged Betsy. "I'll never forget you! Please don't forget us."

Betsy wiped away her own tears. "How could I forget you? I will always remember you. I promise!"

Uncle Andrew picked her up and swung her around, just as he had done the day she arrived. "I love you like you were my own, lassie. We'll all miss you and your bright smile."

Aunt Dora hugged her tight and handed her a small flask. She winked at her and said, "Here. You might need this to warm you on your trip. It gets cold at sea, even in the summer, and you have a long way to go. Uncle Andrew and I look on you as one of ours now, so if you ever want to come visit, we'll welcome you with open arms."

"I hope I can visit again someday. And thank you for your kindness."

Betsy left quickly before the tears started again.

Abel brought the carriage down and Betsy took her valise and got on board. The whole family waved as the carriage pulled away.

For a few awkward moments, neither Betsy nor Abel said anything.

Then Abel said, "Betsy..."

She interrupted him before he could say anymore. "Abel, I'm sorry about the things I said and all the questions I asked. It's really none of my business. I want you to know the secret is safe with me. I will never mention it again."

Abel threw up his hands in mock surprise. "Why, my little colleen, I really don't know what you are talking about." He smiled wickedly and put his fingers to his lips. "Sshh!"

When the carriage reached the quayside, Abel helped her down. The two of them stood together for a moment and then he leaned down and kissed her softly on the mouth. He looked at her momentarily. Betsy's head spun as he pulled her to him and kissed her hard. Her bonnet fell off and was left hanging askew around her neck. She felt a warm glow move through her body.

Suddenly, Abel released her. "I'm sorry, I had no right. But...I've wanted to kiss you since I first met you. Forgive me!"

Betsy slowly opened her eyes and tried to catch her breath. Awkwardly, she put her bonnet back on and retied it. "Oh, Abel..." she said softly, "Don't apologize...I mean, it's all right...I forgive you..."

Abel picked up her bag and took her down to the little ship that would take her to Wick. When they reached the gangplank, he helped her on board and escorted her to her small cabin. He started to leave when she grabbed him around the neck and kissed him. They stood close together in the semi-dark cabin, feeling each other's warm breath. He began to caress her body with his hands. Suddenly he drew back and whistled softly. "I'll miss you, my little colleen. Think of me from time to time. Maybe we will be destined to meet again someday."

Betsy watched Abel as he climbed the ladder to the main deck. He turned, blew her a kiss, and then he was gone.

She closed the cabin door and leaned against it. Those kisses had aroused feelings she had never experienced before. She liked this new feeling.

It was getting hot in the cabin so she partially undressed and stretched out on the bunk. She lay there thinking about the feel of his body against hers and how his arms felt around her. She curled up, smiled to herself, and waited for the feelings to subside.

-o-

CHAPTER 5

The ship took three days to reach the Scottish coast and the village of Wick. Betsy checked into a small inn and learned that the mail coach was not due for another two days. She spent her time wandering the streets of the village and walking by the seashore.

Betsy loved the smell of the sea. For some reason, she always felt safe when she was near the sea. She could sit for hours and listen to the sounds of the waves washing against the shore. It was relaxing and somehow reassuring to her. She wondered if other people in other parts of the world loved the seashore as much as she did.

She discovered a beautiful old arched stone bridge that crossed the River Wick to Pultneytown, an old area that was home to most of the fishermen in the area. She learned that both villages were involved in herring fisheries.

Hmmm, she thought, *I wonder if the fishermen here have a profitable sideline like my Uncle Andrew and my father!*

The Royal Mail Coach arrived on schedule and soon Betsy found herself bouncing down the road with three other passengers.

Sitting next to her was a middle-aged refined English woman with gray hair and a pleasant smile. She was returning to London after having visited relatives in the John O. Groats area, which is on the northern most tip of Scotland.

Betsy liked this woman. She had met other English people and had decided that, even though they were polite, they still wanted to lord it over everyone who was not English. But this lady did not have the fault of superiority. She was just nice.

A farmer in his late fifties, who was not at all talkative, occupied the seat across from her. The last seat held a pompous British Officer. Betsy thought he must have been somewhat important because there were two soldiers on horseback riding along with the coach.

Betsy and Mrs. Jane Bowen fell into an easy conversation.

"I'm curious, Mrs. Bowen. Could you tell me, please? How did John O. Groats get its name?"

Mrs. Bowen laughed. "That's a very interesting story, my dear. You see, the village and surrounding area was named for a Dutchman by the name of Jan de Groot. He was one of the first to operate a ferry to and from the Orkneys. It was a very profitable business. In fact he built an expensive eight-sided house for his eight sons who were constantly bickering with each other. That way, each would have his own room and his own entryway."

"That's a wonderful story," Betsy exclaimed. "I wonder if it cut down on the bickering."

"Decidedly so!" Mrs. Bowen assured her, "Unless, of course, they ran into each other in town!"

Betsy glanced at the British officer. He made her feel uneasy. She caught him staring at her. She noticed that he was a little careless in his dress, and kept sipping from a flask he carried in a side pocket. The more he drank, the more he interrupted the conversation between Mrs. Bowen and Betsy.

"How do you like Scotland, Mum?" he asked Mrs. Bowen.

"Oh, it's a beautiful place," Mrs. Bowen responded pleasantly.

"And the people, Mum?" the officer continued. "What do you think of the people of Scotland?"

"I find them most pleasant and very hard working. Those are traits I admire, I must say."

"But you are English born, are you not?" the officer went on.

"Why, yes, I am. What does that have to do with Scotland?"

"Well, Mum, I think that those of us who are true-born Englishmen find this country tedious and the people only slightly better than savages." The young officer tipped his hat to Mrs. Bowen. "Present company excluded, of course."

Mrs. Bowen glanced over at Betsy and could see she was getting angry. She placed a reassuring hand on Betsy and looked directly at the impertinent English soldier.

"Well, sir," she said. "I am a freeborn English woman who is able to make up my own mind. And I certainly do not agree with your opinion. You are also insulting this sweet young lady who is in no position to defend herself or her country from your insults. It is obvious to me that your training in courtesy is sorely lacking and you sully the uniform you are wearing because of it."

The lieutenant felt a little ill at ease. "Madam…I am a serving officer in th…"

Mrs. Bowen didn't hesitate to interrupt this rude, young officer. "So is my husband, Lieutenant. He is a Rear Admiral in the Royal Navy and is presently serving in the Admiralty in London. I doubt that he would be happy to hear about the manner in which you treated his wife. I demand to know your name and regiment!"

"I am Lieutenant Oliver Pennington of the Buffs, Mum." He again tipped his hat and nodded toward her. "And I apologize to you. No disrespect was intended."

"I think you had best apologize to my companion, Lieutenant Pennington," Mrs. Bowen said as she pulled herself upright and looked Pennington straight in the eye. "She was the one you insulted with your outrageous remarks."

"As you wish, Mum." He looked at Betsy. "I'm sorry if I offended you, Miss." He didn't sound the least bit contrite.

Betsy took her lead from Mrs. Bowen. "Well, sir, you did offend me and I do not wish to speak to you again." She turned her head away from him and looked out the coach window.

The farmer, who to this point had not said anything, made his opinion clear to everyone. "You have a lot to learn, young man, about honor, integrity, and plain old good manners. With your haughty attitude, I venture to say you won't live to see another year before someone challenges you…and you'll lose! Enough said!" He nodded to the ladies, leaned back in the coach and closed his eyes.

The foursome rode in silence and soon Betsy dozed off on Mrs. Bowen's shoulder.

Betsy awoke as the carriage came to a stop. She looked confused for a moment. "Where are we?" she asked.

"We're in Helmsdale, dear," Mrs. Bowen said. "We'll spend the night here." Betsy lifted the curtain on the coach window and looked out.

"Not much here," Mrs. Bowen said. "This is just a fishing village. It's not much different from all the other North Sea villages.

Betsy climbed down and watched as the coachman and the hostlers moved the luggage inside the inn and up the staircase to the ladies' respective rooms. Betsy noticed that the two military escorts who had ridden behind the coach took special care with a wooden chest that was bound with metal bands. The chest had a padlock on it and was marked with a crown.

Kings money! Betsy thought as she looked at it.

She entered the inn and headed upstairs to find her room. Mrs. Bowen was waiting for her.

"Betsy, dear," she said. "I wanted you to know that I am staying here in Helmsdale for a few days to tend to some of my husband's investments, so I won't be traveling on with you."

Betsy was disappointed. "Oh, I'll miss your company on the coach tomorrow."

Mrs. Bowen looked around to see if anyone was close enough to eavesdrop. She lowered her voice. "I want to warn you to be careful of that loutish lieutenant. He learned he couldn't intimidate me, but I'm worried about his treatment of you. Be very careful. I have a feeling he can be a cunning and dangerous man."

"Thank you for your concern," Betsy said. I think the lieutenant might be surprised at how formidable I can be if I have to."

"Well, sweet girl. Be careful anyway. Please!"

"Thank you, Mum. I will be." Betsy opened the door to her room.

"I feel better now. Meet me in fifteen minutes and we'll go down to dinner. My treat!" Mrs. Bowen smiled and entered her room that was adjacent to Betsy's.

When the two entered the main dining room, a large fire was burning in the fireplace. It was a cozy, comfortable room and they were seated at a table where they could feel the warmth of the fire. Mrs. Bowen looked around and immediately spotted Lieutenant Pennington and his companion soldiers seated at a table across the room. Betsy saw them, too. When their eyes met, the soldiers stood up and bowed courteously.

The ladies acknowledged the gesture, then turned away.

"Well," Mrs. Bowen said softly, "That's more like it!"

Betsy tried hard not to giggle.

Mrs. Bowen ordered a bottle of wine. Betsy hadn't much experience with wine but since this was a special occasion, she decided to indulge. She sipped it slowly and found the flavor to be quite enjoyable.

Soon they were served a fine meal of roasted mutton with a large bowl of hot oatmeal as a side dish. There was brown barley bread and some jam in a small bowl.

By the time they finished their dinner, they noticed that the soldiers were nowhere to be seen.

"Thank you so much for dinner, Mrs. Bowen, but if you'll excuse me, I think I'd like to go up to my room now." The long journey had taken its toll on Betsy and she was ready for a good night's sleep.

"I'm right behind you, child. We'll say our goodbyes in the morning."

~~~

The next morning, Betsy was awakened by a knock on the door. She opened her eyes. It took her a few moments to realize where she was.

"It's time to get up, lass," someone said. "The coach will be ready in about an hour and a half. Get dressed and come down to breakfast."

Betsy rose up on one elbow. "Thank you. I'm awake."

She washed up and packed her bag. Before she left the room, she decided to heed Mrs. Bowen's warning to be careful. She loaded her pistol and put it in her pocket. She slid her dirk into her sleeve with its handle pointing down so she could grasp it easily. She tested her ability to draw it from its scabbard and found that she could do so with ease.

By the time she went downstairs for breakfast, she still had plenty of time to spare.

Mrs. Bowen joined her for breakfast. When they finished, she warmly embraced Betsy. "Perhaps we'll meet again someday. But remember my warning, dear child. God speed!"

When Betsy boarded the coach, Lieutenant Pennington and another passenger were already seated.

"Good morning," the lieutenant said without a smile.

The other passenger was well dressed and polite. He was a young man of about twenty. "Allow me to introduce myself. My name is Will Reed."

"Good morning to both of you," Betsy said and seated herself across from the young man.

Will Reed was obviously English and very pleasant. The two enjoyed a lively conversation. Lieutenant Pennington had nothing to say.

When they stopped in the town of Brora for lunch and to change horses, Mr. Reed kissed Betsy's hand and said goodbye. "I've enjoyed my journey with you, Miss Betsy. I hope the rest of your journey is pleasant."

When Betsy re-boarded the coach, Lieutenant Pennington sat opposite her. This time he was leering at her. She ignored him, closed her eyes and tried to sleep.

After a while, Lieutenant Pennington cleared his throat. "Ahem…"

Betsy opened her eyes.

"Well, Missy. What are you going to do now that there is no one around to hold your hand and protect you from the big bad wolf?" he asked sarcastically.

Betsy refused to make eye contact with him. She lifted the curtain and looked out the window. "I'm sure I don't know what you mean," Betsy replied.

The lieutenant crossed the narrow space between the seats and sat next to her. He started to reach for her hand when suddenly there was shouting from the rear of the coach. Betsy jumped when she heard gunshots. The coach lurched then gained speed.

Lieutenant Pennington pulled the window curtain back and stuck his head and shoulders out the window. "What the hell's going on back th…"

He never finished his sentence. The lieutenant fell backward and slumped into the seat. Betsy looked at his puffy face and saw blood streaming down both sides of his nose. There was a hole between his eyes. Lieutenant Oliver Pennington of the Buffs was deader than a doornail.

The shouting and shooting continued for a few moments. Betsy held on for dear life as the coach sped forward and then suddenly went downhill at a very high speed. The coach lurched and fell onto its side. Betsy and the dead lieutenant tumbled inside as the coach rolled over and over. As the coach smashed into the trunks of two large trees and came to an abrupt stop, Betsy was knocked unconscious.

When Betsy regained consciousness, she laid quietly for a few moments; afraid she might be dead. When she heard a bird sing, she felt it was safe to open her eyes. She was lying on top of Lieutenant. Pennington who had softened her fall with his dead body. She repositioned herself and saw that the coach was on its side in a ravine that was a considerable distance from the road. The doors of the coach had been torn off. Betsy crawled out and carefully lowered herself to the ground. She looked around. Her valise was lying a short distance from the coach. As she went over to pick it up, she saw the chest bearing the Royal insignia. She stopped to listen for other voices. Maybe someone else had survived, too. She heard nothing except the cheerful sounds of songbirds.

Where are all the others? she wondered. She started to climb back up the hill and had only taken a few steps when she saw the coachman and the co-driver lying like crumpled rag dolls near the top of the hill. She could tell from the angle of their necks that they were both dead. She returned to the chest and tried to move it but it was too heavy for her to lift.

She thought for a minute, M*aybe I could drag it somewhere where no one could find it.*

The hill that led back to the road was too steep. She turned around and looked at the opposite hill. It was not as steep and in fact seemed to level off at a distance about one hundred yards to the right.

Now, where would be a good place to hide it? Then she saw it. About fifty feet up the hill at about a 45-degree angle from the wrecked coach, Betsy saw a jagged rock ledge. *That should do nicely,* she said to herself, *if only I can get the chest up to it.*

She climbed back into the coach and found a blanket. She laid it next to the box and then rolled the chest onto the blanket. Ever so slowly, Betsy dragged the chest up the side of the hill to level ground. She found some soft soil beside a large rock.

The chest was extremely heavy and it took all of Betsy's strength to move it. She kept pulling the blanket and the chest moved upward. She stopped to rest, then she pulled some more. *Keep going, Betsy,* she told herself. *Just a little farther.*

Finally, she was within a few feet of the rock. She examined the area around it and discovered that the soil beneath the rock was soft and moist.

This will be a perfect hiding place, she thought.

She used her dirk to dig a shallow hole, pushed the chest in, and then covered it up. In an attempt to do away with any signs of digging, she swept the ground around the site.

She stood for a few minutes and committed the location to her memory. Later, she would return to claim her prize and she needed to remember exactly where it was buried.

Betsy returned to the coach and found a water barrel that had been broken open but still contained a small amount of water. She washed her hands and used her knife to clean the dirt out from under her fingernails.

As she brushed the hair from her eyes, she cried out. "Ouch!" She ran her fingers over a bump on her forehead that was tender to the touch.

Betsy started shaking. The trauma had taken its toll on her. She knew it was only a matter of time until she would be rescued. When the coach carrying a king's ransom didn't arrive at its next destination on time, a search party would be dispatched immediately. She knew the safest place was for her to go back inside the coach. She did not want to go back inside with the dead Pennington but she had to. It would look better if she was found inside the coach. But first, she took the pistol from her pocket and put it and the dirk inside her valise underneath some clothing. She thought it would be better not to have the weapons on her person when she was found.

It started raining, so she quickly climbed back inside and curled up a few inches away from the dead man and promptly fell asleep.

The rain fell steadily and wiped out all signs that Betsy might have left when she moved the treasure chest.

Several hours later, she heard noises above the ravine. There were lanterns swinging in the darkness and she knew that someone was coming. She lay very still and waited for them to discover her. She could hear them coming closer and closer. Finally, one man climbed up onto the coach and, using his lantern, peered down inside.

"Hey, Sergeant! Looks like there are two people still inside. They're probably dead, though."

Betsy took this opportunity to moan softly.

"No, wait! I think the girl may still be alive! Someone help me get her out of there."

While one man held the lantern, another climbed up the outside of the coach and gradually let himself down inside. He moved the dead lieutenant out of the way and pulled Betsy to a sitting position.

"Are you hurt, Miss?" he asked.

Betsy whimpered a little and didn't say anything for a few moments.

"Where...where...am I?" she stammered.

"There's been an accident, Miss. I hope you aren't badly hurt. Can you move?"

"Yes, I...think so." She touched the bump on her forehead. "Oww! I think I hurt my head...and I feel kind of woozy."

"All right. Take it easy now," he said gently, "Let me help you get out." He lifted her gently to the arms of another man crowded on top of the wrecked coach. "Easy with her, mate. She may be hurt."

Two soldiers carried her to the ground and held onto her while she tried to stand.

"Does anything hurt?" one asked. "I see you have a nasty gash above your eye."

She wobbled and grabbed the soldier's arm. "I'm kind of sore... and my head hurts, but other than that, I think I'm all right."

The sergeant offered her a drink of water. "I'm sorry, M'am, this might not be a good time to ask, but can you tell me what happened here?"

Betsy didn't realize how thirsty she was. She drank the full cup of water without stopping. "Thank you, sir. I was very thirsty." She handed him the cup and he refilled it from his canteen.

She took a few more sips. "I heard shooting but I was inside the coach and couldn't see what was happening outside. The lieutenant... the one in the coach...put his head out the window and was shot. He was killed instantly and he fell back inside. The coach started to speed up. It started swaying back and forth. I could feel it falling over. Then it started to roll over and over. That was the last thing I remember."

"Thank you, Miss," the sergeant said, then turned to two of his men. "Take her back to the village before she drowns. And for gods sake! Wrap her up in a blanket! The rest of you men keep looking for that strong box."

When Betsy awoke the next morning, she was in a clean, comfortable bed in an Inn in Golspie, which would have been the next stop for the coach. A middle-aged woman sat next to her bed.

"Ah! You're finally awake. How do you feel?" she asked.

"I feel very weak," Betsy answered truthfully. "And my head still hurts."

"Well, I'm not surprised. You looked like a drowned rat when they brought you in last night. By the way, I'm Erma MacLain. My husband and I own this inn. And what is your name, dear?"

Betsy tried to sit up. My name is Betsy Stewart. Thank you for taking me in."

"I don't mean to be nosey," Mrs. MacLain said, "but why is someone so young traveling alone? And where might you be goin'?"

"I had been visiting family in Kirkwall. Now I'm on my home to Banff. My parents are waiting for me."

"Well, don't try to do too much today. You need to rest," Mrs. MacLain said. "Oh, yes, dear. They delivered your bag when they brought you in last night. Do you need anything from it now?"

"I don't think so." Betsy paused before continuing. "Mrs. MacLain, do you know what happened to us yesterday?"

"I certainly do! It's the talk of the town!" Mrs. MacLain couldn't wait to tell Betsy all the details. "It was a big robbery! You see, the robbers were looking for gold and they knew the Royal Mail Couch was carrying some. But they found a lot of trouble first. They killed the two coachmen and both of the soldier escorts, but some of them got killed, too. They found two...or was it three dead outlaws. They think the others grabbed the gold and high-tailed it out of there. The Army is scouring the country right now. But, I think the rascals got clean away. They took to the mountains I'll wager." She leaned closer to Betsy and lowered her voice. "Personally, I wish them well!"

Betsy was surprised. "Why do you say that?"

"Well, our Dutch King got his nose pulled hard yesterday and I don't think any true Scot will feel badly about that. Do you? You know, after Glencoe and all."

Betsy tossed her head. "Well, I don't know about those things," she answered quite innocently. "I leave that to the men."

Mrs. MacLain nodded. "No doubt you are better off not worrying about such things, you still being a wee tyke and all." Mrs. MacLain stood up. "I'll go down and fetch you some porridge, bread, and milk so you'll get your strength back. You rest now." She patted Betsy's hand and smiled.

After Mrs. MacLain left, Betsy stretched out luxuriously and smiled to herself. *"Sooo...everyone thinks the robbers got the gold. Good! The soldiers can look all they want. They won't find it. It's MY buried treasure now!* She frowned and absent-mindedly chewed on her bottom lip. *Just one little problem. How will I ever retrieve it and get it back home without anyone finding out?* She had several days to think about it before another Royal Mail Coach arrived.

When the coach arrived, Betsy was ready. She had a plan and she was ready to put it into action.

-o-

CHAPTER 6

The driver helped Betsy into the coach. "You're a brave lass to be traveling all alone, especially after what happened the other day."

"Yes, I heard about the robbery," Betsy said quite innocently.

"That's probably why no one else is traveling right now. Everyone's afraid," he said and closed the door of the coach. "Don't you worry. I'll take good care of you."

Betsy was glad she was alone. Now she would have time to perfect her plan, down to the smallest detail. She paid attention to the road they traveled because very soon she would be doubling back this way when she came to claim the King's chest and its contents.

The coach headed south and stopped in Dornoch for lunch. It was a small town but Betsy noted there was a general store close by the inn. In front of the store, there was a pony cart with a "For Sale" sign propped against a wheel.

Her eyes opened wide. "Oh, that is just what I need!"

It was late evening when the coach rumbled into Bonar Bridge for the overnight stay. The driver opened the coach door and helped Betsy down.

"Have a nice evening and a good night's sleep, lass. The coach will leave at 8 a.m. sharp."

"Thank you, sir, but I have relatives in this town," she lied. "I'll be staying a few days."

"Good luck to ye, then." He tipped his hat as she walked toward the inn.

Betsy didn't want to draw attention to herself so she ate a quiet supper, then went to her room for the night.

The next morning, she approached the innkeeper. "Can you tell me when the next north bound coach will arrive?"

The innkeeper frowned slightly. "Hm. Let me see." He walked over to a desk covered with papers. He licked a finger and then picked through one stack in the center. "Aha!" He pulled out one sheet that apparently listed the mail coach schedule. "Here it is. Umm.

Tomorrow. It will arrive about noon. Would you like to book passage?" He looked up at her with raised eyebrows.

"Uh, no. You know I just arrived from Dornoch yesterday. Why would I wish to return so soon?" She had to think fast. She didn't want anyone to remember her much less remember her travel plans. "I'm going to meet my brother…here…tomorrow. We're planning on settling here…maybe."

The innkeeper looked at her strangely. As he walked away, he mumbled, "She's a funny one. Wonder what she's *really* talking about."

Betsy had planned on changing her appearance when she returned to Dornoch but decided now was a better time. She spent most of the day walking about town and buying new clothes and a broad-brimmed hat.

After supper, she paid the innkeeper for her two-night stay. She told him she was meeting a relative in the morning and together they would wait for her brother's arrival.

The innkeeper was quite busy and obviously uninterested in Betsy or her explanation, but he nodded his acknowledgement.

Before retiring, she arranged to have breakfast sent to her room the next morning. That way she wouldn't have to deal with anyone in the dining room.

She didn't sleep well that night. Restful sleep was interrupted with frightful dreams of being chased, and running for her life.

A knock on her door announced that morning had arrived and so had her breakfast. Wearily, she answered the door and moved aside as the server placed a tray on a sideboard. The smell of the coffee aroused her appetite and she ate heartily except for two rolls and an apple which she put aside for later.

She bathed from a basin that had been filled the night before, and then pulled out the clothes she had purchased the previous day. Betsy put on the full-sleeved shirt and peasant trousers and tucked her hair under the broad-brimmed hat. She stepped over to the looking glass above the sideboard and was surprised at her reflection.

"Why!" she said aloud. "I do look like a boy! I really do!" She turned halfway around and tried to see herself from the back. She giggled. "Now, if I had a brother, what would his name be?" she wondered. "Hmm!" She faced the mirror again and looked at her reflection. "I look like someone whose name is Rob. That's it! If anyone asks, I'll tell them my name is Rob. Robbie Brown."

Satisfied, she packed her valise and quietly left the inn through the rear entrance. She didn't want to be seen by the innkeeper or anyone else.

Betsy walked to the edge of town, found a large shade tree and sat down to wait patiently for the coach that would take her back to Dornoch.

She heard the coach before she saw it. She ran into the road and saw the horses and the coach followed by a cloud of dust. She jumped up and down and flagged down the driver.

"Kind sir," she said in as low a voice as she could muster. "I must get to Dornoch. Can I buy passage from you?"

The driver seemed a little hesitant. "Well, young man. You should have bought your ticket back at the inn. But," he didn't want to miss out on a fare, "Oh, well, climb aboard."

Betsy handed him the fare. She threw her valise on top of the coach, and then climbed inside. An old man was sprawled across one seat. His eyes were half-closed and he reeked of the smell of whiskey. He raised his head slightly and mumbled, "Top of the mornin' to you, sir." He belched loudly, then fell back and started snoring.

Betsy held her nose. Not only did the old man smell of whiskey but it was obvious he hadn't bathed in some time. She pulled back away from him as far as she could.

Oh, my, she said to herself, *this is going to be a very long day!*

Later, Betsy was glad she had saved the rolls and apple. It was the only food she had until the coach pulled into Dornoch later that evening. She got out of the coach first, and then watched as her fellow passenger stumbled out of the coach and staggered down the street. He had sipped from a flask throughout the day and was still feeling no pain.

"Drunker than a skunk," Betsy observed then turned to enter the inn.

After a tasty supper and a good night's sleep, Betsy was ready for her adventure. Today was the day she would find out if there was really gold inside the chest she had so carefully buried.

Still dressed like a boy, Betsy walked to the general store where she had seen the pony cart for sale. She was relieved when she saw that it was.

She went inside and bought some food, since she had no idea how long it would be before she had a decent meal.

Remembering to lower her voice, she said, "I'd like to buy the pony cart you have for sale, but I'll need a horse to pull it. Would you know where I might buy one?"

The storeowner seemed like a friendly chap. He smiled broadly. "You've come to the right place, laddie. I have several in the barn out back. Come take your pick."

Betsy followed her benefactor. Indeed, she had no trouble choosing an animal sturdy enough for the work ahead. She paid for the horse and the cart and while she was at it, she bought some tools, some nails, and some boards. Now she had everything she needed and she was anxious to be on her way.

A few minutes later, Betsy climbed onto the pony cart and heaved a sigh of relief. "So far so good!" She snapped the reins and the horse moved forward toward Golspie and the mysterious chest.

There was little traffic on the road, only an occasional carriage or horseback rider. They just waved and continued on their way.

About an hour before sunset, Betsy pulled over and parked in a secluded grove of trees. There was a small pond in the center, so she unhitched the horse and tied him to a tree next to the water. She took time to enjoy a cool drink and wash some of the dust from her face and hands.

There was work to be done before it got dark and Betsy wasted no time. She took the tools, nails, and boards out of the cart and laid them in front of her. Silently she thanked her father for teaching her skills that he would have taught a son. She wondered at the time why he bothered to teach her. His answer was simple.

"First of all, it's not a bother to me. Secondly, you never know when a skill will come in handy. I want you to be as prepared as possible for any circumstance."

Now it was time to get to work. She constructed a box about several inches high, shaping the boards as carefully as she could so that the box would take up only about a third of the floor of the cart. When she finished, it looked as though a step had been built to make it easier for a short person to handle the horse's reins. She gathered handfuls of mud from close to the pond and smeared the areas that had been fresh cut to make them look worn. It was late when she completed the work. Before she slept, she realized how hungry she was so she ate some dried herring and bread and hoped it wouldn't sit on her stomach like a stone.

When Betsy awoke in the morning she loaded the cart with her belongings, hitched the horse to the cart, and climbed aboard. Once again, luck was with her as there was almost no traffic along the way. She made good time and soon found herself in the outdoor market in Golspie where she stopped to fill up her jugs with water and buy some food. She saw no one she recognized and she left town as quickly as possible.

Now comes the hard part, she thought. *Am I going to recognize the place where the coach was ambushed? What if I can't find it?*

She remembered the innkeeper's wife, Mrs. MacLain, telling her that the robbery had occurred about ten miles north of town. She drove slowly for about an hour, looking at the left side of the road for clues to where the accident might have happened. She remembered how hard it had rained that night and was afraid the tracks might have been washed away.

She needn't have worried. Up ahead she could clearly see a break in the brush along the roadside. She stopped the cart a few yards behind and jumped out. Carefully, she walked to the area and looked at the ground. There were wheel marks. She stepped closer to the edge of the ravine. In the trees below, she could see the wreckage of the coach. Her heart was in her mouth but she had presence of mind enough not to do anything foolish. She went back to the cart and as she did, she wiped out her footprints in the dust of the road. She didn't want anyone coming by to notice she had even stopped to look at the wreckage.

Betsy drove on about a hundred yards where she found a track that turned off to the right side of the road. It led to a wooded area with trees and brush on both sides. It proved to be a perfect spot for a hiding place. She unhitched the horse and retied him to a bush so he could graze.

Betsy returned to the cart and picked up a short shovel and her small bag of powder and shot she used for her pistol. She walked back up the track and looked to see if there was anyone on the road. Satisfied that she was alone, she crossed the road and went down the bank to the bottom of the ravine and walked to where the remains of the coach lay. She turned around and looked up the opposite hill to try to get her bearings. Close to the top, she saw the jagged rock.

"That's it! She said. "That's where I buried the chest." Hurriedly, she climbed the hill using her hands as well as her feet to move faster.

She soon found the spot where the chest was buried. Carefully, she removed the dirt covering it. She dragged it out of its hiding place and studied the lock on the box.

If only I had the key! she thought. *It's a sturdy lock. Looks like only a blacksmith could cut through this lock.* She rested on her knees for a moment. "I know!" she said out loud. "I'll shoot it off!" She loaded her pistol with ease and fired. Her first attempt taught her a serious lesson. The ball she fired ricocheted off the metal lock and went whizzing back close to her head and did absolutely no damage to the lock.

Now what? Betsy wondered. *What would my father do?*

She looked closely at the lock again. It contained a large keyhole.

"I wonder what would happen if I put a little gunpowder directly into the lock?"

She took a chance. Very carefully she poured a little gunpowder into the keyhole. Then she poured in a little more. She stood up and laid a gunpowder trail from the lock to a tree about ten feet away. She stood behind the tree, reached out using her flint to make a spark and lit the powder trail.

Banners of Honor

Within moments, there was an intense explosion. Startled, Betsy jumped back. She peeked out from behind the tree. She waited for the smoke to clear then ran and kneeled down beside the box. There was no sign of the lock. It had been blown to pieces. Luckily, the box itself suffered only minor damage.

Betsy was elated. Slowly she lifted the lid. She took a deep breath. She couldn't believe her eyes. The box was filled with gold bars. There were dozens of them. Betsy lifted one out of the chest. It was heavy!

Her heart was racing. "Oh, dear Lord," she exclaimed. "This must be worth thousands and thousands of pounds!"

As she replaced the gold bar, her eye fell on the top of the chest. The outside was arched but the inside was flat. *A false bottom?* she wondered.

She pulled out her dirk and carefully pried the edges of the wood. It moved. "It is a false bottom," she declared and continued to pry the compartment open.

Inside, there were four leather pouches. She untied the drawstring of one of them and peeked inside. It looked like stones. She poured some of the contents into her hand. Once again, Betsy couldn't believe her eyes.

"Jewels!" she shouted to the world. "A King's ransom in jewels!"

She didn't know exactly what kind they were, but she did know they must be extremely valuable.

She opened each of the four pouches and found they all contained a variety of sparkling jewels. Red, blue, green! Each was more beautiful than the one before.

Betsy was excited. She knew she had a fortune in her hands and if anyone found out about it, she would be killed in the blink of an eye. She had to work fast. She couldn't afford to be seen by anyone.

First, she took the four leather pouches and ran around the hill and across the road to where her cart was hidden. She hid the bags under some leaves at the base of a tree a short distance away from the cart.

As she started to return for the gold, she heard a carriage approaching. She stayed hidden, hoping the carriage wouldn't stop.

As it passed close to her, she heard a child crying. Then a woman's voice, "We'll be home soon, son. Papa is going as fast as he can."

Soon the sounds faded. Betsy looked both ways but the only dust cloud she saw was of the departing carriage. Quickly, she ran directly across the road and angled down the hill to the treasure chest. Using her shawl as a makeshift bag, she loaded six bars of gold into the shawl and carried it around the hill and back across the road to the waiting cart. She opened the box she had built inside the cart and, one by one, she placed the gold bars in their new hiding place. She repeated the process until all seventy-two bars were safely hidden in the pony cart. Betsy was exhausted by the time she had loaded the last of them. She was hungry, too, but before she could rest, there was one more thing to do. She took several long drinks of water then returned one final time to the King's Royal Chest, which was now as empty as a bird's nest in winter. She re-buried the chest and removed all signs she had been there. As she crossed the road for the last time to return to her hiding place, she could see in the distance another cloud of dust announcing more travelers. Her heart thumping, she ran toward the trees and safety. Soon the carriage rumbled past Betsy and her treasure. It didn't even slow down. She took a deep breath. She was safe, at least for the time being.

She ate a quick meal and fell into a dreamless sleep.

When morning came, Betsy felt refreshed. She knew the most dangerous part of her journey was ahead of her. She didn't want to have to explain herself to anyone. Being dressed as a boy would help. People would be less likely to stop and question her.

Her plan after leaving Golspie was to go through Dornoch and, rather than go to Bonar Bridge where she might be recognized, she would travel south to Nairn, store the cart, sell the horse, and take the Royal Mail Coach to her home in Banff.

She hitched the horse and headed back toward Golspie. This time she wouldn't stop in town. She thought she had enough food and water to last until she reached Nairn, although she had no idea how long it would take.

No matter, she told herself, *I'll make it last.*

Travel was slower now because the pony cart was bearing much more weight than it was designed to carry. She took her time and watched the road for ruts and other hazards that could cause damage to the wheels. This proved to be no problem and soon she had passed through Golspie and was back out in the country headed toward her next goal which was the village of Dornoch.

She drove until it was almost dark and found a spot where she could take the cart off the road and hide it in a small valley with a stream flowing through it. Betsy was delighted that finally she could bathe herself and wash her clothes. She hung them on bushes to dry overnight, curled up in her shawl and fell asleep, her pistol and dirk within easy reach.

The next day she passed through Dornoch and continued south to Nairn. It took Betsy another day and a half to reach the village. After inquiring, she was told the coach would arrive in two days. This would give her time to find safe storage for her cart. She befriended the wife of the innkeeper who told Betsy, "I wish I had a son just like you, Robbie."

The woman took pleasure in feeding and caring for her temporary son and cheerfully agreed to keep the pony cart for as long as necessary.

"I'm glad you plan to return, Robbie," she said. "Maybe next time you can stay a little longer." She kissed him on the cheek. "Why, Robbie, you're blushing!"

Before Betsy boarded the coach to Banff, she placed the four leather pouches in the inside pocket of her valise. She chuckled to herself. "I have to leave the gold, but if I left the jewels, Father would think I was daft!"

-o-

CHAPTER 7

The Royal Mail Coach arrived in Banff at sunset. Betsy stepped down from the coach and took a deep breath. Clutching her valise tightly in her arms, she ran the short distance to her home and burst through the front door. Her father and Uncle Roy were sitting at the kitchen table eating supper.

Ewin Stewart jumped up and stared at the person who had entered his home. Betsy saw his look of bewilderment. She dropped her valise and laughed as she whipped off her hat. Her long auburn hair fell around her face and shoulders.

"It's me, Father...Betsy!"

Relieved as well as surprised, Ewin started laughing. "Child, why in the world are you dressed like a lad?" He quickly moved toward his daughter and caught her in a strong embrace.

"It's a long story, Father. I'll join you for supper...I'm famished ...and tell you all about it." She looked around. "Where's Mother?"

"She's in France visiting your grandparents. That, too, is a long story."

Roy filled a plate with food and handed it to Betsy. "We've all been worried about you, lass. Praise the Lord you got home safely. Now sit down and tell us all about it."

Ewin and Roy sat mesmerized as Betsy related, in great detail, her harrowing story. When she finished, she looked first at her father, then at her uncle, and then back again to her father. Each of them looked at each other, and then slowly shook their heads in disbelief.

Roy spoke first. "My God, child, you do get yourself into fixes, now don't you?"

Ewin reached over and squeezed his daughter's hand. His face looked serious. "I am so very sorry for what you've gone through the last few months. I feel I am much to blame. You are much too young to be away from home for so long. I see that now. I won't make that mistake again. From now on, you'll be with me and your mother."

Betsy understood what her father was telling her. "Father, you taught me well. If you hadn't, I never would have survived. I have tested my skills and am stronger and more confident because of it. Besides," she stood up and turned full circle a couple of times. "Don't I make a fine looking laddie?"

"You do, indeed!" Her father's face relaxed and he smiled at his brave daughter. "Aye! You do indeed!"

Betsy walked over to her valise. She reached inside and took out the four leather pouches. She handed one to her father and one to her Uncle Roy. After she opened the other two pouches, she carefully poured the contents onto the kitchen table.

Eyes wide, both men whistled their surprise.

"Will you look at these?" Ewin declared. He picked up a large emerald with one hand and an even larger ruby with the other. "I don't know much about precious stones," he admitted, "but I'll stake my life on the fact that these are worth thousands of pounds." He looked at his brother who was fingering several diamonds. "What do you think, Roy?"

Roy looked up with a twinkle in his eye. "I think, my brother, that your little girl is now a very *rich* little girl.

"Lassie," Ewin said, "do you have any idea what you have done this time?"

Betsy scooped the jewels back into the pouches. "What I have done is to relieve King William of some of his wealth," she said flippantly.

Ewin sighed as he looked at his daughter who somehow looked older than her sixteen years. "Well, let's see what you have accomplished during the last six months. First, you killed two of the King's soldiers, and second, you robbed that same King of God knows how much gold and jewels. Do you realize how ruthless the English are? They will search until they find out where the treasure is. Rest assured, they have not forgotten their two dead Campbells. There will be a bounty on your head. If you are ever found out…or if you are ever caught…" He hesitated. "Justice will be swift. No matter that you are just a girl." He paused and took a deep breath, then let it out. "It is my job to protect you…and protect you I will! We must leave Scotland for a safer land."

Betsy knew her father was right and suddenly she felt afraid. "But where, Father? Where can we go?"

Ewin looked at his daughter, then took her in his arms and hugged her. "Since neither you nor this treasure can remain in Scotland, we will go to France to be with your mother and grandparents."

Betsy was surprised but pleased with her father's decision. "When shall we leave?" she asked.

"We'll leave in the morning to first get the gold, and then we'll sail for France. Now, let's pack as much as we can for we won't return here for a very long time...if ever." He turned to his brother. "Roy, you'll come with us, I hope. We'll need your help."

Roy's lips turned up in the faintest smile. "I wouldn't miss this for the world!"

The next morning, the three boarded *The Cormorant* and set sail for Nairn.

~~~

It was sunset when they arrived at their destination. Roy stayed with the boat. Again dressed like a boy, Betsy and her father walked to the inn to fetch the pony cart.

"By the way," Betsy forewarned her father, "the innkeeper and his wife think my name is Robbie Brown." She skipped a few steps. "Good name, don't you think?"

Ewin smiled at his creative, and daring, daughter. "Aye, laddie, I do!"

When Maggie Owens saw Robbie, she couldn't contain herself. She ran to him and smothered him in a bear hug. "Oh, Robbie, me boy. It's so good to see you again. I hope you are staying for a few days."

"No, I'm afraid not. My father and I just came to collect my pony cart," she said in her deepest voice.

Maggie's lower lip jutted out in an exaggerated pout. "Oh, I'd so hoped you could stay a while." She looked at Robbie's father. "Mr. Brown, you have a wonderful son here. I do hope you appreciate him."

Ewin didn't miss a beat. "Oh, yes, M'am. I appreciate my son more than you'll ever know."

She seemed relieved. "Good, then! Now!" She clapped her hands together, "Let's go get your cart and you can be on your way."

When they reached the barn, Ewin pulled Maggie aside and smiled at her very cordially. "Thank you for helping my son. He speaks highly of you. He said you remind him so much of his beloved grandmother. And indeed you do."

Maggie's face reddened and she fanned herself with her hands. "Oh, he's such a dear boy! Just like one of my own."

Ewin slipped a few coins in her hand. "Would it be possible to borrow a horse just long enough to help us get the cart aboard our boat? Then I'll return him immediately. I promise!"

She quickly pocketed the coins. "Why, of course," she agreed. "That won't be a problem at all."

As Robbie and his father climbed aboard the cart, Maggie took out her handkerchief, blew her nose and waved goodbye.

Under the cover of night, the three carried the bars of gold onto the boat and placed them inside a strongbox in the lower cabin. When the last bar was removed, Ewin took the empty cart out of town and pushed it over a cliff where it broke into small pieces that tumbled into the surf below. He rode the horse back to the inn, placed him in his stall, and ran back to the boat. As soon as he was aboard, *The Cormorant* cast off and drifted toward the open sea.

The weather was clear and prevailing winds made the sailing effortless. Within a few days, they anchored in Aberdeen to take on supplies. While there, Ewin posted a letter to his wife telling her of their planned arrival and what she needed to do before that could happen. He asked her to send her response c/o General Delivery in Poole, England. He hoped the weather would hold and he would be in Poole when it arrived.

Soon they sailed south past the mouth of the Thames River and proceeded down the coast of the English Channel to the small, protected port of Poole. They dropped anchor and awaited Heather's reply.

~~~

Ewin had suggested three possible dates for a rendezvous in the area of the French village of St. Val'ery Sur Somme. When Heather's reply finally arrived, the weather was still miraculously clear and it looked as though the first alternate date would prove to be possible.

Since he had to cross the Channel to St. Val'ery, Ewin waited a few days to be sure the weather was just right.

It was late at night when they made landfall at the mouth of the Somme River. As planned, three signal lights were in place to guide them. A horse and wagon were waiting. As per Ewin's instructions, no one was with the wagon. They beached the boat and carried the treasure up to the waiting wagon. When they were finished Ewin and Roy pushed the boat back into the river where Roy would wait for the tide to turn so he could take the boat up river to the port of St. Val'ery. Ewin and Betsy climbed into the wagon where they found a map, held in place by a stone under the wagon seat. The map showed them the way to the farm Heather had been told to purchase. The map was clear and they only had about three miles to travel. The road was well traveled and easy to follow. When they reached the turnoff, Ewin was pleased to see the farmhouse sat a good distance back from the road on good level ground. They pulled the wagon into a large barn adjacent to the house. Ewin took Betsy's arm and together they went up to the farmhouse that was obviously in good repair. They entered through the side door that led to the kitchen. There were food supplies on the table. As they walked into the sitting room, Ewin led Betsy to the couch.

"I want you to lie down and sleep for a time. I'll stand watch."

Betsy started to object.

"Do what I tell you, lassie," he said gently. "I expect your mother will be along soon. I'll wait for her.

Betsy did as she was told. "All right, Father. Oh, it feels good to stretch out," she admitted. "But do let me know when Mother gets here. I'm so anxious to see her."

"Rest assured, I will. I want to see your mother's face when you tell her everything you've been up to."

He covered her with a blanket that was thrown across the back of the couch. Betsy patted her pocket to make sure her pistol was handy and was asleep before her father left the room.

She slept for almost three hours when she was awakened by the sound of a horse's hooves. She jumped up and grabbed her pistol on the way to the window. Although it was not quite daylight, she looked out and could make out the silhouette of her mother astride a fine looking horse. Betsy ran outside to meet her. Her father was coming from the direction of the barn and they both reached Heather at the same time. Betsy clung to her mother and started sobbing. Without Betsy saying a word, Heather understood her daughter's emotions. She cradled Betsy's head in her hands.

"I know, sweetheart," she cooed. "It's all right. We're together again. You're safe now. Let's go inside and you can tell me everything that happened."

In vivid detail, Betsy told her mother how she managed to steal King William's treasure.

Heather was alarmed. "My God, child, you're lucky to be alive! The English would have hanged you if you had been caught. You took a terrible chance!" Eyes wide, she looked at her husband. "Ewin, do you think she is safe? Do you think *we* are safe? For the second time this year, this child has placed herself in grave danger."

"Just relax, Heather," he said to his wife. "Betsy was very clever. She hid her trail well. No one even suspects her. The King's men are chasing their tails and I doubt they even know what to look for, much less where to look for it! I believe that Betsy is safe now and none of us have anything to fear. As long as we don't do anything foolish, of course," he added. "Now, dear wife," Ewin continued, "Tell me. Were you able to buy this farm or did you rent it?"

"I was able to buy it, but it took all the money I had plus I had to borrow some from my parents."

"How large is this farm? How many acres did you buy?"

"Fifty," Heather answered.

"Good! Did anyone ask questions about why we are moving here?"

Heather laughed. "Oh, my, yes! There were lots of questions. I simply told everyone that you are having some health problems and needed a warmer climate. I also told them that we want Betsy to attend a good girls' school. I purchased the land from the brother of the local magistrate. He is the mayor of Le Tre'port. It's just down the coast from here. Both men are long time friends of my family and are pleased that we bought the farm."

Ewin hugged his wife. "Heather, I'm so very proud of you. You did wonderfully! 'Tis no wonder I love thee so much!"

Heather kissed her husband. "I'm glad it's all over and we are together again. I don't want to let you and Betsy out of my sight for a long time."

"Keeping Betsy out of trouble will be a round-the-clock effort, I fear," Ewin said with humor. "Now, back to business. Let me know how much you borrowed from your parents and I'll write them a bank draft this very day." He hesitated, "Do you think they suspect anything?"

"I doubt it," Heather replied. "They probably suspect that you smuggled something into France. That's really not unusual. Everyone in this part of the country smuggles something from time to time. Don't worry," she tried to assure him, "They won't ask questions. They are loyal to us both." She looked at her daughter, then at her husband. "How are we going to take care of Betsy's fortune? It is her money after all. She risked everything for it."

"Don't worry. We'll find a way." He held out his arms. "Come here, both of you." He took his wife and daughter in his arms and hugged them tightly. "We're a family again. That's all that really counts."

Betsy caught her breath. "Father, what about the gold? We can't leave it in the wagon?"

"I've already taken care of that, Betsy. While you were asleep, I buried the gold...and the jewels as well. Except for these," he said and pulled out two large gold bars and two large diamonds.

Heather's mouth dropped open. "I've never seen anything like this! What do you think they are worth?"

"Probably enough to support a man and his wife for the rest of their lives…if they lived frugally," he said with a smile. "I really don't know their value but I will find someone who will put a price on them for me."

"How do you plan to do that?" Heather asked.

"For now, I won't do anything. I believe it would be easier for the Crown to trace jewelry back to Betsy rather than the gold." He placed the gold bars on the table. "Come here, both of you. I want to show you something." He picked up one of the gold bars and turned it over. "Look here," he said, pointing to a seal imprinted on the bar. "This is a crown seal and is easy to identify. I must melt these bars down into small bars before I try to sell them. We must be very, very careful. No one…and I mean *no one*…must even suspect we have any new wealth."

Heather and Betsy understood and nodded their agreement.

Quietly he said to his daughter, "Your mother and I have money saved so I know that by using good judgment we can secure this treasure for your future. Do you trust me to do that?"

Betsy took hold of her parents' hands. She looked at each one. "Mother, Father. I want you to know that all this gold, all these jewels are not just mine. They are yours, too. When I decided to keep the contents of the King's chest of gold, I did it only for revenge. Revenge for what happened at Glencoe. Revenge for Aunt Sheila and Uncle Dougal. I did it for all the MacDonald clan. I don't want it for myself. I never did. I trust you both. Do with it as you will." Tears ran down her cheeks. "I don't even want to think about it anymore…I just want to live a normal life again…like I did before. Ever since Glencoe, I've had enough adventure and danger to last my whole life!"

Heather wiped away her daughter's tears. "I know I speak for your father when I tell you that we won't speak of this again and we will carry the secret of the treasure to our graves."

Betsy looked at her loving parents and knew that a tremendous burden had been lifted from her mind, as well as her heart.

-o-

CHAPTER 8

Lieutenant Dirk Campbell had just received a new set of orders. A Royal Mail Coach had been ambushed outside of Golspie and a chest filled with the King's gold had been stolen. Lieutenant Campbell was ordered to take three soldiers and investigate the crime.

Dirk was always eager to accept a new challenge, especially when it involved murder. He hated for murderers to go unpunished.

This time, there were five victims murdered. In addition, three of the outlaws had been killed as well. There was only one surviving witness. The report included the names of the soldiers who had first been on the scene.

Well, he thought, *that should make my investigation easier.*

Dirk picked up the folder containing the complete report of the Golspie incident and perused it. Before arriving in Golspie, he would have the details memorized.

There was a knock on his office door. Dirk stood up just as the Colonel opened the door and entered.

Dirk saluted. The Colonel returned the salute.

"Lieutenant," he said, "before you leave, please give me the folder on your investigation of the two Army soldiers killed at Glencoe."

Lieutenant Campbell looked uncomfortable as he opened a desk drawer and pulled out the heavy folder. "Sir, as you know, I haven't completed this investigation. I would like permission to follow through on a few leads on my way to Golspie.

"Good! An excellent idea!" the Colonel said. "We need to move forward on this as quickly as possible. If too much time elapses, the trail will grow cold. Go ahead and keep the file with you, but I will want a full report on both investigations when you return."

Dirk was not at all happy with himself. He had not made much progress in the Glencoe case at all. His visit to the MacTavish farm several months ago had been futile. When he arrived, the family was in deep mourning over the recent death of Mrs. MacTavish. In fact, the day he arrived the MacTavishes were planning the funeral. He quickly realized that no one in the family cared about the death of the two Campbell soldiers and Mr. MacTavish angrily asked the soldiers to leave.

Mr. MacTavish's words rang in his ears. "Have you no feelings? Have you no compassion? My wife has just died. My sons have lost their mother. Go away and leave us alone."

Dirk was more angry than embarrassed. "Don't you understand? I am on the King's business. A murderer is on the loose and it's my job to identify him and bring him to justice."

MacTavish's eyes narrowed and he took several strides toward the lieutenant. "Don't talk to me about justice until you punish the cowards who slaughtered the fine people at Glencoe." He moved to within inches of the lieutenant's face. "Now, get off my property!"

Dirk had planned to return to the MacTavish farm but it seemed like something always kept him from it. Now fate had intervened and nothing could stand in his way.

Within twenty-four hours, he was ready to leave. He decided he would first go to Ballachulish where, dressed as a civilian, he could renew his investigation of the events surrounding the massacre.

He found lodging in town and went to a local pub. Above the door there was still a sign that read, "If your name is Campbell, you are not welcome."

It was easy to strike up a conversation with the locals. They were friendly and talkative. He introduced himself as Charles Henry, traveling from Glasgow to Inverness. After a few pints, they were eager to talk about Glencoe. Emotions still ran very high.

The publican was quick to give his opinion. "I think every MacDonald throughout Scotland should join together and kill all the Campbells. The Bible says, 'An eye for an eye.'"

A customer sitting at the bar spoke up. "My name isn't MacDonald but I'd join them anyway."

Dirk spent several days in Ballachulish gleaning as much information as he could. On the day before he was to rendezvous with his troopers, he met a teamster named Richard who had taken supplies to the families of Glencoe on a weekly basis. He had gotten to know them well.

Dirk bought Richard a pint. Then another. The more Dirk bought, the more Richard talked.

"There were so many fine people there," Richard said, "but my favorite was Dougal MacDonald and his family."

Dirk's face lit up. "Dougal MacDonald? What was so special about his family?"

Richard sipped his beer and looked at Dirk. "Ah!" Slowly he shook his head back and forth. "They had three of the finest little boys you ever saw. And that little girl who was visiting…"

The muscles in Dirk's neck tightened and he sat up straight. "Girl?" He had to be careful and not seem too curious.

Richard nodded. "Aye! And a comely lass she was, too, with that fiery hair of hers."

Dirk leaned back in his chair and folded his arms. "It's a real shame, isn't it? That they were all killed?"

Richard nodded, and then held out his mug to the publican for a refill. "It's strange though. I went up there afterward and I saw all the graves. But I never found hers."

Dirk continued to bait his informant. "Well, maybe she went back to her home before…you know."

"I don't think so," Richard said. "I was there just a couple of days before the killings. In fact I talked to her. "Betsy, I said, when are you going home? Not till spring, she told me." He took a deep breath. "Such a shame, too. Her family will probably come lookin' for her grave, but it isn't there. Unless maybe someone forgot to put a marker on it."

"Maybe so," Dirk said. "Was her name MacDonald? If it wasn't, maybe the soldiers let her go."

Richard looked at Dirk as if he was crazy. "She wasn't a MacDonald. She was a Stewart. But do you think those soldiers cared? They didn't ask any questions and they showed no mercy. Tsk, tsk! She was just a young girl. Couldn't have been more than sixteen years old. She didn't deserve to die. None of them did." Richard stood up. "You know what Mr. Charles Henry? I don't want to talk about this anymore. Thanks for your company and the drinks, but I'm going home now." Richard plopped his hat on his head and staggered toward the door.

Dirk couldn't believe his luck. *Thank you Richard-whoever-you-are. You've been more help than you can imagine.* He stayed a few more minutes and finished his pint, then returned to the Inn.

He pulled the Glencoe folder from his briefcase and reread the details.

Quinn Campbell, stabbed. He was lying on the ground with his trousers halfway down. Sean Campbell, shot and then stabbed through the neck with his own Claymore.

And now Dirk could add another piece to the puzzle. He laughed excitedly. "Now there is a missing girl to add to the equation," he said out loud. "But I think I know what really happened."

Quinn took her down to rape her and somehow she was able to stab him. When Sean came toward her, she pushed Quinn off, pulled out a pistol and shot Sean. He fell to the ground, mortally wounded. She grabbed his Claymore and drove it through his neck.

That makes sense, Dirk thought. But he was still puzzled. *What was she doing out there by herself in a snowstorm? She must have been on an errand of some kind...an important errand. But where was she going?* He paced the floor trying to come up with a plausible scenario. *The soldiers had been told not to let anyone pass. They decided to rape her before they killed her. She would have been terrified. Probably asked them why they were doing this. Thinking they were in total control, and being stupid as well, they probably told her about the impending massacre.*

Dirk's heart was racing. *I've got this figured out! After she killed them she couldn't go back to Glencoe or she would be killed, too. The only choice she had was to continue on. But where? Where did she go?* Dirk clapped his hands together. *She went to the MacTavishes! That has to be the answer!*

I've got her name, her age, even the color of her hair. Suddenly he remembered the one piece of physical evidence he had. *Her scarf! I have her MacDonald neck scarf. Probably belonged to her aunt or uncle, but nevertheless...*The puzzle was almost complete. All he had to do was go back to the MacTavish farm for verification.

Dirk couldn't get to sleep that night. His mind was whirling about all the possibilities involved here. He'd probably get a promotion when this case was all wrapped up. Now if the Royal Mail Coach robbery investigation was as fruitful, he could write his own ticket in the military.

Oh, life is good, he said. Relaxed now, he closed his eyes and slept.

In the early morning, even before the sun came up, Dirk put on his military uniform and left town before anyone was up. He rode to the campsite where he was to rendezvous with his troopers. Together they rode out to revisit the MacTavish farm.

When they arrived, they found the farmhouse deserted. Dirk searched the area and found a grave with a headstone that read,

Ian and Mary MacTavish
Together in life,
Together in death

Dirk threw up his arms in frustration. "Damn!" he said and quickly walked away. MacTavish could have given him some valuable information as well as verification of the girl's identity. He knew that finding the right Betsy Stewart in Scotland would be like finding a needle in a haystack.

Undaunted, he changed his focus and headed toward Golspie. Perhaps this new mystery would prove to be easier to solve. He wasn't finished with the Glencoe case, but he would file it away again, at least temporarily, and concentrate on finding the missing gold.

When Dirk and his troopers rode into Golspie, they had no trouble locating the soldiers who had found the wrecked coach and rescued the only survivor. They were still on duty in the area. They corroborated the information Dirk already had. The driver and co-driver and two soldier escorts had been shot. Three outlaws who had ambushed the coach had also been killed during the crossfire. In addition, a lieutenant who had been a passenger had been shot between the eyes.

Dirk questioned each of the soldiers separately. He was especially interested in the survivor. Their answers were the same. No one had asked her name. It was dark and a heavy rain was falling. The girl had a gash on her head and seemed disoriented. She was cold and wet and the sergeant felt it was important to get her to safety as quickly as possible. They asked her what had happened and then they took her to an inn in Golspie and they never saw her again. During the next few days following the robbery, the soldiers spent hours searching the area around the accident but found no chest and no gold. The consensus was that one of the robbers got away and took the gold with him.

Dirk intended to interview the innkeeper himself.

"Mr. MacLain, I'd like to talk to you about the young girl who survived the ambush a few weeks ago."

The innkeeper busied himself with entries in an accounting book. He didn't bother to look up at the lieutenant. "Can't you see I'm busy, officer? Go talk to my wife. She's the one who cared for the girl. I can't help you."

Before seeing Mrs. MacLain, Dirk talked to some of the inn employees. No one seemed to remember much about her except for one of the maids.

"What can you tell me about the girl?" Dirk asked politely.

The maid seemed a little hesitant. "I don't want to get nobody in trouble," she said.

Dirk smiled pleasantly, hoping to encourage the frightened girl. "Why, don't you worry. No one is going to get in trouble. Won't you please help me?"

The maid smiled nervously back at Dirk. "She...she was young...15 or 16 maybe."

"Do you know her name?"

"Yes."

Dirk was getting impatient but couldn't let it show. "Well...what was her name?"

"Betsy. Her name was Betsy."

Betsy! Dirk hid his surprise. "Did Betsy have a last name?"

The maid shook her head. "I don't know."

Quick to jump to a conclusion that might link the two cases together, he continued. "Could her last name be Stewart?"

The maid backed away from Dirk. "I don't know, sir. Really I don't...Can I go now?"

"Just one more question and then you can go. What color was her hair?"

"That's an easy question. Her hair was red, a very dark red. It was really very beautiful...Now can I go?"

Dirk didn't bother to answer the girl. He needed to find the innkeeper's wife.

Erma MacLain didn't like soldiers. As far as she was concerned, they were all pushy and arrogant. After the robbery, soldiers swarmed all over town asking questions. Over and over, they asked the same questions.

Now they are back again, she thought. *Well, they won't get any help from me!*

Dirk was on his best behavior. He removed his hat and bowed politely. "Good day, M'am. I understand you might be able to help me."

"Why, of course, officer," she said sweetly. "How can I help you?"

She's putty in my hands. This will be a piece of cake, he thought to himself. "I'm investigating the recent mail coach robbery. I wonder if you can tell me what you know about the young girl who survived."

You'll get nothing useful from me, she vowed. She cocked her head slightly and blinked her eyes ever so delicately. "What would you like to know?"

"Her name?"

"Uh, let me see. It was Betty. Yes, that's it...Betty."

"Betty?" Dirk frowned. "Are you sure it wasn't Betsy?"

"Hmm. It could have been Betsy. Betty, Betsy, they both sound alike to me."

"What was her last name?"

Mrs. MacLain pursed her lips. "Uh...I don't remember her last name." She looked at him so sweetly. "I'm sorry, Lieutenant, I'm not real good with names."

Dirk didn't intend to let up. "Was her name Stewart? Does that sound familiar?"

Erma shook her head. "It could have been. I'm sorry. I just can't remember for sure. And I certainly don't want to give you false information."

Dirk was getting frustrated. "Can you describe her to me? What did she look like? How old was she? Do you know where she was going?"

"My goodness! So many questions!" Mrs. MacLain smoothed her skirts self-consciously. "Let me think. She was short and looked to be 12 or 13. She had brown hair…and I think she was going to her home in Inverness. Yes, that's right! Inverness."

Now Dirk wasn't sure if this was the same girl or not. This wasn't turning out the way he had hoped. "You said her hair was brown. Could it have been red?"

"Red?" Mrs. MacLain thought for a moment. "It looked brown to me. Now, if you will excuse me, officer, I really must get back to my work. She turned and walked away; satisfied that she had him totally confused.

Dirk ran his fingers through his hair, and then put his hat back on. He stared after Mrs. MacLain long after she was out of sight.

Erma MacLain watched as the soldiers rode away. *I hope that pretty young lass isn't in any trouble. Perhaps I helped throw him off in a different direction.*

Before returning to Fort William, Dirk and his troopers searched the hillsides all around the wrecked coach. He had a strong feeling that there were clues just waiting to be found.

Inch by inch they examined the soil looking for signs that it had been recently disturbed. One of the troopers called to Dirk.

"Lieutenant, come over here." He leaned over and picked up a piece of metal. He turned it over in his hand. When Dirk reached his side, the trooper held out his hand.

"What do you make of this, Lieutenant?"

Dirk took the piece and looked at it closely. "It looks like it could be a piece of a lock. Maybe the lock was blown off the chest." He looked around. "Let's concentrate on searching this area within, say, twenty feet or so of where you found this." *I don't know what I'm looking for,* he mumbled, *but I'll know it when I see it.*

Just then, something caught his eye. He kneeled down and looked closer. *The soil here has been washed away.* "Something is buried here," he shouted. "Bring me a shovel!"

Just barely visible was the top of something made out of wood. Heavy rains had begun to wash away the dirt placed so carefully on top of the box.

Within minutes, Dirk had uncovered the chest. He pulled it out of the ground and flipped open the top. "Empty!" he exclaimed.

"Guess the outlaws came back and took the treasure," one of the troopers said.

"Someone took the treasure all right," Dirk said, "but I'm not so sure it was an outlaw." He didn't believe an outlaw would bury the gold and then return for it. After the ambush, he would have grabbed the chest and left the area as fast as he could. He smiled to himself, *No...someone else buried that chest of gold.*

Dirk's intuition convinced him that somehow Betsy Stewart was involved with both incidents.

The trip had ended on a high note and Dirk Campbell was ready to return to Fort William to file a report that would please the Colonel.

Indeed, the Colonel was pleased. He quickly forwarded the new information to King William, who was so pleased that he promoted Lieutenant Dirk Campbell not to Captain but to Major. Further, he sent Major Campbell a letter of congratulations along with his personal request that Dirk continue the investigation until justice was served.

The King did not really expect the treasure to be recovered but he was aware that Major Campbell had shown unique enterprise. The King needed men like that around him.

"I need ferrets working for me," the King said. "And Dirk Campbell is the best kind of ferret!"

Dirk was feeling very proud of himself. Maybe before this was all over, he would be promoted to Lieutenant Colonel. All he had to do was find the right Betsy Stewart.

-o-

CHAPTER 9

Betsy was anxious to see her grandparents. She remembered the last time she had seen them. It had been three summers ago. They came to Banff and stayed for four weeks. Uncle Dougal and Aunt Sheila and their three young boys came from Glencoe and stayed a week. She laughed to herself remembering how crowded the house had been with all the visitors. There was an extra bed in her room so Thomas and Charles shared one bed and little Brian slept with her. It had been a happy time. She remembered the laughter, the long summer nights, long walks though the woods, and lazy days of fishing, not caring whether they caught any fish or not.

That was the summer her grandmother taught her to knit. Betsy loved to knit! After her grandparents left, Betsy knitted caps for her parents and Uncle Roy and gave them as Christmas gifts. The following Christmas she made a cap for her grandfather and a scarf for her grandmother. Last Christmas, while she was in Glencoe, she knitted caps for her cousins. Little Brian was especially excited. After he opened his gift, he looked at Betsy with his bright shiny eyes. "You made this all by yourself? Just for me?"

Betsy felt an ache in the pit of her stomach. Tears filled her eyes and she swallowed a lump in her throat as memories of Glencoe once again flooded her mind. She shook her head back and forth, as though to erase those awful memories and forced her mind away from that awful day. She thought again about her grandparents, Angus and Lisa MacDonald. They were such wonderful people and after all these years, they were still in love.

Heather saw her daughter's tears and the far-away look in her eyes.

"Betsy, dear," she said softly, "Why don't you freshen up a bit. We're almost ready to go to Grandpere's."

Betsy nodded. "Mother, tell me again about how they met. I need to think about something pleasant for a change."

~~~

Angus MacDonald had been born and raised in Scotland. He fully intended to die in Scotland. But fate has a way of changing plans, sometimes for the better, sometimes not. Like his father, he became involved in the shipping business and had made some good investments in cargoes from the West Indies. He was a frugal Scot who watched his pennies. Instinctively, he knew how important it was to earn more money than was spent. Putting aside a little on a regular basis meant that there would be funds available when income slowed down or stopped for whatever reason. As a young man, his focus was on making as much money as possible and living on as little as possible. He wasn't a tightwad, but always concentrated on what was coming in rather than what was going out.

Angus traveled a great deal, always looking for new ship builders, new ports, and new products to buy and sell. He had heard about St. Val'ery on the coast of France as a potential source for the exportation of wine.

On his first visit to the small port city, he met Lisa Bonne. Angus MacDonald was a brash young man who always knew what he wanted, and he wanted Lisa Bonne.

When first introduced to the beautiful, shy young girl, he bowed and said, "How do you do, Mademoiselle. Will you do me the great honor of marrying me?"

Lisa laughed out loud. She couldn't help herself. This was obviously the most outrageous and presumptuous person she had ever met. "I will do no such thing, Monsieur MacDonald! How dare you ask me such a question! Hmmf!" She turned on her heel and quickly walked away.

Angus persisted. He brought her a bunch of wild flowers. "Will you marry me now?" he asked with a smile that went ear to ear.

Lisa's frown furrowed her brow. "Of course not!" she said, but accepted the flowers anyway.

As she turned to walk away, he called after her, "I'm not leaving St. Val'ery until you say yes!"

Although his business interest in the town proved to be fruitless, his personal interest eventually became successful.

Lisa Bonne found it impossible to resist the charm of the handsome Scotsman. After days and weeks of being wooed with gifts of flowers, hand-written poems, an armful of bottles of wine, a bolt of bright calico fabric, even a baby kitten tied up in a pink bow, she caught him by surprise.

When once again he approached her carrying not so much as a single blossom, he looked at her and opened his mouth to speak. She silenced him by placing two fingers against his lips. She stood tall and smoothed her dress. "Ahem!" she began. "For weeks you have been courting me and all you have ever said is, 'Will you marry me now?' Well, I'm tired of that question and I never want you to ask me that again! Do you understand?"

Before Angus had a chance to respond, Lisa continued, "I've decided that the only way I'll ever get a decent conversation out of you is if I accept your silly proposal. Therefore, Angus MacDonald, I agree to be your wife." She planted a kiss on his open lips then brushed past him and hurried down the street.

Angus stood there, dumbfounded, trying to absorb what she had said. It was a full five seconds before he could react. He turned and ran after her.

During the next few weeks, Angus and Lisa became inseparable. Angus wanted to know everything about Lisa.

"Tell me your life story, sweetheart. I want to know what I missed the last eighteen years." Tenderly, he stroked her cheek with the back of his hand.

"It's a short story, my love. My mother died giving birth to my brother, Francois. I was only eight years old. My father was left with a new infant plus my four year-old brother, Henri, and me. He needed me…and I needed my mother." Her eyes became moist with tears. "We found a wet nurse for the baby and mon pere found a housekeeper. I loved my little brothers, but life without my mother was never the same."

Angus could see the sadness in her eyes. "I, too, lost my mother at an early age. But my father became my mother, too. He never left me alone…and he taught me everything I know."

Lisa looked off in the distance, remembering. "My mother taught me everything, too. She taught me the English language. She told me that it was important for me to know other languages. She had planned to teach me German, too, but she died before she had the chance."

They were sitting on a large smooth rock overlooking the Somme River. Lisa pulled her knees up and hugged them with her arms. "I don't remember her face…mon pere tells me I look like her…but I remember her soft, gentle voice and her laughter. It was like music to my ears. Oh, Angus, I still miss her."

Angus pulled her to her feet and held her in his arms. "Oh, my darlin' girl," he said and gently held her chin so she had to look him in the eye. "I promise you that our life together will be happy. And if it's in my power, you will never cry again."

Angus was true to his word. He took his bride back to Scotland and they started a new life together. Two children were born. First, a son they named Dougal. A few years later, their daughter Heather was born. Lisa was a caring and loving mother. Her sadness and the empty feeling she had carried for so many years after her mother's death was finally gone. She and her husband were devoted to one another. The children were bright and healthy and grew rapidly. Indeed, life was good and the years passed swiftly.

Then they received the tragic news that Lisa's father and both of her brothers had drowned. Unrelenting rain had flooded the Somme River. Families clung to rooftops as their homes were swept away in the rushing waters. Lisa's father and brothers had tried to save one such family but a torrent of muddy water killed them all.

Lisa, being the only surviving heir, inherited all of her father's land. She would have to leave Scotland and return to St. Val'ery. Their son, Dougal, now eighteen years old, decided to stay in Scotland. He offered to handle the sale of his father's holdings. Angus agreed and he, Lisa, and their daughter, Heather, left for a new life in France.

Two years later, Dougal sent his parents a letter informing them of his betrothal to a girl named Sheila. After their wedding, they planned to join the MacDonald clan in Glencoe.

It was late afternoon when Betsy and her parents arrived at the MacDonald farm. Before the wagon came to a complete stop, Betsy jumped down and ran to the front door.

"Grandmere!" she called.

Lisa MacDonald opened the front door. She grabbed Betsy and almost squeezed the life out of her. In a moment she was enveloped in the arms of her grandfather who lifted her up off the floor, as if she was a feather. His smell was so familiar to her. He always smelled the same. There was a faint odor of whiskey and a stronger scent of pipe tobacco. When she was little, Betsy had told her mother how her grandfather smelled to her.

Heather had laughed. "Angus MacDonald has always smelled like that! Sometimes the whiskey smell is stronger than the pipe tobacco," her mother had said.

Betsy's father had always smelled like the sea. It was a fresh smell except on the days when he had been handling fish. Betsy laughed to herself when she compared the two. *I wonder how the man I will marry will smell?*

Angus put his granddaughter down. "Spin around for me, child. I want to see you from every angle…Now, let me look at you…Why, you've grown so much. You're no longer a child. Indeed, you are quite the young woman." He pinched her cheek playfully. "And a pretty one at that!"

Betsy suddenly felt self-conscious. "Oh, Grandpere, I'm glad you noticed. I'm sixteen now, you know."

"Aye, I know. And now you'll probably find some handsome young man and want to get married soon," he teased.

"Papa," Heather interrupted. "Don't put foolish ideas in her head. She still has a lot of growing up to do."

"Come," Lisa said. "Let's all sit by the fire and enjoy some wine."

When all the glasses were filled, Lisa raised her glass high. "I have something to say. Here's to you, my beloved family. I thank God you are here with us now and I pray your future is bright and successful. My dream…for us all to be together again…has come true. Praise God!"

She sipped her wine and the others followed.

"Hear, hear!" Angus cheered.

Betsy looked at her parents and grandparents. She was surrounded by people who truly loved her and would take care of her and protect her and even fight to the death for her. A warm feeling filled her whole body. She relaxed and, for the first time in months, she felt completely safe.

She just listened as the adults carried on idle conversation and enjoyed refills of the hot wine.

Soon the family adjourned to the large kitchen with its glowing fireplace. In the middle of the room there was a lengthy table covered with food. Two French women scurried about serving more wine and fresh bread still warm from the oven. There were four large meat pies on the table and plates of fried rabbit. When the main course was finished, the meal was topped off with warm fruit pies and flaky pastries.

After dinner, they returned to the sitting room for a nightcap. This was too much for Betsy who closed her eyes and fell asleep.

Angus leaned toward Ewin. "Ye canna go home tonight." He nodded toward Betsy. "The lass is already asleep. We have room for you to stay the night."

Ewin's first thought was to protest. He remembered the buried treasure with no one there to protect it. Silently he chided himself. *The treasure is safe. Heather and Betsy don't know where it's buried and no one else even knows it's there. Relax,* he told himself.

"Thank you, Angus. We'll accept your kind offer. The hour is late and we've all had too much to drink."

The women took Betsy and left the room. Ewin took the opportunity of being alone with Angus.

"Angus, I would beg your help over the next few days as I need to buy some things for our new farm and I hope you will accompany me. Also," Ewin took out a note he had written on the London Counting House that held his money. "I hope you will accept this note in repayment of the five thousand francs you loaned Heather when she purchased the farm."

Angus looked at the paper. "I will," he said and pocketed the note. "You and I will go to the village tomorrow. I'll cash the note and then we'll spend the day getting your farm outfitted."

"Good. I'm very anxious to get started. By the way, do you know if there is any more available land adjacent to our farm?"

"I don't know, but I'll find out. How much more land are you considering?"

"As much as I can get. I have some kinsmen in Scotland that I would like to bring here. I'm thinking of three families in particular. They are my cousins and are very fine people. As you know, Angus," Ewin had to chuckle, "wherever Scots gather, they bring grace, honor, and a lot of humility with them."

Angus laughed loudly. "Lad, you are beginning to sound like an Irishman!" Angus stood up. "We can talk more tomorrow. I don't know about you, but I'm an old man and I need a good night's sleep."

When Ewin crawled into bed next to Heather, she rolled over and kissed his nose. "I wasn't eavesdropping, but did I hear you say you want to buy more land?"

"Yes, I do. Don't you remember what it was like at home? Many farmers didn't own enough land to raise sufficient food for their own families. If we own enough land we can not only feed ourselves, but also help to feed others. With my cousins here, we can continue to fish, not only to supplement our food, but also to make additional money. The lesson I have learned is that large farms survive. I want to be successful for Betsy so she can someday be in charge of a large and profitable business so that she won't have to rely solely on her buried wealth."

"That's all well and good, Ewin, but maybe our daughter will have other plans. She's headstrong and will make her own decisions even if they don't agree with yours. If Betsy wants to have her day, let her."

Ewin hugged his wife. "I will, lass, I will."

The next morning, Betsy was awakened by a rooster crowing. She dressed and walked into the kitchen. Her grandmother and one of the servants were making flour cakes for breakfast. She watched as they kneaded small pieces of apple into the dough. With the heel of their hands, they flattened the cakes and placed them on a broad, flat pan to cook. Soon the smell of apples and cinnamon filled the air.

"I'm hungry," Betsy announced just as the rest of the family sauntered in.

Lisa wiped her hands on her apron. "Good morning, everyone. Breakfast is just about ready."

"And we're ready for breakfast," Angus said. "Ewin and I have much to do in town before we think about another meal."

As hungry as they were, the men waited until the women were served before they filled their plates. Betsy watched in amazement as her father and grandfather ate non-stop until all the food Lisa had prepared was gone.

"Men certainly do have huge appetites," she muttered to herself.

Angus stood up first and patted his stomach. "Whew! That was a fine breakfast, little wife. I thank you!" He turned to Ewin. "Whenever you are ready, lad, let's go hitch up the wagon."

Ewin wiped his mouth and pushed away from the table. "I can't eat another bite, so we might as well get to work." He kissed Heather's cheek. "We'll be back in time for supper."

After the men left and the kitchen was cleaned up, Lisa asked Heather and Betsy to join her in the sitting room.

"Betsy…" Lisa said hesitantly. Her eyes were moist as she took her granddaughter's hands and looked deeply into her eyes. "Dear child…you have been through a terrible ordeal. I don't know if you can…or even want to talk about what happened at Glencoe. But can you tell me about your Uncle Dougal and…"

Betsy turned her head away and bit her bottom lip. She tried hard to keep her composure. After taking a deep breath, she turned to face her grandmother.

"I try so hard to keep from thinking about it because every time I *do* think about it, it's as though I'm right there again…as though it's happening right this very minute." She sobbed deeply and fought back unwanted tears. "I don't want to talk about what I did…what I had to do. But I will tell you about my visit with your son and his family."

She took a few moments to quiet her emotions and centered on remembering the happy days she spent there.

Betsy smiled now at her grandmother and squeezed her hands. "I am so very grateful for the time I spent with them. I was like a big sister to the boys, especially Brian. He followed me around like a little puppy dog. Aunt Sheila taught me how to make Christmas cookies and Thomas and I were able to help Uncle Dougal with some of the chores. Charles was the brightest of the boys and wanted me to help him learn to read." Her chin quivered as she became lost in her memories. Then she lifted her eyes. "Uncle Dougal was a wonderful man and he had a very loving family. I'll always miss them. I'm sorry, Grandmere. I'm so sorry I couldn't save them!"

Lisa held Betsy in her arms. "Sshh, now. Don't cry. There was nothing you could do. I thank God everyday that you were spared."

Heather had listened quietly. She wiped away her own tears before she said, "I know how hard it is for you to speak of these things, Betsy. But now you can finally put it all behind you once and for all. We needn't speak of it again. We can't change the past although it becomes a part of who we are. Scotland, with all its good as well as bad memories, is part of our past. Now we have the opportunity for a fresh new life here in France. I'm ready for it. Are you?" She took her daughter and her mother by the hand. "Food always makes me feel better. Let's go have another apple turnover!"

It was late when Angus returned home. The supper dishes had been cleared but Lisa had kept his dinner warm.

Heather was surprised Angus was alone.

"Don't worry, my dear," he said. "Your husband is safe and sound. We had a full day buying everything that was needed. It was late when we finished so Ewin decided to go straight to the farm so he could get the animals settled. He wants you and Betsy to spend the night here and then I'll take you home in the morning. I'll be taking some hired hands with me, too, because there will be enough work for a dozen men."

Angus awakened Heather and Betsy early the next morning. After a quick breakfast, the three, along with three hired hands, climbed into the wagon and headed toward the new Stewart farm.

When they arrived, Ewin was already hard at work. He greeted his wife and daughter with a big grin. "I think we're in business!"

Betsy looked around and saw a new wagon by the barn. She could hear the bleating of goats so she hurried over and looked inside the barn. There were three horses, one cow, several sheep and goats, and a dozen or so chickens scurrying around.

"Mother!" she called excitedly. "Come look!"

As Heather came to see, Betsy ran back to her father. "Can I help? Is there anything I can do to help?"

"Well," he said as he leaned against his shovel, "you can say hello to your Uncle Roy."

Betsy whirled around. "Uncle Roy! You're back!" She ran to him and gave him a quick kiss on the cheek. "Where have you been?"

Roy gave his niece a big hug. "Let's see now. I had to find a place to dock our boat. Then I cleaned her up. Then I waited for your father. And now…here I am!"

Ewin took Betsy's arm. "Now, my dear daughter, I want you and your mother to go inside the house. You two can take care of the inside and we men will take care of the outside."

The day was well spent. Fences were built to keep the goats and sheep separate. A large area was corralled for the horses. Ewin started building a shed to be used as a blacksmith shop. He had been fortunate to find everything he needed. This included a large bellows, several bags of charcoal and coal, an anvil, a large wooden barrel to hold water, a crucible, several assorted hammers, and two horseshoe nail pullers. He made sure the door would be wide enough to allow him to drive a wagon inside in case he needed to do repairs. Secretly, he knew he had other uses for his blacksmith tools, but that would come later.

Heather and Betsy prepared a large supper knowing the men would be famished when the day's work ended. They both ate first, so they would be able to keep the men's plates and glasses filled.

Betsy couldn't help but stare. She had never seen six grown men at one table before. There wasn't much conversation. The men ate heartily and only stopped long enough to wash down the food with glasses of wine. Almost in unison, they finished eating, took one last gulp of wine, and wiped their mouths. One by one, they stood up, thanked her mother for the fine food and left the house. Angus took a few minutes to talk to Ewin and Roy, then kissed his daughter and granddaughter and waved goodbye.

After the table was cleared, the family sat down by the fire.

Ewin told Roy about his plan to buy more land and bring their cousins to France to share it all with them.

Roy was impressed. "Sounds like you've given this a lot of thought. I must admit the possibilities here seem endless."

Ewin lit his pipe and drew on it deeply. Little puffs of smoke floated around his face. Betsy took a deep breath. She loved the smell of pipe tobacco.

"The possibilities *are* endless, Roy. And we hope you'll stay and be a part of all this, too."

Heather leaned over and kissed her brother-in-law on the forehead. "You know how much we all love you. You have always been a friend to us as well as a brother. On more than one occasion you have risked your life for us. Can you not see that we wish you to stay here with us?"

Betsy had to have her say as well and was not as subtle as her parents. "Uncle Roy, we won't take no for an answer."

The outpouring of genuine affection touched Roy. "If you put it that way, dear lass, I have no choice. Besides, I want to stay here with you. You are my only family, you know. And, Betsy dear, I have to be around to see what new trouble you'll get yourself into."

"My days of getting into trouble are over!" Betsy assured him. "I promise!"

Ewin leaned over to shake Roy's hand. "Done then. You know, Roy, if our cousins agree to come, we'll have our own Stewart clan right here in St. Val'ery."

Roy laughed. "Do you think France is ready for a Stewart clan? They might chase us out of the country!"

The next morning was another workday. They repaired the barnyard gate and continued fencing an acre of paddock area.

Later that morning Angus, along with his hired hand Jack, came by with a wagonload of hay.

"I knew you'd be needing this. Anything else you might be needing right now?" Angus asked.

Ewin wiped his brow. "I could use about a fifteen minute break and maybe a couple of wagonloads of lumber as well."

"That's no problem." Angus smiled. "I brought some mortar so Roy and Jack can work on the stone walls and build them up. I can see that last year's frost tumbled them. Meanwhile you and I will fetch some lumber."

The men quickly unloaded the hay, then Angus and Ewin left for a nearby sawmill.

While the two men loaded the lumber, the mill owner approached them with a shepherd puppy under each arm. He was grinning broadly.

"Today is your lucky day," he said to Ewin.

Ewin stopped for a moment. He was curious. "Why is that?" he asked.

"I understand you are new here and in the process of establishing a farm."

"That's right." Ewin didn't make the connection. "Why does that make it my lucky day?"

Angus laughed. He knew what was coming.

"Because," the mill owner continued, "every farm needs a dog or two." He handed the puppies to Ewin. "You'll be doing me a favor if you take them off my hands. No charge! It's my gift to you."

Ewin wasn't sure what to say.

Angus didn't hesitate in accepting on Ewin's behalf. "Thank you, sir. That's very kind." He took one of the puppies from Ewin. "Won't Betsy be thrilled?"

Ewin shook his head and laughed. "How can I say no?"

"Hold on just a minute." The mill owner ran over to his barn and hurried back with three black and white kittens. "Here's a bonus. Guaranteed to keep the mice out of your house and your barn."

Betsy was elated when she saw the new puppies and kittens. She played with them all until suppertime, and then took the kittens out to the barn with a big bowl of milk. Heather allowed the puppies to spend the first night in a box in Betsy's bedroom with the promise that building a doghouse would be the first thing on tomorrow's agenda.

The family quickly settled into a comfortable routine. They became acquainted with other farm families and, until the weather became too cold, enjoyed occasional social gatherings at each other's farms.

As the Christmas season approached, the Stewart family started attending mass at a small church near the site of the sawmill.

Pere Francis was a very friendly and humorous priest and soon became a frequent guest in the Stewart home.

One evening after supper, the conversation centered on Betsy.

"Have you thought about a school for the child?" Pere Francis asked.

Ewin looked at Heather. "Why, yes, Father, we have."

Pere Francis smiled at Betsy. "There's a wonderful convent school in Amiens. I might be able to get you enrolled there."

Betsy shook her head. "No!...I mean...yes, I want to go to school but I don't want to leave home...not now." She looked at her parents frantically.

Heather understood her daughter's fears. "Thank you, Father, but our family was apart for much of last year. We are only recently reunited and—to tell you the truth—we're not ready for Betsy to be away from us again."

Betsy was relieved. "Maybe there's a school here in St. Val'ery I could attend."

Now it was Pere Francis' turn to shake his head. "No, no. That school won't do at all." He thought for a moment then looked at Betsy's parents. "I know! Would you agree to let me tutor her? I have an extensive private library she could use at her discretion. In addition, I could tutor her in mathematics."

So it was decided. Betsy went to Pere Francis' library three days a week. She delighted in reading books about ancient Greece, Socrates, Aristotle, and Plato. Books about ancient Egyptian civilization taught her about the pharaohs and the giant pyramids. Geography books showed her a world map. She could locate Scotland, France, and the faraway countries of India and China. Betsy had developed a thirst for knowledge that was visible to everyone, especially Pere Francis. It was easy to see that Betsy was an exceptional girl. Her mother had taught her French when she was very young and impressed upon her that French was the language of culture. Except for the nobility in the Highlands, not many people spoke French fluently; therefore, Heather and Betsy were respected because of their knowledge of the language. Thanks to Heather who had taught her daughter addition and subtraction, it was not long before Betsy mastered all the math basics including the use of decimals and percentages. The priest polished Betsy's skills and taught her the practical use of all of her math skills.

By late spring, the priest was so pleased with Betsy's progress that he began to teach her algebra and geometry. The girl was like a sponge and soaked up knowledge as fast as it was revealed to her. Pere Francis required her to read at least one book in French every two weeks. By the end of summer, he began to teach her Latin as well.

While Betsy was expanding her world through education, her father had developed his farm and acquired an additional two hundred acres of land. Although farming took up much of his time, he decided that now was the time to start melting down some of the gold bars that were still safely buried. He and Heather discussed it with Betsy.

"Father, I told you I don't want to have to make any decision about that gold. As far as I'm concerned, it's yours and Mothers."

Ewin was patient with his daughter. "Betsy, it's important that you understand the tremendous responsibility that owning such a fortune demands. There is enough gold to take care of all of us for the rest of our lives. But I still must be careful. No one must ever question our expenditures. I need to take action now. Even though you say you want no part of it, it is yours. So I ask your approval if I begin to sell it."

"Of course I approve. I trust you completely." Betsy frowned slightly. "I fear I will be cursed by that gold for the rest of my life."

Gently, Heather held her daughter's face in her hands. "No, sweetheart, I promise you the day will come when you don't see it as a curse but as an opportunity to accomplish great things."

That night, Ewin went out to the barn and unearthed several bars of gold. He went to his blacksmith shop and lit a bed of coal. When it was red hot, he placed the gold bars in the crucible and watched as, slowly, the gold melted into a puddle of liquid sunshine. Carefully, he poured it into small forms. He lit his pipe and sat quietly until the liquid once again became solid.

In a few days, I will leave for Paris, he said to himself. *When I return, I'll have enough cash to see to all our needs...and then some.*

Gold was always in demand in a city that depends on commerce, so Ewin wasted no time in going from counting house to counting house converting his gold to francs. He was glad he had made the effort to learn French because, even though he spoke with an accent, no one seemed to pay particular attention to him.

Within two days, he had exchanged all his gold and had seen enough of Paris to last a lifetime. It was not the kind of city he would like to live in.

As he left the city behind, he couldn't help but feel a little smug. He had converted the King's gold without any suspicion. He had enough money so that he wouldn't have to worry about melting any more gold for some time. Now that his pockets were well lined, he was anxious to return home and once again become a hard working farmer, knowing full well he would never again have to worry about making ends meet.

-o-

CHAPTER 10

After the third full year, the farm showed a little profit. There were times when things ran so smoothly that Ewin and Roy could still enjoy fishing. Now it was more of a hobby than a way to make profit. It provided food for the family. What they couldn't eat, they sold and that, too, added coins to the coffer.

Because of their success, some of the lesser nobility began to invite them to their homes. They met many of the more influential people in the area and their circle of friends expanded.

Betsy liked most of the people she met, but the nobility did not impress her. She was used to the clan system, where everyone was extended family. It was hard for her to understand how many of the French could be so indifferent to the people who served them. Many of her new acquaintances seemed shallow. They were more concerned with the style of their clothes and judged others solely on their social status. Betsy made an effort to befriend those who, like herself, tried to follow the Golden Rule.

One day in late summer, Heather came out of the house just as a post rider came galloping up toward the house waving something above his head.

"Madame! I have a letter for you," he shouted enthusiastically.

Mail was a rare and much anticipated occurrence. Heather looked at the envelope. "Oh, it's from Kenneth Stewart," she said excitedly and tore open the envelope. Quickly she scanned the contents. She picked up her skirts with one hand and started running, frantically waving the letter with her other hand. "Ewin! Ewin! I have news!" She continued running. "Come quick! I have good news!"

Ewin came out of the barn just in time to catch his wife as she stumbled into his arms.

"Oh!" she gasped. "I'm out of breath. Here!" She thrust the letter into his hands. "They're coming!"

Ewin let out a whoop. "The letter says they'll be here in October. We've got a lot to do before then."

Several months before, Ewin had received an answer to his query. His two cousins and their families agreed to come to France and were very excited about the prospect of financial independence that Ewin had promised. So, he immediately made plans to build a place for each of them to live. He and Roy were almost finished with a cottage for Roy. The timing was perfect because Roy had been seeing a young woman named Jeanette Blanchett.

Betsy really liked Jeanette. She came from one of the better families in the area but she had none of the phony airs that many of Betsy's acquaintances had.

Although no formal engagement had been announced, Betsy knew it was only a matter of time. Personally, she believed that Roy would propose as soon as his house was finished.

Her life was changing and she relished each of those changes. She thought about everything good that had happened to her since she came to France: seeing her grandparents on a regular basis, having Jeanette as a friend, her tutoring with Pere Francis, and now her cousins would be coming soon. She was excited about the future and the memories of Glencoe seldom surfaced.

Saturday there was to be a picnic at her grandparents' farm. It was to be a grand event. She couldn't wait. There would be food and drinks, of course, but her grandfather promised her there would be entertainment, too.

She worried about what to wear. Not that she had many choices. Jeanette helped her to decide on a colorful calico dress.

The day of the picnic dawned bright and sunny. Before her parents were ready, Betsy was dressed and ready to go. When Ewin saw his daughter, he whistled his approval.

"You look charming, lass. You'll knock all the young laddies clear off their feet."

Betsy seemed surprised. "What young laddies?" she asked.

Ewin put his arm around her shoulder as he led her toward the front door. "Oh," he teased. "I think there just might be several young men for you to meet. Perhaps one might catch your fancy. Or maybe two!"

Heather came up behind them. "Now, Ewin, don't go putting any ideas in her head."

Ewin smiled. "Tisn't me, my love. It's your father who is the matchmaker."

When they arrived at the MacDonald farm, Betsy could see there was quite a crowd of people. They seemed to be gathering around a dozen or so young men arrayed in Highland dress, complete with swords and pistols.

Angus saw the wagon approaching and hurriedly came out to meet them. "Finally you are here! I've been waiting." He helped Betsy down from the wagon. "Come to the house. There is someone I am anxious for you to meet."

Angus took Betsy's arm and led the way. Ewin and Heather followed.

As they crossed the yard, a tall muscular young man came out of the farmhouse. He walked toward them in long deliberate strides. His blond hair was long and curled around his face. He had a well-trimmed moustache and eyes that were steel blue and riveting. Dressed as a Highlander, he was also wearing a traditional hat with long pheasant plumes stuck in the hatband.

Angus took the young man's hand. "Sir John MacDonald, may I present my daughter, Heather, her husband Ewin, and their daughter." He added proudly, "My granddaughter, Betsy Stewart."

Sir John doffed his hat and bowed. "I am so pleased to meet you. Angus has told me so much about you."

He looked at Betsy. Betsy looked at him. Ewin and Heather looked at each other. The silence was deafening.

Finally, Ewin came to his daughter's rescue. "We are very pleased to meet you, too, Sir John. Tell me, is there any chance we will hear you play the bagpipes today?"

Sir John laughed. "I'm afraid not. That is one skill that I can't master. But I guarantee you will hear the pipes this day." He turned to Betsy. "May I have the pleasure of your company today? As your escort, I mean."

Betsy looked at her father for approval. "Father?"

Ewin saw that Angus was smiling and nodding his head. Heather's expression was one of approval as well.

"Sir John," he said, "Guess it's unanimous."

The young man bowed again and offered Betsy his arm. As they walked away she turned to look at her parents and grandfather. They were all standing together, grinning like Cheshire cats.

Sir John was completely attentive to Betsy. He introduced her to the other Highlanders and never left her side.

Betsy had never before been the center of a man's attention, so although she was thrilled, she was also a little uncomfortable and self-conscious. She caught herself staring at him whenever she had the opportunity to do so. He was the most handsome man she had ever seen. She loved the way he laughed and when he looked at her, she felt her heart skip a beat. He seemed quite regal, but she noticed he treated his men as equals in the tradition of a Highland chief.

The day was filled with festivities, eating, drinking, foot races, horse racing, tossing the caber and the stone. In the late afternoon, a large bonfire was lighted and some of Sir John's soldiers began to play the bagpipes. Soon, some of the young people began dancing traditional Highland dances. Betsy loved to dance and eagerly joined the circle of dancers.

Feet spread and arms folded, Sir John watched Betsy. As she danced, her thick auburn hair reflected the firelight. It looked as though it was on fire, too. It was a magical, almost ethereal moment for Sir John. Somehow he knew that this was just the beginning of something that would prove to be bigger than anything he had ever experienced before.

Betsy felt the magic, too. As she danced, she could almost feel the wild music float out beyond the firelight into the star-filled sky.

When the music finally stopped, Betsy was out of breath. She twirled a few more times, then stopped. She leaned over, placed her hands on her knees and took a couple of deep breaths. When she stood up, Sir John was standing in front of her.

He smiled and handed her a glass. "I think you could use a cool drink and a short rest." He led her away from the bonfire. They walked in silence for a few minutes, each enjoying the warm autumn evening.

Finally, Betsy broke the silence. She didn't really want to talk about Glencoe, but she had to ask the question. "Tell me, Sir John, are you in any way related to the MacDonald clan who were so brutally massacred in Glencoe?"

"Why, yes, I am," Sir John admitted. "But the division of the MacDonald clan to which I belong was not part of the resistance to King William," he explained.

Betsy was fascinated. "Tell me more."

"All right, I will. I'll start at the beginning. My grandfather fought with King Charles II against Cromwell. In fact, he was at the Battle of Worcester. In appreciation for my grandfather's loyalty, the King made him an Earl and gave him lands in the far north of Scotland. Because of that, he was able to make a great deal of money in trade and other ventures and became a favorite of King Charles in court. My grandmother came from a wealthy family so together my grandparents built up quite a fortune. Later when my father became of age, he moved to London to handle the family businesses. It was only natural that I follow in my family's footsteps and fully support our King with our respect, loyalty, service, and even money when necessary. Thus we have always been in favor. Our family was greatly saddened when King Charles died."

"And now we have King William," Betsy said. "I don't know much about King Charles, but honestly, Sir John, I don't see how you can honorably serve a king who murders your clansmen," she said sharply.

"Och, lass, I do not blame King William for Glencoe."

Betsy's eyes flashed with anger. "He signed the order for the massacre! In fact, he signed it twice!"

"That's true," Sir John admitted, "but the blame lies with John Dalrymple and the Campbells who lied to King William about the MacDonalds. They are the ones who are guilty. You have to understand that the King had his hands full with many other matters on the continent. Therefore, he must rely on the truthfulness of his advisors. Unfortunately he listened to the conniving Campbells. That resulted in a serious mistake that almost caused a war in Scotland. Even the English were up in arms about what happened at Glencoe."

Betsy was not convinced that Sir John was correct, but it was his opinion and she didn't challenge him. Instead, she changed the subject.

"Why are you here in France?" she asked. "Are you here on holiday?"

"Not quite," he said. Actually, I am here as a soldier on the King's business. Seems like we are trying to keep the Catholics and Protestants from killing each other in the Lowlands." He hesitated before continuing. "It just might be an impossible task."

Betsy frowned. "I don't like the Protestants," she said. "I believe they are trying to destroy the True Church."

"Well, I don't know about that. Personally, I favor neither religion and I resent fighting wars to protect the clergy's politics."

Betsy raised her eyebrows in disbelief. "You are not a Catholic? Nor are you a Protestant? Then are you a non-believer?"

"No, no," Sir John assured her. "I am a Christian but I have a hard time understanding how one Christian group can kill another Christian group over nothing but minor differences."

Betsy was surprised by his answer. She was unaware that Protestants believed in the same God she did. She had been well indoctrinated by her Church about evil Protestants who performed pagan rituals and killed and tortured Catholics. Now she was being told that the two religions *did* believe in the same God. She had to admit that she had often suspected that priests were too zealous, although she had accepted what they said without question because it was a Catholic's duty to never question the Church's teachings.

The discussion with Sir John left Betsy with many questions and she was sorry when he and his men rode out the next morning and headed back to the Low Countries.

Just before he left, Sir John took Betsy aside. His blue eyes looked deeply into hers. Once again, she felt her heart skip a beat.

"May I visit you again when I return in two months?" He didn't take his eyes off her.

"Yes, Sir John," she answered, "I would like that. Will my being a Catholic bother you?" she asked softly.

"Of course not. But do be advised," Sir John teased, "that is one reason I worry about you. If you can accept me as I am, I will certainly accept you as you are. I already know that I will get the best of the bargain." He kissed her hand, turned abruptly and joined his fellow soldiers.

Betsy watched as they rode away. "Two months!" she pouted. "He'll forget all about me by then."

The next day Betsy told her mother what Sir John MacDonald had said.

"I like him very much, Mother, but it worries me that he doesn't seem to follow any religion...although he says he is a Christian."

Heather sat down across the table from her daughter. "My dear, this may be hard for you to understand right now, but religions are created by man, not by God. I think of our Church as a large kingdom, and its leaders—like our kings—are just men. Sometimes the Church does great good. Sometimes it does great harm. I'm sorry to say that many of our Popes have been very corrupt men. Likewise, I am certain that many Protestant leaders have been corrupt as well. I'm afraid that many church leaders are only interested in wealth and power, but they call it God's work."

Betsy was confused. "But don't you believe the teachings of the Church?"

"Sometimes, but not always. You know I was raised a Catholic. Your father never was a very religious person but he is such a good and honorable man. It made me think. And I came to the conclusion that everyone creates his own belief system. I don't want you to make the mistake of quibbling over religion with those around you. It only leads to arguments and ill feelings. You can't change anyone else's beliefs. You can only change your own. At this point in your life, I think most of the Church's teachings are worthy of your beliefs. Practice your faith, as you understand it. Remember, your faith and your beliefs are between you and God."

Now Betsy was really surprised. Her mother had been a practicing Catholic all of her life and she had come from a strong Catholic family. Now her mother had as much as told her that she saw flaws in the church. When she stopped to think about it, she herself had questioned some things. Betsy had never believed in blind obedience and had always had trouble with the idea that Popes were infallible and thought of as 'God on earth.'

Sir John and her mother had given her a lot to think about.

-o-

CHAPTER 11

Betsy couldn't stop thinking about John MacDonald. She could see his eyes and remembered how they looked at her. His hair was always neatly pulled back and tied, but wisps of curls framed his face. Just thinking about him made her tingle. She loved the sound of his voice which was deep and resonant. Betsy smiled when she remembered his hearty laughter. Somehow it always made her feel happy inside.

This is silly, she admonished herself. *I hardly know the man. We just spent one evening together. It doesn't mean a thing. I'll probably never see him again.*

So Betsy did the sensible thing. She went back to her studies with a vengeance. It was the only way she could keep her mind off John MacDonald.

If course it didn't work very well. How many times had she opened up a book and just stared at the pages? She kept seeing John's smile. But she kept trying. When she wasn't trying to study, she kept busy with crocheting, a new skill she had recently learned from her grandmother. In fact, she was hoping to complete an afghan as a Christmas gift to her parents.

Betsy loved Christmas, even more so now that she was in France. Her extended family made it very merry indeed. She always looked forward to baking Christmas treats with her grandmother. Since there was so much to do to prepare for the holidays, Heather gave Betsy permission to spend a few days at the MacDonald farm.

"Grandmere needs another right arm!" Betsy told her mother.

On the first day, they baked oatmeal cookies and cinnamon rolls. The house smelled good all day and Betsy ate as many cookies as she could.

After dinner, Angus asked Betsy to walk to the barn with him so he could finish milking the cows.

"We seldom get the chance just to talk, lass," he said. "I just wanted to know how you're doing." He looked at her with loving eyes. "Have you been able to put Glencoe behind you?" Angus placed the milk bucket under the cow and began milking.

Betsy nodded. "Most of the time, Grandpere. But I must admit it still haunts me at times." She kneeled down next to her grandfather and rested on her heels. "I don't know if I will ever forget it. It's always close in my thoughts. I remind myself over and over *not* to remember it."

"That's true, child. But as time passes and you move farther away from that awful night, you'll be able to put it in perspective as an event that, even though you can't change it, helped to make you who you are. Your actions were simply self-defense and nothing more. You just did what you had to do to save your own life."

"Grandpere, who do you think is more to blame—the King who signed the order or the Campbells who carried it out?" Betsy had never been able to resolve her own feelings about who was to blame. Maybe her grandfather could.

Angus picked up the stool and bucket and moved to the next cow. Betsy followed.

"Blame is usually not a simple thing," he said. "In this case, there was a disastrous chain of events that led up to it. First, it was the MacDonald clan chief who refused to sign the oath of allegiance until after the deadline. Then Scotland's Secretary of State, who hated the MacDonalds, lied to the King by telling him the chief had not signed. Finally, the Campbells completed the vicious cycle by carrying out the King's order of genocide. There is blood on many hands, I'm afraid."

Angus stopped for a moment, then handed Betsy the pail of fresh milk. He stood up and Betsy could see his eyes were narrow and his face was flushed with anger. "I blame the Campbells, lassie, and I will do everything in my power to avenge the death of my son, his wife, and my three grandsons! If it takes the rest of my life, I will get revenge!"

Betsy was surprised at her grandfather's fury. She understood the pain of losing his son and his family was buried deep inside and he truly believed it could only be healed by revenge.

"Revenge, Grandpere?" She repeated the word, "Revenge?"

"Aye, lass, revenge! Do you think for one moment I could forgive such an outrage against my family? Only heartless creatures would leave women and children to die in the snow!"

Angus said no more. He took the pail of milk from Betsy and headed back to the house. She followed close behind.

I wonder what he means by revenge. The word aroused deep feelings within her. She remembered that her father had told her revenge was never a solution, but she understood her grandfather's desire for revenge. He had lost precious family who could never be replaced. She admitted that regardless of what her father had said, she wanted revenge too!

The next day she had an opportunity to question her grandfather again.

"Yesterday, Grandpere, you mentioned you wanted revenge. May I ask what kind of revenge do you mean?"

Angus was not pleased with her question. He frowned and answered her sharply. "No, girl, you may not! Mine was a slip of the tongue. Forget what I said."

Betsy realized she had been out of line so she asked no more questions. Once again, she pushed memories of Glencoe from her mind. She had other important things to occupy her thoughts. Christmas was fast approaching and she refused to allow anything to dampen her festive Christmas spirit.

When Christmas day arrived, Betsy jumped out of bed and looked out the window. The sky was clear and it was easy to see it would be a bright day full of sunshine. She opened her window and breathed in the crisp cold air. She laughed and rubbed the tingle from her nostrils. A light snow had fallen during the night and the ground was white.

"This is going to be the best Christmas ever. I just know it!" she said. Betsy closed the window and hurriedly got dressed. She didn't want to waste one minute of this wonderful day.

Before they left for the MacDonald farm, Ewin put sleigh bells around the horses' necks so that the bells jingled merrily with each step. She snuggled next to her mother and pulled the blanket tight around them.

When the Stewart family arrived, Uncle Roy and Jeanette met them at the door.

"Come in, come in! Everyone is waiting for you," Uncle Roy exclaimed.

After the hugs and kisses and wishes for a Merry Christmas, Grandmere brought in a tray of hot beverages. She could see that Roy was extremely excited about something. "Here, Roy, have a drink. You need to calm down."

Roy shook his head. "I will in a minute. But first, I want everyone to come into the parlor and sit down." He took Betsy and Jeanette by the hand and led them to the couch. Then he changed his mind. "No, Jeanette. You sit over here." He led her to an overstuffed chair close to the fire. Then one by one, he led Ewin, Heather, Angus, and Lisa to their places around Jeanette.

Betsy thought he looked awfully nervous. He was smiling from ear to ear, but he kept clasping and unclasping his hands as he paced back and forth in front of the fire.

"I just can't wait any longer…and I wanted all of you here." He pulled a small pouch from his pocket and dropped to one knee in front of Jeanette. "My darling, I love you. Will you do me the great honor of becoming my wife?" He held the pouch upside down and the contents fell into his hand. He picked up the delicate cameo ring and held it up for Jeanette to see. "This ring belonged to my grandmother and now I give it to you with all my love."

Jeanette's eyes grew wide as her hand covered her mouth. She gasped, "Oh, Roy! Yes! I love you, too! I mean…I will…I will marry you!"

Roy slipped the ring on her finger and kissed her softly.

The rest of the day was filled with laughter, gaiety, and wedding plans. Betsy was right. It was the best Christmas Day she had ever had.

In mid-January, Sir John MacDonald and some of his soldiers returned to the MacDonald farm. Angus sent for Ewin and Roy. The men spent hours behind closed doors.

Lisa was naturally very curious. "Angus, what in the world is going on in there?"

Angus looked serious. "Sorry, my love, it's nothing I can discuss with you now. Later, perhaps. You'll just have to trust me."

Lisa knew not to press her husband for details. She knew he would inform her when the time was right. In the meantime, she kept busy keeping their mugs and their stomachs filled.

Betsy was disappointed and hurt when she learned that Sir John had been in the area for a full week and had not come to see her. Nevertheless, the day he rode to the Stewart farm, her disappointment disappeared and she felt giddy.

"I've had urgent business to attend to and I'm afraid there's much more to come before I leave," he explained. "But I had to come see you, Miss Betsy. I've missed you, you know."

Betsy was honest. "I'm glad to see you, too, Sir John." She felt awkward. He seemed sincere but she couldn't help but wonder if she had read too much into the day they had spent together.

His warm smile helped to put her fears to rest. "Please, just call me John."

She relaxed a little and returned his smile. "Just call me Betsy."

They talked for more than an hour. She noticed that he never took his eyes off of her. It made her nervous, but she didn't want him to stop.

As he stood up, he reached for her hand and pulled her to her feet. "I must leave now. More meetings to attend." He grinned. "I plan to see you again soon…if that's all right with you, of course."

Betsy liked the warmth of his hand holding hers. "Yes, I'd like to see you again. How long do you think you'll be staying with my grandfather?"

"Several weeks, I imagine. We are planning a very important endeavor." John released her hand and bowed slightly out of respect. "I take my leave now…until we meet again."

"Yes," Betsy said softly. "Until we meet again."

Betsy had no way of knowing how very important the endeavor was. It not only involved many hours of planning but also was followed by many hours of learning to sail a boat. Ewin and Roy were in charge of training Sir John and his soldiers. Once they had mastered handling *The Cormorant,* it was time to look for a larger ship, one that could insure them the success of their mission. They sailed down the coast to Le Havre where they purchased a sixty-foot schooner with exceptionally clean lines. After returning home to St. Val'ery, the new sailors spent many days at the Stewart farm.

Fascinated, Betsy watched as the men put up ropes on the barn rafters and practiced climbing them. The students were divided into two groups. While Roy taught one group how to tie knots, Ewin taught the second group nautical terms. Then they switched. It soon became clear to Betsy that these men were being trained to be seaworthy sailors. *But why?* she wondered. *What in the world does this mean?*

She was curious enough to ask her mother.

Heather shrugged her shoulders. "I don't know what's going on, child."

Betsy couldn't accept that answer. "Mother, you must have some idea. You and father have no secrets. I'm no longer a child. You can tell me."

Heather hesitated a moment. "Yes, Betsy, you are no longer a child. Besides if anyone has a right to know, it's you. It's a long story. And it's all about revenge."

"Revenge?" Betsy didn't understand. "Revenge on whom?"

"Sit down, dear, and I will tell you everything." Heather poured two cups of coffee and handed one to Betsy.

She cradled the cup in her hands, and then took a long, slow sip of the hot liquid. Heather sighed deeply. "This is hard for me to talk about, but I will try to make you understand. You know that neither your father nor I believe in violent revenge. Not an 'eye for an eye or a tooth for a tooth' kind of revenge. What we do believe in is justice."

"Mother, I'm not following. What are you talking about?" Betsy asked.

"I'm talking about revenge for my brother. Revenge for his family. Revenge for all the MacDonalds of Glencoe."

Betsy started to speak. "I still…"

"Let me continue, Betsy. When I'm finished, you will understand. Your father and Uncle Roy have trained Sir John and his soldiers to be good sailors. They aren't going to kill any Campbells but there is a way to cripple them financially. We have learned that the Campbells own several cargo ships. One is loaded with cargo from the West Indies and will soon be returning to England. Sir John and his men will sail to Spain to load cannon and shot. There, professional Scottish sailors will join them. Later, they will intercept the Campbell ship and take its cargo."

Betsy understood all too clearly. "Mother, Sir John is in the military! If he pirates a ship under the English flag, he'll be committing treason! He'll be hanged!"

Heather held up her hands and tried to calm Betsy's fears. "Wait a minute, Betsy. Sir John is not in the English military. He is a mercenary employed by the King. They won't sail under a British flag. The captain of their ship is a French privateer and the ship will sail under the French flag. You need to understand that Sir John wants to do this. He wants revenge, too."

"Is Grandpere aware of this plan?"

"Yes, dear. Your grandfather is the one who came up with the plan. You see, we are not alone in our desire for justice. There are men all over Scotland, and even in the new American colonies, who will let us know about any ship on which Campbell wealth travels. Sir John plans to intercept all of them."

Finally, Betsy understood her grandfather's meaning of revenge. Maybe the success of this plan would satisfy her own desire for revenge and she could put memories of Glencoe behind her forever.

-o-

CHAPTER 12

Betsy didn't know if Sir John was alive or dead. It had been weeks since he and his men sailed out of Le Havre harbor. No one mentioned his name. It was as though he didn't exist, had never existed. Sometimes she wondered if it had all been her imagination. But she knew better. She remembered his eyes and how she felt when he was close to her. She could take a deep breath and smell him. Sir John always smelled clean. She couldn't identify the combination of scents that were unique to him, but knew it was something she would always remember. At night she prayed for his safety. During the day she scanned the landscape for a cloud of dust that always followed someone on horseback.

Then suddenly he returned. Once again Betsy's world began turning.

This time, he came to see her first. He seemed a little ill at ease as he removed his hat and turned it round and round in his hands.

"Betsy, could we go for a walk? I need to talk to you."

"Certainly," she agreed and picked up a shawl to cover her shoulders against the chill of the evening.

As they walked he held her hand. She liked the feeling of this strong man strolling beside her. They walked in silence for a few minutes before John spoke.

"Betsy, although I am just a soldier, I am not without means. I understand that I may be rushing things and possibly I should have come to you first, but I felt I should ask your parents for your hand first."

"You have talked to my parents?" Betsy's surprise was genuine.

Now it was John's turn to show surprise. "Of course. Didn't they tell you?"

"No. They never said a word."

"Perhaps they waited to be sure I was serious. And I am serious, Betsy. I want to ask for your hand in marriage."

Betsy stopped dead in her tracks. "Marriage!" She thought there would be time for courting, time to get to know each other. Betsy didn't know what to say. His sudden offer made her realize he was a serious suitor and that she would not have the luxury of time in making up her mind.

She wanted him to kiss her. Then maybe she could believe he was really serious. She did not have long to wait. Slowly, he leaned down and kissed her. It was a warm, soft kiss and she felt herself responding to it. She reached up on her toes and he embraced her and kissed her again. This time she threw her arms around his neck and her body arched against his. His kisses became longer and harder. Each time her desire for him grew. He stopped and gently tilted her chin up. She caught her breath and slowly opened her eyes.

"Lass," he asked, "Will you consider being my wife. I promise to love you for the rest of my life."

If these delicious feeling sweeping through her whole body were any indication, she knew she was head-over-heels in love. Breathlessly she answered, "Yes."

John was elated. He picked her up in his arms and swung her around and around until they were both dizzy.

"C'mon! Let's go tell your parents." John grabbed her hand and together they ran back to the farmhouse.

~~~

During the next few weeks, John and Betsy were inseparable. They took advantage of the time to really get to know each other and to fall more deeply in love.

John had not been looking for a wife. He was very happy with his exciting and adventurous life. It suited him. He was a restless young man who wanted to leave his mark on the world. Being loyal to the monarchy was an excellent way for him to achieve his goals. It had worked for his father and grandfather before him and he just naturally followed their lead.

Then he met Betsy and his thoughts for the future began to change. From the moment he first saw her, every waking thought was of her. He had never seen anyone with hair so rich, so alive with highlights. His hands could get lost in that hair. And her eyes! Her beautiful eyes were framed with long, thick lashes. They were definitely gray but could change to stormy blue when she was angry. There was so much to learn about her and now that he had made a lifelong commitment to her, he could take his time to discover and enjoy every facet of her personality. John was not worried. Betsy would make a wonderful wife. She had a natural grace in her movements and an elegance that others admired.

Betsy, however, *was* worried. John was a nobleman. She was a country girl. How could she possibly fit into his world? John was such a handsome man. He could have any woman. Why would he want her for a wife? Did he see something in her that she couldn't see? Whatever he saw must be good because every time he looked at her, his face lit up and his eyes shone with love. She could actually see that love and in return, knew she would do anything for him. *Worry? So what! A little worry will just keep me on my toes!*

Soon after posting their own marriage bans, John and Betsy attended the wedding of her Uncle Roy and Jeanette. It was a small service with only immediate family present.

This was the first wedding Betsy had ever attended. John noticed the tears streaming down her cheeks.

"Are you all right?" he whispered.

Betsy smiled through tear filled eyes. "It's so beautiful, John. I can't help myself. I'm so happy for them both."

John didn't understand, but he smiled anyway. "Are you going to cry like this at our wedding?"

She looked at him a little sheepishly and nodded.

Following the reception at the Stewarts, Betsy pulled John aside. "There is something very important we need to discuss. I've been worried about it for some time."

John showed concern. "By all means. Tell me."

"We'll have to talk to Pere Francis soon about our wedding. What will you tell him about your religion? If you don't confess to being a Catholic, he won't be able to marry us."

John took her hands in his. "I guess I haven't been totally truthful with you about that. It's true, I don't follow any one religion faithfully but I was baptized Catholic."

Relieved, Betsy blew out a slow breath. "Good! That's one more worry to cross off my list." She kissed his cheek.

John grabbed her and pulled her close. "No, no. Not good enough!"

At first his kiss was soft and warm. Then his arms tightened around her. His tongue parted her lips and he kissed her deeply. Betsy's response was immediate. Her knees buckled and her body was delirious with wonderful new sensations.

Worry? She thought, *what worry?*

The next day, John had a surprise for Betsy. "I want you to close your eyes and hold out your arms."

Betsy did as she was asked. John placed something heavy across her arms. She had no idea what she was holding.

"Open your eyes," John instructed.

Betsy opened her eyes. Her mouth dropped open and her eyes widened. She was holding a bolt of pale yellow silk. She was speechless.

John wasn't sure of her reaction. "It's for your wedding dress. I thought you'd like it."

Betsy stared at the fabric, then looked up at John. Very carefully she placed the bolt of silk on a nearby table, then turned and jumped into John's arms. "It's the most beautiful thing I've ever seen! Thank you! My wedding dress will be the most beautiful dress that was ever made!"

She ran back to the table and unrolled a yard of the fabric and held it across her chest, close to her face. Her eyes sparkled. "Well, what do you think?"

John couldn't help but laugh. "What do I think?" he repeated. "I think I love you. I think you're the most incredible woman I've ever known. And I think you'll be the most beautiful bride the world will ever see."

When Heather saw the silk she was awed. "Betsy! Where ever did he get such a beautiful piece of silk?"

"He bought it when he was in Spain last year. He said that when he saw the fabric, he could see me in it. That's when he knew he wanted to marry me!"

Heather slid her hand over the smooth fabric. "It's a good thing we have several weeks before the wedding. It will take me and your grandmother that much time to get it ready for the wedding."

The wedding preparations were joyful with lots of singing and humming and laughter. The men stayed as far away from it as they could.

In the evenings, John and Betsy took long walks and talked about their future.

"After the wedding," John told her, "I want to take you to London. You can buy some ready made clothes there and I can introduce you to some of my friends."

Betsy liked the idea. "London! How wonderful! The only large city I've ever been in is Edinburgh but I was very young and I really don't remember much about it except it was noisy and the streets were dirty."

"London is noisy, too…and dirty, I'm afraid. But I'll show you some of the finer points of the city."

Betsy's insecurities surfaced. "John…I'm still concerned about one thing. Will I fit in? I'd rather die than embarrass you."

John placed her head on his shoulder. "There is no way you could ever embarrass me. Why, those fine London ladies will pale in comparison to you."

Betsy jerked her head up. "You're teasing me!"

John kissed the tip of her nose. "Just you wait, my darling. I'll be the envy of London when you are by my side."

~~~

The wedding was just a week away. Betsy's stomach fluttered every time she thought of it. She knew the time had come for her to tell John about Glencoe. She dreaded having to relive the nightmare once again but John needed to know.

Her mother had agreed. "The sooner the better," she said. "It's not a good idea to have any deep dark secrets from your husband, except for…"

"I know, Mother, except for…" Neither one of them wanted to mention the other secret.

That night at supper, the conversation was light and centered, of course, on the wedding. John noticed that Heather was always smiling these days. This day was no different.

"The dress is almost finished!" Heather beamed. "Tomorrow, Betsy, you must try it on for a final fitting." Still beaming, she turned to John. "The fabric is exquisite. You chose well, John."

"I'm glad you like it." he said, then turned his attention to Betsy.

Heather, still smiling, got up from the table. "Ewin, I need your help with something." She started gathering plates and motioned for Ewin to do the same. "Betsy, dear, you and John run along now. I know you have lots to discuss."

Betsy looked up at her mother and Heather nodded slightly.

John could read Betsy well. He noticed that something was bothering her. She was definitely preoccupied. Whatever it was, Heather was aware of it, too.

As soon as they were alone, he asked. "What is it, Betsy? Something is bothering you." He leaned closer to her and tried to encourage her. "Remember, you can tell me anything." He covered her hands with his own. "Betsy, look at me."

Slowly she raised her eyes. "It's about Glencoe, John." She waited for a reaction.

A slight frown furrowed his brow for a moment. "Go on," he said, "I'm listening."

Betsy told John the story, leaving out no details. At times her eyes glistened with unshed tears. She had cried enough about Glencoe and refused to give in to any more tears.

John listened to the incredible story and his heart swelled with compassion. She had been a child. No child should ever witness violence and bloodshed much less become a part of it.

When she finished her story, John softly caressed her cheek, then drew her into his arms. Gently he rocked her back and forth. "I'm so sorry, my darling, for what you endured. As long as I am alive, you never again will face such danger. I promise."

For the very first time, Betsy felt free, really free. She had said it before but this time she was convinced that memories of Glencoe could safely be put to rest. She had John. Their growing love and their bright future was a promise for many happy tomorrows. She could finally look forward to those tomorrows and forget about all the sad yesterdays.

John cleared his throat. "Now, it's confession time for me."

"What do you mean?" Betsy asked.

"I had no idea how personally involved you were in Glencoe. But now that I do, you might like to know that your family and I have taken steps that will make some of the Campbells wish they'd never been born."

"Oh," Betsy said offhandedly, "you mean when you pirated a Campbell ship filled with valuable cargo?"

John's face showed his surprise. "You know?"

Betsy's eyes twinkled with amusement. "Yes, I know. Mother told me. Tell me, are you going to do it again?"

John burst out laughing. "You amaze me, Betsy. Really you do!"

Betsy joined his laughter. They laughed so loud, Heather poked her head into the room and watched. *Laughter is good for the soul,* she thought. *I hope they never forget how to laugh.*

Betsy's wedding day was warm and sunny. She had all day to prepare because the service was scheduled to begin at sunset.

Pere Francis had strongly objected to an evening wedding.

"Weddings are always in the morning," he told her.

"My wedding will be in the evening with lots of candlelight," she told him.

"That's not possible," he said.

"Why not?" she countered.

"Well…just because all Catholic weddings are in the morning."

Betsy stood firm. "My wedding will be in the evening. If you won't agree, I'll find another priest who will!"

Pere Francis looked at this headstrong young woman whose mind was made up. Reluctantly, he agreed. "All right…but only because it's you!"

Betsy beamed. "Thank you, Pere Francis." She took his hand and kissed it. "It'll be the most beautiful wedding you've ever seen!"

And it was. The church was aglow with candlelight. Baskets of bright flowers lined the communion rail. When Betsy came into the back of the church, the organ began to play. John took a deep breath and his heart began to pound as he watched his bride, escorted by her father, walk slowly down the aisle. He had never seen anyone so beautiful. It was as though he was seeing a vision. His heart skipped a beat as he realized this was real. This moment they had both been waiting for, was finally here.

With every step, Betsy's gown shimmered in the soft candlelight. The design of the dress was perfect for her. The bodice was cut low enough to frame modest cleavage. Sleeves were full at the shoulders, then slimmed below the elbows and ended in points at the tips of her fingers. The skirt was exceptionally full so as to make her already small waist look even smaller. A choker of yellow silk banded her throat and was highlighted with a small gold brooch. Piled high on her head, her hair was covered with a sheer, pale yellow veil that reached her shoulders.

As Betsy slipped into place beside John, the music swelled and then fell silent. She looked into her bridegroom's eyes and saw the love that was written all over his face. The butterflies in her stomach quieted as he took her hand and they stepped forward to face the priest and repeat the most important vows they would ever take.

Her worries disappeared and she knew that this day, this moment, was what she had waited for, for her entire life.

~~~

For their wedding night, John had rented a room at an inn in St. Val'ery. It was a large, comfortable room. John had seen to that. He knew how much Betsy loved candlelight, so he made sure there was an abundance of lighted candles throughout the room.

Betsy was surprised when she entered the room. She had never seen anything like it. "Oh, it's magnificent," she said.

The first thing she noticed was the mahogany four-poster bed. The satin bedspread was the color of port wine. Across the room were two comfortable-looking chairs upholstered in stripes of ecru and wine velvet. Between them was a round table that held a vase of fresh flowers and a silver bucket containing a bottle of chilled champagne. There were two windows behind the chairs. The light colored curtains provided privacy but were sheer enough to let in light. The top half of the walls were covered with cream colored damask that reflected the glow of candlelight. The bottom half of the walls were paneled mahogany. Oriental rugs in various shades of blue, cream, and deep red were scattered across the highly polished floor.

John wrapped his arms around his new wife. "Do you like the room?" he asked and kissed the top of her head.

"John, it's the most beautiful room I've ever seen. It's fit for a king!"

He turned her around so he could look at her face. "You are glowing," he said.

"Of course I am," she said, "I'm so happy I could burst."

"Well, before you do and ruin that beautiful dress," he joked, "why not change. While you do that, I'll uncork the champagne."

She looked at him helplessly for a moment before he realized what the look meant. "Turn around, love, and I'll unbutton you."

She shivered when his fingers touched her back. One by one, she felt the buttons release.

When he finished, he slapped her behind. "You can handle it from here."

She lifted her skirts and glanced at him over her shoulder. He smiled and winked. "Go on, now. I'm getting thirsty...aren't you?"

She returned his smile and slipped behind the privacy screen. When she had changed, she stepped in front of the screen. John was sitting in one of the chairs. He whistled low when he saw her. She was wearing a pretty pink cotton chemise that hugged her curves. The low neckline was trimmed with lace. The long sleeves gathered at her wrists. They, too, were finished with lace.

Slowly she stepped toward him. John jumped out of the chair and met her halfway. "The hell with the champagne! We'll have it later."

Swiftly he picked her up and carried her to the bed that he had carefully uncovered. He sat alongside her and just looked at her. Her hair was still pinned but some of the curls had escaped and were framing her face. Carefully, he reached up and removed the pins. Her hair fell in shiny cascades around her shoulders.

"My God, Betsy, you are incredibly beautiful!" He held her head in his hands and ran his fingers through her thick hair. He kissed her mouth lightly at first then with a passion that made him quiver.

Betsy's body responded with sensations she had never before experienced. She allowed the delicious feelings to guide her mouth. Her hands ran over his arms, his shoulders, his chest.

Suddenly John stopped. He hurriedly removed his clothes. All she saw was skin and hard muscle. Gently he pushed her down onto the pillows and lifted her gown. She raised her arms and he pulled it off and threw it aside. He rose up on his arms and drank in her beauty. The candlelight threw shafts of light across her hair and her face. He rolled to his side and began caressing her. His fingers traced the shape of her face, her throat, and her shoulders. He leaned close and kissed the curve of her throat. His breath was hot and his kisses were warm and moist. She took a deep breath and filled her nostrils with his musky, masculine scent. She memorized this smell and would always associate it with love. Then his hands went lower to caress her breasts, her stomach, and her thighs. Instinctively, her legs parted. He answered by placing his fingers in her most private place. She jumped at the intense sensation it gave her.

"It's all right, my darling. I'm going to take you to a place you never dreamed existed. Trust me."

She did trust him. Soon they were both lost in a sea of tangled arms and legs. Their hands touched and explored every crevice, every curve. His lips were hot and tasted every part of her body. Her mouth felt bruised but she didn't want to stop. She couldn't stop. The crescendo was building and she thought she was going to die. Just then, she cried out and experienced the place she never knew existed.

They drank the champagne at 4 o'clock in the morning. When the bottle was empty, he took her by the hand and led her again to that wonderful place that before tonight she never knew existed. After tonight, she knew she wanted to visit it often.

~~~

Goodbyes are never easy, but this time when Betsy said farewell to her parents and grandparents, it was with a happy heart. She promised to keep in touch and let them know when she and John would return.

Ewin insisted on taking the newlyweds across to Southampton on the *Cormorant*. It was a beautiful day and the channel crossing was smooth.

John helped Betsy disembark. Ewin followed, and then squeezed his daughter tightly.

"Oh, dear child, I will miss you so. But I leave you in good hands." He kissed her cheek, shook hands with John, and jumped back into his boat. He waved a last farewell, and then pushed the boat away from the dock.

Betsy and John stood arm in arm and watched until the boat became a dot on the horizon.

It was late in the day when they arrived in Southampton, so they agreed to spend the night in an inn before traveling on to London. After securing a room, John made arrangements with the innkeeper to book passage on the morning coach to London.

John was asleep when Betsy climbed into bed. She lay quietly and listened to his rhythmic breathing, then she curled up against his back. Her hand slid up his arm and rested on his muscle.

Instantly he was awake. He raised his head and covered her hand with his own. "Are you all right?" he asked sleepily.

"I can't sleep. I'm excited about tomorrow, I guess, and wondering what it will be like to actually be in London."

Now wide-awake, John turned onto his back and put his arm underneath her head. "You will love London and London will love you. But first, get some sleep."

She rose up on one elbow and delicately traced his lips with her finger. "I will, my love, but not right now. First things first!"

~~~

Betsy enjoyed the ride to London. While John carried on a conversation with the other passenger, Betsy kept looking out the coach window at the scenic countryside. Each time the coach passed by a garden or a park, Betsy would "ooh" and "aah."

Soon she could see the outskirts of the city. She was amazed at the number of buildings. People were everywhere! There were so many carriages criss-crossing the roads she wondered how they kept from bumping into each other.

The coach stopped and John jumped out and assisted Betsy as she stepped down. He removed their luggage from the hold, then stood until the coach moved on.

John pointed at a building across the street. "See that big gray house? That's my father's." He couldn't help but add, "Someday, it will be ours."

Betsy stood in awe. The house was much larger than those around it. It was three stories high. Window boxes filled with bright red and white flowers were mounted beneath every window. She counted nine. The window frames and the front door were painted a shiny black. Two large white urns overflowing with red flowers flanked each side of the front door. It was a clean, well-kept house that looked very inviting. She was anxious to see inside.

As they walked across the street and climbed the front steps, the door opened wide. A short, plump woman wearing a gray dress with a white bib apron and a white dust cap greeted them with open arms. Betsy couldn't help but notice that her maid's uniform matched the house. Could that be a coincidence?

"John!" she cried excitedly and threw her arms around him. "It's so good to see you again. It's been too long, you know. Come in! Come in!" She looked at Betsy warmly. "Now who is this, John? You rascal! Did you get married?" She pulled them away from the door and closed it.

"Annie, I've missed you too!" John had to talk fast as he could see Annie was ready to talk again. "I want you to meet my wife, Betsy Stewart."

Annie dropped a curtsy then stood with her hands on her hips as she assessed her new mistress.

"She's a beauty, John and I hope you know you're lucky to have her. She'll brighten things up around here. We've needed that since your mother passed. The place needs a woman's touch. Yessiree! Now come along, you two. I'll take you to your room. I'm sure you're tired from your long trip and would like to freshen up and rest a while." She took Betsy by the arm and looked over her shoulder at John. "Only bring the bags you need. I'll have Frederick bring up the rest." She returned her attention to Betsy as they climbed the staircase. "If you ever want to know anything about this new husband of yours, you come to me. I can tell you stories that will curl your ears. You see, I've known him since he was a wee tyke."

When they were alone in their room, they both laughed quietly.

"Is she always so talkative?" Betsy asked.

"Always!" John said. "I never remember a time when she didn't have a lot to say."

After they had rested, John took Betsy on a tour of the house. She could easily see it was as lovely on the inside as it was on the outside. The first floor consisted of a large stone entry hall. A large parlor entered from the right.

"It's mostly for entertaining guests," John explained.

To the left of the entry hall was a large dining room with a table that looked like it could seat eighteen people.

John watched as Betsy silently counted the possible number of guests.

"Actually, it will seat twenty," he said.

Behind the large dining room was a smaller dining room, not so elegantly addressed.

John turned up his nose slightly. "Just for everyday family dining. Nothing fancy."

Betsy gasped when she saw the huge kitchen. A long table for food preparation ran the length of the room. Against the outside wall were three large fireplaces for cooking. This was a different world for Betsy. It would take a lot of getting used to.

"How many cooks do you have?" she asked.

"Usually just one. If there is a big party, we bring in one or two more."

Betsy just shook her head in amazement. She wandered back into the entry hall and looked around. There was a beautifully hand-carved curved staircase on either side.

"I guess one is for going up and the other is for going down," Betsy mused.

John laughed. "You know, that's pretty much how it works. We usually go up on the right side and come down on the left side."

Betsy made a mental note to do just the opposite. Just to see if it would get a reaction.

The second floor contained the family's living quarters. There was a large comfortable sitting room. Shelves along one wall held more books than Betsy had ever seen. Even more than were in Pere Francis's library. Betsy counted four bedrooms, not including the one she and John shared.

She looked at the less formal staircase that led to the third floor.

John answered her silent question. "The third floor is for the staff."

"How many staff are there?" she wondered.

"You met Annie, of course. Then there is Frederick. He's kind of the man of the house, inside and out. He does repairs, weeds the garden, tends to the horses, oils squeaky wheels and anything else that needs to be done. Emma is the full time cook." He thought for a moment. "That's about it, I guess."

Betsy wasn't sure she understood the need for three full time servants. "But John, what do they do when your father's not here? And when you are not here?"

"The house is rarely empty of guests. Father opens the house to close friends and business associates who use the house as their own private inn, you might say, whenever they are in London for business or pleasure."

"Is it safe," Betsy wondered, "to have strangers in your house when you are not even there?"

"I'm surprised at you, Betsy, my love." John feigned concern. "You are a Scot. You know how hospitable we are. And that goes for here in London as well as in the Highlands."

Betsy nodded her understanding. "I see what you mean. But you'll have to give me time to adjust to all this. You've taken me to a whole new world. And," she admitted, "one I think I'm going to like very much."

While they were eating dinner that night in the small dining room, Annie came in carrying a silver tray that held an embossed envelope.

John quickly opened it. A smile spread across his face. He handed the folded paper to Betsy. "You're going to like this."

Betsy read the message, then looked at John. Her face drained of color. She placed her hand over her heart to stop the sudden palpitation.

"The Marquis of Staffordshire is inviting us to dinner…at his home …*TOMORROW?*"

John tried to reassure her. "He's a friend of mine. We've known each other for years."

She was not comforted. "A Marquis!"

John couldn't help but laugh. He had never seen her flustered before.

"Don't get caught up in titles. Everyone in London has a title. You'll get used to it soon enough." He reached over and tried to calm her by patting her hand. "Do you realize, my darling, that you have a title?"

"Me? A title?" She wanted to laugh. "I have a *title?*"

"Yes, you do. You are Lady MacDonald."

This was almost too much to comprehend. She burst out laughing. "You aren't serious! Me? A Lady?"

When she saw the strange look on her husband's face, she stopped laughing. "You *are* serious. I am now…Lady MacDonald." She tried to grasp the idea that it was really true. Her face reddened with embarrassment. "John, forgive me. I never made the connection. Remember that, until today at least, I was a small town country girl. I should have known. You are Sir John MacDonald and your wife... that's me," she giggled, "shall henceforth be known as...*The Lady MacDonald!*" Seriously she added, "And I promise I will never embarrass you...ever!"

"On the contrary," he said dramatically, "You will be my shining star. Any light that I might have had will surely dim in comparison whenever you waltz into a room!"

"You are silly, Sir John MacDonald...but don't stop. I love hearing it. By the way, if you really want my light to shine, I'm going to need some clothes appropriate for the occasion."

~~~

The next day they went shopping.

"I never knew there were so many shops to buy dresses!" Betsy's face was flushed with excitement.

John enjoyed watching her wide-eyed expression as she went from dress shop to dress shop.

"I want you to help me choose," she insisted.

He was having as good a time as she was as he watched her expressions change from serious, to indecision, to sheer delight when she found a dress she really liked. She tried it on and waited for John's approval. He smiled and nodded and she added it to her growing wardrobe.

In amazement, he watched her every move. His heart swelled with love for his new bride. *She has no idea how lovely she is,* he thought. But it was more. He liked her, he trusted her. *She doesn't know it,* he realized, *but she was a lady long before she ever married me.*

Betsy was understandably nervous as she dressed for her first introduction to London nobility.

If these people were anything like the nobility in France, she knew she'd be highly disappointed.

"What do you think, Annie?" Betsy asked as she stepped into the light blue satin gown she had chosen for tonight's affair. She wriggled until it felt comfortable, then Annie began fastening the back buttons.

Annie didn't mince words. "I think it's the most beautiful dress I've ever seen. Your husband's mother dressed very well, but I never saw her wear anything as elegant as this." She finished the task and then turned Betsy around. "There now. Don't you look fine! Did you know the color of this dress changes the color of your eyes from gray to blue? What do you think of that?" Her fingers fussed at the high neckline. "Doesn't that choke you? It would me. But then, I'll never have to wear anything so fancy." She guided Betsy toward the vanity chair. "Now you sit right down and let me fix your hair. I'm pretty good at it, you know. Used to fix Lady MacDonald's hair all the time."

Annie proved to be as expert as she claimed. She brushed Betsy's long hair then deftly twisted it up and secured it, letting a few loose curls fall around her face and neck. As a finishing touch, she wove a blue satin ribbon through her hair so there was no beginning and no end.

Betsy was aware that while she was fixing her hair, Annie didn't say one word.

John stepped into the bedroom just as Annie finished. Betsy stood up and turned. He didn't have to say a word. His smile said it all. He offered her his arm and headed toward the 'down' staircase. Betsy stopped. With a mischievous look in her eye, she said sweetly, "Let's go down the 'up' staircase tonight."

"The way you look tonight, I can deny you nothing. The 'up' staircase it is!"

When they arrived at the dinner party, they stood in the entrance and were announced by the butler. His loud voice boomed across the already crowded room.

"May I introduce Sir John and Lady MacDonald."

Conversation quieted and all eyes turned toward the new arrivals.

Betsy clung tightly to John's arm. Without moving her lips she asked, "What do I do now?"

John smiled acknowledgement to several of the guests, "Just smile and hold tight."

The Marquis was obviously pleased to see John and took long strides to his side. He took John's hand and pumped it up and down vigorously.

"John, my old friend! It's so good to see you. It's been too long."

"Yes it has, Geoff. I'll be in London awhile. Perhaps we can get together without all these fancy trappings." He grabbed his old friend's shoulder in a warm gesture. "Geoff, I'd like to introduce you to my wife, Betsy." To Betsy, he said, "May I introduce my very old …and very good…friend, Geoffrey Burns, our host and Marquis of Staffordshire."

Betsy curtsied politely. "My pleasure, Sir."

The Marquis eyes never left hers. He took her hand and brushed his lips against it ever so lightly. "You are wrong, my dear," he said warmly, "It is definitely my pleasure. Please call me Geoff. I know we will become good friends." He took her other arm. "Come. Let me introduce both of you to my other guests."

As he made the rounds, the Marquis did most of the talking. Betsy and John were polite and contributed amicably to the impersonal conversation.

Betsy thought most of the men seemed stiff and the ladies were aloof, as though they felt threatened by the newcomers. No one made much eye contact. They seemed to be looking past Betsy and John to see who else of more importance had arrived.

Betsy was relieved when they were called to dinner. She quickly discovered that guests were seated in order of rank. John, who was only a knight, was seated with Betsy at the far end of the table. One of tonight's lessons, it seemed, was for Betsy to learn about the rank and file and customs of the nobility.

She also learned that a well-planned dinner could take several hours from start to finish.

First, there was the wine. When everyone was served, the Marquis toasted his guests. Then, in turn, the guests toasted the Marquis and each other. Appetizers were served. Glasses were refilled and there were more toasts. Soup was the next course followed by a salad. A different wine was served before the generous entrée that included lamb, fish, and roast beef. A cordial liqueur accompanied the dessert tray of puff pastries.

Betsy was so full; she could hardly stand up. When the gentlemen retired to the smoking room for cigars and brandy, the ladies were escorted to the very large sitting room.

That's a misnomer, she said to herself. *No one is sitting.* The ladies stood in small close circles as though they were afraid someone less welcome might try to join them.

While she was standing close to one group and only half-listening to their idle chatter, she suddenly felt a hand on her arm. She turned to face an elegantly dressed woman.

"Excuse me, my dear, but haven't we met before?"

Betsy was thrilled at seeing a familiar face. "Why, yes, of course! We met on the Royal Mail Coach several years ago. Your name is... Mrs. Bowen, I believe."

"That's right. And you are Betsy. Betsy Stewart. I would know you anywhere. Your beautiful hair is a dead giveaway. I doubt that anyone in the world has hair like yours." She took Betsy's arm and led her to a settee. "Let's sit a while and get reacquainted."

Betsy was delighted to have someone so pleasant to talk to. "I loved your story about John O. Groats and his eight angry sons. I've never forgotten it."

Mrs. Bowen laughed. "It is a good story, isn't it?" Tell me, my dear, did that loutish lieutenant give you any trouble after I left?"

"Not really," Betsy said matter-of-factly. "You see, he was killed in a robbery the very next day."

"Can't say I'm sorry." Mrs. Bowen patted Betsy's hand. "He was trouble!" She noticed the ring on Betsy's finger. "Oh, I see you are married! He is a very lucky man, you know. You have grown to be a very beautiful young woman. Now, tell me all about that wonderful young man."

"Why thank you, M'am." Betsy's face lit up. "I will tell you about my husband. He *is* wonderful! His name is Sir John MacDonald. We've only been married a short time."

"Is he a soldier in the King's service?"

"No, he is not in the regular army but he does serve the King in the Low Countries."

Mrs. Bowen looked around. "Now, before it gets too late, I want you to meet some of my friends."

As they walked around the room, Betsy was introduced to wives of Earls, Dukes, and other members of the nobility. Some she had briefly met earlier when the Marquis introduced her. She couldn't help but notice that all the women deferred to Mrs. Bowen and that she herself was treated more kindly now.

As soon as Betsy saw the men enter the room, she gestured to John, hoping he would join her. He saw her immediately and walked toward her.

"John, dear, I'd like you to meet Mrs. Jane Bowen. She and I met several years ago when we were both traveling in northern Scotland."

"It's a pleasure, M'am," John said as he bowed.

After a few minutes of pleasant conversation, Mrs. Bowen spotted her husband. "Charles! Charles! Would you please join us for a moment?"

A tall white-haired man in a naval uniform came to her side.

"Sir John and Lady Betsy MacDonald, may I present my husband Admiral Charles Bowen, Duke of Stratford and Knight of the Garter."

John had heard of the Duke on several different occasions. He had a reputation of fairness and great intellect. In addition, John knew he was probably the most highly regarded naval officer in the Royal Navy.

"Your Grace," John said and bowed appropriately.

Betsy curtsied but looked stricken. "I'm sorry, M'am. I didn't know you are a Duchess. Forgive me!"

"There's nothing to forgive." The Duchess wrinkled up her nose. "Don't worry about it. I'd prefer you call me Jane anyway." Her smile was genuine and Betsy felt better about her blatant faux pas.

"So," the Admiral said to John. "You are a Scot. I know the Scots are among the best sailors and fighters in the world. I would wish there were more of you except," he paused for effect, "I'm never sure whose side you will come down on in a fight!"

John laughed. "I'm afraid you are right about that, sir."

The Admiral continued. "We need to keep the union between England and Scotland firm." His face became serious and he clasped John on his shoulder. "On a more personal level, let me apologize for what happened to your kinsmen in Scotland. I assure you that all of England was outraged by that massacre. I dare say a few heads rolled because of it but the punishment was not strong enough."

"Charles," Lady Bowen suggested. "Don't talk of such things now. John and Betsy are newlyweds and should only be hearing about pleasant things."

"You are right of course, my dear." Easily, he changed the subject. "Where do you live in Scotland, Sir John?"

"We don't live in Scotland, sir. We live in France. We met there and we were married there."

The Admiral raised his brows. "Ah! Many of the royal Stuarts have lived in France throughout the years. Are you allied with any of them, by chance?"

"As a matter of fact, I guess I am." John smiled at Betsy then at the Admiral. "You see, my wife Betsy is a Stewart."

"Well, upon my word!" the Admiral laughed. "Guess I put my foot in it that time, didn't I?"

Betsy quickly put the Admiral back at ease. "Don't worry about me, sir. I am not the least bit political. Besides we spell our name differently from the royal Stuarts."

Betsy noticed that Lady Bowen kept looking from Betsy to John and back again. She couldn't help but wonder what she was thinking.

"Charles," she said. "I have the most *wonderful* idea. I would like to invite this young couple to spend the season here in London this year. I feel a strong connection with Betsy. I felt it the very first day we met several years ago. It will give them an opportunity to meet people of influence and perhaps Sir John could profit from your contacts."

The Admiral smiled agreeably at his wife. "Whatever you wish, my dear. Consider it done." He put an arm around Betsy and another around John and looked at each of them. "You are invited to join us for the social season this year as our guests." He chuckled. "You may as well give up any plans you might have because Jane will fill all your waking hours."

The music started playing and couples started leaving for the dance floor.

"Come," Lady Bowen said, "Let's join the merriment."

The remainder of the evening was a blur. Betsy danced until she could dance no more. She was not aware that her sudden popularity was based on the Bowens obvious approval of them. John was more astute. He knew that the attention he was receiving was due to his old friendship with the Marquis and his new friendship with the Duke and Duchess of Stratford.

And all because of my wife's chance encounter with a Duchess. He watched as his wife twirled round and round on the dance floor. *The world is a very strange place,* he thought, *and at the moment, at least, our future looks very bright indeed!*

-o-

CHAPTER 13

Life with the Admiral and Lady Bowen became a daily schedule of activities for both Betsy and John. The Admiral took John under his wing. Everyday was a new experience for John. He was taken to the Admiral's office and was shown around the London dockyard. From time to time, the Admiral asked John to take notes for him. John was happy to oblige. Wherever the Admiral went, he insisted John accompany him. This included morning meetings, afternoons at the Club for smoking, libations, and spirited discussions of current events. John was getting a valuable education. He liked the Admiral and admired his candor even when it made others uncomfortable with his no-nonsense approach to delicate matters. John was flattered when the Admiral casually introduced him to influential people.

Meanwhile, Lady Bowen and Betsy attended luncheons and card parties as well as charity functions at least twice a week.

In the evenings, there were frequent dinner parties and balls that the Bowens encouraged their protégés to attend.

One night after an exhausting evening of too much food, too much wine, and too much dancing, Betsy sat on the bed and rubbed her sore feet.

"John," she said, I've come to the obvious conclusion that I need a lady's maid of my own."

John sat beside her and picked up one of her feet. "Here, let me do that. Lie back and relax."

Gratefully, she laid back and closed her eyes. "Oh, that feels wonderful. Don't stop."

"Now, what's this about you needing a servant of your own?"

"Well," she said, "Lady Bowen has kindly let me use her girl to help me with my hair and my clothes. But now that the social season is at its height, it isn't fair to make Dora work doubly hard. Lady Bowen says she knows someone we could hire. Her name is Claudette and, by sheer coincidence, I learned that she is from Le Tre'Port."

John picked up her other foot and began massaging it. "That's practically in our own back yard. I trust your judgment, Betsy. Do whatever you think is necessary."

Claudette proved to be worth her weight in gold. She not only helped Betsy with her hair and her clothes, she also helped choose her wardrobe. Betsy took her shopping and Claudette was a keen observer as to colors and fabrics that would enhance Betsy's skin color, hair color, and natural beauty. Claudette paid attention to detail. She could anticipate Betsy's requirements each day and always remembered to perfume Betsy's bath water. She knew about Betsy's love of candlelight so whenever possible she made sure there were plenty of lighted candles, even around her bath. Betsy liked having someone her own age around and the two young ladies found common ground to enjoy many conversations and exchange ideas.

Several weeks into the social season, the Admiral took John to a pub for lunch. The Admiral wanted privacy, so he located a table in the back of the room.

He ordered a mug of ale for each of them. "Now," he said. I have a proposition for you."

John looked intrigued.

"During the last few weeks, I have watched you carefully and I have learned a great deal about you. Naturally, I have also made some outside inquiries about you. I find that you are not only brave but a good leader of men as well. I know you led a large number of mercenary Scots in the Low Countries. With your family's position, I realize you could be appointed to the King's regular service with no difficulty. Now," the Admiral stopped for a moment and took a long drink of his ale. "My long time secretary—I call him that but he's much more than that—has just informed me that he will be leaving my service sometime next year. I need someone to replace him; someone with a great sense of honor and integrity. He must be a man of discretion and good judgment. I believe you are that man. I want you to replace him. Are you interested?"

Stunned, John leaned back in his chair and placed his mug back on the table. "I'm flattered…and very surprised. You say your current secretary is leaving next year. When would his replacement begin?"

"Not before next summer…possibly even the fall."

John's head was spinning. "To be honest, I don't think King William is very fond of the MacDonalds. Will that present a problem for you?"

The Admiral shook his head. "I don't believe that is an issue anymore. You see, with the increasing strength of the King's military forces, Scotland is virtually neutralized and could not possibly win a war with England, even with the most charismatic leader. Besides, England and Scotland have been a United Kingdom for years and they must always remain united. With all the enemies we have in the world, being divided would be a disaster for us all. We have to always consider the welfare of everyone on this island. You are a smart man. I think you can see that. A new century is almost here, you know. What we do now will determine the Kingdom's role, and indeed, its very existence in the future."

John never doubted that the Admiral knew what he was talking about. Nevertheless, he was still uneasy about casting his lot with the English. Although, he had to admit, his father and grandfather had done it before him.

"Sir, you have given me a lot to think about. I am aware this is the best opportunity I have ever been given and I thank you for it. You will have my answer soon."

The Admiral affectionately patted John's arm. "Good! Now let's have some lunch."

~~~

John couldn't wait to get Betsy alone so he could tell her about the Admiral's offer. Betsy could see his excitement before he opened his mouth to speak.

"This is an opportunity of a lifetime," he said. "I can't even begin to imagine what this could mean to our future."

Betsy was surprised he was even considering it. "What it means is that we would stay here in London."

He could see she was not enthusiastic. "Would that be so bad?" he asked.

"I...I don't really know, John. "I always thought we would go back to France and live."

"Betsy, you know I'm not a farmer. And I'm not French. As much as I care for your family, I don't really care for the French, their culture, or their attitudes. You and I are Scottish. If we can't live in Scotland, then England is a good second choice."

"It sounds as though you've made up your mind." This was all happening so fast. She wasn't sure she wanted to stay in London.

"No, I haven't. I plan to give it a lot of thought." He pulled her close and held her against him. "I promise, my darling, I will only accept this offer if I am convinced it's the best choice for us both."

The next day, Betsy consulted Lady Bowen, who was very surprised when Betsy told her the news.

"Charles didn't mention a word of it to me. Perhaps I'll just play dumb until John gives him an answer." She looked at Betsy and could see she was troubled.

"I understand your problem, my dear. You're homesick for one thing, aren't you?"

Betsy nodded and bit her lower lip. "I thought we'd be going home after the holiday, home to stay. But now I don't know."

Lady Bowen was sympathetic. "I really do understand, Betsy. But remember you are married now. Things are different. Your husband must come first."

"I know, but maybe..."

Lady Bowen shook her finger. "No maybes...You must learn that you cannot change any man anymore than a man can change you. You are a soldier's wife. I am a sailor's wife. We must come to grips with that fact every day. If we do not give our men support they might look for it elsewhere. I know you truly love your husband."

Betsy nodded.

"Then you must love him enough to support him in his decisions. Am I right?"

Again Betsy nodded. "Yes, I'm sure you are right."

"I know, child, that I'm being selfish," Lady Bowen admitted, "but I like having you around. The idea of your staying in London pleases me. You know, Betsy, Charles and I were never blessed with children.

Charles has told me he thinks of John as the son we never had. Well, my dear, I think of you as the daughter I *might* have had."

Betsy was touched. "Thank you, Lady Jane. You've been a wonderful friend. I appreciate your advice. It's a little frightening when I realize how much I have to learn."

"It takes time…and time is one thing you have plenty of."

~~~

The rest of the social season was a whirlwind of festivities. John's friend, the Marquis, hosted another party and this time John and Betsy were included in the inner circles of London society. Rumors were flying about who would be replacing the Admiral's secretary.

Geoff pulled his friend aside, "Is it you, John? Tell me. I can keep a secret."

John was noncommittal. "I'll let you know just as soon as I know who it is."

He turned to look for his wife. She was in the center of several ladies who were commenting on her dress.

"Where *do* you get your clothes, Lady MacDonald?" one asked. "Do you go to Paris?"

Betsy was a little annoyed with all the fuss over her clothes. "Why would I go to Paris when London has so many wonderful shops?"

Betsy and John were both glad when the Christmas holidays ended. They were exhausted and anxious to go back home for a well-deserved rest.

As they packed their bags, John said rather offhandedly, "By the way. I gave the Admiral my answer."

Betsy stopped and looked up at her husband. "And…?"

"I've decided to take his offer."

Betsy had known what his answer would be. They had not discussed it anymore but she caught him occasionally daydreaming with a hint of a smile on his face. She watched the way John hung on the Admiral's every word. She knew. She was waiting for him to admit it to himself before he could tell her.

"Does my decision anger you, Betsy?"

Betsy closed one bag and began packing another. "No, I'm not angry." She stopped and looked at John. There was real concern on his face. She knew he wanted her to be happy about his decision. Now it was her turn to reassure him.

"I'm your wife and I believe in you. I know you want me to be happy…and I will be, as long as we are together." Her face brightened. "Besides, we're on our way home! Nothing can make me sad today! Now would you tell Claudette I need her to help me finish the packing? Then you and I can say goodbye to the Bowens. They've changed our lives, you know."

"Yes, I know. And all because you were once traveling companions. By the way, what were you doing on that coach anyway?"

Betsy quickly turned back to her packing. "Oh, it's a long story… and a boring one. Someday, when we have nothing better to do, I'll tell you all about it."

-o-

CHAPTER 14

Claudette was as excited as Betsy was about returning to France to see her family.

"Stay in Le Tre'Port as long as you like," Betsy told her. "I think John and I will be in St. Val'ery for some time. I'll keep you informed of our plans." She giggled, "as soon as *I'm* informed."

The homecoming was a happy one. Betsy's mother, grandmother, and Jeanette all wanted lots of details about the parties, the people she met, and her new wardrobe.

"Hobnobbing with nobility, are you?" her mother teased.

Jeanette joined in. "I guess we call you Lady Betsy now."

Lisa hugged her granddaughter. "She'll always be my little Betsy, no matter how many titles she has."

"London is truly a different world." Betsy tried to make them understand. "Some of the people were kind and polite, others were tedious and boorish. Lady Bowen and the Admiral are not only good friends; they have became surrogate parents." She looked at her mother and grandmother. "I think you both would like them. I hope you have the chance to meet them someday."

While the ladies enjoyed endless discussions of the do's and don't's of London's social circles, Angus, Ewin and Roy were anxious to talk to John about matters that were not in the least frivolous.

Angus took the lead. "John, we have no time to waste. A ship commissioned by the Campbells and flying a Danish flag is scheduled to leave Charleston in the colony of Virginia in just one week."

That grabbed John's attention. "Where is she bound?"

"She's bound for Glasgow. That's why we're in such a hurry. With favorable winds it'll only take her a week or so to cross. We've again hired Captain Renau."

Ewin took over with more details. "Roy and I, and we hope you as well, will be aboard. We hope to seize the Campbell vessel before she enters St. George's Channel. We would have a good chance of intercepting her there since there is less chance of other ships being in the area."

"What happens after we capture her?" John was getting excited.

"Then we run out into the Atlantic before turning for the southern coast of France across the Bay of Biscay."

"What's her cargo?" John wanted as many details as he could get.

Roy smiled broadly. "That's the good part. She'd loaded with tobacco and rum. Both can be easily sold for a good profit."

John felt a sudden rush of excitement. He had enjoyed the last sea adventure and the idea of a new challenge made his heart race.

"How soon do we need to leave?" he wanted to know.

"As soon as possible. Tomorrow even," Ewin told him. "We have a crew just waiting for our command."

"Angus, will you be going this time?"

"No, laddie," Angus answered. "I'm getting too long in the tooth for such adventure. I leave such things to you young scallywags."

Roy was anxious for a reply. "Are you with us, John?"

"I'm with you, Roy." John stood up. "I need to tell Betsy. Somehow, I don't think she'll be real thrilled with my leaving." He walked toward the door, then turned around. The grin on his face went from ear to ear. "Revenge can be a beautiful thing. Right, mates?"

The others laughed and got up to follow John.

John was right. Betsy was not happy about his leaving. "How long will you be gone?" she asked.

John was honest. "I don't really know. No longer than absolutely necessary."

"Dare I ask the purpose of this new endeavor?"

"All I can say now is this: Justice is not reserved only for a courtroom. Justice can be found on the high seas as well."

Betsy knew what he meant and she didn't sleep well that night. Each time she rolled over, she woke up. Each time she did, John reached out to hold her, to comfort her, and to tell her he'd return safely.

Before he left, John sent for two of his soldiers to stay at the Stewart farm as protection for the women, just in case anything went wrong.

The swells from the Atlantic were slow and even, as the ship stood ready to pursue her victim. But first she had to be found, and that was the hard part. Finding another ship on the high seas is never easy.

For several days now, the crew had been standing double watches, looking for any sign of a sail heading east toward them. They had seen ships, but they, too, were heading west. The waiting was boring and tried the men's patience.

John was standing close to the bow, one foot resting on a wooden barrel. He gazed at the rise and fall of the silvery ocean. He turned so that his face was bathed in the mist of sea spray. John inhaled deeply. The smell of the sea filled his nostrils. The feeling was exhilarating. From his very first day as a sailor, John knew he was meant to be at sea.

Captain Paul Renau came up behind John. He raised his foot on the same wooden barrel and used his telescope to scan the ocean.

"Do you think she slipped by us, Captain?" John wondered.

"Oui. It is possible. As you can see, it is a very big ocean."

John laughed. His patience, too, was wearing thin. "How long are we going to give her to show up?"

The Captain shrugged, "As long as it takes."

Suddenly the lookout on the masthead shouted, "Sail ho!"

Everyone standing within earshot took out telescopes to try to locate the ship.

The Captain squinted then raised his scope to get a better look. "I see her!" he said, and then shouted to the crew, "Prepare to come about, all hands." He told the helmsman the course he desired. As the ship turned, the wind caught the sails and she picked up speed.

The Captain looked encouraged. "If we have luck, Sir John, I estimate we will intercept that ship about two hours before dark. She is riding low in the water. That means she has a heavy load."

Ewin joined them. "Do you think it's our prey, Captain?

"It's really too soon to say for sure, but I'm betting she's the one we've been waiting for."

It was a gray day and the clouds were low in the sky. A strong wind filled the sails and the ship moved swiftly across the water.

Some of the crew took time to eat while others tried to sleep. Most of them were anxious to see action and used their scopes to view the oncoming ship.

Soon Roy came up from below. The four men stood and watched as the distance between the two ships narrowed. Captain Renau was very accurate as to the time they would be ready to go into action with the merchant ship. Once again, he lifted the telescope to his eye. "I can see her flag! Her colors are Danish."

Roy grabbed his brother's arm. "Good, Ewin. The English can never accuse us of pirating an English ship."

Ewin looked at Roy and grinned. "Not if she's flying a Danish flag!"

The Captain shouted to his crew. "Raise our colors!" Then to his partners, "Men, she's going to be ours!"

With perfect timing, the Captain pulled his ship close alongside the other vessel. As the ships passed each other, the Captain ordered a shot to be fired across her bow.

"Heave to!" the Captain commanded.

The merchant ship responded immediately and dropped her sails.

Captain Renau shouted across the water and ordered the Captain to come aboard the privateer. The hostage captain wasted no time. His men quickly lowered a long boat to row him across to the privateer.

Captain Renau reminded his men to remain silent and to put on their masks so they couldn't be identified later.

When the Danish captain climbed aboard, Renau faced him.

"Sir," he said in a stern, no-nonsense voice, "I am taking your ship but there will be no bloodshed if you cooperate. As a gesture of good will on my part, I will allow you to retain your sword. I want your men to leave their arms and go below decks and stay there until we come to get them. We will sail your ship close to the Irish coast. There you will disembark into your own long boats and row to shore. Mark my words though. If there is *any* resistance, we will not hesitate to kill all of you. Do you understand, Captain?"

The hostage captain stood erect. "Yes, Captain, I understand."

"Relay my orders to your men…*now!*"

The captain turned and leaned against the ship's rail and shouted to his men what they were to do and the consequences that would occur if they failed to follow orders.

Renau continued, "Now, some of my men will go to your ship to see that my orders are carried out. You will stay here on my ship as my captive until your vessel is safely under our control."

"We are a simple merchant ship, Captain. I will do whatever is necessary to save the lives of my men."

Captain Renau sent Ewin, Roy and two other armed sailors with the boat that was returning to the captured ship, then he gathered the rest of his crew and together they waited for the signal indicating all was secure on the captured ship. When the 'all clear' signal was given, Captain Renau boarded one of the privateer's boats and headed for the captive ship, taking her captain back with him. Three crew members accompanied him. Three additional crew followed in a second longboat.

The Captain searched every area of the ship both topside and below. When he was convinced that all was secure, and that all sailors including the captain were locked away, he put Ewin Stewart in charge of sailing her to the Irish coast. He returned to his own ship and, with a full moon overhead, set sail for Ireland.

Forty-eight hours later and under the cover of night, the two ships came within a few miles of the Irish coast. The merchant ship's boats were lowered and all captive crew got on board. The Danish captain was the last to leave his ship.

The two ships turned and headed out into the Atlantic before changing direction toward a small fishing village on the French coast.

Soon after arriving, the sailors were paid their wages. Most of them were quick to offer their services to Captain Renau for any future expeditions.

While in port, Ewin arranged to have the hull of their ship painted a brilliant white.

"Never hurts to cover your tracks," he explained.

Several trusted crewmen agreed to stay on board until arrangements could be made to sell the cargo and the merchant ship as well. Profits would be divided at a later time.

Before heading home, the four partners walked to a local pub.

Captain Renau insisted on buying a round of ale. He raised his glass high and the others followed. "Here's to another successful adventure and to the best damned crew I've ever had!"

They tipped their mugs and quickly drained the contents.

"Fill them up again, Publican," Ewin shouted. "We're just getting started."

John stood up and placed his hand over his heart in mock sincerity. "Here's to the Campbells. May they never again feel safe on the high seas."

"Not as long as we're alive," Roy added.

"Three cheers" Ewin insisted.

They raised their mugs and chanted in unison, "Hear hear! Hear hear! Hear hear!"

It was several hours before they stumbled to their quarters and fell into a deep sleep.

-o-

CHAPTER 15

Betsy missed John terribly, especially at night. During the days, her mother kept her busy with activities. She knitted, she crocheted, and she increased her knowledge of cooking. Sometimes she went on long walks, always accompanied by her two dogs. They shadowed her; wherever she went, they were close by.

Claudette had only spent a couple of weeks in Le Tre'Port with her family before she joined Betsy at the Stewart farm. There wasn't much for her to do as a lady-in-waiting so she, like the dogs, followed Betsy. Their friendship deepened. Betsy even taught Claudette to knit.

One day when the two girls were walking, one of the soldiers John had left behind found the courage to approach Claudette. From that moment on, the two spent hours together. Betsy recognized the signs. The couple found excuses to be alone. They stared at each other endlessly and had the silliest smiles on their faces.

Were John and I that obvious when we were falling in love? She wondered.

One day when Claudette and her beau were out walking, Betsy, her mother, and Jeanette decided to go horseback riding. As they walked toward the stable, Betsy heard a thunderous sound in the distance. She turned in the direction of the noise and saw three horsemen stirring up a huge cloud of dust. Then she recognized them.

"Mother! Jeanette! Look!" Her heart raced. She lifted her skirts and ran toward her husband. When John rode close, he slowed his horse but didn't wait for it to stop. He jumped off the animal's back and ran toward Betsy, arms outstretched. He grabbed her and squeezed her so tight she couldn't breathe. But Betsy didn't care.

"John, you're home! You're home!" she whispered. He looked at her for a moment, then his lips found hers. It was a hard, bruising kiss. Betsy didn't care. He was home!

No one spoke. Then she realized her parents and Jeanette and Roy were locked in tight embraces as well.

She smiled at John. "Aren't homecomings wonderful?"

That night when they were alone, they lay close together. John rose up on one elbow and just gazed at his beautiful wife. The moon threw shafts of light across the room; he adjusted her head so one moonbeam lit up her face and hair.

Although John's face was in shadow, Betsy could always see him clearly, even with her eyes closed. She breathed in his familiar scent. Time stood still. They were lost in their own thoughts of love. Then slowly, John lowered his head and kissed his wife softly, tenderly. Then long pent up passion erupted. The moon and stars could have fallen from the sky. They wouldn't have noticed or even cared because they were lost in each other and didn't want it to ever stop.

~~~

John had not told Ewin about his career opportunity with Admiral Bowen until they were on their way back to St. Val'ery. Ewin had been very supportive of John's decision.

"John, you have always shown great promise," Ewin told him. "And I'm sure this is just the first step to a very successful career. I'm proud of you, son."

"I know you don't want to see Betsy go, but I promise, I'll take good care of her. She can return for a visit as often as possible. And, of course, you and Mrs. Stewart can visit us whenever you want."

"You are right about one thing, John. Her mother and I will hate to let her go. But you know, son, we don't own our children. We just borrow them for a little while. You'll understand what I mean when you have children of your own."

When the time came for John to return to London, he released his soldiers except for Brian Cahill who had decided to leave the military and wed Claudette. The couple planned to accompany John and Betsy back to London and would remain in their employ.

Memories of her own wedding flashed through Betsy's mind as she watched Claudette and Brian exchange their vows. She watched helplessly as poor Claudette, so nervous she was visibly shaking, giggled throughout the ceremony. Pere Francis kept frowning but Brian was oblivious. He never took his eyes off his blushing bride.

The next day, it was once again time to say goodbye. This time it was easier for Betsy because, strangely enough, she had really missed the excitement of London. This realization surprised her and pleased John when she told him.

When the foursome reached Le Harve harbor, they took passage on a small ship that made frequent channel crossings and boasted cabin spaces for passengers. The weather was deteriorating when they set sail for England. Before they were half way across the channel, they encountered a heavy gale that blew them considerably off course. John and Brian were used to the sea, but Betsy and Claudette endured terrible seasickness. They both remained in their cabins with buckets close by.

Betsy had never experienced such nausea. At times she hoped she'd die. John tried to comfort her but there was really nothing he could do.

Brian, as a new bridegroom, felt like a failure in his first test as a protective husband. He couldn't stand hearing his bride moan. He held her hand, put a wet cloth on her forehead and prayed for the storm to end.

The storm lasted throughout the next day but finally subsided before they reached Southampton.

It only took a few hours after landing for Betsy and Claudette to recover from their sickness. They were weak, but at least their faces lost their green color.

When they arrived at the MacDonald's London house, Annie gave them a warm welcome. She could see Betsy wasn't feeling too well and insisted she go upstairs to rest.

"Don't you worry, Lady Betsy, I'll take good care of things down here."

John introduced Annie to Brian and Claudette and explained their new roles in the household.

Annie crossed her arms and gave them both a quick once-over. "They're so young," she declared, "and good lookin' too. I'll find plenty to keep them busy. Don't you worry, Sir John, I'll show them the ropes in no time." She stared at Claudette and moved closer to her.

"Missy, you have the shiniest eyes I've ever seen. Looks like there's stars in them."

John leaned close to the couple and whispered loud enough for Annie to hear. "You're in luck. I think she approves."

"Oh, pish-tosh!" Annie said. "You run on along to Miss Betsy. I'll get this young couple settled in."

John rushed up the steps two at a time. Betsy, dressed only in a camisole and pantaloons, was brushing her hair when he came into their bedroom.

He smiled as he pretended to wipe perspiration from his forehead.

"Brian and Claudette passed the 'Annie-test' with flying colors."

Betsy laughed. "Oh, John, Annie loves everyone."

"Not true, my love," John corrected her. "She doesn't like my friend Geoff."

Betsy stopped brushing. "Geoff? Your friend Geoff, the Marquis?"

"That's the one!"

"But why? He seems like a pleasant chap."

"Annie thinks he's a phony and an opportunist."

"And what do you think?"

"The more I am with him; the more I think she's absolutely correct." He took the brush from her hand, turned her around and started brushing her hair with long, gentle strokes.

"Um," Betsy murmured. "You spoil me."

"That's because I want something from you." He paused before continuing. "I want you to agree to stay here in this house this season instead of going to the Bowens."

Betsy turned around and faced her husband. "Oh, I do agree, John, especially now that we have Claudette and Brian. I think it would be an imposition to move in with our friends right now."

"Oooh, you're sooo easy, Lady MacDonald. I can play you like a violin," John said and brushed her lips with a quick kiss.

Betsy grabbed the brush and swatted him. "So! You admit you were buttering me up. The next time I won't be such a pushover, John MacDonald."

He picked her up and held her close. "I love your eyes when you are a little miffed." Unceremoniously, he dropped her on the bed and lay alongside her.

"We should go see the Bowens now, I guess," John said and pushed the camisole off her shoulders.

"Uh, huh," Betsy responded and unbuttoned his shirt.

John loosened his trousers. "Do you think we have time to…?"

Betsy's answer was physical. From past experience, he knew it meant 'yes.'

~~~

Lady Jane and the Admiral were in the sitting room when John and Betsy were announced.

They were overjoyed to see them. Lady Bowen held out her arms to Betsy. "We've missed you both! Come in and sit down." She turned to her maid. 'Dora, bring our guests some refreshment…Now tell me all about your time in France. I want to hear everything." She looked around. "Where are your bags? You are staying with us, aren't you?"

Before Betsy could say anything, John spoke up. "I hope you will understand, but Betsy and I plan to stay in my father's house for the time being. We have hired extra staff and we do need to be there to supervise, at least until they are comfortable with their new routine."

"Of course, I understand," Lady Bowen said. "But the offer still stands, if you should change your mind. But we'll still see a lot of each other. Betsy, dear, I have big plans for you and me."

The Admiral chimed in. "And I have big plans for you, John. Starting tomorrow, your education begins."

The next morning, the Admiral took John to his office and closed the door.

"John, some things have happened since you left for France and I need to keep you informed of any and all changes. I have just received a promotion along with the command of twenty warships. One of my new jobs will be to patrol the Mediterranean and try to stop the destruction of international ships by the Ottoman Empire. That being said, I can now offer you an immediate promotion."

John was pleasantly surprised. "Promotion? What kind of promotion, sir?"

Admiral Bowen cleared his throat for effect. "As I see it, you have three choices. You can accept your new position as a civilian. But if you do, you would probably never be taken seriously by any military personnel or trusted by anyone on my staff, so I think we can eliminate that choice.

"Second, I can appoint you a senior naval lieutenant, which means you would have to command a warship and I don't think you qualify for that right now. The third, and obviously the best, choice is for you to become a major in the marines. For this you will need extensive training but it offers more opportunities as well." He paused and smiled. "Which do you choose, John?"

John didn't need time to think about his decision. "Sir, my choice is to be a marine officer. Having been a soldier, I am already prepared to fight in the field but I eagerly look forward to learning the obligations of a marine officer."

"I don't want you to rush to a decision, John, but if you are sure this is what you want to do," he patted his chest, "I happen to have your commission right here. All you have to do is sign it."

The Admiral reached inside his coat and took out a scroll, unrolled it and showed John where to sign.

John did not hesitate. "I am sure, sir." He took the proffered quill and signed it.

The Admiral quickly countersigned the document and blotted the paper dry. "There! Congratulations, Major!" He shook John's hand enthusiastically. "I'm very proud to have you on board."

John felt a rush of pride. "I'm ready for an assignment, Admiral."

"I'm glad to hear you say that because that's the next order of business. Next week you will report to the Royal Marine Barracks in Plymouth where you will be outfitted and learn the basics of being a marine officer. The training will last one month. Upon completion of that assignment, you will return here to London and work with me."

"Sounds good," John said.

"Wait. There's more. Your next assignment will be a long one. Do you want to hear about it now? Or should I wait for another time?"

John was anxious to hear more. "Now is the perfect time, sir."

"Upon your return, you will be appointed commander of the marine detachment on the HMS Aggressor. She's a sixty-four-gun ship of the line, and is scheduled to depart for the Mediterranean on January 2 of next year. I'm proud to say she will be the first English war ship in that area in ten years. Now for the hard part...You will be gone for up to a year."

John could feel his blood rise. He had always believed the military was his destiny and the breadth and the depth of this opportunity gave him a heady feeling.

After leaving the Admiral, John headed home to share the news with Betsy. He was so happy and excited but had a nagging feeling that Betsy would not share his joy. He was right.

"You'll be gone for a year?" It wasn't as much a question as it was a statement of disbelief. "John, I can't believe what you are telling me!" Betsy was getting angry. "And what will happen to me while you're gone? Do I just put my life on hold?"

"Of course not. You can..."

She wasn't listening. "I thought our marriage meant as much to you as it does to me...that we would be together...always!" How can you just walk away from me?" Tears ran down her cheeks. She picked up a pillow and threw it at him.

"Betsy, wait a minute." John had never seen her so angry. He was at a loss as to what to say, or what to do.

She didn't give him a chance. "I think you are the most selfish person I've ever known! Don't talk to me anymore. Right at this moment, I think I hate you!" Betsy stormed out of the room and down the stairs. "Frederick!" she called, "Get my horse!"

John started to run after her but realized she would have to calm down before they could talk reasonably. For the first time, he knew what it was like to be happy and sad at the same time. But he had to admit that the sadness was winning out.

Betsy rode straight to Lady Bowen.

"What is it, dear child? What has happened?" Lady Bowen feared the worst.

"It's John! We've had a fight. I don't know what to do." Betsy wiped her tear-stained face but fresh tears kept falling.

Lady Bowen steered Betsy toward the library. "Let's go in here where we will have some privacy and you can tell me all about it." She poured a glass of water. "Here, drink this. You need to calm down a little bit."

Betsy drank the entire glass of water, and then took a deep breath.

"That's better, my dear. Now sit down and tell me what happened."

Betsy told Lady Bowen what John had said. "How can he do this to me? How can he just leave me for a whole year?" Her chin quivered as she tried to control her emotions.

"First of all, Betsy. He's not doing anything to you. He's made a career choice and you say he's excited about it. You knew he was a soldier when you married him, didn't you?"

Betsy nodded.

"Well, soldiers spend a lot of time away from home, don't they?"

"Yes, but I thought after we were married..."

"That things would change?"

Again Betsy nodded.

"Let me explain something to you. Marriage is a commitment made by two people who want to share their lives. But that doesn't mean sharing every waking moment or even every day. Each of you still has your own life separate from the other. Think about this for a minute. If you could convince John not to go away, he would have to quit the military and find another job. He would do it Betsy, because he loves you and he wants you to be happy. But his heart and soul wouldn't be in it. In time he would become very unhappy and he would resent you for it. You would feel guilty and then *you* would be unhappy. Your marriage would suffer. Do you understand?"

Betsy dried her eyes and blew her nose. "Yes...I think I see what you mean."

"I have a better suggestion. Let John go with your blessing. It's not only what he wants to do: it's what he needs to do. While he is gone you must start to make a new life for yourself. Don't make the mistake of living your life *through* his. Live your life *with* him. Yes, it will be hard, especially when you are apart for a year. But take advantage of the time he is gone to develop yourself. Learn more about who you are. Are you just an extension of your husband or can you stand beside him on your own merit as a person? The nights may be long and lonely, but fill your days with meaningful involvement. Parties and social events are fun and offer a pleasant diversion, but you will need more than that. You don't realize it yet, but you have much to offer others; others who are in need or who are less fortunate than you."

Lady Bowen knew exactly what Betsy was feeling. She had been there, too. She looked at the young girl and knew she had to make her understand how important her own life is.

"It's a funny thing about giving, Betsy. When you give of yourself, you find that you receive much more than you give. And that, I promise, will not only enrich your life but will give you personal fulfillment as a person. John will see the difference in you when he returns and will love you all the more for it."

For the first time since she arrived, Betsy's lips turned up into a little smile. "You've given me a different way of looking at things, Lady Bowen. But I'm not sure I'm up to it...becoming the kind of person you are talking about. I really don't want him to go."

"I didn't want Charles to go either. But he did. He didn't ask for or need my permission. What he needed was my understanding and my promise to stand by his side as a trusting and loving wife. This I have always done. And I've never regretted it. Think long and hard about your decision. The happiness of your marriage will depend on it. You can't change John. All you can do is change the way you feel."

Lady Jane walked Betsy to the door and gave her a reassuring hug.

"Take your time in returning home and think long and hard about what you will say to John."

John was waiting for Betsy when she returned home. The knot in his stomach tightened as she entered the room. He had no idea what she would say.

She just looked at him for a moment, then burst into tears and ran to his arms.

"I'm sorry!" she cried. "Oh, John, I'm so sorry! I don't hate you! I love you! I acted like a spoiled child. Please forgive me."

He held her tight with both arms, then one hand smoothed her hair. His voice was soothing. "Don't cry, my love. I don't ever want to hurt you." He cupped her face with his hands and looked into her eyes. "I'll leave the military if that's what you want me to do."

"No! I don't want you to quit. I knew you were a soldier before I married you. Now I am the wife of a marine. Be patient with me, John. I'm learning and I'm growing. Yes. I'll hate it while you're gone but I'll be here when you return."

John was so relieved. "And I *will* return...I promise." One side of his mouth turned up into a crooked smile. "Now tell me, little wife, is our first fight over?"

She looked a little sheepish. "Yes, I guess it is."

"Good! Let's kiss and make up!"

～～

All too soon, John left for Plymouth and his intense marine training. There was little time for rest. During the first week, he spent long days mastering a multitude of tasks he would be expected to perform at sea.

The second week he learned and practiced how to drill his men in the marine style. Every night after dinner, he spent hours before lights out reading about life at sea. The last two weeks he mastered the battle drills he and his men were required to perform at sea. John was not only a fast learner but he had the knack of converting what he learned in books to the reality of command.

The days were long and so crammed with learning activities that there was no time for idle thoughts. But at night, before he fell into an exhausted sleep, he thought of Betsy.

While John developed new skills and a deeper understanding of his career's direction, Betsy spent the month thinking about her own future. She spent many hours with Lady Jane who provided her with insight about the responsibility of being a military wife as well as being a perfect example of combining the role of successful wife and as a successful person separate from her husband.

At the end of his first month as a Marine, John returned home, resplendent in his uniform and full of pride in his accomplishments. He was proud of being a Royal Marine and grateful to Admiral Bowen for making it happen.

The London social season was in full swing when John returned, but this year, Sir John and Lady Betsy MacDonald were not a part of it. John was busy with Admiral Bowen during the day but the nights belonged to Betsy. They wanted to be together as much as possible because they both knew that during the year they were apart, they would have to live on memories of today.

The Christmas holidays were bittersweet. The joy of the season shadowed the knowledge that each day was one day closer to their long separation.

Betsy tried to reassure John that she would be fine and that Lady Bowen would see that she was kept very busy.

In return, John reassured Betsy that he was well trained and would return safely.

As planned, John departed for Plymouth on January 2. There was a steady rain falling as Betsy kissed her husband goodbye and watched him walk down the steps of the house, board a cab, and disappear into the rain. She had tried hard to appear strong and confident while John was home. Now that he was gone, her resolve disappeared. She returned to her room, closed the door and cried until there were no more tears.

-o-

CHAPTER 16

It was late morning when Betsy woke up. She opened her eyes and realized this was the first day without John. There would be so many more to come. Slowly she sat up and rubbed the sleep from her eyes.

"Oh, John," she whispered out loud. "I miss you already."

She slipped out of bed and walked to the window. Overnight the rain had turned to snow and gave way to a gray and foggy day. Betsy sat on the window seat and watched the snowflakes fall silently to the ground.

Claudette knocked on the bedroom door, turned the knob and entered the room. "Miss Betsy? Are you up? Would you like breakfast now?"

Betsy continued to stare out the window. "I'm not hungry, Claudette. In fact, I'm not feeling very well. I think I'll go back to bed for a while."

When she awoke, she realized how hungry she was. After a hearty lunch, she felt so much better that she began working on her first project. Betsy was taking Lady Bowen's advice about doing for others. The church had expressed a need for warm blankets to be distributed to the poorer parishes. She had always enjoyed needlework of any kind; this included sewing as well. It was much faster than knitting or crocheting. Her goal of a blanket a day was easy to achieve. It kept her busy and her mind off of John, at least part of the time. At night, though, before she fell asleep her thoughts were always about her husband.

The days went quickly. Sometimes Lady Bowen came and they sewed together.

One day during Lady Bowen's visit, Betsy complained that she hadn't been feeling very well. "It's a very strange malady," Betsy said. "I'm sick when I wake up every morning, but after lunch, I feel fine."

Lady Bowen stopped sewing. "Every morning?" she asked. "And how long has this been going on?"

"I noticed it right after John left. I wonder if it has anything to do with my missing him so much. I don't really know, but I can't seem to shake it. In fact, it's getting worse. Sometimes I feel like I'm going to throw up."

Lady Bowen smiled and gave Betsy a quick hug. "I think I know the problem. Excuse me a minute, my dear, I'll be right back."

She hurried downstairs to find Annie. Lady Bowen wasted no time with small talk. "Annie, Miss Betsy needs a doctor. Please fetch one immediately."

Annie didn't ask any questions; she grabbed her coat and ran out the door.

When the doctor arrived, Lady Bowen alerted him to her own diagnosis and then escorted him to Betsy's room.

Following the doctor's examination, he called Lady Bowen back into the room. He winked at her and said, "Madam, would you like to tell our patient the diagnosis?"

Lady Bowen's eyes were bright and she clasped her hands together. "Betsy, dear. You're going to have a baby!"

Betsy bolted upright. "A baby?" She couldn't believe it. "I'm going to have a baby?" she repeated. She looked at the doctor, then at Lady Bowen who was nodding her head and grinning, then back again to the doctor. "Are you sure?"

"Oh, yes. I'm positive," the doctor assured her. "In fact, I will predict that your baby will be born the end of September."

Betsy was stunned. She looked down at her stomach and gently ran her hands across her abdomen.

"Well, young lady," the doctor said as he packed his medical bag. "I want you to take it easy. No lifting of heavy objects. Eat three hearty meals a day. And," he paused, "Start thinking about names." He closed his bag and turned toward the door, then stopped and smiled at Betsy. "You know, I believe in having babies. They are God's way of telling us the world should go on."

Lady Bowen escorted the doctor back downstairs and Betsy was alone for a few minutes. "Her mind started spinning. *A baby!* She thought, *I just never dreamed*...She was happy about the idea but wondered if she knew enough to be a good mother. She was excited about how this would change her life but felt frustrated that John wouldn't be here for the delivery. He wouldn't even know about the baby until he came home a couple of months later.

Just then, Annie and Claudette burst into the room. "A baby! How wonderful!" Annie announced. "Now, Miss Betsy, you listen to me. I know just how to take care of you and don't you make any mistake about it, I *will* take care of you."

Claudette had to offer her congratulations, too. "You can count on me for anything, night or day. It won't matter. I'll be here for you."

Just then, Lady Bowen came into the room. All three just stared at Betsy with smiles that lit up their whole faces. Betsy couldn't help it. She looked at these three wonderful people and burst out laughing. "You'd think I was the first person to ever have a baby!"

Annie quickly answered for them all. "Not the first baby, just the *best* baby!"

~~~

That night, Betsy had a hard time falling asleep. She thought about the new life she carried inside. *Girl or boy? I don't really care. I just pray it will be healthy.* Her heart ached that John wouldn't be here to share in the birth of his first child. *Maybe I could write him a letter to let him know.* She decided against that idea. If he knew, he would feel guilty for not being here with her and he would worry about her constantly instead of concentrating on his job at hand. No, she wouldn't tell him. She would wait until he arrived home and let it be the biggest and best surprise of his life! Somehow, the thought comforted her and she soon fell asleep.

~~~

As soon as they read their daughter's letter that began, "Dear Grandmother and Grandfather to be..." Betsy's parents booked passage to London.

By the time they arrived at the MacDonald home, Betsy's morning sickness had subsided. In fact, she felt wonderful.

"Betsy, you are positively glowing," her mother said and pulled her into an embrace.

Ewin had to agree. "I've never seen you look more beautiful," he said and kissed her on both cheeks.

Betsy's eyes misted when she saw her parents. "I've missed you both so much. "How long can you stay?"

Heather smiled at her daughter. "Why, we'll be here until John returns…if that's all right."

Betsy's face showed relief. "Thank you, Mother. I'd hoped you would say that. Come now, I'll introduce you to the staff and take you to your room."

A few days later, Lady Bowen invited Betsy and her parents to dinner.

Betsy was anxious for them to meet. She had told each of them so much about the other that meeting face to face was almost like old friends saying hello after a long separation.

The evening was pleasant with most of the conversation centering on Betsy, John, and the new baby.

In the ensuing weeks, Betsy was delighted as she watched her mother and Lady Bowen develop a close friendship. She was equally delighted and a little bit surprised when the Admiral took time to show her father around London and the naval dockyards.

One afternoon while the two men were at lunch, the Admiral said, "Ewin, I feel the two of us know each other pretty well now. Do you agree?

"Yes, of course, Admiral. I do agree."

"Ewin," the Admiral paused a moment find the right word. "I have information that leads me to believe that you might be placing yourself and your family in some danger."

Ewin was stymied. "I don't know what you mean."

"Well," the Admiral continued. "I am speaking about possible… illegal activities…bootlegging and smuggling for example."

Ewin tried not to become defensive. "How would you know that, Admiral?"

"As an Admiral in the Royal Navy, it is my job to know about such things. But that's not what troubles me the most. I have recently been informed that you, your brother, and Sir John have engaged in a privateering venture. Although these accusations are difficult to prove, I strongly advise you to drop these activities now before there are any major political ramifications related to what you have done."

Ewin wasn't sure how to respond so he kept silent and listened.

"As far as I can tell, you no longer are engaged in the smuggling and whiskey trade. That's good. Thus far, the privateering has been legal because the ships you took were flying a foreign flag. I am sure you are aware how easy it is to prosecute a privateer if he is targeting British subjects. That would be considered piracy and is punishable by death. Do I make my point?"

Ewin could not deny what the Admiral had said. "Aye, sir, you do."

The Admiral continued. "Lady Bowen and I want to see Betsy and John prosper. I am in a position to make that happen, but there must be no scandal that could cloud my efforts. I am telling you this for your own good as well as theirs. Do I have your word?"

"I thank you for your candor. I assure you those activities are a thing of the past, Admiral, and I will take steps to sever all relationships with questionable associates."

That night, Ewin and Heather talked well into the night. He told her what the Admiral had said.

"I'm glad, Ewin," Heather admitted. "I've been worried for some time about the same things. We have money now. More money that we will ever need and we don't have to take chances anymore. Besides, you have had your revenge on the Campbells. It's time to put that to rest as well. Soon we will have a grandchild to consider. I want us both to be around to watch him grow."

"Or her," Ewin offered. "Tomorrow I'll talk to Betsy, then I want to go back to France to tie up some more loose ends."

~~~

"Lass," Ewin began when he and Betsy were alone. "The time has come for us to change the form of our treasure so that it can never be connected to us in any way."

Betsy had almost forgotten about the gold. She was glad her father was taking charge. "Good, Father. Can you do that?"

"I'm going to try. I know someone in Le Harve who may be able to help me. First, though, I need to know what you want me to do with it."

"That's simple," Betsy replied. "I want the money divided between you and Mother, Roy, and me. We have all taken chances to keep the money safe and I would not have it any other way."

"Your mother and I have discussed this at length. We want you to have half. If your mother and I keep one-quarter and Uncle Roy keeps one-quarter, that's more than enough to support us for the rest of our lives. Betsy, you risked your life for that treasure. And remember, you have a wee one on the way and you will want to provide for him as well as any other children you may have."

"Thank you, Father. I'm relieved that the matter will finally be resolved. I really don't want to think about it anymore."

The next day, Ewin left for France.

It was early morning when his ship docked in Le Harve. He ate breakfast and then went in search of the man he was told might be able to help him. He quickly located Levine's Counting House, just off the main street.

The only person in the room was a gray haired man wearing a traditional Hebrew skullcap. "Good morning," he said, "How may I help you?"

Ewin closed the door behind him. "I'm looking for Jacob Levine."

The man smiled and extended his hand. "I'm Jacob Levine. How can I help you?"

"My name is Ewin Stewart." Ewin reached out and shook the proffered hand. "Our mutual friend, Pierre Francois, told me you are the best in the business."

Jacob Levine chuckled. "And what business is that? Yes, I'm good at what I do, but I'm sure Pierre exaggerated. Again I ask. How can I help you?"

"Well, it's really about my friend. Let me explain." Ewin seemed nervous as he laid out a hypothetical problem.

Jacob listened intently. "Tell your friend I can definitely help him. By the way," Jacob looked serious but his eyes were smiling. "Is your friend's name Ewin Stewart by any chance?"

Ewin looked sheepish. "Am I that transparent?"

"Yes, I'm afraid you are. But I like you and I think we can work together very well." Jacob wasted no time. "Now, let me tell you what I can do. I can take the gold, convert it, and then place it into banking houses that only you, the owner, can tap. All transactions will be made using numbers. The Hebrew people, at least some of us, have specialized in finance for a long time and we are happy to provide this service to you."

"Sounds interesting," Ewin said. "Tell me more."

"You see, your money helps to keep our businesses going. It's really simple. We help you; you help us, thereby establishing trust on both sides. After a transaction has been made, we don't even know where the resources went and we cannot withdraw them. Only you hold the withdrawal numbers. Let me suggest that you experiment with us first with a small amount. If you are satisfied, we can continue with larger amounts."

Ewin didn't admit that he was confused by all the talk of transfers but he decided he would test the water. He told Mr. Levine that he would soon return with some of his resources so he could see firsthand how the system worked.

When Ewin arrived back at St. Val'ery, he and Roy began melting the gold bars and reformed them into small bars each weighing about one pound.

Ewin gathered up all the gold they had transformed and headed back to Le Harve. In the meantime, Roy continued the process, so that they would be ready when Ewin returned.

Jacob was genuinely impressed with the amount of gold Ewin had with him. "It's none of my business, Mr. Stewart, but you have a small fortune here."

"Yes, I know," Ewin said. "Let's just say I've had a run of good luck."

"Extremely good luck, I'd say. And this is only part of what you want me to diversify?"

"Yes, there is much more, but I want to fully understand this diversification before I bring more."

"I understand," Mr. Levine said. "Now if my calculations are correct, you have brought me 60,000 pounds sterling. My fee for this transaction and all other transactions will be five percent. Is that agreeable to you?"

Ewin was pleasantly surprised. He had thought it would be more. "Yes, that is a fair price for all your work."

"To begin with, Mr. Stewart, I will give you your 60,000 pounds—less commission of course—in bank notes on the Bank of England and the Bank of France. That way you will have ready cash while you are in London and when you return here to France. With subsequent transactions, I will deliver your money to various banks throughout Europe where it will always be ready whenever you wish to access it. We use only the oldest and most solvent money storage houses throughout the world."

"One moment, Mr. Levine," Ewin interrupted, "I'm overwhelmed with what you've said and a little confused. Are you telling me that I will have no trouble accessing my money even if it is in a bank in Switzerland?'

Mr. Levine nodded. "That's right, my friend. To my knowledge, there has never been a problem in moving or retrieving money within this system." Mr. Levine paused. "But you will have to have faith in me."

"I like what you've told me, Mr. Levine. You look me straight in the eye when you talk to me. That's the mark of an honest man. I trust you. Besides," he couldn't help but smile, "could our mutual friend be wrong about you?"

On Ewin's next trip, Levine provided him with bank notes from Paris and Rome. "I'm at your service," he told Ewin. "And I will act as your agent whenever it's necessary.

Ewin was convinced that Levine's system of placing the money in bank notes was working, but he wasn't certain that he trusted the numbered account system. He needed to test it.

At Ewin's request, Levine deposited a small sum in the bank at Le Tre'Port. A month later Ewin went to the bank and gave the clerk the account number. The clerk returned in a few moments and told Ewin the exact balance.

"Would you like to make a withdrawal, sir?" the clerk asked politely.

Ewin withdrew a few francs and walked out shaking his head.

Roy accompanied Ewin on his next visit to Jacob Levine. He explained that his money was to be deposited in English and French banks only.

"That's no problem at all," Levine answered, "but may I suggest to you both that banks are only one way to invest your money. Land is another good investment.

Roy's eyes lit up. "That's my dream," he said. "I want to own large parcels of land."

Ewin was surprised. "I thought your heart belonged to the sea. I expected you to buy a good sturdy fishing boat one of these days."

"That was true at one time. Since I married Jeanette, I've learned to love farming. So does she."

Mr. Levine looked at Roy. "Well, young man, it so happens that the best buys in land now and in the foreseeable future are in the Virginia colonies."

"The new world?" Roy grinned broadly. "Now that's what I call exciting!"

Once again, his brother surprised Ewin. "Roy, you would consider going to the Americas?"

Roy nodded. "Jeanette and I have talked about just such a move. Land is plentiful there and probably very inexpensive. It's a new world with new opportunities. It would be a wonderful place to raise a family and there would be countless opportunities for them to build a good life."

"Roy," Levine said, "If you are serious, I will get more information about the Virginia colonies and let you know.

"Thank you. I would like that very much."

Jacob watched as the brothers left the counting house. "Life is strange," he mused. "Their good fortune has become my good fortune. I'll have to remember to thank Pierre for the referral."

-o-

CHAPTER 17

Far away in another part of the world, the HMS Aggressor was hove to in the midday heat of the Mediterranean sun. Her wooden decks were almost too hot to walk on. There had been no wind for several days and the ship wallowed in the slick, greasy, swells of the hot afternoon.

In spite of the heat, Major John MacDonald made his marines run in place for thirty minutes every day. He believed it was good for the body and good for morale. John always led the exercise that was especially difficult today because of the heat. After the workout, the men were allowed to go over the side for a swim. Although it felt refreshing, the water was almost as warm as the air. Fitful breezes blew against the ship but offered no relief from the heat.

John stood at the rail and watched his men carouse in the sapphire blue water. He looked at the horizon where the water and sky blended into one. His mind drifted and he thought about Betsy. She had changed his life. Without knowing it, she had given a new purpose to his very existence. Before he had met her, there had been no direction, no goals. He took each day as it came and seldom thought about his future. That all changed the day he met her. Now they were oceans apart. John took comfort knowing his wife was safe and well cared for and was surrounded by people who loved her. Even so, there was an undeniable feeling of guilt. He wanted to be with her. He needed to be with her. And he would. Just a few more months to go.

Suddenly John felt a puff of air. This time the puff turned into a steady stream of air and finally a breeze. The Captain felt it too.

"All hands on deck!" he called loudly.

The sailors were soon climbing in the masthead and out along the lines on the yards. The mainsail was let go and the ship came up into the wind and began making headway. Additional sails were set and the ship began to increase speed as the sails were artfully trimmed. She soon settled into a steady rhythm.

Captain Gray stood by the tiller and observed as his officers gave the sailors directions. The captain believed in the chain of command;

therefore, he instructed his officers. They, in turn, were responsible for instructing and controlling those under their command. Generally, he was a soft-spoken man and few had ever seen him angry. His reputation of being a firm taskmaster preceded him and no one wanted him to get angry. He ran a tight ship and expected his men to know their jobs. Patient with his new officers, he always took time to bring the new men up to speed.

The captain turned his attention to the marine major. He had to admit that this fellow knew what he was about. Although he worked his men hard, it was obvious that they respected him. Captain Gray was pleased that Major MacDonald attended all the midshipmen classes even though he wasn't required to do so. He duly noted that John even took time to train his marines in seamanship. The first officer, Lieutenant Worley, commented that the major knew more about navigation and ships drills than most of the naval officers on board. In a way, the captain was sorry to hear that John would become Admiral Bowen's secretary at the end of this voyage. He would hate to lose this officer.

The meal that night was pleasant but a little rowdy. The men were celebrating that the Sea Gods had once again smiled on them with a steady wind. The wine was flowing generously and most of the officers over indulged. John was content with his usual one glass of wine. He was frequently teased about being a Scots Puritan and this night was no exception. After a few minutes, the captain became annoyed and put a stop to the teasing.

"Gentlemen," he said. "As I look around me, I see only two men at this table who have the discipline to always be ready to do their duty. I am one of those men and Major MacDonald is the other. You are all grown men and I don't want to preach but I want you to understand that there is no profit in being muddled with drink when you are serving aboard one of His Majesty's ships. You would all do well to think on that. Danger surrounds us constantly and you can be sure the Turks are just waiting for an opportunity to sink us or discredit us. Mind that you are ready, if such a trial comes." He excused himself and returned to his cabin.

Things quieted down after the captain left and most of the wine bottles were corked.

The ship took a long swing to the tip of Italy where they re-provisioned before beginning the long beat back to Gibraltar. As they approached, they did not sail into the straight, but turned north along the coast of Andalusia until they came off the coast of Barcelona. The captain then reversed the ship and retraced their steps back to Gibraltar. No ship, friend or foe, was sighted but after their many sweeps through the Mediterranean, their presence had certainly been noted.

Merchants at most neutral ports welcomed ships of the Royal Navy but the governments of most nations forbid the crew to land; therefore, although they were permitted to re-supply, the men were not allowed to go ashore. Captain Gray had solved this problem previously by making arrangements with merchants to send food and grog along with women to secluded areas along the coasts where the captain could anchor and let the men go ashore in longboats. Strict watches were kept on board and lookouts were sent to high ground on the shore to keep an eye on the weather and to look for potential danger from other ships.

As the ship sailed close to the eastern shore of Spain and dropped anchor, the ship's sailors lined up quickly to go ashore. This was the first stop the ship had made in several months and the men were anxious to be on firm ground.

John's marines were the backbone of the ship's security force. He divided them into four two-hour watches. One would go ashore while the other three stayed aboard. John, too, stayed onboard to supervise. He noticed as the first group of sailors returned, they smuggled grog on board for themselves and their shipmates still on watch. Although he observed this, he was not in a position to stop it. Soon, both of the Navy watches on board were drunk as were the men returning from the shore. He couldn't understand why none of the Navy officers attempted to prevent the situation. Perhaps it was because many of them were drunk as well.

Early in the afternoon, a lookout stationed on the masthead shouted, "Sail ho!" What looked like a warship was sighted approaching from the south.

The Captain had been in his cabin writing reports. He heard the call and rushed to the main deck and quickly ordered all men back to the ship. Some were so drunk they resisted being returned to the ship. Many of those on board were also drunk and some were simply unable to perform their duties.

Captain Gray was furious when he saw the condition his crew was in. He shouted to his first officer, "Prepare the ship for sea!" His face was so red it was almost purple. He paced the deck, arms swinging rapidly.

John knew the Captain was in trouble. He came forward and snapped a salute.

"Sir, my men are well-trained and stand ready to demonstrate their skills as seamen. They have been training for a long time. I would ask that you allow them to demonstrate what they have learned."

The Captain squared his jaw. "Are they sober, Major?"

"Aye, aye, sir!"

The Captain's anger gave way to tremendous relief. "Very well, then. Call your men and I will command them myself." He picked three of his most reliable and sober sailors and told them to direct the activities of the marines. The order was given to begin preparations for sea.

Without hesitation, the sailors relayed orders to the marines. Some went aloft and others manned the capstan and began to haul the anchor aboard.

The Captain shouted orders. They were instantly obeyed. Captain Gray took note of the speed and the agility of the marines. Soon the sails billowed and the ship moved along smartly in the afternoon sun.

The Captain kept his telescope focused on the ship to their south. It soon became obvious that she was rapidly falling astern. The marines on the masthead verified the Captain's conclusion. The mystery ship was no longer a threat, if indeed she ever had been.

By late afternoon, the majority of the drunken sailors were back on duty. The Captain was able to relieve the marines and John sent them back to their regular duties.

After things had returned to normal, Captain Gray called John aside.

"Major, I think your men performed admirably today. They may well have saved the ship as well as my career. I was busy today in my cabin and unaware of what was going on. I realize that is no excuse for dereliction of duty. I can assure you that this will never happen again."

"I'm glad that we were able to assist, sir. Don't be too hard on yourself. I think everyone on this ship learned a valuable lesson today."

"Let's hope so," the Captain said. "John, I am very much aware that you sometimes have to walk a tightrope on this ship because you are outranked by every naval officer on board. But today your ability to handle situations was clearly seen by everyone on board." He extended his hand to John. "Thank you for a job well done."

John grasped the Captain's hand. "Thank you, Captain." John saluted and turned sharply. He needed to find his men.

When they were all together, John shook each man's hand.

"I'm proud of you men. You performed superbly today. The Captain was impressed with your skills and asked me to extend his appreciation for all your efforts. He was truly caught off guard today and you men have become his heroes." He paused. "God bless you. Always remember you are marines. Duty, honor, country. In that you will always have personal pride. Stand tall, but remain humble. Pass no judgment on the poor blokes who faltered today. They are their own worst enemy. I doubt the events of today shall ever be repeated."

That night at dinner, there was little conversation. The officers had all been chastised by their Captain for their failure to control themselves or their men and they were feeling somewhat subdued.

John couldn't help but smile to himself when he realized that the only beverages consumed that night were water and hot coffee.

-o-

CHAPTER 18

When the last of the gold had been melted, Ewin and Roy returned together to Le Havre and Mr. Levine's counting house.

"Welcome back, gentlemen," Jacob said warmly. "I see you have brought more work for me to do."

"This is the last of it," Ewin said and opened his satchel.

Roy placed his bag on the counter and began unloading its contents.

"And how is this to be deposited?" Jacob asked as he began weighing the bars.

"Just as before," Ewin said. "Half in the one account and one-quarter in each of the other two."

When Jacob finished with the accounting, he presented them with three sets of keys. "Let me again explain how this works. When large amounts of money are deposited in numbered accounts, they are always placed in secure, locked storage boxes and kept in the bank's vault. When you want to make a withdrawal, you give your account number to a clerk. He retrieves your box and takes you to a private room where you use your key to unlock the box. When you have completed your transaction, you relock the box and it is returned to the vault." Jacob looked at his clients for their reaction. "Simple, isn't it?"

They both agreed. "Sounds foolproof to me," Ewin said, "As long as I can remember my account numbers, that is."

"Ah, don't worry about that. Since you are my client, I have a record of those numbers here under lock and key using a code only you and I can identify." He realized Roy hadn't made any comment yet. "Roy, what do you think about this system?"

"If I move to the colonies, I probably won't need such a sophisticated system."

Jacob smiled. "Glad you mentioned that. That was my next order of business." He placed a sheaf of papers on the table in front of him. "It seems as though there is widespread fever in the tidewater area of Virginia. The information I have for you is in regard to the piedmont area that is somewhat inland but boasts rich fertile soil. My agent in Virginia has located several large farms for you to consider. By the way, in Virginia, farms are called plantations." He smiled, "Sounds fancy, eh? After evaluating the properties, my agent strongly recommends a twenty-seven hundred acre parcel on..." He flipped through the papers until he found the word he was looking for, "the Appomattox River. There is an existing house and several outbuildings and..." He paused and perused the material, "It looks as though it is ready for occupancy."

Jacob put the papers together and handed Roy the large packet. "Information about each of the properties and the asking prices are all included. If you decide to go to Virginia to look at the various properties, I will escrow some of your money. Then, if you decide to buy, just tell my agent there. He'll have the bill of sale and the paid mortgage in your hands within days. I can arrange for the rest of your assets to be transferred to a bank in the colonial capitol in Williamsburg. That way you may begin working on the farm, excuse me...I mean plantation, immediately and have the resources you need at your immediate disposal."

Roy was excited. "This sounds perfect. I can't wait to share this information with my wife."

"Is Jeanette really ready for this?" Ewin wondered.

"We've talked about doing this ever since we were married. We're both ready. Don't be surprised if we leave in the early spring."

Ewin smiled at his brother. "Yes, I can see you now," he said. "You will build a great house on a plantation in the Virginias and live like a king!"

Roy laughed. "You know me better than that, brother. I will always be a frugal Scot trying to figure out ways to make more money than I spend."

Jacob agreed with this sound philosophy. "It doesn't have anything to do with being a Scot. That's the only way to increase wealth. Make more, spend less. It's the only way to financial success."

"Now, Jacob," Ewin said, "we have one more piece of business before we leave." He reached inside his jacket and pulled out two leather pouches and placed them in front of Jacob.

Roy added two more pouches from his pocket. The brothers exchanged glances and smiled as Jacob emptied the contents of the pouches onto a black velvet cloth.

As the jewels tumbled out, Jacob raised his eyebrows. "Whew! There's another fortune here." He fingered several stones then reached for a magnifier. One by one, he lifted each jewel, held it close to the magnifier, and looked deeply into its center.

"Hmm...beautiful...flawless." Jacob put down the magnifier. "It's going to take some time to determine the value of these gems. I'll need a day or two. But I have a friend in Italy who will be excited about getting so many jewels at one time."

"Take your time," Ewin said. "We're in no hurry."

Roy sorted through the stones and picked up a sparkling ruby. "Jacob, I'd like to keep this one as a gift to my wife."

"I understand," Jacob said, "but it would be smarter if I traded you one of mine instead. That way, you'll have a bill of sale and no one could every question its origin."

"I see your logic," Roy agreed. "We'll do it your way."

Ewin started looking at the stones. "I have a wife and daughter who I know would love to have one as a keepsake." He selected a sapphire for Betsy and an emerald for Heather. He handed them to Jacob. "Have you got something that compares with these?"

Jacob walked over to a locked cabinet, inserted a key and withdrew a drawer. "Here, gentlemen, take your pick." The drawer contained a variety of necklaces, earrings, brooches, and bracelets.

Ewin chose an emerald brooch for his wife and a gold necklace with one large pear-shaped sapphire for Betsy. Roy selected a delicate ruby necklace for Jeanette.

Two days later, all the jewels had been evaluated and Jacob distributed the cash exchange into the three respective accounts.

With a bounce in their step, Ewin and Roy left the counting house feeling as though a great weight had been lifted from their shoulders.

Finally, the treasure had been dissolved and the traces of it had been very efficiently wiped away.

Roy returned to St. Val'ery and Ewin booked passage for London. He couldn't wait to see Heather and Betsy's faces when he handed each of them a leather pouch representing the final retribution for Glencoe.

-o-

CHAPTER 19

The HMS Aggressor had entered the east end of the Straights of Gibraltar and was waiting for the tide to turn. She was at rest, just drifting, when the lookout announced that a cutter was approaching from the Spanish coast. A midshipman notified the Captain, who ordered a cannon salute to be fired. By the time she came alongside, John had his marines ready by the ladder.

The cutter's boatswain cupped his hands to his mouth and shouted, "Ahoy the Aggressor! We have His Majesty's representative to the Bey of Tunis board. He wishes to transfer to your vessel."

As the representative ascended the ladder, the marine drummer began a drum roll and John called his men to attention. When the visitor's head came over the rail, the boatswain piped him over the side and the marine guard presented arms. Captain Gray greeted the new arrival who presented his credentials and introduced himself as Lord Ralph Bennett. By this time, his assistant was on deck and the Captain invited them both to his cabin.

That night at dinner, the Captain presented his officers to the honored guests. Lord Bennett was King William's unofficial envoy to the court of the Bey of Tunis.

There was no doubt that Lord Bennett was an important man in government. He stood tall and straight like a soldier. His thick grey hair was pulled back and neatly tied at the nape. A handsome man, he had a square jaw and piercing blue eyes. Over his right shoulder, he wore a sash bearing the cross of St. George.

His assistant, introduced as James Marks, was a nondescript person who wore dull brown colors. Everything about him indicated that he didn't want to call attention to himself. Even his looks were ordinary. Slightly built, he had mousy brown hair and hazel eyes. Although he looked like a clerk, John suspected he might also be an intelligence source for the government.

During dinner, John noticed that Lord Bennett kept glancing over at him. He never spoke to John since the other officers peppered him with questions. When dinner was concluded, the officers rose to leave the table.

The Captain caught John's eye. "Major MacDonald, would you stay for a moment, please?"

"Of course," John replied.

After the table was cleared and they were alone, Captain Gray said, "Sit down, John. Lord Bennett has something he wants to discuss with you."

John nodded to Lord Bennett and took a seat opposite him.

"Captain Gray speaks highly of you, Major."

"Thank you," John said. "I return the compliment."

Lord Bennett continued. "I understand that you are a friend of a very close acquaintance of mine, Admiral Charles Bowen."

John wondered where this small talk was leading. "Yes, sir. I have the pleasure of serving the Admiral."

"May I ask why you are on the Aggressor?" Bennett asked.

"In a way, I am serving an apprenticeship. Previously, I was a mercenary soldier in the Low Countries for King William. I met the Admiral in London through my wife. We became friends and he offered me a regular commission that I accepted. It became necessary for me to learn the role of a marine officer rapidly so that I could serve as the Admiral's secretary as soon as possible."

"I see. The Captain assures me that your apprenticeship has been more than successful. In fact, he believes you could take command of this ship today."

"I don't know about that." John laughed and looked at the Captain.

"Captain Gray is well known as a skillful seaman. If he believes you could do it, then I believe it, too." Lord Bennett leaned closer to John and lowered his voice. "But now, Major. Let's get down to business. I will tell you what I need done and then you tell me how to accomplish it."

John was fascinated as the story unfolded.

"Months ago, King William made a generous proposal to the Bey of Tunis hoping to keep his Corsairs from preying on English ships. The Bey refused and we had no hope of reaching any kind of agreement with the man." Lord Bennett glanced at Captain Gray. "Your Captain has agreed to take me to Tunis where I might once again try diplomatic solutions with the Bey. But now, we have an international problem. This is where you come in, Major. You see, six English subjects and their wives have been captured and are being held as prisoners. They were on holiday and were sailing from Italy to Cairo. Their plan was to visit the pyramids and then travel on to Jerusalem before returning to England. Their ship was pirated by the Turks. They killed the crew and took the passengers hostage. King William learned of their capture and that they were being held in Tunis. Then two days ago, my intelligence sources informed me that the Bey plans to move the prisoners to the inland city of Batna, where they will remain until the Bey decides their fate." Lord Bennett hesitated. His eyes narrowed and his chin jutted slightly. "Major, those people must be rescued now, while this ship is in Tunis. If not, there is no hope for them. The women will be raped and brutalized, the men will be tortured and then they will all be slaughtered. The Turks are merciless and cruel and they hate the English. You and your marines offer the only hope we have to rescue them. Now we've learned that they will be moved in just eight days, so there isn't much time."

John needed some more facts. "How reliable are your intelligence sources?"

"Extremely reliable," Lord Bennett assured him.

"How good are the Bey's intelligence sources?" John asked.

Lord Bennett's face drained of color. "He is cunning and extremely thorough. He knows everything about our ship, even to how many men we generally carry on board. He is so good that he probably even knows your address in London," he said sarcastically. He put his hand over John's. "You must realize how dangerous this mission is. If you or any of your men are caught, not only will the captives suffer for it, but your men will be tortured and humiliated in every way imaginable. Their final revenge will be boiling you in oil." He paused. "Am I clear on this?"

John paled slightly. "Yes, sir. I do understand."

Lord Bennett reached into his coat pocket and pulled out some folded papers and handed them to John. "Here are some maps of Tunisia including the route to Batna. Study them very carefully. If and when you come up with a plan, let me know. I'll be anxiously awaiting your summons."

John returned to his small cabin. His heart started racing. He took a deep breath and then mentally reviewed the mission as he understood it. He had to get his men ashore, attack a caravan that would be heavily guarded, rescue the prisoners and transport them back to the sea and then get them on board the Aggressor for the get-away. He shook his head in disbelief of the monumental task facing him.

"Well, I'll just take it one step at a time and see where that takes me."

First, he studied the maps. The road to Batna looked to be twenty miles inland except in one place where it was about half that distance.

"That's it!" John said aloud. "That will be our route!" He made notes that included a time frame, supplies needed, and possible glitches they might encounter. He worked feverishly throughout the night and through most of the next day. By late afternoon, he had a workable plan. He sent word to the Captain and Lord Bennett. They wasted no time in requesting John to come to the Captain's cabin.

John cleared his throat. "Before I explain my plan, let me assure you that the goal is to rescue the prisoners and lose no marine in the process."

Lord Bennett and the Captain exchanged encouraging looks.

John continued. "I plan to take fifteen marines with me. The other fifteen will remain on board and perform duties as usual. Now, gentlemen, I want to share with you some things that seem to be in our favor. Fortunately for us, the rescue falls within the dark of the moon. We should be able to make landfall without detection. Next, the Bey probably does not know that in addition to the regular crew, there are thirty marines on board. So when they do learn there are fifteen on board, they will see nothing amiss. I checked the sail locker and found an old sail we can use to make hooded cloaks for all the men." He smiled. "A little disguise will be helpful. Of course we will need food, water, and some medical supplies—just in case. I want two pistols for every man, plus cutlasses, and as many muskets as we can get our hands on. I will need two longboats to transport everyone back to the Aggressor. I think it would be a good idea for the ship's carpenters to construct two dummy boats so that it will appear as though all the ship's boats are on board." He stopped. "Any questions?"

"Not so far," the Captain said.

"Please continue," Lord Bennett replied.

John rubbed his hands together in anticipation. "Now, let me outline my plan."

The Captain and Lord Bennett listened intently. When John finished, Lord Bennett looked at Captain Gray. He raised his eyebrows and his eyes brightened.

"This could work!" he said.

The Captain smiled. "John, you almost make this sound easy. I can get you everything you request except for the pistols. Let me see how many I can come up with." He closed his eyes and counted mentally. "I can count eleven plus two dueling pistols I have." He walked across the cabin to his arms cabinet. There were ten pistols in the rack. "It looks like you can plan on twenty-three."

"Thanks, Captain. That's close enough. Guess we can't have everything." John said with a smile.

He returned to his cabin that night with his head spinning. In spite of the fact he had not slept the night before, John dozed fitfully and was up early the next morning. He mustered his men and told them that they had been given a dangerous mission that would require fifteen volunteers. All thirty men stepped forward. John was pleased.

"Thank you, men. I'm proud of you all. But now you force me to eliminate some of you. All new recruits and family men are dismissed."

That brought the number down to twenty. From those, he chose the fifteen he thought were the fittest and the best marksmen. He took the chosen fifteen aside and briefed them on the mission at hand. They spent the next few days training and exercising.

The night before the Aggressor arrived at the Port of Tunis, John and his fifteen marines left the ship and began rowing to shore on the first leg of their life saving mission.

~~~

The next day when the Aggressor entered the port, she fired her obligatory salute and received a salute in return. James Marks was sent ashore to notify the Bey of the arrival of Lord Bennett who carried letters from the English king.

The Bey was not impressed and wanted to get rid of the English warship as soon as possible. He was worried. Was it just a coincidence that the ship arrived this day, the day he was moving the captives? Could they possibly know about their capture and plan to bargain for their release? He wasn't sure but he had to find out.

Abruptly, he told Marks. "Tell Lord Bennett to be here at 2 p.m. this afternoon. In the meantime, no one is to leave your ship to come ashore while you are in port. Is that understood?"

"Yes, sir. I understand." Marks bowed slightly out of a respect he did not feel. The Bey was arrogant and unpleasant but he couldn't afford to anger him. "May I request that you allow us to re-supply our ship with water, food, and other supplies?"

"Of course. That can be arranged. That is all!" He dismissed Marks with a wave of his hand.

As soon as Marks left, the Bey summoned two of his most reliable officers. "Make sure no one leaves the English ship. I want patrol boats to circle the ship at all times. Make sure no one comes ashore!"

The Bey could not resist the golden opportunity to make close up observations of the English ship.

"The Aggressor has requested water and food supplies. I want you and your officers to accompany the supply boats and take a headcount of those on board. Also, look around to see if you find anything unusual. Report back to me immediately." Again, a simple wave of his hand dismissed his men.

~~~

Meanwhile, the captives were chained together and told that they were going for a long walk. The commander stood in front of them with an air of superiority. His feet were spread and his arms crossed. He looked at the faces of the prisoners before he spoke. His lips curled into a sneer.

"You English think you are so much better than anyone else. Well, look at you now. No better than any other slave." He moved closer to their faces. His eyes narrowed and he gritted his teeth. "I take great pleasure in assuring you that if any one of you tries to escape or if anyone foolishly tries to rescue you, you will first pay dire consequences and then you will be killed. We have several ways for you to die. It depends on our mood at the time."

Having made his warning speech, he led the captives down the dirt road in the already hot morning sun.

~~~

It was still dark when John and his men landed on the beach. Using the maps, John had selected what looked like the most deserted shore as a landing place. The men were wearing the hooded cloaks and in the darkness they looked like specters. The masts and sails that would be used later were taken ashore and hidden.

Two men were sent ahead as scouts. Two others swamped the boats so no passerby could see them. Just before sunset, they would float them again so they could all make a quick escape.

The rest of the marines moved out in three groups of four. They hurried along; not knowing what hidden dangers might await them. They planned to reach the road by dawn so they would have time to prepare for the rescue. Everyone remained alert as they moved swiftly toward their destination, never knowing what lay ahead. John secretly hoped for the best but prepared for the worst.

Just as the sun broke over the horizon, they arrived at the rendezvous point. The two scouts reported that they had seen nothing at all.

John posted a lookout while the others dug trenches back from the road. The purpose of the trenches was two-fold. The first purpose was to keep the men hidden until the attack. The second purpose would come later.

The hard part now was waiting. John tried hard not to speculate too far ahead. He knew his marines could do the job. They were well trained and most were crack shots. What he didn't know was the enemy. How many guards would there be? Would they be armed with pistols, swords, or both? He had been told that the Turks were cruel and would have no mercy on the hostages. They would be particularly merciless to the rescuers.

John didn't have too long to wait. As mid-day approached, the lookout reported seeing a small caravan about a half-mile away. John looked through his telescope and could clearly see the hostages walking single file. Two guards led the way and two flanked each side of the group. All were on horseback. He could see two camels with riders bringing up the rear. John crouched down and quietly gave instructions to his men. He told them there was a total of eight guards.

"Robert, you shoot the two soldiers in front; Andrew, you take out the two on the left and Thomas, you get the ones on the right. Kenneth and Geoff, you aim for the riders at the rear. The rest of us will be backup. They aren't expecting any trouble, so we will probably catch them unaware. At least I hope so. Wait for my command; then let's surprise the hell out of them. And send them there to boot!"

The waiting seemed endless. John's heart was pounding, partly in anticipation and partly in fear of the unknown.

As the group approached, John could see the women were in front of the men. "Oh, my God," he whispered. "They're chained together!"

He put his head down and waited. The only sounds were the horses' hooves and an occasional shout from one of the guards.

The men were ready and kept their eyes on John as they waited for his command.

"Now!" John shouted. The marines jumped up and took quick aim. Volley after volley of gunfire erupted. The hostages fell to the ground and covered their heads. The Turkish guards took direct hits and fell from their horses. Within seconds, the two guards on camelback were killed. Quickly the marines moved in to make sure all the guards were dead. If there was any doubt, they were put to the sword. John quickly spotted the highest-ranking soldier and was rewarded when he found the keys to the hostages' chains on a ring tied around his waist.

Some of the women hostages sobbed as their chains were released and they realized they were free. Some stood up, but others seemed too weak to move.

While John and several of the marines helped move the hostages off the main road, the others dragged the dead bodies from the road and buried them in the trenches they had dug for the ambush. The second purpose had been fulfilled.

There was no time to lose. They had to move quickly. Each female was lifted onto a horse and she placed her arms around the waist of the marine horseman. They left immediately on their long ride back to the beach. Two marines led the male hostages who followed on foot.

John and the remaining marines stayed behind long enough to cover all the blood signs. They took blankets off the camels and swept the road clean. The camels were useless to them so they removed the saddles and let the beasts wander away over the sand dunes. The saddle packs were searched for anything of value. Several bags of gold and silver coins were found and given to John for safekeeping. The saddles were then buried in the sand. After all hoof marks and footprints were swept away, John and the remaining marines left to follow the others. Two scouts were left behind to make sure no one was following.

By late afternoon, the two marines acting as rear guards caught up to the group.

"No sign of anyone following us," one reported. "We stayed back for an hour and no one came down the road in either direction."

John was not relieved. "You can be sure the Turks know the hostages and the guards are missing. We need to move swiftly now."

By sunset, John could see the ocean and knew they were within minutes of the rendezvous point. He encouraged everyone to walk faster.

When they were within one hundred yards of the beach, John signaled the two marines who had stayed with the boats.

They answered the signal.

John gave out a whoop. "We've made it! Let's hurry and get out of here."

Everyone started running. Several marines helped the hostage into the boats. Others removed the saddles from the horses and smacked their rumps to release them. The horses galloped away. The saddles were thrown into a gully and the last of the marines jumped aboard.

The boats were pushed into deeper water and as quickly as possible, the sails were hoisted. Soon they were leaving the coast of Tunisia behind. The rescue had gone extremely well so far. John's only concern now was about finding a needle in a haystack. He took comfort in the fact that the Aggressor was looking for a needle too.

~~~

Lord Bennett's audience with the Bey had not gone well.

"Once and for all," the Bey almost shouted," I reject your King's proposal. We don't need or want his money, his jewels, or any of his goods." He turned away in anger, then stopped and turned to face Lord Bennett. He had to find out now if there was an ulterior motive to Lord Bennett's visit. Did he know about the English hostages?

"Is there any other reason you are here in Tunis at this time?"

Lord Bennett played dumb. "I'm not sure what you mean, sir. I came with a proposal from our King. That is the purpose for my visit."

Inwardly, the Bey was relieved. He wanted no trouble. He could kill all of the Aggressor crew if he had to, but that might cause such uproar that war would be declared. He certainly didn't want that. He liked things just the way they were. His Corsairs were doing a fine job of pirating and keeping the coffers filled. No, the best course of action now would be to just get rid of the English ship.

Calm now, the Bey smiled at Lord Bennett. "Then since you have no more business here in Tunis and your ship has been re-supplied, I suggest you weigh anchor as quickly as possible. I grant you safe passage this time, Lord Bennett, but I make no such promise in the future." With a smirk, he snapped his fingers. "You are dismissed."

An officer accompanied Lord Bennett and then informed the port captain that the English ship had the Bey's permission to leave port.

The Aggressor prepared for sea. Well before sunset, she slipped her anchor and was towed out of the harbor by the crew in longboats. When the tide turned, the ship had cleared the harbor and was being carried out to sea.

About an hour after darkness, the Captain was relieved to feel the first stirrings of the nightly off shore breeze. The longboats were recalled, sails were raised and the ship headed for the open sea.

Captain Gray knew he had a difficult navigational problem. He needed to sail along the coast to the area where he had dropped the marines. He would have to locate them in the dark. His dilemma was that he had to sail close enough to the shore to take advantage of the off shore wind, and stay far enough out so he could not be detected by anyone on the shore. He gave orders that the ship's port lights be extinguished and then proceeded with fingers crossed and a silent prayer on his lips.

Lord Bennett sat in his small cabin and sweated. He was angry and his stomach was in a knot. His meeting with the Bey had been disastrous. *What an arrogant fool he is,* Lord Bennett thought. *And dangerous, too.* He was sure that if the rescue party was captured, the Bey would unleash terrible cruelty on them all. Lord Bennett wasn't a praying man but he did take a moment to look up and whisper to the unseen and unknown power above.

James Marks, on the other hand, was very relaxed. He was the one who had made the contacts in Tunis and gave Lord Bennett the information about the prisoners being moved to Batna. John had been right about this man. Marks was a player in the dangerous game of espionage and was an important spy for Great Britain. He was a Levite whose family had been slaughtered by the Turks. Lord Bennett was angry with the Turks, but James Marks hated them with a passion. His only goal in life was to make them pay.

Marks liked Major MacDonald. He saw him as a highly capable and honorable young man who was flexible in his thinking and seemed to be always open to new ideas. Personally, Marks believed the rescue effort would be a failure. *Who knows,* he thought, *it might even start a war.* On the other hand, he admitted, if anyone could make it work, it would be the major.

He offered a prayer, too. It was not for the hostages or their rescuers. His prayer was that every Turk alive now would spend eternity in hell.

~~~

The night air was cool and the freed captives began to feel exhilarated. Their nightmare was almost over and for the first time in days, they felt hope. They were extremely grateful to the marines and let them know it.

They didn't want to talk about their ordeal except to say they never thought they'd live through it.

The night sky was streaked with clouds and offered only filtered moonlight. After several hours of sailing north, John felt a little more confident that they were not being chased. Now if only their course would lead to contact with the Aggressor. If not, John concluded, they would sail for safety in Spain.

Meanwhile, the Captain stayed on deck and scoured the sea. If all went well and as planned, the rendezvous would occur in just an hour or more. The plan was to pick them up at the same latitude and longitude where they were dropped. The Captain had the advantage of using his charts. His ship sat higher in the water and that afforded him a wider view. Every available man was on deck, telescope to eye, searching the vast sea for two tiny bumps that would indicate the longboats were in sight.

There are long moments just before dawn when the eastern sky begins to brighten. But the Captain strained his eyes toward the west where the night still kept hold.

"We're close," he said to his first mate. "We should see them anytime now."

The first mate squinted, also trying to glimpse anything that looked like a sail.

Lord Bennett and James Marks came up on deck and scanned the horizon, too.

The darkness was lifting and visibility increased. Suddenly, the lookout on the mast shouted joyously, "Ahoy, Captain! Sails! Two points on the larboard quarter!"

The Captain swung around and adjusted his telescope. "By jove!" he grabbed Lord Bennett's arm and handed him his telescope. "It's them! See for yourself! Hallelujah! Praise the Lord. "Ring the ship's bell. Let them know we see them. Keep ringing it!"

The two longboats were still a mile away but the distance between them closed rapidly. John ordered the sails to be dropped and they drifted until the Aggressor came alongside.

The wives were first to be hoisted aboard. Husbands followed. The Captain warmly welcomed each one. For the first time since their capture, the hostages were able to smile.

John came aboard, grinning ear to ear. He saluted the Captain. "Sir, I am pleased to report we were able to free all twelve captives and return them safely without casualties. The enemy has been destroyed. Mission accomplished, sir!"

The Captain's eyes became misty. He could barely contain his profound relief and joy. "Well done, Major MacDonald. Well done!"

Lord Bennett shook John's hand. "Congratulations, Major. This is indeed a happy day for us all."

The Captain addressed the six English couples. "I know you are exhausted from your ordeal. Let me assure you that you are finally safe. We will now sail for the French port of Marseille. From there it will be easy for you to return to England. The galley crew is prepared to feed you a hearty breakfast after which we will show you to your quarters where you can get some undisturbed rest. Welcome aboard!"

After the new passengers went below, John mustered his marines in front of the Captain.

"Marines," the Captain said. "I salute you. You have accomplished a mission that seemed impossible. Congratulations to each of you. You've earned a much-deserved rest. Go below; get some food, then rest. Dismissed!"

John stayed behind. The Captain put his arm around John's shoulder. "Words can't express our tremendous gratitude. I want you to join me for dinner tonight. Everyone will be anxious to hear how you accomplished the world's greatest rescue. I'll need a written report of course, but tonight, I just want to hear your story." He squeezed John's shoulder. "Now, go below, son. Get something to eat and get some rest. By dinnertime tonight, we'll be well on our way to Marseille."

John went to his cabin to freshen up and ordered the steward to bring him some food and beverage. There was a rap on his door. One of his sergeants stepped inside.

"Excuse me, sir. But before you rest, the lads and I would like to do up your kit. When you have dinner with the Captain tonight, we want you to look your best, boots blackened and collar washed and starched." He grinned. "Believe me, sir. When we are through with you, you will shine like a star."

John was surprised but pleased. "Well, thank you, sergeant. I sincerely appreciate that."

The steward arrived with a tray. The smell of the food made John realize how extremely hungry he was. Before the steward left, John took the plate and began shoveling the food in his mouth, hardly chewing before he swallowed and shoveled in more. The food lay like a stone in his stomach. He didn't care. His appetite was sated and now the next order of business. He fell into his bunk and went to sleep.

That night, John did shine. His uniform was as close to perfect as it could be. He felt proud of what he and his men had accomplished but realized there was a lot of luck involved. Something deep inside him disagreed with that theory. He knew it wasn't luck at all. It was divine providence.

During dinner, the conversation was light at first and then became political as Lord Bennett praised the King and supported all his decisions. James Marks and Bennett remarked that the Turks were a menace both on land and on sea. Captain Gray had to agree.

John picked up a wine bottle and refilled his glass. He was not in the mood to discuss politics.

The Captain picked up on John's cue. "Now that the table has been cleared, I want very much to hear about the Major's remarkable adventure." He looked at each of his tablemates. "And I know you do too. But first, a toast." He raised his glass and the others followed. "To Major John MacDonald and a job well done!"

John felt a little uncomfortable. He took a sip of wine and then started his oral report in detail. When he finished, he pulled the bags of coins from inside his jacket pocket and presented them to the Captain. "Bounty, Captain Gray." He smiled with satire. "Compliments of the Bey of Tunis. Only he doesn't know it!"

Laughter filled the room. It was a fitting end to a remarkable story.

Within days, Captain Gray arrived at the French port of Marseille. He turned the former captives over to the British Consul who promised he would make immediate arrangements for their transport home.

As was the custom in many foreign ports, no one from the ship was permitted to go ashore and the ship had to clear the port within twenty-four hours. The Aggressor left on time and sailed west toward Gibraltar.

One evening as the setting sun splashed the sky with shades of orange and pink, John joined the Captain on the quarterdeck. They stood with their backs against the ship's rail. Both of them were awed by the magnificent rock of Gibraltar.

"You know what I wish, Major" The Captain spoke as though he was thinking out loud. "I wish that someday Gibraltar will belong to England."

John was curious. "Why do you say that, Captain?"

"Because I know that this could become the most important naval station in the world. I would trust the British to occupy it a lot more than I trust the Spanish."

John chuckled. "It would surely be a thorn in the Turks side, wouldn't it?"

"Aye, John; it would inconvenience them severely."

"You know the Spanish won't give it up without a fight."

"Aye, John. You're right again. But that's a battle for another day."

Both men fell silent, lost in their own thoughts. The Captain was visualizing a British naval base at Gibraltar.

John was visualizing sailing around the Atlantic side of Portugal and heading home to Betsy.

-o-

CHAPTER 20

It was a beautiful fall morning. Betsy marveled at the scenery around her. The sky formed a bright blue backdrop for acres of trees whose leaves boasted hues of red and gold. The grass was still green and summer flowers continued to bloom profusely.

Betsy loved the fall. It was her favorite season. Days were still warm and the nights were crisp and cool.

She and her mother were arm-in-arm, strolling through the park. Betsy stopped for a moment and took a deep breath.

"Isn't it wonderful, Mother? I can smell fall in the air. Can't you?"

Heather took a deep breath, too. "Yes I can, Betsy. For some reason, it reminds me of my childhood when I scampered through the woods and felt the crunch of the falling leaves beneath my feet."

Betsy looked down at her feet and laughed. "I can't see my feet anymore, Mother," she quipped.

Heather patted her daughter's large protruding belly. "Well, it won't be long now. That baby should be ready to come any day now."

Betsy was unsure. "The doctor said the baby would be born at the end of September. Here it is the second week of October and still no baby."

She felt a tightening in her abdomen and linked her fingers around it.

"I know I'm ready! I'm more than ready. The drawers are filled with little sweaters and blankets. I don't think there's room for one more piece of baby clothing." She felt another tightening in her stomach.

"Mother, I think we should go back now. I'm feeling a bit strange."

Heather frowned. "Are you all right, honey?"

"I think so. I just want to go home and lie down."

By the time they reached the house, Betsy had experienced more sporadic contractions.

"Annie!" Heather called as they entered the house. "Help me get Miss Betsy upstairs. I think we might be having a baby later today."

Annie voiced her surprise. "Oh, my goodness!" she said and took Betsy's other arm. "C'mon, Miss Betsy. Don't you worry about nothing right now. Your Mama and I will take care of everything. Claudette!" she called loudly. "Turn back Miss Betsy's bed. She needs to lie down."

Claudette threw her arms up in alarm. "Yes, Mum! Right away Mum!" She ran ahead of them and had the bed properly turned by the time Betsy came into the room.

"Ooh!" Betsy cried out and grabbed her stomach. "I think the baby's coming!"

Her mother wasted no time. "Claudette, you go get the mid-wife. Annie, you gather up as many towels as you can find. Here, Betsy, let me help you get undressed and into bed."

Betsy looked tense. "Is the baby coming now, Mother?"

Heather shook her head. "Not for a few hours. The first baby usually takes a long time. I want you to lie down and rest as much as you can. The pains will get stronger and closer together after a while. You'll need your strength then." She took hold of Betsy's hand and smiled reassuringly. "In the meantime, just rest. I'll be here with you. Don't worry about a thing."

Betsy's chin started quivering and tears welled in her eyes. "I wish John was here. I've missed him so much, but now I *need* him. I want him here when our baby is born." Tears spilled down her cheeks. "Oh, Mother! He doesn't even know!"

Heather's heart ached for her daughter but there was nothing she could do but to try to comfort her.

"I know, sweetheart. You have been so strong, so brave. Just a few more weeks and John will be home. Think how surprised he'll be!"

"Ooh!" Betsy bolted upright when a strong contraction ripped through her.

The mid-wife rushed into the room and immediately took charge. "Please move out of the way, Madam," she said to Heather. "I need room to take care of this young woman." Gently, she pushed Betsy back onto the pillows. "Hello, dear. My name is Martha Tudor—yes, like the royal Tudors, but no, I'm not related."

Betsy smiled and relaxed. She knew she could trust this woman. "I'm glad you're here. My name is Betsy."

"Now," Martha said and looked at Heather. "I want to examine Miss Betsy and I want you and," she nodded toward Annie and Claudette who were standing in the doorway, "the other two to leave us alone for a short while."

Betsy protested. "Please! I want my mother to stay with me."

"That's fine with me," Martha said. "She can return a little later; but first, you and I need to talk."

Heather kissed Betsy's forehead. "I'll be back soon." As she left the room, she closed the door softly behind her.

Martha pulled a chair close to the bed and sat down so she was eye to eye with Betsy. "I know this is your first baby, so I'm going to explain what will be happening. Then I want to examine you. If you have any questions, just ask me. I'll be here with you throughout the delivery."

Quietly and thoroughly, Martha explained what would happen between now and the moment of birth.

Betsy cried out as another pain gripped her body. "That was the worst one yet," Betsy said when the pain subsided.

"The pains will get stronger, my dear. But remember, each pain brings you a little closer to the end."

Gently, she moved Betsy's legs apart. "I'm going to examine you now. Let me know if you have another pain and I'll stop."

Betsy closed her eyes and held her breath. Martha noticed.

"Breathe, child. Keep breathing."

She finished the examination and pulled the sheet over Betsy's stomach. "You're about half way there, I'd say," she said in a positive voice.

"What does that mean?" Betsy wondered.

Martha walked over to the door and called to Heather. "You can come in now." To Annie, she said, "Bring in the towels and other items I requested as soon as possible."

Heather sat next to Betsy. "How you holding up, sweetheart?" Betsy started to answer but she arched her back and moaned as another contraction hit.

By late afternoon, the contractions came one on top of another. Betsy's head thrashed from side to side. Her hair was damp from perspiration. Heather placed a cool cloth on her daughter's forehead. She looked at Martha beseechingly. Martha understood.

"It won't be long now. Just a few more minutes."

Annie and Claudette stayed close to the closed bedroom door. Whenever they heard Betsy cry out, Annie would bite her lip and wring her hands. Claudette buried her face in her hands and cried.

Martha could see the baby's head. "Push, Betsy! Push harder!"

In agony, Betsy bore down as hard as she could. "AAAAH! AAAAH!"

"Good girl!" Martha said. "Take some short breaths, Betsy… Good! Good! Now, one more push!"

Betsy pushed until she thought she would explode. "AAAAH!"

"The baby's head is out!" Martha cried. "Now the shoulders. Push, Betsy! Harder!"

Betsy's face turned red as she held her breath and pushed again. With that, the shoulders emerged and the rest of the baby slipped out.

Panting, Betsy fell back onto the pillows and closed her eyes. She was exhausted. She couldn't think clearly for a moment. Suddenly, her eyes popped open. "Is my baby here? Is he all right?" Betsy looked at Martha and then at her mother.

As Martha cut the umbilical cord, the baby gave a lusty cry. The child was quickly wrapped in a cloth. Martha handed her to Heather.

Heather took the baby and just looked at her. She couldn't find the words, but the tears she shed said a thousand words. She walked over to her daughter and carefully laid the child in Betsy's waiting arms.

"Meet your daughter," Heather smiled through her tears. She is the spitting image of you, Betsy."

Betsy looked at her tiny, wrinkled daughter. She had a round little face and a shock of dark red hair. Emotions filled every fiber of her body: joy, excitement, relief, and wonder. "It's a miracle," she said in a whisper. "This child is the greatest miracle in my life."

Within minutes of the baby's birth, Ewin quietly came into the room. He was grinning from ear to ear. As he kissed Betsy, he whispered, "I'm so proud of you, lass."

"Would you like to hold your granddaughter, Father?" Betsy, too, was beaming.

Ewin cradled the infant in his arms and rocked her gently from side to side. "What a beautiful baby girl you have now. I love her already!"

Betsy named her daughter, Meggie. The child quickly became the center of attention. For Betsy, the infant became her whole world, her whole reason for being. The bassinette was placed next to Betsy's bed. The only time she allowed her mother or Annie to take her out of the room was after a feeding when Betsy tried to catch up on some sleep.

Lady Bowen became a frequent visitor and could always be counted on to "ooh!" and "ah!" each time she saw little Meggie. Then there was Annie and Claudette who hovered over the bassinette every chance they had.

Betsy laughed as she watched her parents coo and baby-talk many times throughout the day. There seemed to be a constant parade of on-lookers eager to watch the baby's every move.

Within a week, Betsy had healed and could feel her levels of energy rise. She quickly adjusted to motherhood in spite of the fact Meggie was a fussy baby. She couldn't seem to sleep more than two hours without waking and crying. Betsy never became upset. She would just hold the baby and sing quiet lullabies until Meggie fell asleep.

The new baby was surrounded with love and Betsy was grateful. She had been blessed with a healthy baby and a loving extended family.

Betsy kissed her baby daughter. "You think you are loved now. Just wait until your Papa gets home!"

-o-

CHAPTER 21

The Bey of Tunis was furious. His face turned purple with rage when he thought about how he had been duped by the British. His pride couldn't take such a blow.

"The Aggressor has not heard the last of me!" he bellowed. "I will make them pay! They will regret the day they sailed into my harbor!"

When he had been told the English captives and the guards were missing, he couldn't believe it. Eight of his best soldiers had been put in charge of moving the prisoners. What could possibly have happened? Then he remembered and made the connection. The English ship had sailed into Tunis the very same day the prisoners were moved.

He shook his head in disbelief. "It's impossible! No one could have accomplished a successful rescue. It's just not possible!"

He had been ranting for hours before he finally came to the conclusion that he had to find out exactly what happened. He ordered a company of men to search every inch of the road between Tunis and Batna.

"Twenty people could not have vanished into thin air," he said to the captain of the guard. "Don't return until you have some answers. If you return empty handed, you will all be shot!"

The captain addressed his men. "If such a rescue did take place, I know the exact spot it would have happened. Follow me!" He knew the road like the back of his hand.

There was one area where the road turned north and angled toward the sea. At that point, it would have only been a ten-mile journey to the inlet.

When they reached the area in question, the men spread out and scoured the road. After several hours of searching, they found nothing.

"Continue your search, men. There must be something they left behind."

The captain took a contingent of men and headed toward the beach. They found nothing along the way to indicate anything unusual had occurred. Frustrated, the captain stood with hands on hips, his back to the sea and looked around. Ahead about 100 yards and to his left, he saw an area that looked like it dropped away. He snapped his fingers at two of the soldiers closest to him.

"Come with me," he said and started running. He reached the drop off and looked down twenty feet. He squinted at what he saw there.

"Men," he ordered. "Bring those saddles up here to me." The captain leaned back on his heels and laughed loudly. "Well, I'll be damned! There's our proof, gentlemen. Indeed there was a rescue and they even used our own horses! The Bey will be pleased with what we have found."

By the time the captain returned to the main road, his officers had more news. They had found the bodies of the eight murdered guards buried not far from the main road.

They loaded the guards' bodies onto horses and returned to Tunis.

The captain smiled to himself. "This will make the Bey a happy man. He'll probably give me a promotion!"

He spurred his horse to a faster gait. He was anxious for his reward.

~~~

The Bey felt vindicated when he was shown the proof that there had been a rescue. Now he was more determined than ever to have revenge. It didn't take him long to come up with a plan. He was convinced that this time he would successfully destroy the infidels once and for all.

He immediately ordered six small but fast dhows to cross the Mediterranean and locate the HMS Aggressor, then instructed them to return to Algiers with that information. Meanwhile, the Bey took two galley ships, readied them for sea, manned them with the best captains, soldiers, and crew available and gave them their mission. The ships were already lightly armed but more cannon were placed on board. Each ship held fifty galley slaves whose rowing strength provided reliable and certain speed even when the sails were not in use. The ships were to wait in Algiers until they were informed of the enemy ship's location and then stalk her. The Bey's order had been clear. Surround the HMS Aggressor, sink her, and leave no survivors.

When the British ship was spotted headed east away from Gibraltar, two dhows turned to report the sighting to the galley ships waiting in Algiers. The other four dhows continued to track their prey. They stayed well back, out of the view of the larger ship. Even though they could still see the Aggressor's masthead, they knew that because they were so much smaller and rode lower in the water, the earth's curvature hid them from view.

When the Bey's two galley ships and six dhows reached a rendezvous on the southern coast of Sicily, the galley captains formed their strategy. They would plan their attack just before dawn when many of the Aggressor's crew were still sleeping. One galley would hit the starboard side and one would attack on the port side. As soon as the enemy was fully engaged, the smaller ships would close in for the kill.

~~~

The HMS Aggressor's lookout, high on the masthead, was not asleep. He rotated 360-degrees. As he again looked westward, he thought he saw something. He rubbed his eyes, then lifted the telescope again to his right eye. The lackluster moon was low in the night sky but provided just enough light that the lookout was sure of what he saw.

"Ahoy! Captain. Ships astern!"

The Captain had just come on deck and taken the helm. Now the first mate took the wheel as the Captain rushed to the stern for a closer look.

"Ah, yes. I see them. God! It looks like a small fleet!" He sounded the alarm for all hands on deck.

John was the first to stand by his side. "What is it, Captain?" He lifted a telescope to his own eye and answered his own question. "Looks like we've going to be attacked."

The Captain continued to keep an eye on the approaching vessels. "Yes, it does. If I were a betting man, I'd say our friend, the Bey of

Tunis, has learned about the rescue and has sent his navy to retaliate. Look at the smaller ships coming up behind the galleys. I think they intend to smother us. Not if I can help it, by God! John, order two of your men to the masthead to pick off as many as they can, especially those who might be climbing the rigging for better shots of their own. Your other marines should stand at the ready by the rails. At my command, they will sweep the enemy's decks and shoot anyone in sight."

John ordered his men into positions and then he turned back to listen to the Captain as he gave orders to his other officers.

When they were within one hundred yards, the galleys fanned out so one could come up on each side of the Aggressor.

Captain Gray steered the ship to the starboard so that it looked as though she might intersect the path of the galley approaching on the starboard side. Then deftly, he turned the ship ninety degrees to port and crossed directly in front of the other galley's bow.

"Open fire!" he shouted.

A roar filled the air as cannons fired at the bow of the enemy ship below. Soon, the galley stopped dead in the water.

The Aggressor didn't hesitate. She made a short loop around the damaged galley and continued her barrage. Because the galley sat low in the water, like a sitting duck, the guns from the British ship shot away her mast and killed or wounded many of her crew.

Next, the Captain headed the ship straight for the center of the fleet of smaller boats that were fast approaching. He shouted new commands to his first mate and John.

"Kill every man who shows his head."

The gunners showed no mercy. In a few passes, they destroyed all that, a moment ago, might have represented a threat. The ships out of range turned to run for cover.

With the dhows no longer a threat, the Captain turned his attention back to the two galleys. He felt confident he was winning this battle. With determination, he approached the remaining galley at extreme range for his guns. Some of the rounds fell short, but many hit home. He knew the enemy's guns could not reach him so he smoothly turned across the galley's stern and raked her with all his port cannon.

Now, the Aggressor was posed mid-way between the two galleys. From each side, she pummeled the ships with cannon fire and gunfire until they both raised a white flag of surrender.

Within minutes, the marines boarded each vessel and first removed the galley slaves who had not been killed. The surviving crew were set adrift in the galley's own boats. Helplessly, the Tunisians watched as the marines set mines in the galleys and detonated them. Moments later, the little ships exploded into a thousand pieces and sank to the bottom of the sea.

The HMS Aggressor, fresh from another victory at sea changed her course and sailed to the coast of Sicily where she released the non-Christian slaves. Days later, the Aggressor sailed into Marseille and released the Christian slaves to the British consul.

Captain Gray was well satisfied. He had not lost the life of one of his men in the battle with the Bey's fleet.

The Bey, on the other hand, had lost his men, his ships, and his pride.

~~~

When the Aggressor reached Gibraltar, she was met by a courier vessel with good news. She was to immediately return to her home port in Plymouth.

There was sad news to. Several months ago, King William had been thrown from his horse and had later died. Queen Anne, daughter of King James II had ascended the throne.

The King is dead! Long live the Queen!

-o-

CHAPTER 22

"Miss Betsy! Miss Betsy!" Annie yelled as she lifted her skirts and started up the staircase. "Come quick! He's home! Sir John is home!"

Betsy handed the baby to Claudette and ran to the top of the staircase just as the front door opened. Her heart raced as John, all smiles, came through the doorway.

"John!" Betsy couldn't believe her eyes. He really was home!

John saw Betsy at the top of the stairs. He dropped his bag and ran to the steps, taking them two at a time. He met her halfway and threw his arms around her. His bear hug squeezed the air from her lungs and she couldn't say a word. She didn't have to. He said it all.

"Oh, Betsy, my darling wife. I've missed you so much. I'm so glad to be home." He released his grip and held her at arm's length. "Let me look at you. You're even more beautiful than when I left."

Finally she could breathe. "You're home! Thank God you're home!"

They stared at each other for a few moments; afraid to blink for fear this was all just an illusion. Then his lips met hers; hesitant at first, then with a hint of the passion that would come later when they were alone.

Annie broke the spell. "Okay, you two. You need to be alone because *I know* there's a lot for you to talk about." She winked at Betsy knowingly. "I'll call you when supper is ready."

Their eyes stayed locked on each other as, arm-in-arm, they climbed the stairs to their quarters. John closed the door behind them and kissed Betsy again and again; soft, moist kisses that sent chills through her body.

He needs to stop, she thought, *I have to tell him.* She wanted him to keep kissing her until her lips were raw, until her body screamed for more. With every bit of strength she could muster, she pulled away from him.

His eyes were glassy and he reached for her lips again.

She pulled back and took both of his hands in hers. "Darling," she said. "Let's sit down. I have something to tell you."

He pulled her close again. "You can tell me later. But first, I need to kiss you again."

This time his kiss was deep and his hands began caressing her.

"John, wait!" Betsy moved across the room to the settee.

John frowned as he followed her. Just then, Meggie started crying. Puzzled, John glanced toward their bedroom.

"It's all right, Claudette. Bring her to me." Betsy hurried to the bedroom door and took the baby from Claudette's arms. With tears in her eyes and a smile on her face, Betsy walked toward her husband.

John sat still, staring at his wife. His face paled and his mouth dropped open.

Betsy sat beside him and pulled the blanket away from the baby's face.

"This is your daughter, John," Betsy said softly. "Her name is Meggie."

John was tongue-tied. He looked at Betsy, and then at the baby, then back again at Betsy. Finally, he found his voice.

"How…when…why didn't you…?"

Betsy giggled. "I didn't find out until after you left. I wanted to tell you but I knew you'd worry."

John's face softened. "When was she born?"

"On Sunday, October 8."

John felt a lump in his throat. "May I hold her?" he asked.

Betsy nodded and placed the infant in his arms. Meggie opened her eyes and focused on John. Almost on cue, as though she already knew how to twist this man around her finger, she cooed.

That was all it took. Now there was another love in John's life. Tenderly, he kissed her fingers. It must have tickled because Meggie responded with a tiny laugh."

John looked at Betsy with tears in his eyes. "Thank you, my darling. You have given me the greatest gift of my life."

~~~

Dinner that night was especially merry. John didn't eat much. He held his baby daughter in his arms and couldn't take his eyes off her face, except for the times he looked at Betsy with adoration and complete devotion.

Heather and Ewin kept the conversation lively. It centered on John and his adventures, Betsy's pregnancy and delivery, and the plans for Christmas which was just a week away.

When dinner concluded, Heather reached for Meggie. "John, you and Betsy need time to be husband and wife again. Ewin and I will keep Meggie with us tonight." She stood up and pulled on Ewin's sleeve. "C'mon, Grandpa. Time for us to retire for the night." She threw a kiss to Betsy and John and quickly left the room.

John reached for Betsy's hand. He squeezed it gently. "My heart is overflowing with unspoken words and feelings I can never express. I am in awe of you and our daughter. I want to hear every detail of what you endured while I was gone. And then," he squeezed her hand again, stronger this time, "I want to hold you and kiss you and love you until we die from the ecstasy."

Betsy pushed her chair back and smiled coyly. "I think you must be reading my mind."

~~~

John didn't have much time to shop, but this was a very special Christmas; therefore, it required very special gifts. He was lucky. He found the perfect gifts as though they had been there just waiting for him to come along.

Meanwhile, on Christmas Eve morning while John was running errands, Betsy visited the local bank that held some of her funds in a numbered account. She withdrew a generous amount of cash and placed it in a large leather pouch. After returning the strongbox to the vault, she made arrangements for a bank courier to deliver the pouch to a church in the poor section of London. The giver was to remain anonymous. She smiled as she left the bank with a feeling of satisfaction. It was her way of making sure that at least some of the King's resources would be used for the people who needed it most.

And she planned to do the same thing next year and every year thereafter.

This year, Christmas was all about Meggie. It didn't matter that she was too young to appreciate gifts. Everyone in the household had gifts for Meggie.

The Admiral and Lady Bowen were delighted when Betsy invited them to spend Christmas Day with them. They, too, came bearing gifts for their godchild.

The gift exchange took place in the later afternoon just before dinner. John waited until all the gifts had been opened before he handed Betsy two red velvet boxes.

"The large one is for you; the smaller box is for Meggie," he said with a broad smile. "Merry Christmas to my two favorite girls."

Betsy anxiously opened her gift. "Oh, John!" she cried in delight as she lifted a diamond-cut gold cross necklace from the box. "It's beautiful!" she exclaimed. She lifted her hair. "Would you place it around my neck, John?"

"With pleasure," he said and stole a kiss in the process.

"Now, open Meggie's." John seemed more excited than Betsy.

Slowly, she lifted the lid. Her eyes grew large with surprise. "Look, everyone!" She held up a miniature of her own gift. "John, I love it and Meggie will love it, too. Thank you darling. It's the perfect gift."

Now it was her turn to steal two kisses from him. "One from me and one from Meggie. I'd like to give you the honor of placing it around her neck."

When John approached the baby's bassinette, Meggie recognized him immediately. She flailed her arms, kicked her legs and gave him a smile that warmed him from head to toe.

Annie came in to the parlor. "Christmas dinner is now being served. Miss Betsy, would you like for Claudette to take the baby during dinner?"

John spoke up quickly. "No thank you, Annie. We'll take the bassinette into the dining room and place it next to me."

The baby slept through the festive Christmas dinner, but John kept stealing glances at her, just to make sure she was all right.

When dinner concluded, Heather and Ewin excused themselves. The Admiral turned to John.

"I wonder if you would join me in the library for a brandy. There's something I must discuss with you."

John looked at Betsy.

"Go ahead, sweetheart," she said. "I'll take Meggie upstairs now."

"Wait, Betsy," Lady Bowen said, "I'll come with you."

Annie served the brandy, and then discreetly closed the library door behind her.

The Admiral sat down in an overstuffed leather chair, leaned back, and unbuttoned his jacket.

"Fine dinner. I always eat too much," he said and patted his stomach.

John sat across from the Admiral and waited for him to speak.

Admiral Bowen sipped his brandy, then smacked his lips. "Nothing like a stiff brandy to aid digestion." He took another sip.

"Now, John, I'll get right to the business at hand."

John squirmed in his chair. He had no idea what was coming.

The Admiral placed his brandy on a table alongside his chair, and then laced his fingers across his waist.

"This may sound like an impertinent question, but I have my reasons for asking."

John was curious. "Go ahead, sir. Ask me anything."

"Are you Catholic or Protestant?"

"I don't consider myself either, sir. I do not attend church but I certainly have a deep abiding belief in God."

"Good! Good!" The Admiral nodded his approval. "And what about Betsy?"

"Betsy was raised Catholic and I think she believes in their teachings. We were married in a Catholic church. I was baptized in that religion, but I've never followed it." He paused for a moment. "What is this all about, sir?"

Admiral Bowen picked up his brandy snifter. "Let me give you a little history lesson here. King Henry VIII split with the Pope in Rome and became head of a new Anglican Church of England. There have been papist Kings since then but the true Church of England has become powerful through the years. Our Queen Anne is Protestant. She is so strong in her belief that she never wants to see another Catholic on the throne of England. She considers it a pledge of allegiance if those around her are Protestant."

"But how does all of this affect me? I have no dealings with Her Majesty." Now John took a big sip of his brandy.

"For the moment, that is true." He leaned toward John and lowered his voice. "Trust me now, John. You know I have your best interests at heart and I wouldn't lead you astray."

"Of course I know that, sir."

"All right, then. Talk to Betsy as soon as you can. I can tell you this…it will be in your best interest if you and your wife become members of the Church of England as soon as possible."

Later when they were getting ready for bed, John told Betsy about his curious conversation with the Admiral.

"What do you think, John?"

"He made it sound as though we really don't have a choice. I never realized politics and religion were so closely entwined. But I trust him, Betsy. He assures me we'll understand all of this later. Now I'm going to ask you the same question. What do you think, Betsy?"

She climbed into bed and pulled the covers up to her chin. "When I married you, I promised to love, honor, and obey. Maybe you trust the Admiral, but I trust you, sweetheart. Whatever you decide is fine with me. I'll adjust."

Heather and Ewin returned to France just before John and Betsy were inducted into the Church of England. Betsy was sad to see her parents go, but she was glad she didn't have to explain why she switched her church loyalty. Heather was a strong Roman Catholic and Betsy knew her mother would never understand. She wasn't even sure *she* understood.

~~~

John was spending his days at the Admiralty. He was amazed at how much there was for him to learn.

One afternoon when he was knee-deep in paperwork, there was a knock on his office door.

"Come in," he said and looked up as the door opened. He was surprised to see James Marks. John stood up.

"James! What a pleasant surprise!"

The two men shook hands and exchanged pleasantries.

"How have you been, John?"

"I've been very well, thank you. Did you hear that my wife had a baby girl while we were at sea?"

James smiled pleasantly. "No, I hadn't heard. Congratulations!"

There was an awkward lull in the conversation.

"Tell me, James, what brings you here?"

"Well, I'm on official business and I need to ask you a few questions."

"Uh oh," John said. "Does this have anything to do with the rescue in Tunisia?"

"Only indirectly. Relax, John. Actually, I'm on very pleasant business. I'm not being nosey, but I have to ask you. Are you and your wife members of the Church of England?"

John couldn't believe his ears. "Why is it that everyone wants to know my religion?" He was getting a little upset.

"Simmer down, John."

"Yes! The answer is yes!" he said adamantly. "My wife and I belong to the Church of England. Anything else you want to know?"

"Just one more question and then I will give you an explanation. I know you swore allegiance to King William. Do you likewise swear allegiance to our new queen, Queen Anne?"

"I am trying hard not to take offense to your questions, James. Yes. I am a loyal British subject and I am proud to be a major in the marines. Queen Anne has my complete loyalty. I would die for her if need be." John was more than a little annoyed. "Does that answer your question?"

"It does, and thank you, John. Now let me explain both as an advisor and as a friend. There will soon be some changes in your life that will demand your loyalty. I ask you now to draw you sword, and with me as your witness, swear that you will be loyal to your Queen and this nation as long as you live. If you so swear, I know you will keep your word because you are a man of honor."

Without hesitation, John drew his sword and held it chest high between his hands. "I do so swear," John said and kissed his sword.

James was relieved. "Thank you, John. Well, that's all for today." He rose to leave. "Oh, yes," he said over his shoulder, "did I tell you your big day is coming very soon?"

John was totally bewildered. He spoke out loud although there was no one to hear him. "All this secrecy. First with the Admiral and now with Marks. Joining a church, kissing my sword. And what did he mean, 'my big day?' I have no idea what is going on!"

He didn't have to wait too long. A week later while having dinner, Annie interrupted.

"Sir, John. There are two men at the door. They say they are representatives of the Queen. I showed them into the parlor."

John almost ran to the parlor door. "Gentlemen, I am Sir John MacDonald. How can I help you?"

The gentlemen introduced themselves as Lord Wells and Lord Carrington.

"It is our pleasure to inform you that you and Lady MacDonald are scheduled for an audience with Her Majesty two days hence at eleven o'clock in the morning. It will be necessary for you to wear your uniform." Lord Wells handed John a scroll tied with ribbon. "This will outline the proper protocol. A Royal Carriage will arrive to escort you at ten o'clock."

With that, the two gentlemen shook John's hand and departed.

John was nervous when he returned to the dining room and told Betsy. "Some very strange things have been going on recently, but this is the strangest of all."

"Don't you have any idea why the Queen would summon us?" Betsy, too, was getting nervous. She couldn't help but wonder if her past was catching up to her.

John sat down and started drumming his fingers on the table. "My mind is blank, unless it has to do with my being promoted to Colonel. But why so much fanfare for a simple promotion?"

The next morning after breakfast, John and Betsy rode over to the Bowens hoping they could give them some clarification.

As always, the Bowens were delighted to see them and excited with their news.

Lady Bowen looked at her husband before she spoke. "We, too, have been invited to be there. I guess it's going to be quite an occasion. Am I right, Charles?"

Charles nodded. "Yes, my dear. It will be quite an occasion. John and I are going to talk in the library. Don't you ladies have some shopping to do?"

Lady Bowen was invaluable in helping Betsy choose the right dress. She must have tried on a dozen before they both agreed on a rich blue velvet dress that draped across her shoulders.

Claudette pinned up Betsy's hair but left some tendrils loose around her face. As a finishing touch, Betsy put on her necklace with the pear shaped sapphire. She smiled to herself. *Fit for an audience with a queen, I'd say!*

John whistled low when he saw her. "Betsy, you take my breath away." He spotted the necklace. "Your necklace is exquisite. Is it new?"

She reached up and touched the gem with her fingers. Her eyes were large and innocent. "Father gave it to me soon after he found out I was expecting a baby. I'll probably give it to Meggie someday."

John kissed her lightly. "Well, it's beautiful and so are you."

Betsy looked at her husband with approval. "And you are one handsome marine, Major MacDonald."

Annie called upstairs to say the carriage had arrived.

John clicked his heels together and offered his arm. "Shall we go, Lady MacDonald?'

"Of course! We can't keep the Queen waiting!" Betsy quipped.

When the carriage arrived at Kensington Palace, the MacDonalds were ushered inside and told to wait in a large anteroom filled with finely dressed men and perfectly coiffed women showcasing elegant dresses. Betsy wanted to pinch herself to believe she was actually waiting to see the Queen. She looked around and then spotted the Admiral and Lady Bowen who were in deep conversation with another couple. When Lady Bowen saw Betsy, she waved. Within moments they excused themselves and came over to Betsy and John.

"I have to say you are the most attractive couple here," Lady Bowen said and kissed Betsy's cheek.

The Admiral kissed Betsy's other cheek. "You look absolutely beautiful, my dear."

John felt ill at ease. "Admiral, can you tell me what's going to happen? I have no idea why we have been called here."

Admiral Bowen chuckled. "First time at court is a little overwhelming. Wait till your name is called. Then you will be escorted inside where you can wait some more. After a while, the Queen arrives. When your name is called again, you approach the throne. There's really nothing to it," he said with a sly smile.

At promptly eleven o'clock, the first names were announced in order of rank. Soon the Bowens were called.

"Here we go," Lady Bowen said as she took her husband's arm and headed toward the open doors.

One by one, the names were announced. Finally, they heard their own names announced.

"Major John MacDonald, Earl of Krieth, and Lady Betsy MacDonald.

Hearts racing and heads held high, John and Betsy entered the large throne room. Others who had entered earlier were lined up on both sides of the room. Everyone stood quietly and waited.

Music heralded the Queen's arrival. Guards in front and guards in the rear protected her. She looked straight ahead and walked between the two rows of her subjects. As she did, men bowed and ladies curtsied. When she reached the throne, she turned quite majestically and sat down.

Betsy's first impression of the Queen was one of great pity. The woman was extremely overweight and her face couldn't hide the sorrow of her personal life. Through the years, she had suffered many miscarriages and stillbirths. Only one child had survived, but he was a weak and sickly child who had died at the age of eleven.

"Oh, that poor tragic woman," Betsy murmured under her breath. She knew without question that being Queen was no compensation for losing so many children.

Several business matters were first on the Queen's agenda. Betsy watched and listened closely as the Queen considered each matter carefully before she gave her decision. Although many thought the Queen was dull, Betsy saw something different in her disposition. The woman didn't smile. Perhaps that's why people thought she was dull. Instead, Betsy saw it as unhappiness.

As names were called, each went to the Queen, bowed or curtsied, then kneeled in front of her. Betsy strained to hear what was being said.

Finally, the MacDonalds were called to come forward. Betsy felt the blood rush to her face and her knees trembled. Her heart pounded so hard she was sure everyone could hear it. It was the longest walk of her life. When they reached the throne, John and Betsy kneeled and dropped their heads in respect.

"Please rise," the Queen said.

Betsy thought she saw a hint of a smile.

"Major, I have very much been looking forward to meeting you and your beautiful wife." She paused to look around the room and slightly raised her voice so everyone in the room could hear what she had to say. "I have called you here today to give you recognition for the great service you performed for your country when you achieved the release of twelve British subjects who were cruelly captured on the high seas and taken to Africa as prisoners. Because of you and your brave marines, they have returned safely to their homes. I am sure you are unaware that two of those you rescued are my cousins. You were so busy affecting their safe return that they were never able to thank you for your courage and heroism."

John was humbled. "Thank you, your Majesty, but I must tell you that I couldn't have done it without my men. I believe they are the true heroes."

"Don't misunderstand, Major. I hold all of your men in the highest esteem. Rest assured, they will all be duly rewarded."

"Thank you, your Majesty," John said.

The Queen turned to Betsy. I understand your maiden name was Stuart."

"Yes, your Royal Highness," Betsy answered.

"Ah, then we must be kinsman. I'm sure you know I am a Stuart as well. How is your last name spelled?"

"S-t-e-w-a-r-t, your Majesty."

Now the Queen did smile.

"Well, now. I really prefer that spelling but my family changed it years ago when everyone was so impressed with the French. Since it is basically the same family, I think I shall call you cousin."

Betsy was surprised and very pleased. "Thank you. You do me great honor, your Royal Highness."

The Queen nodded to Betsy and then looked at John."

"Major," she said. I believe that you should be rewarded for your courage and your service to my family and all of England. Therefore, I invest you with the title of Marquis of Steddenham and all the properties and revenues presently associated with that title. My secretary will see that you have all the papers soon. Congratulations! I wish England had a thousand more just like you. Now," she clasped her hands together, "I am inviting you and wife along with a few others to join me for dinner this evening. You may withdraw now and my staff will soon take you to the palace drawing room where you will be served some light refreshments."

John and Betsy bowed low and started to withdraw to the station they had occupied when they had entered. A marshal stopped them and escorted them to a position closer to the Queen.

"You will stand here M'lord and form a reception line.

John and Betsy exchanged looks of disbelief. Betsy pointed at John, "Marquis!"

He pointed at her, "Marquise."

They tried to stifle their excitement until the Queen departed. Soon they were swarmed with well-wishers. One of them was James Marks who pumped John's hand up and down several times. He was all smiles.

"Didn't I tell you your big day was coming?"

John had to laugh. "I had no idea how big. I'm still in a state of disbelief. For whatever part you played in all this, James, I thank you."

The Admiral's pride showed on his face. "You deserve it, John. I'm so proud of you, son. Sincere congratulations from both of us."

~~~

That night, John and Betsy almost fell into bed. They were both emotionally drained. It had been exhausting, but probably the most exciting day of their lives.

They turned on their sides and stared at each other.

"Just think, John, this morning I was simply Lady MacDonald. Tonight I'm a Marquise."

"Oh, the difference a day makes," John said. "Tell me, Marquise, are you too tired to celebrate?"

She put her arm around him and answered him with a long, warm kiss.

-o-

CHAPTER 23

A few days later, a Queen's courier delivered the title and deeds. Betsy was as excited as John as he read the documents.

She bounced up and down like a child and tried to read over his shoulder. "Read it to me, John. Don't make me wait. Tell me! Tell me!" she begged.

"There's a note here from the Queen herself. She explains that the previous owner of the estate died a few months ago and left no heirs, so it was returned to the Queen to be used at her discretion...Oh, Betsy!"

"What John? Don't keep me in suspense!"

"Betsy!" John was obviously in disbelief. "The estate is situated fifty kilometers northeast of London and encompasses *seven thousand acres!*"

"Seven *thousand* acres?" she repeated.

"That's what this says. And along with the three thousand acres I will inherit from my father as Earl of Krieth, that's a total of ten thousand acres! And the best part is that both the titles and the land are hereditary."

Betsy was beginning to see the scope of this. "That means our children will inherit them."

"Exactly! Betsy, God has smiled on us." John couldn't stop grinning.

"When can we go see it?" Betsy wondered.

"Soon. Very soon." Mentally, he was already making plans.

While John made arrangements to inspect the property the following week, Betsy packed one bag for each of them and two bags for Meggie.

John looked at the baby's two bags. "Do you think the baby will be all right?" he asked. "She's never traveled before."

Betsy wasn't the least bit concerned. "I've packed everything she'll possibly need. Now that she sleeps through the night, she's become a very good baby. Don't worry. She'll be fine."

It was raining when they left London but by evening, the sky was clear and they were only twenty kilometers from their destination.

John was relieved that Meggie was such a good traveler. She slept a lot, cooed and smiled when she was awake, and seldom cried. It had been a very pleasant day. They spent the night in an inn and hurriedly left the next morning, eager to reach Steddenham.

There wasn't much conversation. The baby slept and Betsy and John were each lost in their own thoughts.

As they approached the entrance to Steddenham, Betsy felt a rush. On either side of the driveway was a high stone wall. A ten-foot high stone archway bridged the driveway. Across the arch hung a weathered sign that read "Steddenham." The carriage turned off the main road and rumbled under the arch. Both sides of the driveway were lined with giant oak trees. Betsy could see that the branches had been trained to form a canopy over the drive.

I can't wait to see it in the summer, she thought.

She handed the baby to John and leaned over to look out the coach window.

"I see it, John! I can see the manor house. It's huge!"

The carriage continued for another two hundred yards before the driveway ended and then circled around to the front of the house. A large stone portico extended over the front drive so that family and visitors were protected from the weather.

At first glance, the three-storied stone structure seemed to be in good repair. There were more windows than Betsy could count at the moment. The entrance consisted of mahogany double doors, each with a large brass knocker.

John handed Meggie back to Betsy. "Well, Marquise of Steddenham, would you like to see the inside of your new home?" he said as he guided her toward the front door.

"Indeed, I would, Marquis of Steddenham."

The doors swung open as they approached. An elderly, white-haired gentleman welcomed them.

"Welcome to Steddenham. My name is Oliver Stanton. I am the estate manager. Please come inside."

Betsy noticed how stooped he was. His complexion was sallow and he coughed frequently. Mr. Stanton seemed extremely ill. She looked around. The foyer was expansive, but she noticed that the floor looked dull and scuffed. Worn chairs were lined up like soldiers around the perimeter of the room. Betsy thought it looked like a large waiting room of some kind.

Centered high above was a massive chandelier hung on chains that could be lowered so the fifty candles could be easily lighted. Faded tapestries hung on walls on either side of the foyer. A wide staircase curved to the second floor. Betsy was awed. She couldn't wait to see the rest of the house. Her reverie was broken by Oliver Stanton.

"The staff will take your bags upstairs. Meanwhile, I will show you the house. Would you like some refreshments first?"

John glanced at Betsy and answered for them both. "Thank you, Mr. Stanton. I think some refreshment would be well received after our long journey."

Mr. Stanton smiled at the bundle in Betsy's arms. "Your baby is beautiful, M'Lady. Please follow me."

He led them to a large drawing room off the foyer. This room, too, was large but looked inviting. The focal point was a large fireplace with a roaring fire. A large area rug covered the center of the oak floor. Windows were heavily draped and let in very little light.

They sat in comfortable but worn chairs. Stanton rang for the housekeeper. The tall, thin woman entered carrying a tray.

"Hello, my name is Sylvia. Welcome to Steddenham." She dropped a curtsy. "I knew you'd want refreshments right away. I brought tea and biscuits."

Her long face was framed with steel gray hair. She wasn't a pretty woman but she had a ready smile. Betsy liked her.

"Thank you for being so efficient, Sylvia," Betsy said. "I'm looking forward to getting to know you."

"Thank you, M'Lady." Sylvia curtsied again and left the room.

"Before I show you the house," Mr. Stanton said as he buttered a biscuit, "I'd like to give you some of its history. The previous owner was Marquis Colin Andrews. His family owned Steddenham for generations. But when he died, the lineage ended. He left no heirs.

During the last fifteen years of the Marquis' life, he was in poor health and suffered with failing eyesight. I'm sure you have already noticed that there is much in disrepair. The Marquis just kind of let things go. I think he lost his will to live. He made no effort to replenish stock or increase the crop harvest. Furniture became worn and faded but his poor eyesight prevented him from seeing that. During the last five years of his life, he seldom went outdoors and there were no visitors to the manor house. It was very sad. Once so healthy and robust, he became a living dead man." Stanton smiled. "But now you are here. I feel certain that happiness will again fill the rooms of this house."

John agreed. "I can assure you that if my wife has anything to do with it, happiness and laughter will not only return but will become a mainstay." He squeezed Betsy's hand. "Ready to see the rest of the house?"

Betsy finished her last sip of tea. "I can't wait," she said.

In addition to the foyer and drawing room, the first floor consisted of a large library with bookshelves on each of three walls. It, too, had a large fireplace. The dining room looked as though it could easily accommodate thirty guests. A large candle-lighted chandelier hung above the long oak dining table. The kitchen and pantry took up the rear end of the house. Betsy saw similarities to the MacDonald house in London but the rooms were larger.

The second floor had two wings. The master wing included a drawing room, sitting room, master bedroom, and a nursery with an adjoining room for the nursemaid. The other wing had four bedrooms and another nursery with adjoining quarters for a nursemaid. The third floor consisted of seven bedrooms and was restricted to the servants.

The commonality throughout was the rundown condition that Betsy noticed in every room.

At dinner, John informed Mr. Stanton of his agenda during their brief stay.

"My wife and I only plan to be here for a few days but during that time I want to learn of any and all problems the estate is facing. I'd like an overview of the staff, expenses, and the estate's income. I hope you will be candid with me in giving me your opinion on all matters at hand."

For the first time, Oliver Stanton really smiled. There was visible relief on his face.

"There is so much to tell you I hardly know where to start, but I'll do my best. I'll begin with the staff. Most of us were young when Lord Andrews inherited the estate forty-five years ago. The truth is that we are all getting old and many of us find it difficult to put in a full day's work. I include myself in this category because I have become ill and it is getting very difficult to keep up with so much work.

"The estate still shows a small profit each year but it keeps diminishing every year. After the staff has been paid, there is very little remaining to keep the house and grounds in good repair. Some staff has not been paid full wages in some time. We are now at the point that I will have to terminate at least one staff member so we don't go into the red. You will see for yourself tomorrow when I show you the ledgers."

"Are there able-bodied hands for hire in the surrounding countryside?" John wanted to know.

"Oh, aye, there are but what will become of the old people if they are replaced by younger ones?"

"Don't worry about that. In Scotland, the landlord gives the elderly employees a small fixed income on which to live. They normally stay around and tend the house, garden and the grounds if they still wish to continue working. If not, they are permitted to stay on the premises in their own small cottages.

Mr. Stanton was genuinely surprised. "Is that what you plan to do here, sir?"

"As long as it is in my power, no one will suffer because he is old. I'll meet with the staff tomorrow morning and pay them their back wages at that time. Get a good night's sleep, Mr. Stanton, and we'll continue in the morning.

After Meggie was tucked in for the night, John and Betsy finally had a chance to talk.

"My God, Betsy," John seemed almost overwhelmed. "There is so much to do here. I had no idea! I'm afraid I wasn't really prepared and I'm sure I didn't bring along enough money to really get started on all the necessary repairs."

Betsy pulled her chair closer to John. "I have some surprisingly good news for you. I'm not sure why, but before we left London, I had an impulse to bring some of my money along, just in case."

"Your money? What do you mean? I don't understand," John said honestly.

"I haven't had a chance to tell you until now. You were gone for so long and so much has happened since your return. You see, my family has a considerable amount of money that has been invested wisely through the years. When Father found out I was going to have a baby, he set up an account for me in London and has been making monthly deposits to it ever since. I did not need much money while you were gone, so the balance has grown considerably. Your income is more than enough to support our London residence. We can use my money to finance the renovation of our new home at Steddenham."

She hated lying to him but she knew she could never, never tell him the real truth of the source of her family's money.

"I don't know what to say," John said.

"You don't have to say anything. We are more than husband and wife. We are partners." Betsy got serious. "John, you haven't told me, but I know you have to go to sea again soon. While you are gone, I want you to know I will take care of things here and in London so that when you return, you'll be simply *amazed* at what has been accomplished."

He grabbed her and kissed her hard. "What did I ever do to deserve a gem like you? I have been so worried about leaving you again and worried about what to do here when I can't oversee any of it. You have no idea of the weight you have lifted from my shoulders. "Thank you, my darling."

They both slept well that night and awoke refreshed and eager to meet a new challenge.

After breakfast, John walked around the grounds before heading toward a large solidly built shed. He entered and was surprised to see a coach covered with canvas. He was startled when someone behind him spoke.

"She's a real beauty, M'Lord. I have taken care of her for forty-odd years now and she is as good as new. Would you like to take a look at her?"

John turned to see a man standing behind him just inside the front door. Because the morning light was behind him, the man was in shadow and his face couldn't be seen.

"Yes, I would," John said as he extended his hand. I am Major John MacDonald, the new owner of Steddenham. And your name, sir?"

The man stepped out of the shadows. His face was wrinkled but his blue eyes were bright.

"Skugs, sir, if you please, Toby Skugs. Everyone here calls me Toby." He walked over to the coach. "I'll take the cover off so you can see what she looks like."

John watched as Toby removed the cover. Slowly he walked around her. The coach was classic and in beautiful condition. John was amazed to see the Steddenham coat of arms emblazoned on the both doors of the carriage.

"She looks roadworthy." John surmised.

"Aye, she is. She's my baby and I take great pride in keeping her in tip-top shape. She hasn't been out of the barn in a year but I know she'll perform perfectly," Toby replied proudly.

"Good then," John said with a broad smile. "Bring her around to the house at two this afternoon."

Meanwhile Betsy met with the household staff. There was Sylvia, the housekeeper. Eunice was the upstairs maid, while Stella took care of the first floor. The cook was Alice and her assistant's name was Edythe. The only male in the house was William who handled all indoor repairs and supervised the groundskeepers.

Betsy felt outnumbered. They all looked at her as though they expected to be criticized or even fired.

Their faces relaxed when Betsy assured them their positions were secure as long as they did their jobs. Betsy smiled sweetly.

"I hope you give me time to learn all your names and get to know each of you well. You'll find I am easy to get along with. I hope I find you the same." She was ready to dismiss them when she remembered. "Oh, yes, as soon as my husband returns, you will all receive back wages and our assurance that in the future you will all be paid on a timely basis."

She must have said some magic words because they all left with a smile on their face and a bounce in their step.

~~~

John wanted Betsy with him when he and Mr. Stanton reconciled the books. She agreed.

"If I'm going to take charge of the repairs, I certainly need to know where we stand financially."

The process didn't take long. Mr. Stanton had done a fine job of keeping records. They found only minor errors, probably due to Mr. Stanton's failing health.

When they were finished, Betsy took John aside. "I have made a decision and I hope you approve. This is our home now and it needs our full attention. After you return to sea, I will bring Claudette and Brian here with me to Steddenham."

John looked surprised. "You plan to leave London society?"

"Of course. Our home is here now. We can still go to London whenever the spirit moves us. But we have a family here now. They need to know that they are safe and secure as well."

John shook his head in sheer wonder of this woman. "Betsy, you continually surprise me. You have hit me with several bombshells. I never dreamed you had money and I never thought you would so willingly leave London."

She thought for a minute. "Perhaps I can explain it another way. Our home in London is not *really* our home. It's your father's. Oh, I know it will be ours someday, but Steddenham is *our* home, yours and mine and Meggie's. When we are finished with all the repairs and renovations and when it is once again making a healthy profit, it will become a part of us, we become a part of it and the two can never be separated."

John just kept shaking his head. "You amaze me, Betsy. You really do."

Promptly at two o'clock, a carriage rumbled up to the portico. Betsy ran to a window and looked out.

"What a beautiful carriage," she said. "I wonder whose it is. Are we having visitors?"

"Let's go see," John said with a gleam in his eye.

They grabbed their coats and went outside. John greeted the driver pleasantly.

"You're right on time, Toby. Come and meet your new mistress."

Toby stepped down and doffed his cap. "M'Lady," he said.

Betsy looked from John to Toby. "What a wonderful coach."

"I've taken care of it for years, M'Lady, now it is yours."

Betsy was so surprised she hardly knew what to say. "Thank you, Toby. Thank you, John. It's the most elegant carriage I've ever seen. And it really is ours?"

John and Toby nodded simultaneously. Then John turned his attention to the horses. "These animals look old and sluggish. I think we should plan to purchase four more young, strong, and steady mounts. Perhaps we could buy some chestnuts."

"Well, sir, it so happens there is to be a market in the village the day after tomorrow. Would you care to go?"

"Yes, I would. But I know very little about horseflesh. Is there anyone here who does?"

"As a matter of fact, there is. His name is Harry Leach. He was a horse trader once but had an accident a few years ago that left him with a bad limp. Lord Andrews hired him to tend the horses. He really knows his animals."

"Good! Why don't you both plan on being here at the house and ready to go at 7 o'clock Thursday morning?" He looked at Betsy. "Want to join us? We're going in the coach."

"Just try and stop me!" she said jokingly.

The market was held in a small village nestled in a valley. Sturdy corrals had been built to handle the various livestock traded there. Onlookers stopped and stared as the classy carriage, bearing the

Steddenham coat of arms, rolled up to the outside of the market and came to a stop. Toby and Harry dismounted from the carriage, opened the doors, and lowered the steps for Betsy and John. As they walked toward the horse corrals, people began to whisper but smiled at the newcomers. John doffed his hat to the women and returned their smiles. Betsy also smiled as she bowed her head to everyone. Toby stayed with the coach but Harry Leach followed behind, using his stick to help keep up.

Harry knew just what to do. He first saw four dapple-gray draught horses and took time to carefully examine them.

"These are good horses, Sir John. I recommend you consider them for purchase."

John was obviously disappointed. "I was really hoping we'd find some chestnuts."

"Yessir, "Harry explained, "but you ain't likely to find no better horses wherever you look."

Betsy put her hand on her husband's arm. "John, if Harry thinks they are good horses, let's buy them now. Harry can keep looking until he can find your chestnuts. The carriage needs a good team now. Besides, they will also have many uses around the estate even if you do find your chestnuts."

John brightened. "All right, Betsy. If these animals are reasonably priced, we shall have them hitched right away and lead the others home."

Harry nodded his head and went to bargain with the owners. When the sale was completed, John asked Harry to help him select two good saddle horses, one for himself and one for Betsy.

Before they left for home, they had purchased not two but three saddle horses and had made arrangements for the delivery of a dozen sheep, fifty chickens, two cows and some geese.

"And John, this is just a start," Betsy said. "By the time you return to Steddenham, we'll be turning a tidy profit."

"I don't doubt it, my love. I don't doubt it one bit," John said and gave her a pinch on her backside. "Now! Get on your new horse. I'll race you home!"

Friday, Saturday, and Sunday were busy days. Betsy made a list of repairs to be made in order of importance. Outbuildings, fences, and corrals were high on the list, along with road repairs. Next she compiled a list of immediate repairs to the house. Painting projects could wait until warmer weather. Landscaping, too, would be a spring and summer project.

Before they returned to London on Monday morning, Betsy told Mr. Stanton she would notify him when she would return to take permanent residence.

John let Betsy know how impressed he was.

"If I didn't know it before, I surely know it now. You *are* the Marquise of Steddenham in every sense of the word. I am so proud of you. Steddenham will one day be returned to her former glory. All because of you."

When they arrived in London, their attention was quickly turned to other matters. Betsy sorted through the mail and was excited when she opened an invitation to a late winter party scheduled for the end of February. She quickly responded to the R.S.V.P.

Admiral Bowen kept John busy with his venting about the fact there had been countless delays with his ships and only two of his squadron had actually entered the Mediterranean.

"Dammit, John! I was supposed to have twenty warships but now I only have ten. I wanted a real show of force on land *and* on sea. Those ten ships won't carry the number of men I need. I don't suppose you have any ideas, do you?"

John thought for a minute. "Well," he said and paused. "What if we put as many extra marines as possible on four of the largest ships? They would present a large striking force for any necessary land action. Of course, I would need a few weeks to train them. What do you think?"

The Admiral nodded enthusiastically. "It sounds practical. Let me run it past the Admiralty for their input. By Jove, John, I think it will work."

The Admiralty was looking for a solution, any solution, and quickly approved the idea. However, they did stress to Admiral Bowen the importance that all military branches be prepared to defend against future attacks by the Bey of Tunis on land as well as on the sea.

"The western Mediterranean is a hotspot now, Charles," he was told, and we must stand ready."

Once John received approval, he began intense training of the new recruits.

John and Betsy knew the time was fast approaching when John would once again board the HMS Aggressor. In the evening, John stayed close to Betsy and held Meggie until she fell asleep.

Although he hated to leave for even one evening, John was looking forward to the party his friend Geoff Burns was hosting. It would be their last chance to attend a social evening for many months to come.

The party seemed especially festive. There was dancing, much laughter, and bottomless glasses of spirits.

As the evening progressed, Betsy became increasingly uneasy. She noticed that a man kept staring at her. Wherever she moved in the room, he seemed to be there, too. She tried not to notice, but out of the corner of her eye she could see him watching. Once she noticed he leaned close to a companion and whispered as he gestured in her direction.

John was preoccupied with a friend and she tried to get his attention. "Who's that man in the uniform over there? He keeps looking at me."

John took a cursory glance. "He's a major in the Queen's service, but I don't know him." He looked at her lovingly. "You're beautiful, Betsy. Every man in the room looks at you."

His words weren't comforting. For some reason she couldn't explain, the major made her skin crawl.

At her first opportunity, she cornered Geoff. "Who is that soldier over there? Is he a friend of yours?"

Geoff looked casually toward the soldier. "Oh, that is Major Dirk Campbell."

Just hearing the name Campbell sent a chill through her.

Geoff continued offhandedly, "He's a new acquaintance. He's on business here in London so I thought I'd introduce him to a few of my friends. Would you like an introduction?"

"No thank you, Geoff. I was just wondering," she said and moved away quickly. His explanation did little to ease her mind.

John noticed her slight frown and took her arm. "Come, my darling, let's dance once more before the night comes to an end."

She looked into her husband's loving eyes as he twirled her round and round. She soon forgot all about the strange Major Dirk Campbell.

~~~

Time was running short. John would soon be leaving for sea duty and he and his wife had a lot to discuss before he left. Betsy was eager to share her plan for the renovating of Steddenham.

"If things go well, most of the work will be completed by the time you return," she told him.

John took out a pocket ledger and showed it to Betsy. "This is how much cash you have on hand right now. I've made arrangements for my pay to come directly to you. I calculate that your income together with mine should be enough to complete most of the repairs."

Betsy took the ledger and looked at the figures. "Indeed, John. I'm sure I'll have enough money." Her eyes locked on his. "Meggie and I are going to miss you terribly, you know."

"This is hard for me, too," he assured her. "Now there are two of you for me to miss." He held her in his arms and kissed her tenderly. "One more thing, Betsy. I have hired two of my best men to stay with you at Steddenham during my absence."

"Who are they? Do I know them?" she asked.

"You might have met them once before. We were soldiers together when I fought in the Low Countries. Their names are Robert Keith and Stanley Bruce. I trust them completely. They will contact you soon after I leave."

It was another rainy morning when John left. This time she and Meggie stood at the door and watched him as his carriage disappeared into the morning mist.

Although she hated seeing him go, it was different this time. Now she had Meggie. And she had Steddenham. Between the two, there wouldn't be time for her to mope around. Except for the nights, after Meggie was asleep. In the quiet moments before she fell asleep, she knew her heart would ache for her husband.

~~~

Since the Admiral was also at sea, Lady Bowen spent many days with Betsy. She loved watching Meggie grow and was grateful to be an important part of the child's life.

She enjoyed listening to Betsy talk about Steddenham.

"How soon do you plan to return?" she asked.

"Within a fortnight, I would say. There is a lot of packing to do. Claudette and her husband Brian are coming with me, too. Then there are my two bodyguards," she said with a chuckle.

"Bodyguards?"

Betsy explained why John had hired them. "I must admit, I'll feel better having them around. So many of the staff at Steddenham are quite elderly and couldn't provide much protection should we ever need it."

"I've been thinking about this for some time, Betsy. What would you think if I came along, too? With Charles gone, there's nothing to tie me to London. I think if we put our artistic minds together, we'll turn Steddenham into a masterpiece."

"Lady Bowen!" Betsy was thrilled. "What a wonderful idea! I'd love to have you as my companion. You can stay as long as you wish."

"There's only one thing, my dear." Lady Bowen became stern but there was a twinkle in her eye. "You must call me Jane."

Betsy started to protest.

"Ah ah ah!" Lady Bowen held up her hand. "I insist."

Betsy smiled at her good friend. "I'm happy and proud to call you Jane. I love you as much as I love my own dear mother. You are the kindest friend that anyone could have." Betsy's own eyes misted as she saw the tears in Jane Bowen's eyes.

Jane tried to lighten the mood. "Besides, you need to have someone launch your social life in the region and you can be assured that when the word gets out that there is a Duchess and a Marquise in the area, they will come flocking to your door!"

Their relationship now took a new direction. The age difference and social status were no longer important. They could simply relate to another on a deeper level, one of love and friendship.

Betsy was surprised the next morning when the butler announced that her father was in the downstairs drawing room. She flew down the stairs and rushed into his arms.

"Father! It's wonderful to see you. I didn't know you were coming? Is Mother with you?"

"No, lass. I'm afraid your Grandmere is ill. Your mother is with her."

"And Grandpere?"

"He is well, dear. And how are you?"

Betsy laughed. "I'm fine. Meggie is growing and John is at sea. What else is new?"

"After I received your letter that was chock full of all your happy news, I decided we needed to talk in person about our finances. I want you to continue using caution so that no one suspects you have immense wealth. Renovations at Steddenham will be costly. I've been thinking a lot about this and here is what I want you to do. I'm sure you have some idea of how much money you will need. I've come up with a ploy that would satisfy any busybody. Each month write a letter to me requesting a portion of the amount you need. I have already discussed this with our banker, Jacob Levine. I want you to give him authorization to withdraw that amount from your Paris account and deposit it into my account. Then I, in turn, will send it to you as a "gift" so no one will suspect that you are financing this yourself. I'm sure you are aware that the English and French are bickering again and in the American colonies, they are even doing battle with one another.

Betsy shook her head sadly. "Sometimes I think humans will never outgrow war. They never seem to understand that war is never an answer. And as to your idea, Father, it's fine with me. I did tell John that I have an income from you so he understands that much of the renovation will be coming from my side of the family."

"He's all right with that?"

Betsy nodded. "Yes, he is. And thank you, Father for all you've done…and keep on doing." She kissed her father's cheek. "I don't know what I'd do without you."

Ewin rose from his chair and pulled Betsy to her feet. "Now," he said, "I want to see my granddaughter."

~~~

Spring was fast approaching and Betsy was anxious to leave for Steddenham. She was careful to buy as many supplies as she could to take with her. This included the purchase of a small carriage that John could use to go to and from Plymouth.

Jane insisted on using her carriage for the trip. For one thing, it was quite large and could carry several trunks. Secondly, it would provide her with easy transportation when she returned to London.

Annie found it hard to say goodbye. She cried and didn't care who saw her tears.

"Miss Betsy, I'll miss you and Meggie so much. The house will seem big and empty without you."

"We'll miss you, too, Annie." She gave her a big hug. "I'll never find another housekeeper as good as you. Are you sure you won't change your mind and come with us."

Annie dried her eyes. "Why, this house would fall apart without me to run things, now wouldn't it?"

Betsy had to agree. "You're one in a million, Annie."

Annie stood by the front steps and waved until the carriages were out of sight.

Betsy, Meggie, Jane, and the two bodyguards rode in the Bowen carriage; Claudette and Brian rode in the smaller carriage.

They rode for several hours before stopping at an inn for refreshments. Betsy took Jane by the hand and led her to a small table against the wall.

She was beaming. "Can you keep a secret?" Betsy asked.

Jane nodded enthusiastically.

"Well, it won't be a secret for long, but I wanted you to know." She giggled. "As usual, John will be the last to know." She stopped and waited for a reaction from Jane.

"Well," Jane said. "Tell me!" Then it dawned on her. "Oh, Betsy!"

Now it was Betsy's turn to nod enthusiastically. "Yes! I'm going to have another baby!"

During the rest of the afternoon, Betsy and Jane exchanged knowing glances and snickered a lot. Robert Keith and Stanley Bruce exchanged glances of utter confusion.

~~~

Oliver Stanton was waiting by the portico when the two carriages arrived. The house staff was lined up just inside the front door. Betsy introduced the staff; then, without hesitation, she took charge.

"Eunice. I would like you to take Mr. Keith and Mr. Bruce to their rooms. I will show Lady Bowen her room. Claudette and Brian will stay in the nursemaid room next to Meggie's nursery.

"Alice, there will be seven for dinner tonight in the formal dining room." She turned to Mr. Stanton. "Oliver, I would like you to join us for dinner tonight if it is convenient."

"Yes, M'Lady," he said. "I'd be honored."

Meggie started crying and Betsy held her against her shoulder and patted her back. "If you'll excuse me, I need to feed my daughter now."

She walked toward the staircase. Jane and Claudette followed. Brian stayed to help unload the carriages.

Mr. Stanton stood by and watched with pleasure as the men quickly and easily moved the luggage, boxes, and crates to their assigned rooms. He couldn't help but smile. "Sure is nice to have young people around again," he said out loud.

Eunice kept Meggie while dinner was being served. Again, Betsy led the conversation.

"Robert and Stanley, I want you both to feel free to investigate and become familiar with the entire estate. If you see anything that needs attention, please let me know. Mr. Stanton, you have served the estate well for many years. Now it's time for you to relax a bit. You can do as much or as little as you want. Brian, along with those we hired when John was here, will do the heavy work. You've earned a rest and I want you to be healthy enough to enjoy it."

"Thank you, M'Lady," Oliver said sincerely. "You are most kind."

"Brian, I would like you to help William around the house as much as you can. Otherwise, I want you to oversee the outside repairs as well as supervise the gardeners."

"Of course, Miss Betsy. I'll do whatever I can."

She turned to Claudette. "Dear, I want you to continue looking after Meggie. She's getting to be a little leery of strangers and she loves you very much." Now she turned her attention to Jane. "You and I, my friend, need a good night's sleep because tomorrow we begin the transformation of Steddenham!"

The next morning, Betsy and Jane put on warm cloaks and walked around the grounds. Spring was definitely in the air and the outside work was well under way. Betsy could see improvements already. Fallen branches had been removed and winter brush was cleared away. Flower beds were cleared and Betsy was delighted to see so many daffodils ready to bloom. Wagon crews had filled the low spots and added new gravel to the driveway.

Both ladies carried notebooks and occasionally jotted down their ideas and comments.

After lunch and while Meggie was napping, Betsy and Jane critiqued the first floor. They agreed the dark heavy draperies had to be replaced by lighter ones that would allow natural light to enter. Perhaps next winter she would re-hang heavier drapes to help prevent drafts. But for now, she wanted an open, airy feel to the house.

They chose new upholstery for worn furniture and new area rugs to replace those that were becoming threadbare. Floors were to be scrubbed, waxed, and polished. Woodwork throughout the first floor was to be cleaned and waxed until it gleamed.

Jane was a tremendous help in coordinating colors and fabrics. She also had good ideas about developing flower gardens especially around the entrance to the manor house. She planned it so there would be daffodils and tulips in the spring, colorful annuals throughout the summer and as much fall color as they could find.

By the end of May, Steddenham was coming alive both inside and out. Crops had been planted and spring hay was ready to be harvested. The flock of sheep had increased because of the birth of several spring lambs. Chickens were providing a daily supply of eggs and the two new cows supplied the household with milk, butter, and cheese.

Jane, too, was pleased with all the progress they had made and knew it was time for her to return to London and set her own house in order.

Betsy promised that she and Meggie would visit in London before her pregnancy prevented her from traveling.

I'm always saying goodbye to someone I love, Betsy thought as she watched her friend's carriage roll away.

-o-

CHAPTER 24

Dirk Campbell had done his homework and it had paid off. Finally, he had been able to connect all the dots. So much time had passed since he first began investigating the murder of the Campbell soldiers and the robbery of the Royal Mail Coach. The trail had grown cold and he was never able to locate the red-haired girl named Betsy. It was the only blemish on his fine investigative career. But now, thanks to a chance encounter with a Marquis and a spur of the moment invitation to his party, Dirk knew he could unravel the mystery and perhaps even arrest the responsible party.

He still couldn't believe his luck. All of the party guests were people of high social status. His head was spinning from meeting and trying to remember everyone. All the faces blurred when he suddenly turned and…there she was, a beautiful young woman with auburn hair. He remembered that a red-haired girl had been present both at Glencoe and at the mail coach robbery. And now here she was. Her age was about right and the hair color was right, now if only her name is Betsy. He had to find out. He quickly found the host and asked the all-important question. Geoff told him her name was Betsy. This couldn't be a coincidence!

During the days following the party, he started asking questions. And he liked the answers he received. He was now convinced this girl was the right Betsy and he couldn't wait to confront her. What's more, her husband was at sea so she would be quite alone.

~~~

It was a beautiful June morning and Betsy was preparing Meggie for an outing. William announced there was a visitor in the downstairs drawing room.

"He's one of Her Majesty's officers, M'Lady," he said.

"Did he give you his name?" Betsy asked.

"Yes, M'Lady. His name is Major Dirk Campbell.

Betsy felt a sudden uneasiness. "What does he want?"

"He didn't say. He asked to speak to the lady of the house."

Betsy called to Claudette. "Please take Meggie for me. It seems I have a visitor." She lowered her voice as she spoke to William. "Go tell Mr. Keith and Mr. Bruce to come quickly and then bring them to the drawing room."

Before she left her room, Betsy took a few deep breaths and tried to calm herself. She didn't trust Dirk Campbell and didn't want to be alone with him, even for a few minutes.

When she entered the drawing room, she forced a smile.

"How may I help you, sir?"

"Are you Mrs. MacDonald?" the major began.

Betsy interrupted him. "My name is Lady MacDonald of Krieth and Marquise of Steddenham. You will address me as Lady MacDonald or our interview is over."

The major turned bright red. This was not starting off well.

"Forgive me, your Ladyship," and he gave a sweeping bow. "I come on the Queen's business."

"You have yet to introduce yourself to me. I doubt Her Majesty would overlook your rudeness, so you better be careful."

It was obvious that he would like to strangle Betsy. "Again I ask your forgiveness. I am Major Dirk Campbell in Her Majesty's service."

"I remember you from the Marquis' party a few weeks ago. You kept staring at me in a very offensive manner."

"You are very beautiful," he said with a smirk, "and your hair is a most unusual color."

Betsy refused to sit, which unnerved Major Campbell. "Why are you here?" she asked.

He handed her a paper he had been holding by his side. "Here are my orders. I am investigating a murder and a robbery that took place several years ago and I must ask you some questions in hopes you can assist in solving those crimes."

"In this house, Major, my husband answers all questions. Regretfully he is at sea. Therefore, I will allow you to question me only in the presence of my husband's representatives who are with me in his absence. They should be here momentarily."

Just then, Robert Keith and Stanley Bruce entered the room and introduced themselves to the major. Robert was blunt.

"What is your business with her Ladyship?"

Betsy answered for him. "Major Campbell wants to ask me some questions.

"Campbell?" Robert snorted and almost spit out the name. He knew the Campbells well and he wanted nothing more to do with them.

Robert spoke in an unfriendly voice. "I don't think much of you Campbells." Then his voice softened as he looked at Betsy. "Your Ladyship, I suggest the major submit all his questions in writing. I will write your reply and Mr. Bruce and I will attest to the accuracy of the report when the interview is completed. The major will do likewise and he will be given a copy when he leaves."

He turned and glared at Dirk. Robert was an imposing figure. He was massively built and towered over the major. His face bore several scars from his battles in the Lowlands.

Dirk had sense enough to be wary of him. He realized he would not be allowed to browbeat this woman even though he knew she was a murderer and a thief. He decided the best tactic would be to pull back and try to regroup.

Betsy looked at Robert Keith with newfound respect. She addressed the major. "Are you willing to accept Mr. Keith's proposal?"

Dirk was in a corner and he knew it. But this could work in his favor. He was good at altering documents and if they bore the signatures of the Lady's own hirelings, what could be better?

"I agree to your terms. I will prepare the questions and return tomorrow."

Betsy was worried. She had no idea what kind of questions he wanted to ask. Was this about Glencoe? It had been so long ago and so much had happened since then. The major had no proof of anything. He was just fishing. Still, she wondered. Did he say Queen Anne sent him? Why would she do that? Just his name…Campbell…brought back vivid memories. She did not want to relive that awful night. Perhaps this was about something else.

She was glad she had two trustworthy friends at her side.

"That was very clever of you, Robert. You sure took the wind out of that weasel's sails."

Robert laughed. "I had a good teacher. My father was a barrister and I read law with him. He showed me how to deal with men like Dirk Campbell."

"But if you studied law, why did you became a soldier?" she wondered.

"Oh, I was younger then and foolish. I felt I needed adventure in my life."

"Well, it's lucky for me that you and Stanley are here. But to tell you the truth, I'll be glad when Dirk Campbell is out of my life."

She relaxed then and tried to put the major out of her mind.

～～～

Dirk Campbell returned the next morning with his list of questions. He gave a copy to Robert who looked at them briefly then passed them to Betsy.

Dirk paced the floor before asking the first question.

"Have you ever been to the village of Glencoe in Scotland?" he asked abruptly.

Betsy's heart fell. She didn't want to revisit that awful place again, especially in front of a Campbell.

"Yes," she answered.

"Were you present when His Majesty's troops subdued the rebellious elements there?"

Betsy looked at the cool, smug man standing a few feet in front of her. She quickly became incensed.

"Do you mean the night when the King's troops, under the leadership of the Campbell clan chiefs, murdered the MacDonald men in their beds then forced the women and children to flee outdoors in their night clothes and freeze to death in the snow?"

He had hit a nerve. He pressed forward. "Please answer the question."

Betsy looked at him with sheer disgust. "If I had been *there,* I wouldn't be *here.* I'd be dead!" She tried to calm herself before she continued. "No, I left for home the day before. But I *was* there when the Campbell troops accepted the hospitality of the MacDonalds before they slaughtered them all."

Dirk couldn't hide his impertinence. "Am I to understand that you disapprove of the action of your King?"

"Major Campbell," she said, "I'm not alone in my belief that all Christian people in Scotland and England disapprove of murder by stealth and deception. Don't you?"

Dirk was getting red in the face again. "We were just soldiers who were following orders," he protested.

We were just soldiers following orders? Oh, my God! He was one of them! Betsy wanted to scream out at him, but somehow she maintained her composure.

"Oh, that may have been the case, Major, but I suspect that it was murder by design by Campbell clansmen who operated under the guise of soldiers in order to weaken and destroy another clan."

Now Dirk was getting angry. "Madam, I take that personally. That is an affront to my family. If you were a man, I would demand satisfaction for that remark."

"Oh, forgive me, Major," she said sarcastically, "You are the one asking the questions and I assumed you wanted honest answers."

Major Campbell realized he had gone too far.

"My apologies," he stammered, "Please let me move forward. Do you have any knowledge of the death of two of the King's soldiers the night of or the morning after the incident at Glencoe?"

"Of course not. How could I? I was already on my way home."

The next question was not on his list but it was a natural follow-up to the previous question. "Did you travel with anyone on your journey?"

"Yes. I was in the company of a young man named MacTavish."

Remembering that the horses of the murdered soldiers were missing, he asked, "Did your traveling companion have any horses with him?"

"Of course," Betsy answered. "The one he rode."

"How did you know the MacTavishes?" Dirk tried to regain the initiative.

"I stopped briefly at their home. The family was friends with my aunt and uncle who were later *murdered* at Glencoe. The son was leaving his family farm to go purchase more sheep for their flocks, so we traveled together."

"How old were you?"

"I was fifteen."

"Isn't that young to be on the road by yourself?"

"No, not at all. I was perfectly capable. Major, that question is not on your list."

Dirk was embarrassed again. This woman was very clever. He had to stay a step ahead of her.

"What was your connection to the MacDonald family at that time?"

"I thought I made that clear. My mother's maiden name was MacDonald and I was visiting her brother and his family."

Dirk exhibited exaggerated shock. "Lady MacDonald, are you telling me you married into your own family?"

This time it was Betsy's turn to become angry but she managed to control her temper.

"Major, you are impudent. I am sure your investigation informed you that my maiden name was Stewart. I am not related to all Stewarts any more than you are related to all Campbells. My husband is the son of the Earl of Krieth and lived near Edinburgh so I don't think your rather nasty implication has any merit, do you?"

Dirk lost that argument. He quickly changed direction.

"What church do you attend?"

"Why is that important?" Betsy asked.

"Just answer the question, please."

"My husband and I belong to the Church of England."

Surprised, Dirk looked up from his list of questions. "I was under the impression you were Catholic."

Betsy was becoming annoyed with these inane questions. "I was; now I'm not."

Dirk continued to press. He had hoped to use her religion against her since Queen Anne disliked Catholics so intensely. "Why did you convert?"

"My husband and I were questioning some of the doctrines. So when some dear friends invited us to learn more about the Anglican Church, we decided to convert."

"Who are these friends?" This question was not on the list either.

"That is really none of your business and should have nothing to do with your investigation. Since I have nothing to hide, I will answer. Our friends are Admiral Charles Bowen and his wife Lady Jane Bowen. They are the Duke and Duchess of Strathford."

In this area, Dirk had not done his homework well and this connection came as a complete surprise. He quickly realized he was up against two peers of the realm, one a Duke and the other a Marquis. He couldn't falter now, so he pushed harder.

"Do you consider yourself wealthy, Lady MacDonald?"

"Major, you are a pompous snod! That question is out of line. Suffice it to say my husband and I are comfortable. I will say no more!"

Robert Keith stepped close to Major Campbell's face. He pointed his finger. "I warn you to be careful, Major. You are treading on thin ice here."

Dirk backed away and changed directions.

"Were you on a Royal Mail Coach when it was robbed several years ago?"

"Yes," Betsy admitted.

"Tell me what happened."

In detail she explained the events of that day.

"When the coach was attacked, did you see any of the assailants?"

"No. I ducked down in the coach when I heard shots. The officer riding next to me looked out the window and was shot dead. Then the coach went off the cliff and I was knocked unconscious."

Dirk didn't know how he was going to use this interview to prove anything against Betsy, but his instincts told him that she had probably not only killed the two Campbell soldiers but was also in someway responsible for the disappearance of the King's money. He would have to dig deeper. Time would always be on his side. Even though she was a practiced liar, she would trip up someday and then he would have his proof.

"That's all the questions for now." He stood up to leave. "I apologize for any inconvenience."

Betsy did not rise. She turned away from the major as she couldn't bear to look at him anymore.

Robert Keith told the major to return the next day for a copy of the transcript.

Stanley Bruce had remained quiet during the interrogation but now he didn't mince words.

"There is a man who needs killing. He means harm to you, Betsy, and I don't think he cares how he injures you. I hope the Queen doesn't have too many more like him in her service."

The next morning Dirk was about ready to receive another surprise.

Robert and Stanley went over the transcripts word for word. Dirk accepted them as accurate and was ready to sign when someone entered the room. Robert introduced him as the Queen's magistrate for this district. He was present to read the documents, sign them and affix his seal to certify their authenticity.

Although this move would prevent any tampering of the existing text, Dirk smiled to himself, knowing he could still insert things as long as they were in context and still make the document damaging to Lady MacDonald. He confidently signed all the documents, said his goodbyes and walked out of the house.

Robert Keith was right behind him.

"Major," Keith said. "I just wanted to tell you that your conduct to Lady MacDonald was despicable. Her husband would have called you out in an instant. As a representative of the Marquis, I am more than willing to draw my saber in her defense. Name the place and the weapons."

Dirk hadn't seen this coming. Fear sent blood rushing to his head. He knew this adversary would take great pleasure in killing him.

Robert took off his glove and threw it down in front of the major. The magistrate came out of the house in time to see and hear it all.

Dirk refused to pick it up. "I don't think you understand," he protested. "I am an agent of the Queen and am acting on her behalf."

"You're a liar, Major Campbell. Our Queen would never condone or even tolerate your behavior for an instant." He turned to the magistrate. "Am I exceeding my rights by challenging this man?"

"I see no impediment in your challenge, Mr. Keith," the magistrate replied.

Dirk held up both hands and backed away. "I will not fight you, Keith. Allow me to withdraw."

"You have proven your cowardice," Robert sneered, "but I warn you, Campbell, if I ever see you on this property again, I will personally take pleasure in cutting your heart out."

The magistrate added his own advice. "I suggest you leave now, Major, and heed Mr. Keith's warning. He is totally within his right, you know."

Dirk Campbell mounted his horse and rode away at a trot. He didn't look back.

As the magistrate prepared to leave, he shook Robert's hand and laughed, "You sure put the fear of God in that little rodent. You take care now."

"I will, and thank you. But I'm afraid we haven't seen the last of Major Campbell."

When Robert returned to the house, Betsy noticed his sour expression. "Did Major Campbell create a ruckus before he left?"

Robert brightened his expression because he didn't want Betsy to be concerned. "No, not really. I just gave him some fatherly advice before he left."

Betsy held the documents close to her chest. "So what do I do with these, Robert?"

"Put them in a safe place in case you ever need them again."

"Of course, the major will have his own copy of these documents, too," Betsy said.

Robert just smiled and slowly shook his head back and forth. "I don't think so. I put a weak acid on the papers I gave to him. It will destroy the ink in just three days and the official seal in five or six. Voila! The documents will cease to exist."

"Robert!" Betsy exclaimed. "You are just wonderful! Did you learn that from your father?"

"No, it's just a little trick I picked up along the way."

"Don't you think he'll return when he realizes what happened?"

"He's way too arrogant to ever admit he was outsmarted. Besides, if the papers disintegrate completely—which they should—he'll probably think they were stolen. By the way Betsy, where did you ever hear the expression 'pompous snod?"

Betsy giggled. "I really don't know. I was very angry at the time and was trying to control myself and it just kind of popped out!"

"Well, lass, I'm going to remember that one. I'm sure I'll find an appropriate place to use it someday!"

Betsy smiled and hooked arms with Robert and Stanley. "Gentlemen, it's been quite a morning. Let's go have some lunch."

-o-

CHAPTER 25

As the HMS Aggressor sailed round the coast of Portugal and entered the Straights of Gibraltar, Admiral Bowen called John to his cabin.

He handed him a cup of coffee and gestured toward a chair.

"Sit down, John. We have a lot to discuss."

John obliged.

"Ever since we left Plymouth," the Admiral said, "I have been studying these charts and maps we've previously made of the Gibraltar coastline."

"For a particular reason, I assume," John said.

"Yes. England wants Gibraltar. And it's going to be our job to take it from the Spanish."

John whistled low. "That's a tall order, Admiral. What are our chances?"

"They're good, I think. But first we have some background work to accomplish before we can make a plan. That's where you come in, John. We have some good intelligence about the area, but I want you to personally go in and chart exactly what we will be up against. The inner harbor is a mystery since the Spanish do not allow any ship to even enter the Bay of Gibraltar. We need to know how well protected it is. Where are the guns? How many are there, etc."

John was still confused. "But attack? Why now, sir? Have there been recent changes that suggests we should prepare an imminent attack?"

"That's it, John! Headquarters has received many reports in recent months from other ships in the area that indicate the Spanish are getting careless with their defense. In addition, you know from personal experience how aggressive the Bey of Tunis has become. No ship in the western Mediterranean is safe anymore. We have to intercede. That means we have to take Gibraltar, fortify it, and make it safe for all ships sailing through the straits. That's why I'm aboard the Aggressor this time. The Admiralty wants me to spearhead the action. And I want you by my side. But before we can continue, I must ask you to perform a dangerous one-man mission…a mission, I believe, only you can successfully complete."

"You know you can count on me, Admiral. Just tell me what to do."

By the time the Aggressor was skirting the coast of Gibraltar, John was fully prepared and ready to go. He knew what he had to do.

The night sky was cloudy when John left the ship and stepped into a long boat that would take him as close as possible to the isthmus, a strip of sand that connected Spain to the Rock. When the boat came within one hundred yards of the shoreline, John waved goodbye to his oarsmen and slipped into the water. Though calm, the water was cold and a chill ran through John's body. He was a good swimmer but as a precaution he had strapped a block of cork to his chest to afford him added flotation. In preparation for this mission, he had hollowed out a place in the cork for a small signal lantern that had a door for signaling but would otherwise not emit light. He had tested it several times and he hoped it would work well this time, too.

It started to rain but he moved smoothly through the water and was soon able to crawl out onto the beach. He turned toward the sea and found that the longboat had disappeared in the blanket of rain. He was alone, in enemy territory and was not at all certain that this plan was very smart but he was committed and had no choice but to go ahead. First, he opened the door of the lantern and, using his flint, he lit the candle. Now if only it could be seen well from offshore. He knew that problem would have to wait until later. His rendezvous with the Aggressor's longboat was scheduled for 4 a.m. That would give him about eight hours to complete his mission.

John climbed a large sand hill close to the shore and hid his gear under some tall grass. He crouched on top of the hill and looked around. The heavy rain made visibility zero and the only sound was the wind and the waves. He headed south, hoping to reach the Bay of Gibraltar. His clothes were drenched and the wind was cold. Rain pelted his face. He used his hand to shelter his eyes so he could see where he was going. Soon he found a road that he thought must have been a supply road from the fortress on the Spanish mainland that lay behind him.

The road was in good repair but was getting slippery from the rain. He continued to follow it south. Visibility was still poor, so he proceeded with caution. Something loomed ahead. He moved closer. The rain had slackened considerably and he could see more clearly. Stone revetments spread east to west in front of him across the isthmus and protected the northern flank of the Rock. As he drew closer, he could see embrasures that undoubtedly held cannons. He could count at least twelve.

John wondered if it would be possible to follow around the western end of this wall and enter the harbor from there. A little more investigation proved that the entire wall paralleled the Bay of Gibraltar and protected the inner harbor.

As he reached the end of the wall, he could see the harbor beyond. Two long earthen docks acted as long arms that hugged the inner harbor in such a way that the opening from the bay to the harbor would only allow one ship at a time to enter. He ran to the water's edge, waded in, then swam to the quay and climbed up onto the road on the top.

The night sky was beginning to clear and clouds parted just enough to allow shaded moonlight on the entire harbor area. John could clearly see sixteen cannons jutting out from the fortification that ran the entire length of the inner harbor. He couldn't help but wonder why there seemed to be no military personnel guarding this area.

Mighty careless, John thought. *Mighty careless, indeed!*

He caught glimpses of the lights from the town nestled at the base of the Rock. Now that he knew first hand what his marines would be up against, his mind started formulating an attack plan. But first, he needed to return safely to the ship.

Just as he started to retrace his steps, he heard someone shout.

"Alto!"

John stopped and stood very still. He watched as a sentry stepped out of the shadows.

"Who goes there?"

John's French and smattering of Spanish plus some basic common sense helped him to understand what the sentry had said.

John wished he had some fishing gear. He answered quickly.

"Pescador."

The sentry lowered his rifle and walked over to get a closer look at John. In the blink of an eye, John grabbed the sentry's arm and jerked it behind him. He spun the man around and put a headlock on him. With a violent twist, John broke the soldier's neck. He searched the man's body but found nothing significant. Hurriedly, he dragged his victim to the edge of the wall, dropped him over the edge and threw his weapon after him. John could only hope that when the Spanish found the soldier, they would think his death had resulted from falling from the wall.

John's heart began racing and he wasted no time in retracing his route. He was profoundly relieved when he finally crossed the isthmus to the Alboran Sea and found his float where he had left it. The candle in the signal lantern was still burning. Exhausted, he sat down in the sand and began to flash his signal out to sea.

It seemed like an eternity before he saw an answering flash. In response, he let his light shine in the direction of the answering signal. When he could see the boat just over the surf line, he hurriedly swam to it.

He was pulled on board and immediately wrapped in blankets. Someone had remembered to bring a bottle of rum and some hard tack. Gratefully, John took a big swig and then another. His body was numb from the wet and the cold but the rum burned his throat and warmed his insides.

"Thanks, Mate," he said and took another swig. Managing a weak smile he added, "I think I'm going to live."

The next morning after less than two hours sleep, John reported to the Admiral and Captain Gray.

"I have a pretty good feel for what we will be facing. The most interesting discovery was that there is very little human defense, at least at night. I saw only the one guard. I think we have two things on our side, the element of surprise and the fact the Rock is so poorly defended." John handed the Admiral a slip of paper. "Here's a sketch of the Rock and location of the fortifications I saw firsthand."

Captain Gray was interested in the drawing too. "You did a good job, John. With this drawing, I think the three of us can plan an attack that will not only be successful but swift as well and," he added, "with a minimum of casualties."

Admiral Bowen was very pleased. "I'd like for our plans to be ready in three days. That's when we should rendezvous with our other warships." He pulled his chair closer to the worktable. "Gentlemen, shall we begin?"

The three worked throughout the day and evening. Meals were brought to the Captain's cabin. They really weren't very hungry. The excitement of planning such an important mission kept their adrenaline rushing and their hunger at bay.

By midnight, the plan was complete. They were all satisfied with the final result.

There would be two simultaneous night attacks. Two warships would cover the isthmus area and deposit one hundred marines there. The marines would secure the area along the sand spit and work their way up to the east-west wall that held the Spanish gun fortifications. A second contingent of marines would land on the southern mole that protected the inner harbor and then attack the town.

Meanwhile, three warships would enter the harbor when the land attack began and lie alongside the mole. Five more warships would patrol the Mediterranean a few miles east of the Rock.

If everything went as planned, there would be a minimal loss of life. John vowed to do everything in his power to make it so.

Three days later, the warships arrived on schedule. Admiral Bowen ordered them to stand-by for orders. That night, all the captains came on board the Aggressor for an in-depth conference.

John was understandably jumpy the day before the attack. He created the attack over and over in his mind. He was confident that his marines would know what to do and could only pray that all the others were as good at following orders as his own marines were.

The evening before the attack, John met with his marines for a last minute review of instructions.

The sky was clear and the moon splashed brightness on the land and on the sea. John hoped this was a good omen. He realized that the moonlight could also work against them and spoil the surprise aspect of the attack.

Throughout the evening hours, the warships moved into place and waited for the command to proceed.

At 2 a.m., the first wave of marines went ashore to cross the sandy area that led to the mainland. Their job was to make certain no Spanish troops reinforced the Rock. Quickly they moved forward. They met no resistance. One group reached the wall and planted mines on the north side.

Guns were held at the ready and bayonets were fixed as the marines stealthily moved west along the wall until they came to the northern mole of the inner harbor.

The Aggressor and two other warships skirted the coastline and approached the southern end of the mole. Ten longboats, each holding twenty marines, were lowered with John leading the way. By the time they reached the inner harbor and landed on the quay, the Spanish sounded the alarm. John could hear yelling and screaming as men were rousted from their sleep and ordered to go fire the cannons at the approaching enemy.

John also gave a command. "Kill the gun crews!"

The night became ablaze with constant barrages of cross fire. Most of the gunfire splashed harmlessly in the water. One British longboat received a direct hit. John watched in horror as bodies flew into the air and the boat split into pieces.

By the time the remaining longboats reached the quay, there were Spaniards everywhere on the beach. The marines were above them on the quay. The Spaniards below them were like sitting ducks, as the marines picked them off one by one. In one persistent volley, most of the Spanish resistance was leveled. Now the entire contingent of marines bounded ashore and headed for the town. The three warships sailed into the harbor and were able to silence the Spanish guns on the revetment above the harbor.

With the marines coming into town from the rear, and the marines attacking from the north, the remaining Spanish quickly ran the white flag of surrender.

By the time the sun was above the horizon, the British had won the battle for Gibraltar. In a matter of hours, the troops brought in by the warships took their position on the Rock.

The rest of the day all the Army and Navy officers gathered aboard the Aggressor for a debriefing.

Admiral Bowen was full of praise. "I want to thank every one of you for a job well done. Each of you men contributed greatly to the success of this campaign. The men who died here are heroes and will never be forgotten. As a tribute to them we must ensure that we will guard this Rock with our very lives so that ships from every nation will sail free and without the constant threat of piracy. The reign of terror of the Bey of Tunis has ended." He filled his glass and held it high.

"Three cheers for Her Royal Majesty's military, the finest in the world!"

There was not much time for celebration for there was much work to be done. Admiral Bowen recommended that, because Gibraltar was a naval base, the Crown create a regiment of marines to man it and supplement them with a contingent of Royal engineers to improve the fortification and crews of naval gunners to man the cannon until soldiers from the Royal Artillery could relieve them. He specifically recommended that John be made commander of the garrison.

In London, the Admiralty quickly approved the appointment and promoted John to the rank of colonel. Of course John was proud of his promotion and he accepted it with great pleasure. Secretly, he had hoped he would soon be going home. That wasn't going to happen. He was quickly immersed in the new operation and all that it entailed.

Now John understood what it meant to represent the Queen. Everything needed to be done at once. It seemed as though he was always needed in several places at the same time. Priorities had to be set. The first one was to assist townspeople who wished to return to Spain. In addition, he assisted British civil service who were sent to do specific government tasks.

It immediately came to his attention that there were no natural springs on the Rock. All water had to either be shipped in or caught in reservoirs to preserve rainwater. The Spanish had attempted to do this but John learned that most water had been shipped in. Work forces soon began the tedious but necessary job of digging cisterns into solid rock. These cisterns would catch and hold the streams of rainwater that flowed down the rock.

Admiral Bowen moved ashore and took a large house that had been vacated by a Spanish family and set up his headquarters there. John moved into the quarters that had belonged to the previous garrison commander.

It wasn't long before Admiral Bowen became even more certain that John was his most able commander; therefore, gave him more responsibility and free reign to deal with day-to-day operations.

Slowly but surely, John began to see progress. This was certainly the strangest and most difficult assignment of his career. He was sure there was no other place on earth like Gibraltar.

Several months later, John was surprised with a visit from James Marks.

"James, you're a sight for sore eyes! I certainly never expected to see you on this God-forsaken Rock. The last time I saw you, you assured me my life was about to change. Is this what you meant?"

James smiled and shook John's extended hand. "Not exactly, but I see that your star is still ascending."

John laughed. "Well, if you call being in command of a Rock with no water an advancement, I guess it is."

James tone changed. "I need to talk to you privately."

John nodded to his clerk, who promptly left the room. "Please sit down, James."

"I'll waste no time. I have reliable information that the Spanish army plans to take this fortress back."

John was alarmed. "When?"

"My best informants tell me it will happen within a fortnight."

"Are you quite sure, James? I've seen no significant Spanish activity. Does Admiral Bowen know of this?"

"Well, in answer to your questions. Yes, I am quite sure. The reason you have not noticed any activity is because it's impossible for you to see far enough into the interior of Spain. They hope to surprise you with a large force before you can prepare. In answer to your second question, No, I have not informed the Admiral for one simple reason. I want you to plan the military and naval campaign and then present it to him. All you have to say is that a trusted informant brought you the information. Lay a big trap, John, and when the attack comes and you are successful, Admiral Bowen will give you all the credit. You know how much he thinks of you."

"Why are you doing this?" John was still unclear on James' motives.

"Simple. You were instrumental in capturing Gibraltar. Along with your other military achievements, you have become an established military hero who has greatly increased the Royal Marines and given them a respected place in the armed forces. You know you are also a peer of the realm. When you return to London don't be surprised if you are asked to rightfully take your place in the House of Lords. Your loyalty to the Crown has been unswerving and you are a credit to your nation."

John was taken aback. "I...I don't know what to say."

"You don't have to say anything. Believe me when I say the amount of support you have at home would surprise you."

Marks stood up and offered John his hand. "Do well in your next endeavor, your Lordship." He picked up his hat, his cane, and left as quickly as he had arrived.

John needed to be alone. When his clerk returned, John excused him for the day. He replayed James's conversation over and over in his mind. *Hero? Peer of the realm? The House of Lords?* This was too much for him to assimilate. He decided there would be time to digest all of this later. For now, he had to concentrate on how his forces would defend the Rock. It would be the first time and he wanted the victory to be so overwhelming that it would be the last time as well. He worked well into the night until he had his battle plans drawn. After a few hours sleep, he made an early morning appointment with Admiral Bowen.

The Admiral listened intently as John told him about the impending attack.

"And you trust this informant? Completely trust him?"

"Yes, I do," John assured him. "The attack will come. I'll stake my reputation on it."

"That's good enough for me, John. Now tell me your plan."

Admiral Bowen studied the plan and made a few suggestions that John readily accepted.

"I think your strategy is sound, John. Give the ships' captains sealed orders that they will open at the appointed time. You know there are people in town who want to see us driven out. Spanish spies are everywhere. If we want to have an edge, we have to play their game and seem unsuspecting."

A week later, several of the largest British warships in the harbor weighed anchor and put to sea with their sealed orders. The remaining warships were fanned out in the harbor, their guns trained on the Spanish coast. At the same time, marines moved more cannon so they pointed across the isthmus toward the mainland of Spain.

Two nights before the expected attack, John increased small boat patrols in the harbor. The next afternoon, lookouts on top of the Rock reported sightings of several large ships up the east side of the Spanish coast.

John sent a note to Admiral Bowen. It simply said, "Guests arriving in the morning."

At ten p.m., message signals were sent to the ships in the harbor. The longboats, all with signal lanterns, rowed out and held a line in front of the warships. Well-trained marines manned the walls of the north fort. All was silent. Everyone waited.

Along the isthmus, marines were hidden along the water's edge where they could hear any movement. About an hour before dawn, they heard the Spanish army approaching and signaled the garrison.

Meanwhile the Spanish war ships had drawn up along the sand bar to support the army's attack. While they were preparing, lights from the fort flashed seaward to signal the British naval squadron facing the Rock as they prepared to engage the Spanish warships.

Out in the bay of Gibraltar, the marine picket boats reported an armada of small craft approaching the warships in the harbor. As the small Spanish boats attacked, the British ships smashed them with volley after volley of grape shot. Most were decimated. A few turned around to find safety on the Spanish coastline. Only two managed to limp to safety. Their crews were wounded and their boats damaged.

John was situated in the fort and watched in the early morning light as the Spanish army now marched onto the neck of land that separated them from Gibraltar. Their artillery moved up behind them as they moved steadily to cover the half-mile that separated them from the fort.

John had faced the Spanish before in the Lowlands and he remembered one thing in particular. The Spanish artillery stayed about fifty feet behind the infantry and it stopped when the infantry stopped. From prior experience, John knew that the infantry would stop short of what they thought would be extreme cannon range.

In anticipation of this very predictable maneuver, John had previously taken pains to indicate the extreme range of the British cannon by firing at targets in front of the fort. After the demonstrations, his marines had elevated guns on parapets to increase their range by forty to fifty feet.

As dawn was breaking, the Spanish army advanced its battle line and reached what they believed was the extreme range of the enemy's cannon. They paused at this point and were pleased to see their warships open fire on the fort. They felt that victory would soon be theirs. In anticipation of a swift victory, the sounds of beating drums and bugles blaring filled the morning air. Suddenly the line began to move again. The marines waited until they had come well into cannon range and then opened fire.

The Spanish field guns sprang into action. What the Spanish did not know was that this field was filled with powder charges containing shrapnel. Marines were dug into camouflaged holes behind them. With perfect timing, they ignited the charges. Suddenly, the earth seemed to explode. Shrapnel splayed in every direction and even wounded men in the rear ranks of the infantry. When the smoke cleared, it was easy to see that the Spanish artillery had ceased to exist as a functioning unit.

After eliminating the small boats in the harbor, British warships turned their attention to the land battle and began bombarding the right flank of the Spanish army that soon began to falter. Simultaneously, the British naval squadron sailed directly toward the Spanish warships. Two of the Spanish ships were driven aground by their vicious bombardment. Only one relatively unscathed warship managed to escape to the north. Now close to the shoreline, the ships opened fire on the remains of the Spanish army. Survivors quickly broke rank and retreated north trying to escape the carnage. John gave the command and the Royal Marines ran out of the fort. With bayonets fixed, they pursued the enemy and gave them no quarter.

The surviving Spanish soldiers ran right into a trap similar to the one that had destroyed the artillery. Hundreds of soldiers were killed or wounded when the secret minefield exploded around them. Thick black smoke clouded the Rock on all sides. The guns became silent and only the moans and cries of the wounded and dying could be heard. The conflict had ended.

The marines captured three sets of Spanish regimental colors that day, but John felt no joy. Too many men had died. Was it worth it? He didn't know the answer to that question. He doubted that he ever would. The only thing he was sure of was that it would be a long time before the Spanish tried to recapture the Rock.

The news of the second battle for Gibraltar reached London in less than a month. Full credit of the victory was given to Colonel John MacDonald who had planned and executed the defense that destroyed the Spanish Army in their fatal attempt to take back control of the fortress.

The Queen wanted to personally thank Colonel MacDonald, so she ordered him to return to London post haste.

-o-

CHAPTER 26

It was a crisp, fall morning and Betsy was walking in the garden with Robert Keith. During John's absence, the two of them had become good friends. Ever since the unpleasant visit from Dirk Campbell, Robert had been a close companion.

Robert didn't trust Campbell and felt a tremendous responsibility for keeping Betsy safe, especially since she was expecting another child.

"Are you going to send word to John about this baby?" he wondered.

"Oh, Robert. This really has been a problem for me. I want to tell him. He should know. But I just can't do it. It was so hard for him to leave us this time. I just can't burden his mind with something out of his control. Besides, it won't be long now before the baby comes. Then I'll really have my hands full and won't have time to worry about whether or not I should tell him. Hopefully, he'll be home soon after."

"Now that Gibraltar is under British control, isn't it possible he'll be home soon?"

Betsy shook her head sadly. "I'm afraid not, Robert. I received a letter from my good friend Lady Jane Bowen. After the battle, her husband sent word to her they would be stationed on Gibraltar for several months. Seems they have a lot of work to do there. I'm hoping he will be home for the holidays."

"John's accomplishments have been remarkable and he has become quite the hero, you know. When he does return, he will probably have a lot of affairs to attend, all in his honor," Robert said. "Betsy, what you have accomplished here at Steddenham is also remarkable. Not just in the physical appearance of the estate but in the general attitude of the staff. They adore you, you know."

"I've always believed in treating everyone with kindness because in some mystical way, I believe we are all connected. I believe most people try their very best to succeed at their jobs and should be respected for that."

Robert laughed. "You've always lived in a gentle world, haven't you? So it's easy for you to see the good in people."

Betsy stopped for a moment and faced Robert. "A gentle world?" She almost spit out the words. "You have no idea how much violence and hatred I've witnessed. I have seen the tremendous strength of evil first hand. Once I was in the deadly grasp of unspeakable danger and survived only because I was safe in God's hands. God's love is more powerful than anything on this earth. I choose to follow in His path. I will love, respect, and honor everyone in my life who chooses the same path."

Robert looked at Betsy with admiration. "I hope John knows how lucky he is to have such a special wife."

The mood was getting too serious. "If he doesn't," Betsy said lightly, "I guess I'll just have to tell him!"

~~~

The next day, Betsy received a letter from Lady Jane.

> "My Dearest Betsy,
> All of London is celebrating another victory. It seems John is once again the hero of Gibraltar. Spain tried to recapture the Rock and John executed a perfect defense and whipped the Spanish once and for all. The Queen is ecstatic and has ordered both Charles and John to return home immediately."

As soon as the ship arrived, Admiral Bowen and John were escorted to the Admiralty where they were debriefed about the capture of Gibraltar and the recent attempt of the Spanish army to reclaim it.

The First Lord of the Admiralty shook both their hands. "Gentlemen, on behalf of Her Majesty, Queen Anne, I commend you for the victories you have bestowed on England. The Queen herself will duly honor you both." He focused his attention on John. "Colonel MacDonald, you have proven over and over the value of a strong marine regiment. Her Majesty has taken notice. Now she is

requesting that you take command, not only of the marine barracks in Plymouth but take command of all of the marines in the Royal Navy. In addition, she wants you to build another marine regiment. If things go as planned, you will subsequently be in command of more than 1600 marines. That little feat will earn you a promotion to the rank of Brigadier General."

John was feeling heady as he stepped into the carriage that would take him home to Betsy. Building a regiment would not only be an exciting challenge but it would keep him at home for quite some time.

While the horses seemed to be moving in slow motion, John's mind was racing. Did Betsy look the same? Would he even recognize Meggie? What changes would he see in Steddenham? Would Betsy see changes in him? He knew he had changed. Every time he fought a battle, he changed a little inside. He had seen enough bloodshed to last a lifetime. There was so much injustice and cruelty in the world. He strongly believed that war was not an answer, but until greed, envy, and a thirst for power were eliminated from the hearts of mankind, history would continue to repeat itself and wars would be inevitable.

He looked out the window of the carriage. It was so good to be home again. He longed for the simple pleasures of life, like watching his daughter grow; spending a quiet evening with his wife; smelling freshly cut hay; listening to the soft bleats of a newborn lamb.

War had taught him one important lesson: Be grateful for each new day and live it to its fullest. Take nothing for granted because life can end or be forever altered in a heartbeat. War is personally defining but it's the little things that make life worthwhile.

As the carriage entered Steddenham and rumbled underneath the tunnel of trees, John felt a tremendous feeling of excitement. He leaned out the carriage window and took a deep breath. Fall fragrance of dried leaves filled his nostrils and made him think of the warm home fires awaiting him.

By the time he stepped down out of the carriage, Betsy stood at the front door, smiling from ear to ear.

John started up the front step. He stopped cold when he saw her and her swollen belly.

'Oh, my God! Betsy, my darling wife. You didn't tell me!"

Betsy held out her arms and in a moment, John was holding her and kissing her.

"It's been too long, my darling, but I'm home now," he murmured. "I'm home now."

Betsy placed his hand on her belly. "We've been waiting for you, this baby and I."

They walked into the foyer and Claudette was waiting with Meggie. John stepped close to his daughter but she turned away and clung to Claudette. John looked stricken.

"Give her a little time, John." Betsy took the child from Claudette. "Meggie, this your Papa."

Meggie looked at Betsy. "Mama?"

Betsy nodded. "I'm Mama." She kissed John's cheek. "This is Papa."

Meggie repeated, "Papa," and reached her arms toward John.

He took his daughter and buried his face in her soft neck. When he looked up, Betsy could see tears in his eyes.

"Welcome home, sweetheart," Betsy said softly and realized tears were spilling from her own eyes.

~~~

As though on cue, the labor pains started during the night. Unlike the first birth, the pains were intense from the beginning. Betsy called for Claudette and the housekeeper, and then told John what to do.

"There isn't time to call for a midwife," she told them. "We're going to have to do this ourselves. This baby is anxious to be born."

Outwardly, John appeared calm and in control, but his insides were jumpy and restless. He sat by Betsy's side and held her hands. With each contraction, she squeezed his hand so hard he thought his fingers would break. She tried to relax between the pains but soon they increased in intensity as the time between decreased. During one of the contractions, John placed a hand on her abdomen and was amazed at how rock hard it felt. As the contraction subsided, the hardness subsided as well.

Betsy cried out as a sudden gush of fluid erupted from her body. John looked at Stella for reassurance.

Stella nodded. "The membranes have ruptured. It won't be long now, Sir John."

Betsy moaned and thrashed her head from side to side. The pains intensified and were coming one on top of another.

Stella gently spread Betsy's legs wider. "I can see the head. Push, Lady Betsy! Push!"

Betsy gritted her teeth and pushed as hard as she could.

"Good!" Stella cried. "Now the shoulders have to come. Bear down again! Even harder this time!"

Betsy cried in agony as she again bore down, harder and longer than before.

"Keep it up, child. Just a little more! Push!"

Betsy screamed as she raised her head up and pushed until she thought it was the last thing she'd ever do.

Stella was all smiles as she lifted the newborn up. "It's a boy! You have a beautiful baby boy!"

Exhausted, Betsy fell back against the pillows and smiled at her husband.

Emotion filled every fiber of John's being. He couldn't speak. He released Betsy's hand and kissed her forehead, then reached for his son. Claudette placed a blanket over John's hand and Stella put the infant in John's arms.

"This is a miracle," John whispered. "I've just witnessed the most incredible miracle I'll ever see."

He laid the baby in the crook of Betsy's arm and sat by her side. For the longest moment, the world stood still as John and Betsy reveled in their newborn son and their reunited family.

They named their son Richard James. From the moment of his birth, he was a wonder to his parents.

John insisted Meggie's crib be moved into their bedroom for a while. He couldn't get enough of his family and wanted them all by his side every moment throughout the day and night.

Betsy healed quickly this time. Having John here for the birth made everything easier. She, too, wanted the four of them to stay close.

During John's absence, she had not allowed herself to admit how much she missed him. Now that he was home again and had been here for the birth, she could recognize those feelings and finally let them go. It happened when Richard was a week old.

She was lying quietly in John's arms when he kissed her tenderly. "Thank you, my darling, for everything you have endured during my absence. Betsy, I don't know how you accomplished so much. I will always feel guilty for not being here with you. Can you forgive me?"

The floodgates opened. Months of pent-up emotion released. Betsy cried until there were no more tears. "We were married...then you left," she sobbed, "then Meggie was born...then you came home ...you left...another baby on the way...repairing Steddenham...now you're home!" The sobs deepened.

John was at a loss. He didn't understand what she was feeling. He never would. So he did the only thing he knew how to do. He let her cry and all the while he soothed her with tender words of love and soft, gentle kisses.

When she finally quieted down, she tried to explain. "All the time you've been gone, I've had to be strong and always in control. All of that responsibility kept me from realizing how much I missed you. If I had admitted it, I would have fallen apart. I couldn't let that happen because then I would disappoint you as well as myself. When you returned home again, it was easy to let down my guard and allow myself to feel weak and vulnerable." She sat up and dried her eyes. "I've washed it all out of my system now. Thanks for allowing me that little breakdown."

John pulled her into his arms and held her tight. "I can't begin to imagine all you've been through. I can't promise you I'll never have to leave again, but I do promise you that I will do everything in my power to keep you and the children as happy and safe as possible. I love you so much. I thank God every day that you came into my life."

They soon fell asleep, each secure in the knowledge there would be many bright and beautiful days ahead before they once again had to think about saying goodbye.

Meggie, too, felt the special bonding with her family. She loved to touch her baby brother, then crawl into her father's arms to fall asleep.

During the days after Richard's birth, the family forged ties of love that would last throughout their lives.

Quietly on Christmas Eve morning, Betsy took the carriage into town and made her annual cash withdrawal with instructions to deliver it anonymously to the priest at St. Stephen Anglican Church.

Shortly after the new year, the MacDonalds were directed to attend an audience with the Queen. This time, however, they were not stationed in the rear, but ushered to the front of the hall.

Betsy was surprised when she saw the Queen who was considerably heavier than the last time she saw her. Queen Anne walked slowly toward the throne and Betsy could hear her labored breathing. There were rumors that the Queen had suffered another miscarriage but her abdomen was so large she looked as though she was ready to give birth. Betsy's heart ached for this woman as she remembered the ease with which she herself had twice given birth to healthy babies. Betsy said a silent prayer for her sorrowful Queen.

When their names were called, John and Betsy moved forward to the Queen with an ease they hadn't experienced the first time.

"Congratulations on the recent birth of your son," the Queen said loudly, then almost a whisper, "I envy you." Awkwardly she stood up and took a few steps toward the couple.

"Sir John Macdonald, you are one of the finest soldiers we have in the realm. I have been told that Gibraltar is now under British control mostly because of you and your fine marines. On behalf of our nation, I thank you, and present you with our most prestigious award, the Knight of the Garter. As a more tangible award, I hereby deed to you the estate that includes Starnes House plus twenty five thousand pounds sterling. Please kneel."

John dropped to his knees.

As the Queen raised her sword, she touched each of his shoulders, "I dub thee Sir John MacDonald, Knight of Gibraltar. Congratulations. You may rise."

John rose to his feet and bowed to his Queen. "Thank you, your Majesty."

For Betsy, the best part of the whole day was later when the Queen ordered John to take two months of personal leave.

On the journey back to Steddenham, John and Betsy had a real chance to talk. Betsy wanted to know all about the two battles for Gibraltar. John's explanation was brief because he realized that war was impossible to understand except for the one experiencing it from moment to moment.

Betsy, however, was eager to explain all the details of the improvements at Steddenham.

"Lady Bowen..." Betsy smiled at John. "...she wants me to call her Jane now...was a great help with the decorating. I think everyone on staff was eager to help out because Steddenham is their home, too, and they wanted it to look top notch like it used to."

"You are all to be commended. It looks wonderful," John assured her. "I'm sure in the spring and summer, I'll see how beautiful the gardens are, too. Now, not to change the subject, but I'm going to. Betsy, yesterday, I ran into my friend, Geoff Burns. He mentioned a name I was not familiar with. A Major Dirk Campbell."

Betsy's face flushed.

"He said Campbell was still nosing around and asking questions. Geoff asked me if the major was still bothering you." John looked worried. "Who is he, Betsy?"

Betsy took a deep breath. "It's a long story, John, and I'm not sure I understand what it all means. Do you remember last year at Geoff's party? Some man was staring at me. No matter where I went, he was close by, staring at me. I asked you about him but you said he was staring because I was so beautiful. Do you remember?"

John nodded. "Yes, I do remember. That man was Major Campbell?"

"Yes." Betsy paused before continuing. "After you left, he came to see me. He said he was on orders from the Queen. He made me extremely uneasy so Robert and Stanley came and took your place beside me."

Betsy explained the major's visit in detail, including his rudeness. "Robert managed to chase him away with his tail between his legs. We have heard nothing since and, truthfully, I had forgotten all about the man."

John's anger flared. "How dare he come to you and make such accusations! And he said he was on the order of the Queen? She would never have condoned such behavior. How did he come up with such nonsense?"

"He is in charge of solving both crimes. Since I was at Glencoe before the massacre *and* I happened to be on the mail coach that was robbed, he's put two and two together and come up with five. He's grabbing for straws. I'm a woman, my husband was gone; so he thought he would able to intimidate me." She laughed. "He was wrong!"

Betsy did not like lying to her husband but her family, who were accessories, had to be protected. Long ago, she had decided never to tell him the truth about how she had single-handedly robbed the Royal Mail. It would remain her secret forever.

"Well," John said, "If he ever comes our way again, I'll be there to make sure he'll never bother you again."

Upon their return to Steddenham, Robert Keith met them with sad news.

"It's Oliver Stanton. He was found in his bed yesterday morning. He apparently went to sleep and never woke up."

Robert had worked closely with Oliver over the last months and knew the man well. He was the obvious choice to give the eulogy. Oliver Stanton was buried with high esteem and gratitude for a life well lived and a job well done.

John and Betsy agreed that Robert should now become the estate manager and Stanley Bruce would be his assistant.

The following day, the eight marines, assigned by Queen Anne to escort John at all times, arrived at Steddenham. She wanted nothing to happen to him and believed this would be assurance.

"If they are to be with us from now on, we had better build some kind of barracks for them," John told Betsy. "I know! They can build it themselves. It will help to keep them occupied. Maybe some of our farm workers can help."

"That's something you and Robert can decide," she said, "In the meantime, we'll put them up in guest quarters."

During John's absence, Betsy had taken the opportunity to meet many of the people in the area. Now that John was home, she wanted to host a dinner and dance and invite as many of the local people as possible.

Betsy sent an invitation to Admiral and Lady Jane Bowen and asked them to arrive several days early so they could enjoy a long visit. She emphasized they were to be the guests of honor.

The Bowens accepted and arrived three days before the scheduled event. Lady Bowen was anxious to assist Betsy in last minute preparations and help instruct her on the important matters of protocol.

While the ladies took care of matters in the house, the gentlemen amused themselves shooting grouse in the hills on the north limits of Steddenham.

John arrived back home in the late afternoon and found Betsy in a quandary.

"I'm very nervous, John. This is my first party and I want everything to go perfectly. Please help me decide what to wear."

She pulled out several dresses for John's approval. He carefully looked at each one, then pointed to a low cut cranberry velvet trimmed with black satin ribbon.

"That's it!" he said with certainty. "I'll wear my cranberry jacket and we'll be perfectly matched."

Betsy made a face. "You're teasing me!" she pouted.

John kissed his wife's protruding lips. "Not at all, my darling. We'll be the perfectly dressed couple hosting the season's most perfect dinner dance." He turned her around and smacked her rump. "Now, go get ready!"

The guests began to arrive at six o'clock. House staff assisted guests as they dismounted their conveyances. Farm staff put up the carriages. Four marines stood on the steps to the main entrance, two on either side.

Inside the manor house, two maids helped the guests with their coats. In the entrance to the great hall, William, the head butler, read the visitors' cards announcing each couple as they arrived. Then they passed through the reception line where they first met John and Betsy. Admiral and Lady Bowen, followed by Robert Keith, his wife Rose, and finally, Stanley Bruce and his wife, Betty.

Geoff Burns and his wife were late arrivals but were greeted warmly by John and Betsy. Betsy made sure the couple was seated close to them at dinner.

When guests had completed the reception line, they were served wine or other beverages of their choice. John and Betsy mingled with guests until dinner was served promptly at eight o'clock.

The main course was tender English roast beef and mutton. A wide variety of vegetables was served along with bread still hot from the oven. Wine flowed freely throughout the meal. The table was cleared for desserts of apple pie, chocolate cake, and a variety of petit fours.

Later, the men adjourned to one of the drawing rooms to smoke cigars and sip port wine or brandy.

John and the Admiral were the center of attention because everyone wanted to know what had happened at Gibraltar and did they know where the British Navy would attack next? Did they think the Spanish would attack again and was the Mediterranean really free from pirates?

The ladies adjourned to another drawing room where the subject of conversations centered on fashion, raising children, and the latest gossip about those not in attendance.

After a half hour, the men were called back to the great hall, as the dancing was about to commence. Just before the dancing began, Geoff pulled John aside.

"I saw Major Campbell the other day. He was being recalled to Fort William. Before he left, he told me he was getting close to an arrest in a couple of old cases. He felt sure that when that happened, he would receive a big promotion. I tried to find out what he was talking about but he would only say one of the Queen's fair haired boys was in for a big surprise."

"Do you know who he was talking about?" John asked.

"He was talking about you."

The music began playing and Betsy, slightly out of breath, appeared and took John's arm. "Excuse me, gentlemen, but the dancing has begun."

John gave a parting look to Geoff. "Thanks for the information. I'll look into it."

The dancing lasted until late that night before guests finally began to leave.

It had been an exhilarating, yet exhausting evening and Betsy was asleep before John climbed into bed.

~~~

Toward the end of John's leave, he and Betsy took the children and went to inspect their new property at Starnes House. It was located near Exeter, about thirty-five kilometers from Plymouth. The estate was in fair repair but would need some refurbishing.

Betsy noticed how moderate the temperature was. Although it was early spring, she saw that flowers were blooming and the trees were green.

"Is it always this warm here?" she asked one of the locals.

"Not always, Mum. But it doesn't get very cold here either. You see here on the southern coast, the warm ocean currents take good care of us. Of course, watch out for fierce winds that blow off the channel. But mostly the weather here is kindly."

Betsy was sure she would like it here for reasons other than the weather. The house and grounds were smaller but seemed homier somehow.

First, the house had to be made ready. In just a matter of days, they hired a man of good reputation as the estate manager. It would be his job to oversee the necessary repairs. He would also maintain a basic house staff and oversee the spring planting.

By the time they left Starnes House, John's leave was over and he had to report to the Admiralty.

Betsy was glad to be back in London. When they arrived at the MacDonald house, Annie couldn't keep her hands off the children.

"Miss Betsy, these are the most beautiful children I've ever seen. I hope you're going to stay a while so I can spoil the dickens out of them."

The next day, John went to the Admiralty to receive instructions.

"Come in, John. Please sit down." The Lord Admiral offered him a chair. "I think you'll be surprised at what I'm going to tell you. The Navy has determined that the port at Plymouth is getting too crowded. We plan to utilize the two thousand acres we have near Exeter on the west side of the River Exe as a new marine base. We want you to gather all your marines at the barracks in Plymouth and proceed along with supply wagons to Exeter and set up new marine headquarters."

"Is this a sudden decision?" John wondered.

"No, John. As your recruits increased, we realized that the marine division was not only here to stay, but would continue to grow. We had the land surveyed for the purpose of setting up a new headquarters. And it's perfect. We couldn't be more pleased with the location."

John couldn't help but laugh.

The Lord Admiral frowned slightly. "Does this idea amuse you, John?"

"No, sir. I mean, yes sir. You see, I have just acquired property near Exeter. So as far as I'm concerned, the location couldn't be better."

The Lord Admiral was pleased. "Good! Then it's settled. You will have two companies of Royal Engineers assigned to you for the building projects. I need you to ready your men and leave for Exeter as soon as possible."

John stood up and shook the Admiral's hand. "Thank you, sir. This is an assignment I am very much looking forward to."

John couldn't wait to tell Betsy.

"Darling, that's wonderful news," she said excitedly. "That means you won't be going back to sea anytime soon and you and the children can really get to know each other."

He put his arm around her and drew her close. "And I'll have lots of time to do this." He kissed her lips, her nose, her eyes, then returned to her lips with a smoldering kiss that shot hot flames clear to her toes.

She pulled away just enough to catch her breath.

"The children are asleep," he murmured, "so I want to spend the next few hours showing you how very much I love you."

"We've got the whole night," she said. "In fact, we have the rest of our lives."

Before John left for Plymouth, he had one more errand to run. He needed to find out more about Major Dirk Campbell. He soon found out that his military exploits were well known throughout London. Army personnel greeted him warmly and were eager to answer all his questions.

It was no secret that Major Campbell was not well liked. He was seen as an opportunist with low morals and little concern for anyone beneath him in rank. The consensus was that everyone was glad he had been recalled to Fort William and they hoped he stayed there for good.

John was well satisfied with what he had learned. When he told Betsy, her response was the same. "I hope he stays in Fort William, too."

~~~

Annie was glad to stay with the children so that John and Betsy could have a quiet evening alone before John left for Plymouth.

Betsy poured a glass of wine for each of them.

"Here's to us, my darling," John said. "I'll count the days until we're together again."

"I'll follow you as soon as I receive word the Starnes House is ready for occupancy. I sent word to Claudette and Brian that I want them to come with me."

John held his glass high. Betsy did the same.

"Another marvelous adventure is waiting for us both. Life is certainly full of surprises."

Betsy grinned. "I'll drink to that!"

The next morning, John left for Plymouth. When he arrived, he discovered he had one hundred and fifty men on the rolls. He selected thirty to remain so they could provide the fleet with any necessary replacements. Posters and handbills had been placed throughout the major cities in England and Scotland and new recruits were beginning to trickle in. It was too soon to measure the impact of the advertising.

John had decided to temporarily set up his headquarters at Starnes House and shelter his men in the empty barns.

Three days later, one hundred and twenty marines marched out of Plymouth toward their new home. Baggage rumbled along behind them. As soon as the troops cleared the town, John ordered the officers' horses to be tied to the back of the wagons along with his own, and they marched with the men. It was a two-day forced march but the weather cooperated and the men were in good spirits when they arrived at Starnes House. After some food and a short rest, work details were assigned to clean out the barns and dig latrines. That was just the beginning. The real work would begin the next day.

After a hearty breakfast that included lots of steaming hot coffee, the men marched to the site that would become the new marine base.

John's first job was to prioritize the jobs that needed to be completed.

There were two large warehouse-type buildings on the government land, each fifty feet by twenty feet. The walls were built of stone and the roofs were thatched. Inside, the stone floors were level and solid. They were perfect for barracks or for training. Before use, they would need to be cleaned and any damage repaired.

When the engineers arrived, John would have them build four more comparable buildings that would form three sides of a square. A smaller officers' barracks and headquarters building would be in the center of the fourth side that paralleled the river.

John hired some roof thatchers from Exeter to repair the existing roofs. In keeping with military tradition, he bought plenty of white wash for the buildings exterior. He purchased lumber to build two level bunks to be installed in the troops' barracks. Tables and benches would be built as well.

By the time the Royal Engineers arrived, the roofs of the existing buildings had been repaired and weatherproofed. The interior and exteriors of the buildings had been painted white. The first problem John presented to the engineers was to provide heat for the buildings. One of the engineer officers suggested building a firebox outside the buildings. The smoke would escape through the chimney and the heat would be channeled into the building through a large vent.

"What about building fireplaces instead?" John asked.

"I believe the ground furnace would be quicker to build, be safer in the long run, and would allow no smoke to enter the room."

Volunteers were assigned to the engineers and the work began immediately.

John insisted that the headquarters and officers barracks be built last. In the meantime, a large tent was erected on the site and he assigned a sergeant and two privates to man it.

Things began taking shape. As soon as it was feasible, John planted an old ship's mast pole in the middle of the square and prepared it for the Union Jack. John was anxious to put the men on a regular training schedule. Since construction was well under way, John divided training into two sessions. While Troop A worked with the engineers in the morning, Troop B began training. Following a lunch break, the troops switched.

The first training exercise was a two-mile run followed by a half-mile swim, providing the river wasn't too swift. The next exercise was hand-to-hand combat followed by a bayonet drill. After that, the men ran a quarter-mile carrying heavy stones. Then, teams of men carried two longboats for a quarter mile. Training didn't end at dinnertime. In the evening, those who were illiterate were taught to read, write, and calculate basic math. Every officer had to participate in at least one of the training cycles each day.

Fridays were short days that allowed the men time to clean their kits for Saturday inspection. On Saturday mornings, rain or shine, officers marched into the square as the drummer sounded assembly and the troops fell out. Each officer conducted an inspection in ranks with a sergeant on his heel. Making notes of everything the officers found wrong, the marines were reprimanded on the spot and made to run around the square carrying their muskets over their heads until the inspection was complete.

Following the inspection, the men were drilled in the square. Soon John introduced the fife and drums to make the drills even more interesting.

The music was so loud it could be heard faintly in town. As residents of Exeter became familiar with the routine, many came to watch the stirring weekly drills.

Betsy and the children, accompanied by Claudette and Brian, arrived at Starnes House at the end of the second month. John was thrilled when he returned home one night and saw Betsy's carriage. He ran into the house and before she could turn around, he swept her off her feet and whirled her around.

"Put me down, silly," she giggled. "The children will think their father is daft."

John obliged, then kneeled in front of Meggie. Gently, he lifted her up and kissed her cheek. 'How's Papa's little angel?"

Meggie just smiled.

Just then, Richard started crying and reached for his mother. Claudette handed him to Betsy.

"He's hungry. John, come with me while I feed him. Claudette, take Meggie for me, please."

When they were alone, John told Betsy about the progress made at the new marine base.

"I'm glad for you, John. But I'm happiest about the fact we'll see each other every night. I really like the way the house looks. We'll be comfortable here. I already feel like its home. Claudette and Brian like it, too."

Betsy took great pleasure in watching the Saturday inspections. She noticed improvement every week and took pride in the positive comments she heard from the townsfolk.

It was obvious how much the marines respected John. They worked hard to please him and it did not go unnoticed.

One day soon after Betsy arrived, John received word from Plymouth that they had over one hundred new recruits ready to join him at Exeter. He had never expected such a flood of enlistments.

When the new men arrived, John was surprised at how young and eager they were. He quickly promoted four corporals from the ranks to help with the training. The day after their arrival, the new men were introduced to the training program, complete with marches and swims.

Betsy was eager to become part of John's world. She could safely leave the children in Claudette's capable hands and began taking a wagon to town to fetch things for the troops. She also spent part of each morning acting as a nurse as she patched up their minor injuries.

In time, the men were given leave to go into Exeter. They all knew that their commander would breech no nonsense from them. They were told to answer 'yes sir, or 'yes mum' and to give a slight bow to everyone they met and to always treat everyone with respect.

In return, the citizens of Exeter welcomed the marines. They quickly learned marines were different from other military men. They were polite, courteous, and spent their money at local establishments. Although they drank in the inn and public houses, they never consumed more than one or two drinks at a time.

~~~

The Royal Engineers had new instructions to build enough barracks for the eventual fifteen hundred men that were to make up the total marine regiment. Recruits were showing up on a regular basis.

By September of 1707, the new barracks and headquarters building were ready to house more than thirteen hundred marines. All of the completed buildings were sparkling white. The square was edged with wide, gravel walks bordered with white stones. In the middle of the square, the flagpole was edged with the same painted stone; its center also filled with gravel.

Stone walls connected the buildings to complete the square. Two gates, one facing the river and one at the back of the compound, were constructed with guard houses at each gate. An offshoot from the main road, a new road circled the buildings. Training areas were improved and a floating dock was now in use.

By the time all buildings, including the stables and outbuildings, were completed, John's regiment was complete. He was proud of what had been accomplished in a relatively short period of time.

Once in a while, he liked to view the new marine base from the eyes of a newcomer: On a typical day, a guest might arrive by small boat or carriage. The first thing he would see were the white washed buildings of the compound; a large Union Jack fluttering above. He would see men in casual uniforms running in formation along the road. More men would be training near the water carrying longboats back and forth. Others were rowing in teams on the river. If he was lucky, he might observe men practicing bayonet drills in the fields surrounding the barracks. As he approached the main gates, marines in full dress uniforms, standing guard, would greet him. After entering the compound, he would see more soldiers in full uniform drilling on the parade ground. There would be no sign of any slackers because these men were obviously dedicated.

John had long been daydreaming about this scenario. Now it was a reality.

When the First Lord of the Admiralty learned that the new marine base was fully operational, he took his staff to visit the Exeter marine Barracks.

It was a fair day in the spring of 1707 when the party arrived. In addition to the First Lord, there were three other Admirals, several Captains, and a few other staff officers as well. John met them in the headquarters building where they were served coffee and rolls before they began their inspection that included records, the buildings, the training areas, and the boat dock.

The troops were to continue routine training when they would then prepare for a full inspection and parade. Officers then had the opportunity to watch several different training sessions and voiced their amazement at the physical demands the training required.

John explained. "Because of the many different kinds of missions they undertake, it is important they be as strong and physically fit as possible. They have to be tougher than the enemies they encounter;

therefore, they need to be expert not just on the land but on the sea as well." John smiled at his captive audience." This brings me to a request, gentlemen. I would like to ask the Navy to send me an old ship with a skeleton crew who can teach our many new recruits basic seaman skills. The time will come when they will need to be as efficient on a ship as they are in the field. If this is possible, perhaps we can also obtain both field and naval cannon so the men can be trained on them as well. My ultimate goal, gentlemen, is to have my marines become the best trained and best equipped military force the world has ever seen."

The four admirals nodded at each other and smiled in agreement. The First Lord reached over and took John's hand in a handshake.

"I'm sure I speak for all of us, John, when I say we are truly in awe of how much you have accomplished. You will get your ship and your navy cannon. I will send you crews to man them until your own men can handle the job. I cannot promise you field cannon, but I will ask some of my Army friends to assist you in that department."

John pumped the Admiral's hand. "I thank you sir, and my men thank you."

"Now, Colonel MacDonald," the Admiral said, "I believe we are all ready for lunch. It's been quite a morning."

Marines brought two coaches around for the admirals and mounts for the other officers. The entourage drove to Starnes House where Betsy and her staff had prepared a hearty lunch.

When the meal was completed, one of the captains approached Betsy.

"Mum, the First Lord has requested that you and your children be present at this afternoon's ceremony."

"It will be a pleasure, Captain. Thank you," Betsy answered.

Betsy and the children waited for the carriage to return from taking the officers back to the marine base. She took the small carriage and reached the compound just as the first drum roll called the men to formations.

Marines rushed out to the parade ground and quickly formed ranks. Sergeants shouted orders and in less than five minutes the regiment was formed.

After forming, the regiment presented arms to the First Lord who sharply returned the regiment's salute.

"Your Lordship," John said proudly, "I invite you to inspect the troops.

The First Lord inspected the front ranks; his aides completed the task while he returned to his place of honor in front of the headquarters.

John was so proud of his men. Their ranks glistened in the sun. He smiled to himself and then gave the order, "Pass in Review!"

He watched the First Lord out of the corner of his eye as the next order was given, "Fix bayonets!"

All musket barrels were thrust forward and bayonets were drawn and fixed.

"Attention! Shoulder muskets!"

Betsy stood to the side of the reviewing stand. Her heart swelled with pride for her husband and the marines' precision throughout the exercise. She turned as the next command was given.

"Right wheel march." At this point, the fifes and drums struck up a tune and the regiment began to move around the edges of the parade field. Orders were shouted and the precision remained intact as the regiment passed by the reviewing stand and then returned to their original formation.

When the troops completed their review, the First Lord stood and faced the troops. "We feel fortunate to have been here today to watch this performance of great precision. Congratulations! Keep up the good work!"

John was surprised when the First Lord then called him to the front of the reviewing stand.

"It is with great pleasure that I announce your promotion to the rank of Brigadier General. Congratulations, General MacDonald."

John beamed as he heard his marines behind him. "Hip, hip, hooray!"

The ceremony ended and the fifes and drums struck up a tune and marched off the field.

Betsy took the children's hands and they ran to John's side. She threw her arms around her husband's neck and kissed him. "John! I'm so proud. Congratulations! You deserve it!"

The officers lined up and, one by one, they offered their congratulations. As the last admiral shook his hand, he handed John an order from the Queen.

"Her Majesty knows about this promotion and requests that you, your wife and children come to her court as soon as possible."

John was overwhelmed. From past experience, he knew an audience with the Queen also brought many changes in his life.

After a day of preparation, he and his family departed for London and Queen Anne's court.

The children were extremely well behaved that day. Betsy was sure they were intimidated by the lavish surroundings. They held tightly to their parents' hands and did not say one word.

Queen Anne smiled sweetly at the children but Betsy could see the sadness in her eyes. Word traveled fast that the Queen had recently suffered another stillbirth and her face bore the sorrow she tried so hard to hide from everyone.

"Your children are beautiful," the Queen said. "I hope you afford me the opportunity to see more of them."

"Of course, your Grace," John said. "Any time at all."

"Now, Sir John, to the business at hand." She placed a jeweled inlaid officer's sword in his hands. "This is in recognition of your achievement at Exeter."

John humbly accepted the sword.

The Queen continued. "Every once in a while, God smiles down on us mere mortals and blesses us with an exceptional leader. You are such a man, Sir John. Our military is stronger and the world is a little safer because of your leadership."

John swallowed hard. "The credit goes to my men, your Majesty. They are the finest I've ever seen. I accept this gift on their behalf."

The Queen now turned her attention to Betsy. "I have chosen a residence close to the palace for you and your family to use whenever you are in London."

Betsy's face showed surprise.

"Oh, there's a method to my madness," the Queen chuckled. "I'm hoping to see more of you and the children. Will you afford me that pleasure?"

Betsy curtsied. "Of course, your Majesty. I'm honored." She really liked Queen Anne and knew she would do anything to bring joy and pleasure into the Queen's life.

The dinner that night at the Royal Palace included many dignitaries. The Queen was not present, but James Marks was.

John laughed heartily when he saw him. "Aha! You again, my friend? Does this mean my star is once again ascending?"

"I guess you could say that," Marks replied honestly. "The Queen, at my request I might add, is sending you to the American colonies. You are to take a personal escort of twenty men and two officers."

"The American colonies?" John had never given any thought to the new world and was truly surprised at this turn of events.

"You probably know there are tensions building between the crown and those colonies. We want you to travel about as an ordinary civilian and try to understand the feelings of the people and then simply report back here with your findings. While there, we want you to survey the ports of Boston, New York, and Charles Town as possible landing places for an expeditionary force of our troops. We want you to be on constant alert for changes in the harbors so we maintain a current status on each of them. He handed John a sealed envelope. These are your orders. I plan to join you in Boston at a date yet to be determined. Then we can sail home together." He slapped John's back cordially, "Our paths just keep crossing, don't they, friend?"

"It seems so, James. When do I leave?"

"In about a week, I'd say. Your ship awaits you in Plymouth."

"James, this comes as a real surprise. I certainly don't question the timing of these orders but there is a matter here that must be handled as quickly as possible. I had hoped to handle it myself."

"Tell me, John. I'll do whatever I can."

In detail, John told James about Major Dirk Campbell and his intrusion upon Betsy.

"What nonsense!" Marks scoffed.

"Of course his accusations are without merit," John assured him. "I just want to be sure that the major leaves my wife alone and doesn't bother her any more."

"Do you know where Major Campbell is now, John?"

"He's back at Fort William. But I'm worried that he could return at anytime and try to make an arrest."

"I think I will have to arrange a reassignment for Major Campbell. How does India sound, John?"

~~~

When the evening ended, John and Betsy took the coach to their new home near the palace. It was small but elegant and beautifully furnished.

"Our home away from home," Betsy said. "I must admit, though, I doubt we'll spend much time here. Don't you agree, John?" She couldn't help but notice the strange look on John's face. "Oh, oh. I do believe there is something I don't know. Am I correct?"

He took her in his arms and held her tight. "Yes, my love. I'm afraid there is. The Queen has requested I do some exploration in the American colonies."

Betsy let out a muffled cry. "The colonies? They are a world away, John. How long will you be gone?"

"I'm not sure. At least seven months." He looked into her eyes filled with unshed tears and spoke softly. "You know I have no choice. I have to go."

She nodded silently, then wrapped her arms around his neck. "Now, I have something to tell you. I think I'm expecting again."

"Oh, Betsy!" John's look of anguish spoke volumes. "How far along are you?"

"Not far. Maybe six weeks."

John did some rapid calculations. "Good! I'll be back before this baby is born. Thank you for telling me this time. Now I have even more reason to complete this mission as rapidly as possible. Count on it, my love," he said and kissed away the salty tears that slipped down her cheeks.

The family returned to Steddenham the following day. John met with Robert Keith and told him that Major Campbell would be reassigned.

"Where to?" Robert asked.

"India, I believe." The two friends enjoyed shared laughter at this welcomed turn of events.

"One more thing, my friend," John said. "Betsy is expecting again. "Please take good care of her until I return.

"Count on me, John. I'll guard her with my very life."

John was comforted, but this farewell was by far the most difficult. His love of adventure was being replaced with a need to be home with Betsy and his children. His life had changed and he had changed along with it. No longer was he the swashbuckling, devil-may-care adventurer. He now longed for simpler things, like a spontaneous hug from his daughter or watching his son somersault across the lawn. The last few years at Exeter had been the most fulfilling of his career because he could be home at night with his family. Secretly, he hoped this would be his last long sea voyage.

Betsy and the children stood in the portico and waved as John's coach left the driveway.

"Will Papa be gone a long time?" Richard asked.

"Yes, son. Papa will be gone a long time. Always remember, though, that he loves you and he'll return as soon as he can.

Betsy knew the separations were getting harder for John. *Funny,* she thought, *it's a little easier for me.* The children kept her days filled with activities. There were also the affairs of Steddenham to oversee. She relied heavily on Robert but the ultimate responsibilities of the estate were hers. It was the nights when Betsy felt John's absence the most. But now that she was again expecting a child, her energy was gone by late evening and she usually fell asleep quickly. Each night before sleep came, she prayed for John's safety and always added, "If it be Thy will, O Lord, could future missions be conducted here at home?"

-o-

CHAPTER 27

When Major Dirk Campbell learned that John MacDonald had been promoted to Brigadier General, his first reaction was anger followed quickly with intense frustration.

"Of course!" he said to no one in particular. "Why wouldn't he get another promotion? He's the Queen's fair-haired boy! His career flourishes and mine languishes. It's not fair! Wait till the Queen finds out his wife is a murderer and a thief!"

Dirk *knew* who had killed the officers at Glencoe and he *knew* who had stolen the King's treasure from the Royal Mail Coach. It was Betsy Stewart MacDonald. He couldn't prove it because the evidence was just circumstantial. In fact, the only 'evidence' was that she was present at both events. Coincidence? He didn't think so.

The major had been satisfied after his interrogation of Betsy at Steddenham but then the documents disappeared and he didn't know why. Frantically, he had searched everywhere but they never surfaced. He didn't know if they were stolen or if he had carelessly discarded them along with other papers. It was a mystery he was never able to solve.

So much had happened since he first began investigating the crimes. His career had been filled with many other investigations, successful investigations that usually resulted in guilty verdicts. In fact, by exacting creative methods, he was usually able to obtain confessions, so his record of solved cases was extremely high.

The only remaining craw in his throat was Betsy MacDonald. He believed that she alone was the reason he had never been promoted to colonel. Maybe there was still time to change all that.

As he was pacing back and forth in his office, a sergeant entered the room and handed the major a summons from Army headquarters in London. He was elated. The timing was perfect. This time he would finagle a confession from her, no matter what.

When he arrived in London, he went straight to headquarters where he met with Colonel Will Farris.

"Thank you for arriving so promptly, Major Campbell." He gestured toward a chair. "Won't you sit down? Your new orders have arrived. You will be leaving London in ten days to assume your new position as Troop Training Officer in India."

Dirk was shocked. He left the colonel's office and wandered aimlessly. He had managed avoiding overseas duty and because of his successful work chasing criminals, he assumed he had friends in high places.

How in the world did this happen, he wondered. He was just a few years away from retirement. India had certainly not been part of his career plan. Then it came to him. It was that MacDonald woman! It had to be. She had reported him to someone in high places and now he was being cast into oblivion. *Not without a fight,* he thought.

Dirk went straight to some of his influential friends to see if they could overturn his new assignment. None of them would even grant him an appointment. He finally realized he was going to India whether he liked it or not. That also meant he would probably remain there until he was eligible for military retirement. Ten days. There was still time to get revenge on Betsy, and he knew exactly what to do.

It didn't take long for him to learn she had returned to Steddenham and her husband had left on another sea voyage. After putting on civilian clothes, he went into the east side of the city and hired three accomplices.

The next day, he hired a coach and the four men drove to the area of the country house at Steddenham where they were dropped off. They hid in the woods and watched for activity by household members. After a few days of observance, he noted a pattern. In mid-morning, Betsy walked to the edge of the woods and picked wildflowers and berries.

"The next time she takes a daily stroll," he told them, "I want you to take her, rape her, sodomize her, and whatever else you want." His face turned red with anger. "Beat her until she's unconscious, but don't kill her. I want that red-haired bitch to live to regret what she's done." Then he gave them specific instructions on the final humiliation for Betsy. "I have to go back to London now. You can handle it from here." He handed them ten pounds each. "Go earn your money, boys."

~~~

The next morning, Betsy wasn't feeling well. It was a lovely day and she had planned to return to the woods to pick wildflowers, but decided just to rest until the sickness subsided.

Claudette came into the room and saw her mistress sipping hot tea.

"I know you aren't feeling well, Miss Betsy. Is there anything I can do for you?"

"I was going to pick some more wildflowers. Maybe another day" she said with a weak smile. "Would you want to do it for me?" she asked.

"Of course," Claudette said. "I'll get my cloak."

"Mine is hanging right there by the door. Take mine," Betsy suggested.

Claudette slipped the cloak over her shoulders and pulled the hood up over her head and went to pick the flowers.

The men hiding in the woods watched with growing excitement as the young woman came toward them. They did not know Betsy by sight, but they assumed this was their prey.

Suddenly, Claudette felt a hand close over her mouth and the point of a knife at her throat.

"Don't cry out," a man ordered, "or I'll kill you."

They pushed and shoved her deep into the woods, threw her to the ground and stripped her. One man tossed a coin to see who would go first.

The man who won pulled down his pants.

"Caleb, you're a lucky son of a bitch!" The other two swilled bottles of wine and watched as their companion fell on top of Claudette.

Using all her strength, Claudette pushed at her assailant. Caleb stopped for a moment.

"Joe, hold her arms down. I can't do nothin' till she stops fighting me."

Joe kneeled down and held Claudette's arms above her head.

When Caleb finished, he stood up. "Give me the bottle, Homer. It's your turn."

As each of them took turns with Claudette, her mind screamed in agony, in fear, in anger, and outrage. Why were they doing this? She tried to close her mind to what was happening to her. *Please God, make them stop!*

When the gag was removed from her mouth and she was turned over, she knew what was coming. She tried to resist but it was useless. The pain was too great. She cried in agony, but she knew they didn't care.

Finally, it was over. One of them pulled her to her feet while the other two pummeled her body. She lost consciousness quickly and slumped to the ground. It was then one of them noticed.

"This girl doesn't have red hair! I think we got the wrong girl."

"It don't matter. We done what we were told," Caleb said. "And we earned our money."

Joe threw an empty bottle of wine to the ground. "Let's finish and then get out of here."

They fulfilled their employer's last instruction, and then scurried away, leaving the naked unconscious girl face up and spread-eagled.

~~~

Betsy took a nap after Claudette left and slept for over an hour. When she awoke, she felt better and went to find Claudette.

"She hasn't returned yet, Miss Betsy," Stella said.

After another hour had gone by and Claudette had still not returned, Betsy went to find Claudette's husband.

"Brian, I'm getting concerned that Claudette's not back yet. Would you go look for her? I want Robert to go with you as well."

Sam, one of the stable hands, asked if he could go too. The three ran toward the woods, calling her name. There was no reply.

"Let's spread out," Robert suggested. "We'll cover more ground that way."

After an hour, Robert found her. She was lying where her assailants had left her. He shouted to Brian and Sam. "I found her! Over here! I found her!"

The three men were shocked by what they saw. It was evident she had been raped repeatedly and beaten. She was lying in a pool of blood. A cucumber was in her mouth and a large dead rat lay between her legs. Her torso was painted with red letters: "Murderer, Thief." Above her head was a wooden grave marker that read: "R.I.P. Lady MacDonald"

Brian rushed to his wife's side. He pulled the cucumber from her mouth and flung the rat into the bushes. Carefully, he wiped away the red paint and then gently covered her body with his cloak. Only then did he drop to his knees and sob.

Robert sent Sam to fetch a cart. He stared at Claudette. Because of all the bruises and the loss of blood, he thought she was dead.

Brian looked up at Robert with a sorrowful expression. "Oh, my God! Who would do such a thing? And why?"

Robert shook his head slowly. "Only bloody monsters, Brian. Only bloody monsters."

Suddenly, Claudette whimpered. Her eyes fluttered, then partially opened. She saw Brian and reached for his hand. Her lips barely moved and she spoke in a whisper.

"Three men...dressed in dark colors...from London...thought I was Miss Betsy."

"Sshh, sweetheart. Rest now. You can talk later." Brian sat beside her and lifted her head on his lap. Gently, he stroked her face and hair, hoping to comfort her.

Sam returned with the cart. Claudette moaned as they carefully lifted her and placed her on it and Brian once again covered her shivering body.

Robert pulled Sam away so Claudette couldn't hear. "Do not speak of this to anyone. If word gets around, Claudette's reputation will be forever blemished. Do you understand?"

"You don't have to worry about me, sir," Sam said reassuringly. Claudette sat with me when my Mum died and then helped me arrange the funeral. She paid for the coffin and gave me ten pounds to tide me over and even told me not to pay it back. I would gladly have died for her."

Robert asked, "Sam, do you know if they still use the Hue and Cry in this district?"

"They do, sir, and it works very well. We don't have much crime in these parts because of it. If we don't find the criminal, the people in neighboring districts will."

"Go raise it then! Tell the Magistrate to be on the alert. Tell him three men, probably from London, attempted to kill a woman near Steddenham. They'll do the rest. Run now. Take my horse and hurry!"

Sam was already running. "Aye, sir. Quick as a wink!"

When they reached the house, Brian carried Claudette up to her room, placed her on the bed, and covered her with a blanket.

In the meantime, Robert found Betsy and told her what had happened. Betsy called for Stella then ran to Claudette's side. Carefully and gently, they bathed her and cleaned her wounds. Claudette stirred and moaned softly. Betsy gave her a sleeping draught to relieve the pain and help her to sleep comfortably.

For the next several days, Brian stayed by her side night and day and nursed her. He fed her and bathed her, and slowly she began to recover.

The attackers were stupid and unimaginative. They found the closest pub and began drinking, while they none-too-quietly applauded themselves for how skillfully they had completed their task. Within hours after the Hue and Cry went out, the three men were located, subdued, and brought to the magistrate who threw them into jail.

While they were awaiting trial, they were interrogated separately. After hours of intense questioning, they were all too eager to confess. Then they had to wait until Claudette was strong enough to identify them.

When everyone was assured that Claudette's healing was well under way, Brian and Robert escorted her to town where she never hesitated in identifying her attackers. She even remembered their names.

The three criminals exchanged surprised glances when they realized how careless they had been to call each other by name.

Brian told the Magistrate. "There is someone else who is responsible too. It's important that we find out who was behind this and why."

"I'm ahead of you there, Mr. Cahill. One of them—Caleb I think—told me he hadn't trusted the man who hired them so he followed him back to a barracks in London. 'The bloke was an officer,' Caleb said. He asked around and learned that his name was Dirk Campbell. Caleb told me that since the man was a major, it probably was on the up-and-up and the three of them agreed to follow through." The Magistrate laughed. "So much for honor among thieves."

Robert flinched when he heard the name Dirk Campbell. Now he knew for sure that Betsy had been the real target.

Three days later, a court was convened in the village. Caleb, Joe, and Homer were found guilty of grievous assault and attempted murder. Justice was swift and they were hung the next morning.

Robert insisted that the entire matter be kept at low key. The villagers were only told that three men had attempted to murder a girl from Steddenham manor house and that they were tried, convicted, and hung.

Within weeks, it was old news and the conflict with the French became the topic of conversation in the village and throughout the district.

During the early days of Claudette's recovery whenever Brian wasn't with her, Betsy was. She felt tremendous guilt about what had happened.

"I am so sorry you had to suffer because a mad man hated me so much," Betsy told her.

"Oh, don't be, Milady," Claudette said sincerely. "I know it sounds strange, but I have a sense of satisfaction that I could suffer this indignity instead of you. I have always believed that part of my responsibility is to protect you in any way I can. You have always been more than an employer to me. When we were girls in France, you always gave me love and friendship. I am proud I could save you from that awful experience."

Betsy embraced her friend. "Claudette, a friend like you comes along once in a lifetime. Thank you. I hope I can be the same steadfast friend as you are."

In the days that followed, Betsy watched and listened to Claudette and began to see a new woman emerging. Claudette seemed to have gained new purpose, courage, and strength from her terrible ordeal. Betsy had already planned to reward her handsomely but now, she decided, that was not enough. She wanted Claudette and Brian in the kind of relationship that would tie them to Betsy and her family forever.

She spoke to Robert about it.

"Robert, you have spent a lot of time observing Brian. I know Claudette well, but not Brian. Tell me about him."

"Well, I know your husband thinks highly of him. They have been friends for many years. I also think highly of Brian. With some additional training and schooling, he could become a fine estate manager. His loyalty to you and John is as deep as Claudette's."

He watched as Betsy's eyes brightened and a small smile turned up her lips. "What are you thinking, my dear Miss Betsy?"

"Oh, nothing I want to discuss right now," she replied. "I have time to think about it until John comes home. Till then, it'll just have to be my little secret." She tilted her head and walked away with a little bounce to her step.

~~~

Dirk Campbell hated India. The people were poor and dirty and the disgusting smell of curry filled the air. The idea he could be buried here for the rest of his career was depressing. But at least once every day, he consoled himself with the fact that Betsy MacDonald was in total disgrace by now, if indeed she was still alive.

A month after he arrived, an English ship came into port. The next day Dirk was on the parade ground supervising the training of a group of native recruits. A lieutenant accompanied by four guards, approached him.

Dirk's heart fell as the guards surrounded him and the lieutenant instructed him to surrender his sword.

"Major Dirk Campbell," he announced loudly, "I arrest you in the name of the Queen for conspiracy to commit murder. Guards, take this man away."

Dirk was stunned when he was marched off to prison to await court martial. *What in the hell happened,* he wondered. No one would give him any details of the indictment. He had to wait for his day in court.

It came just two weeks later.

The evidence was damning. "Three men from London viciously raped, sodomized, and physically assaulted a young woman named Claudette Cahill. After intensive interrogation, the three confessed. Later, the victim personally identified them."

"Who the hell is Claudette Cahill? I don't know anyone by that name." Dirk had no idea what they were talking about.

The statement continued. "Before one of the attackers was hanged, he also confessed that Major Dirk Campbell, previously unknown to them, had hired the three men to brutalize Lady Betsy MacDonald, but they had mistakenly attacked her hand servant."

Dirk slumped in the defense chair. *The wrong woman? They attacked the wrong woman?* he thought. *I hired idiots!* The impact hit home. Lady MacDonald is alive and well!

All of the statements were certified. It did not take the court martial long to reach a verdict.

"Major Dirk Campbell, this court unanimously finds you guilty as charged and sentences you to life imprisonment in a military prison to be later designated. You will be stripped of your rank and all privileges as an officer in Her Majesty's service."

The next morning, he stood in front of a military formation and was formally stripped of his rank. Tears of anger blurred his eyes when he realized that his power base was gone forever. Silently, he swore that somehow, someway, he would exact his revenge on Lady Betsy MacDonald.

-o-

CHAPTER 28

The crossing from Plymouth to Boston took six weeks. It allowed John a great deal of time to think. He had not been happy about making this trip and wasn't sure he understood the need for it. The colonies were growing rapidly and he had not heard of any uprising except with the native Indians outside the villages in the wilderness. Being a loyal officer, John never questioned his orders. Rather, he accepted each one as a challenge and as an opportunity for personal growth. He was sure that this trip, too, would serve an important purpose upon its completion. And then he could go home.

He smiled when he thought of his family. Betsy, with her beautiful auburn hair and luminous eyes, was everything a man could hope for. She was a lover, friend, companion, partner, and nurturing mother to his children. And now another child would soon be born. Whenever John looked at Meggie, it was like seeing a miniature Betsy. She had the same hair, the same eyes, and the same infectious flirtatious laughter. Even little Richard had many of his mother's expressions, though Betsy thought Richard was a copy of his Papa.

John was aware of how much he had changed through the years. He no longer felt complete without his family and wanted nothing more than to be able to tuck his children into bed and kiss them goodnight.

John acknowledged his gratitude every night in his prayers.

He was also grateful to James Marks. Not because of this mission but because of his promise to send Dirk Campbell half way around the world. John was puzzled by Campbell's unorthodox interest in Betsy's actions of so many years ago. It was as though he had a personal vendetta against her. Thanks to James, though, John no longer had to be concerned about that matter.

Now, he would concentrate on the matter at hand, complete the job, and return to England. With luck, he planned to return home in less than six months.

The air was warm and balmy as the ship approached the Charles Town harbor. The town was built on a peninsula that separated the Ashley and Cooper Rivers.

Once ashore, John took great pleasure in learning about the town. Homes were well situated to catch any offshore breeze. There was an abundance of flower gardens throughout the town and the air was sweet with fragrance.

Since the climate was so warm, rice and indigo were the major crops. The locals, mainly English and French, traded amicably with the Indians.

John questioned his Army officer escort about the gallows he saw on the town square near the harbor.

"Oh, that!" the officer laughed. "We call that the Execution Dock. There are many acts of piracy along this Carolina coast. When a pirate is caught, he is brought here and executed publicly. It's not as messy as the guillotine."

John quickly agreed, then asked about the political mood of the townsfolk.

"People here get along well. There isn't much dissention regarding English rule," he said. Every now and then, there's a rumble about the increase in taxation. That's natural. They work hard for their money and don't want the Crown digging into their pockets."

John spent several days talking to the people of Charles Town and found the officer's observations were sound.

After evaluating the harbor, John strongly suggested that the government maintain a strong presence in the Charles Town area because he believed that the present defenses of the harbor would be hard to overcome against an entrenched enemy. It was just a precaution in case attitude against the Crown grew in intensity.

Before leaving this charming place, John carefully penned his findings and his recommendations and posted them to the Admiralty.

John's next stop was New York. It was easy to see the importance of this large port that already boasted about seven thousand people. John found it a confusing city. No one spoke the same language. In fact, he learned there were at least eighteen different languages spoken. He wondered how trading and shipping could be successful with no one understanding what was being said.

He found that many, especially the English-speaking citizens, were trying to learn other languages so communication between them could be improved.

Some complained about taxation, but John believed most were content with their situation.

John's evaluation of the area surrounding New York indicated to him that the best routes of attack would be for the invading fleet to drop anchor on the north side of Long Island and put troops ashore to first attack Brooklyn and then capture the guns commanding the Verrazinano Narrows. This action would allow the fleet access to Long Island where troops could be landed under cover of a bombardment.

At the conclusion of this visit to New York, he again filed a report along with his recommendations to the Admiralty.

When his ship arrived in Boston, he was met by the Army commanding officer, who delighted in giving John a history lesson of the area.

"Boston is the largest colony in New England. There are probably close to ten thousand people here now," Major Smithers said.

John was curious. "Are most of the settlers from England?"

The major continued the history lesson. "The first settlers were British Puritans who came here to find religious freedom. It's interesting to learn that they don't tolerate anyone who disagrees with their religious beliefs. Punishment included whippings. Years ago, they drove out a group of Quakers. When some returned, they were tortured and some were hanged."

John laughed. "So much for religious freedom."

"The community is changing, though. Every month ships arrive carrying immigrants eager to be part of the new world."

Later John took the opportunity to talk to local colonists. He found most of them were loyal to the Queen. The only complaint he heard was that, as freeborn Englishmen, they thought they should have a voice in parliament and colonial councils. John found no fault with that position.

Some mentioned there were also problems with taxations and felt the Crown was not responsive to their input.

One day at a local pub, John overhead a conversation.

"Well, me and my friends think the time will come when we have to break with England."

The drinking partner just laughed. "You and your friends are crazy. That will never happen."

"Never is a long time, my friend. One thing I've learned is 'never say never'"

During the next few days, John and his marines took shore surveys and found favorable landing places with easy access to good roads that could be used if invasion ever became necessary. He noted that Breeds Hill, overlooking Boston, could be used as a defensive point for any rebel force. After investigating, he discovered how it could be bypassed thereby trapping defenders by cutting off their supplies and escape route. Thus, the enemy would be forced to either surrender or starve in a matter of weeks. When he had gathered all the information he needed, he wrote his recommendations then waited for James Marks to arrive.

His work completed, he had time to browse the city. Soon, he felt very much at home. The climate was similar to what he was used to in England. The locals were friendly and seemed interested in learning all the news from London.

Marks arrived in Boston a week later. He couldn't wait to learn John's impressions. Over dinner and drinks, John eagerly detailed his impressions and his findings.

"Do you think we can retain these colonies without force?" he asked John.

"I hope so, James." John became candid. "At this time, I see no united move toward independence. The land is too vast and it would be difficult and expensive to send expeditions into the wilderness to fight. We, of course, have a powerful, well-trained, and very skillful military. We would probably prevail but at a tremendous loss of life on both sides.

"We should view this new land," he continued, "not as a series of colonies, but as part of England, with the same laws and taxes for everyone. If we continue to treat these people differently than their English counterparts, we are courting the loss of this valuable asset which will ultimately be a great and unnecessary disaster for England."

Marks poured them both another glass of wine and held his glass aloft. "Here's to you, John. You have collected valuable information. Once again, you have proven yourself to the Crown. Now," he said and paused for effect. "I want to make a suggestion that I want you to seriously consider. As Lord Steddenham, I believe it is time for you to join the Queen's Privy Council and help guide the policies of our nation." Marks stopped momentarily when he saw John's negative reaction. "Wait a minute, John. Hear me out. This would really not be difficult for you. You would only need to give your opinion on things that you fully understand and have actually seen. Trust me, this would have great impact on the council members. I am certain your input would assist them in making sound recommendations to our Queen. Of course, it would mean living in London and attending frequent meetings. It's time for you to take your place in the House of Lords as well. Queen Anne and I both need you there, John. You can continue to rely on me to be your eyes and ears."

John took a deep breath and blew it out through his mouth. "James, you always amaze me. You have the uncanny ability to turn my life around 180-degrees whenever you appear. You've done it again. This sounds like a ponderous responsibility. I promise you I'll give it a lot of thought."

Now it was James Marks' turn to take a deep breath.

John's brow furrowed. He knew something unpleasant was coming. "I guess that was the good news. Now it's time for the bad news. What do you have to tell me, James?"

James reached across the table and placed a hand over John's. "First let me tell you the news has a happy ending and Betsy is fine. Three men kidnapped, raped, brutalized, and almost murdered Claudette. They thought she was Betsy."

"Oh, my God!" As John jumped to his feet, he spilled the glasses of wine that were on the table between them.

"There is more," James said. "Now for the happy ending. Claudette has recovered. The three assailants were captured, confessed and were subsequently hanged. During interrogation, one of them placed blame on the man who hired them, Major Dirk Campbell."

"Campbell?" John shouted. "I thought you told me he was in India."

"Calm down, John, and I'll explain. Campbell managed to arrange this before he left for India. But he was arrested there, faced a court martial and was sentenced to life in prison for his complicity."

John sat down and ran his hands through his hair. "Where is that bastard now?"

"He's on his way back to England."

John's face reddened and his jaw clenched. I swear I'll kill him."

Again, James closed his hand over John's in order to calm him. "Rest assured, my friend and trust me when I tell you that this chapter in your book will soon end…permanently."

John grabbed the bottle of wine and took a few hearty gulps. "I have to return home." He wasn't asking, he was telling.

James nodded. "It's all been taken care of. We leave on the morning tide."

The favorable winds and the bright blue sky promised a beautiful day. John watched as the Boston harbor faded into the distance.

The ship tacked and headed east toward England and home.

～～～

A half a world away, another ship pulled anchor from the port of Bombay and headed west toward England.

It was a beautiful day with favorable winds and a bright blue sky.

A manacled Dirk Campbell, with two guards close by, stood on deck as the British East Indiaman sailed toward the Cape of Good Hope.

The sea was calm but he could see that sharks were following the ship's wake. He shuddered. *Imagine being torn apart by one of those horrible creatures,* he thought.

Dirk was exercised on deck for a short time every day but he was manacled during those times and then taken back to the ship's hold where his manacles were connected to a large iron ring fastened to the lowest deck. Day after day, he was kept chained in total darkness except for the short exercise time.

There was no ventilation in his cell and the temperature was stifling. Although he could reach a water jug, he was still thirsty most of the time and he was always wet with perspiration.

For the first time in his life, Dirk was frightened. The thought of life in prison terrified him. He knew what happened there. The prisoners were cruel to one another. The guards didn't care. Sometimes they even participated in the cruelty. As an ex-soldier, Dirk knew that he would have to fight for his life every day he was in prison. Prisoners hated each other, but they hated the military more. He had to find a way to escape.

Several weeks before, the long arms of James Marks reached India. In a counting house in Bombay, a deal was struck between a friend and two crew members of the East Indiaman, the ship responsible for transporting Dirk back to London.

Events previously agreed upon were now set in motion.

One night, the ship approached the Cape of Good Hope amid a squall. Dirk could hear the ship creak and felt it surge through the sea.

He rose up on one arm and saw a light. Someone carrying a candle approached him. Soon, the light illuminated the faces of two rough looking sailors as they came toward him.

"Good evening, Mate," one said quietly. "We come to visit you."

When Dirk tried to stand up, the other sailor struck him in the head with a marlin spike. They removed his manacles and carried him to the door of the companionway where they waited until they were certain there was no one around. Then they carried the unconscious Dirk to the rail and unceremoniously dropped him over the side. Satisfied, the two sailors returned to the forecastle to wait for the next watch.

The impact and shock of the water brought Dirk back to consciousness. He fought his way to the surface and gasped for air. Instantly, the surging sea buffeted him. He fought to stay afloat and managed to keep his head above the water by treading water. It took him a minute to fully comprehend where he was.

"Oh, my God! What in the hell happened?"

He could see nothing around him. The rain pelted his head and he wondered why it hurt so much. Swells washed over him and he swallowed salt water and then gasped for air.

Gotta think, gotta stay alert. I'll be rescued. When morning comes, a ship will rescue me.

The night was pitch black but toward dawn the storm blew over and Dirk began to see light in the eastern sky. He turned over and floated on his back to conserve his energy. He knew he would eventually drown unless a ship came to his rescue. Then he felt something brush against his back. Terror struck him when he saw the fins of circling sharks. He was unaware that when he was struck on the head, his scalp had been cut and was bleeding. Frantically, he thrashed the water and screamed for help.

The attack of the first shark took off his left foot. The other sharks, aroused by the presence of fresh blood in the water, tore him to pieces while he was still alive. His agonizing screams were quickly silenced as he gurgled and his mouth filled with blood.

His shirt and trousers were all that remained. Soon they floated silently and aimlessly on the surface of the sapphire blue Indian Ocean.

The next morning, the Captain was notified that the prisoner they were taking to London had escaped and must have gone over the side. The Captain feigned concern, then duly noted the event in the ship's log. Secretly, he was glad to be rid of the prisoner. It was one less responsibility.

~~~

John's homecoming was an emotional reunion. He held his wife as though he'd never let her go. Betsy clung to her husband and let the tears flow freely.

Together they went to see Claudette and Brian. John's face revealed his concern and his sorrow for what she had suffered.

Claudette assured him. "I'm fine, Sir John. Please don't worry about me. Everyone has taken such good care of me. The guilty have been punished and I'm starting to put this all behind me."

John noticed that Betsy seemed ill. She was in her eighth month of pregnancy when she began to suffer severe discomfort and spasms. John became so concerned that he sent for the midwife.

The news was not good. "I think this baby is coming too soon but I'm concerned because these spasms are not normal. At this point, I'm unsure of the outcome. If you prefer, Sir John, I'll stay with Lady Betsy until she delivers."

Betsy was sure everything would be fine, but John insisted the midwife stay.

Later that evening, Betsy delivered a stillborn baby girl. Although she lost a lot of blood, the midwife felt certain Betsy would recover.

Betsy was too weak to cry but the sorrow in her eyes reflected her deep loss. Gently, John cradled her and cried enough tears for them both.

By the time Betsy was strong enough to function again, John was called to London. Before he left, Betsy had something important to discuss with him.

"John," she said. "Claudette was ravished and almost beaten to death because they thought she was me. I've been thinking about this for a long time. I want to put Brian and Claudette in charge of Starnes House and pay them five thousand pounds a year. The estate's profits are more than that every year. Brian could be made your attendant and given the title of Squire. I also want to deed them two hundred acres and build them a house. It is the least we can do for them."

John agreed wholeheartedly. "Why don't we do the same for Robert Keith here at Steddenham? We can make all the arrangements and then surprise them. I shall have Robert and Brian entered on the rolls as my assistants so they will both officially be my Squires. Such loyal service should be duly rewarded."

"I'm glad we think alike," Betsy said.

John returned to London and took his place in the House of Lords. The following month, Betsy and the children joined him. She was present when her husband was named Duke of Barrington and raised to the Privy Council. John was now one of the most influential men in the kingdom.

When Queen Anne heard of Betsy' recent loss she invited her to her private quarters. Together the two women shared grief over losing a child. Betsy noticed that the Queen was slurring her words.

The Queen had always been a drinker but her habit was now so bad that her subjects began to call her 'Brandy Nan' behind her back. She wasn't paying much attention to politics or to the brilliant members of her court. It was said she could not even carry on a conversation. She had gained so much weight; she had to be rolled about in a chair. Her critics were very harsh. Everyone seemed to forget the tremendous loss she encountered every time she lost a child.

Betsy remembered the Queen from better days. She listened as Queen Anne talked about the love she bore for her husband and her personal agony of not being able to give him children. Betsy was always kind to Queen Anne although others around her were not. Sadly, Betsy believed that Queen Anne was on a downward spiral that would probably result in her death.

After the Privy Council adjourned, John and his family returned to Steddenham so John could finalize the purchase of two hundred acres adjoining the estate and put the deed into Robert Keith's name. An agent at Starnes House had done the same thing there for Brian and Claudette.

John and Betsy gathered the two couples in the drawing room and sat them down. Stella presented glasses of wine to each of them and then quietly left the room.

Betsy was as excited as a child. John's face was beaming.

"You go first, John," Betsy grinned.

John grinned. "No, sweetheart, you go first."

After they both gave the news, the two couples were momentarily speechless and sat with their mouths open.

"Wait! There's more," John said and spoke to Robert and Brian together. "I have entered both your names in the list of heraldry as my assistants. That means you are both to be addressed forthwith as Squire. Now, shall we have a drink in honor of Squire Robert Keith and Squire Brian Cahill?"

The merriment and free flowing wine lasted well into the early hours of the morning.

John and Betsy slept late the next morning and remained in bed. They talked quietly about their plans for the future and how they would incorporate Barrington Estate into their lives. It was noon before they finally decided to rise and have breakfast.

They went downstairs and joined the children who were eating lunch. Richard jumped up when he heard a horseman galloping down the driveway, then followed his father to the door. The houseman answered the door then turned to hand a note to Sir John. John came back into the dining room and sat down to finish his coffee.

Betsy was curious. "Open it, John. Who is it from?"

John turned the blank envelope over. "It doesn't say," he replied.

Carefully, John opened the envelope, unfolded the letter and a smile escaped his lips as he read:

"Lord Barrington,

Neither you nor your wife need ever be concerned with Major Dirk Campbell again. He was drowned off the coast of East Africa several weeks ago and his body was never found. All of his documents were accidentally destroyed so nothing of his accusations will ever be raised again.

A Friend

John excused the children and sent them to play, then he gave the letter to Betsy to read. She fell back in her chair and sighed.

John scoffed. "Imagine how silly it was to suspect you of robbing the Royal Mail. Preposterous! And the idea that a little thing like you could kill two of the King's soldiers by yourself is madness isn't it?"

Betsy just smiled and nodded. "Yes. Madness is the perfect word."

The couple exchanged knowing glances. Each had read between the lines and knew that Major Dirk Campbell had been murdered.

The following day, the family returned to their London home.

The morning after they arrived, John was up early. Soon after, Betsy turned the children over to a maid and went to the palace to see the Queen.

Queen Anne had spent a restless night and was somewhat out of sorts until she saw Betsy. Then her behavior changed. "Come here, child. I am so glad you have returned. Are you staying for a while?"

"I will be staying here with John until he is reassigned."

The Queen took Betsy's hand and gave her a teasing look. "The two of you may be going somewhere sooner than you think." She stopped and shook her finger. "I can say no more at this time."

Quickly, she changed the subject. "Tell me, Betsy. Are you happy with your life now that you are a Duchess?"

"Oh, yes, your Majesty. We could not be happier," Betsy answered with a broad smile.

"I know you, Betsy. It isn't being a Duchess that makes you happy. It's having a happy marriage. Titles don't make good bed partners, but the love of a good man does. Am I right?"

Betsy nodded.

"In spite of my grotesque appearance, my husband and I share a deep love, too. It pleases me to see others who are also in love." A look of sadness crossed her face. "I know that everyone thinks I am a fool and perhaps they are right. Aside from that, I can see the quality in people and you are definitely one of my favorites."

The Queen moved around on her couch in discomfort.

"Dear, would you straighten my pillows? I am so tired. I know it is only mid-morning, but I need a nap. Please sit with me until I fall asleep. You are such a comfort to me. After I am asleep, don't tarry. Go home to your husband and children."

"Yes, your Majesty. I will," Betsy answered.

It took a long time before the Queen finally fell asleep and Betsy was able to leave. She arrived home a short time before John. She asked the maid to bring them both a cup of hot tea. Tea was a new import from the Far East that was quickly becoming the rage. Neither she nor John liked to drink wine all the time, so tea was a nice change.

John asked about the Queen's health and was surprised when Betsy indicated that he was going to get a new assignment and that she and the children would be going with him.

John couldn't help but laugh. "Well, I guess I'll find out when James Marks makes another unexpected appearance. Sometimes I wonder if Marks works for the Queen or if the Queen works for Marks. I wonder if she may be controlling more than we all realized," John mused. "One thing I know for certain, she is not stupid. She is smart enough to keep some very bright men beside her at all times."

"Are you referring to James Marks?" Betsy asked.

"Yes. He seems to know everything that is going on and always shows up at some strange times with very accurate assessments about what England needs to know or do."

"I don't think I've ever met him," Betsy remarked.

"Not formally," John admitted. "I like him and I trust him. He is very direct and he always wants a commitment from me. I sometimes believe that he is the Queen's personal representative."

"Hmm," Betsy said. "Sounds like an interesting but mysterious man."

"I've tried to figure this all out and I've come to the conclusion that Government is not directing me nor is the Queen. I believe James Marks is behind it all. And I'm not sure why he has so much power."

"John, I believe you're wrong," Betsy protested. "You produced astonishing results. Everyone is impressed with your capabilities. Marks has watched you and then reported to the Queen. Together they have been helping you ever since. You have earned everything that has been given to you."

"Thank you for that, my love. Got any idea about what's in store for me next?"

"None whatsoever, but I'm certain we will find out soon enough."

Betsy had hardly finished her sentence when the two children bounced into the room.

Meggie was turning into a little beauty. She was all frills and lace but she had a mind of her own and was always ready with an opinion. Richard was a more serious child who emulated his father's every move. He wanted to be a marine just like his father. Generally, the children played together very well but there were times when they almost had to be separated because of their tiffs. The children worshiped their parents and wanted to go everywhere with them. They did so whenever it was possible.

It was hard to find park-like settings in London because of the coal fires that were always burning in the city. The air was often foul, so Betsy often took the children out to the banks of the Thames River to escape the bad air.

After Claudette was attacked, Betsy was never alone. Her coach and footmen were actually marines wearing the house livery so no one would know who they were. They had orders never to let Betsy or the children out of their sight. Betsy took comfort in the safety the marines provided and the children were never aware of possible danger. She believed the children's innocence should be protected as long as possible.

-o-

CHAPTER 29

The Queen was as good as her word. John's new orders consisted of supervising the further expansion of the marine barracks at Exeter. More bright, white buildings were being built to house the headquarters of another regiment. Recruiting throughout England and Scotland began immediately. The fleet force had been expanded, too. John now had three regiments - two in barracks and one at sea.

When it came to his marines, John was a perfectionist. Plans were made to develop an extended training program that emphasized shore missions and raiding. He strongly believed that marines should be equally trained as sailors and as soldiers. In fact, he insisted that his marines become superior in land combat to the average soldier. Spit and shine was still high priority so he redesigned the uniforms to make them even more unique. Officers had to be current on all military matters, so John had them read pre-selected texts describing the typical maneuvers of the European armies as well as books about fighting in North America. He instructed the officers to share their new knowledge with each other before passing the information on to the sergeants. All of the men were required to understand harnesses, saddles, and how to ride and haul equipment with horses.

His high standards paid off in the quality of his officers. By promoting several senior sergeants to officer rank, he tried to discourage the practice of officers buying commissions. This was first accomplished by developing a training course for new officers in whom they had to go through the same training as the enlisted men. The officers who accepted this challenge were far superior to officers in other branches of the service.

When John was satisfied that his three regiments were well-trained, recruitment for the fourth regiment began.

~~~

Betsy was happy to be back at Starnes House. John was home every night and she felt that things were more settled here than at

Steddenham. There were changes though. Claudette and Brian had assumed their new positions as estate managers and would continue to live in the manor house until their new home was completed.

Brian was a quick learner. After some tutoring by Robert Keith, he began his new duties with enthusiasm and finesse.

Claudette was well versed in running a household since she had watched and learned from Betsy for many years. It was strange not to be a handmaiden anymore. The children were a little confused, too. Claudette had been their nanny since they had been born. Now there was a new nanny. The children liked Grace, but sometimes forgot and ran to Claudette out of habit.

Something new seemed to be happening at Starnes House every day. Betsy and Claudette spent a lot of time overseeing the construction of the new house. They walked by the river and watched the children play. The weather was beautiful and sometimes Betsy wondered how life could get any better.

One morning, Betsy was sitting on the front porch watching the children romp across the lawn. Claudette came outside. Her face was smiling but tears were streaming down her cheeks.

"Oh, Betsy, I didn't want to say anything until I was sure. But now I'm sure!" She clapped her hands together. *Finally,* I'm going to have a baby!"

Betsy jumped up and hugged her long time friend. "I'm so happy for you! How do you feel? Does Brian know? When is the baby due?" She was as excited as Claudette.

Claudette laughed. "I feel fine. I told Brian yesterday and he's proud as a peacock. I've got about seven months to go." She stopped for a moment and then confessed. "I didn't think it would ever happen. I can't tell you how happy I am."

Betsy was thinking ahead. "Don't worry. We have lots of time to prepare a layette. We'll make sweaters and blankets and lots of diapers. Let's get started now." She called to the children and then went back into the house.

Weeks later, John received orders to report to the Admiralty in London. Betsy left the children with Grace and Claudette so she could accompany him.

The mood in the Admiralty was somber. When John entered the room, the First Lord was pacing, a deep scowl on his face.

One of the admirals offered John a chair. "Better sit down. It's going to be a long afternoon."

Coffee was served and cigars were lit before the First Lord took a seat.

"There's trouble in North America, John. It's been brewing for some time. But now things are getting critical and I fear we must act as soon as possible.

"What kinds of trouble are we talking about, Admiral?" John wanted as much information as possible. He could see the writing on the wall. He would most probably be commanding another assault.

The Admiral placed a map in front of John and pointed to a circled area. "This is Port Royal in Nova Scotia. It's situated on the Annapolis River. This settlement was founded in 1605 by the French. Later it was destroyed by English colonists but was rebuilt by the French. Since then, it has changed hands between the English and French several times. Now we have learned that the French are fortifying with shiploads of supplies. We believe this port is vital to English interests. We must take it back one last time and break the foothold of the French in that strategically important area."

John wanted to know how he fit into the picture.

The Admiral didn't hesitate. "Troop transports are already headed toward Exeter. We want you to muster two of your regiments for service in this campaign and take personal command of the units. You will be under the command of the Naval Commander for this operation that will include the Army, Navy, and the Marines." He stopped and looked John in the eye. "This is big, John."

"I understand, sir. I'm ready for further orders."

The planning session lasted well into the evening. Before leaving headquarters, John prepared the orders for his command and sent them by courier to Exeter.

When he left for his London home, John was physically exhausted but strangely exhilarated with the idea of taking his men into battle. He was anxious to test his marines against land forces. He knew they would perform brilliantly against the enemy.

John hated to tell Betsy he was leaving again, but this time she took his departure in stride. She was a military wife and had reluctantly learned to accept the necessary separations associated with it.

While John busied himself with preparations, Betsy did what she could to help him. She ordered several cases of his favorite wine and sent them ahead and she made certain he had sturdy protective clothing as well as an ample supply of sundries.

When they returned to Starnes House, John wasted no time in returning to Exeter to insure that his troops would be fully prepared.

On the day of departure, the river bank was lined with families and friends who stood and waved goodbye as the men were ferried out to the waiting transports. One ship-of-the-line and two frigates were standing by as escorts. There was a fair wind in the channel and the convoy soon disappeared from the horizon.

~~~

Betsy felt no need to rush back to Steddenham. The weather was pleasant and the children were able to play outdoors almost every day. Besides, she and Claudette kept busy making baby clothes and discussing possible names for the infant.

At the end of each month, the estate accounts were reconciled. Betsy expressed her pride in the way the Cahills were managing the estate. She noted that all the changes had been positive ones. Claudette and Brian proudly showed Betsy that profits had increased. They wanted to expand by acquiring another two hundred acres of grazing land. Betsy eagerly gave her consent.

The days became weeks, the weeks became months. Betsy was in no hurry to leave. In fact, she decided she would stay until Claudette's baby was born.

After ten days at sea, the convoy was joined by the main force of British ships. The following day, the fleet admiral signaled an officer call. John, as commander of the marines, joined fleet captains in the quarters of Fleet Admiral Sir Roland Stovall. A large chart was spread on a table.

After introductions, the Admiral began. "Our task is to attack and capture Port Royal. The fort there has see-sawed between England and France for years. This time our victory must be permanent. We will be assisted by four regiments of infantry and one of artillery who are already situated in northern Nova Scotia and await our arrival." He placed a hand on John's shoulder. "General John MacDonald will command two regiments of marines who will be put ashore to help conduct the ground attack." The Admiral explained in more detail. "The marines will have to be under the independent command because their job will be to breach the defenses so the Army can enter the fort and capture it. When they reach their destination, John will coordinate with the Army. A plan of attack has not yet been completed. When plans are finalized, we will conduct briefing sessions that will include your ideas as well as your questions."

Each captain was given a preliminary individual assignment before returning to the ships.

John was asked to stay behind. "General MacDonald, I'm proud to have you aboard," Admiral Stovall said. "I commend you on your previous victories at Gibraltar and the way you have almost single-handedly developed a strong marine corp."

"Thank you, Admiral," John replied.

The Admiral handed John a chart of the area. "I want you to study this map and then outline a plan of attack. John, I want to win this battle...no, I *need* to win this battle. It's in a strategic location and is crucial to the future growth of our nation. I have read the accounts of your achievements and I know you can plan a successful campaign and then see it through to victory."

"I'll try my best, sir," John promised.

John went to his assigned cabin and began to study the map. Port Royal was in a bay on the island of Arcadia on the eastern shore of the Bay of Fundy that was noted for its tidal extremes. The entrance to the bay was narrow and protected by two small forts located on either side of the bluffs. During the extreme tidal changes, waters from the Bay of Fundy flowed in and out of the narrow channel and created very strong currents.

Port Royal itself was located on a peninsula between the Bay of Fundy and the inner bay. John looked closely at the map and decided it was actually on the inner bay. He could see that a stream flowed from the vicinity of the fort out to the Bay of Fundy through what appeared to be a gap in the hills. John figured that the stream valley would be well defended and he suspected that the French had fortified the coast and the hills around Port Royal as well as the northeastern approach to it.

As John continued to study, he realized what an excellent position the French had chosen to defend.

He studied distances within the harbor and estimated that it was approximately ten miles from the mouth of the bay to Port Royal. Calculations showed that it was about two miles overland from the Bay of Fundy to Port Royal.

An attack plan began to formulate in his mind. Hours later, he was satisfied with the outline and was ready to present it to the Admiral.

At first, the Admiral said nothing. He folded his arms and closed his eyes. John wasn't sure what he was thinking.

Finally, he opened his eyes and sat upright. "Excuse me, John…I wasn't ignoring you, I was trying to visualize what you proposed. Let me say I think you have thought of every possible scenario. That's good! But I must say, it looks like you have left very little for the Navy to do."

"Not exactly, sir," John replied. "I didn't mention this but I want your ships to commandeer several small fishing boats as we skirt the coast on our approach to Arcadia. We will need your sailors to man them. My hope is that the boats will be big enough to mount at least one cannon each."

The Admiral nodded. "All right. Is there anything else you need?

"Yes. I definitely will need tide tables," he thought for a moment, "and access to about twenty longboats to be used in conjunction with the fishing boats for landing troops. I want the fastest vessel to take a party ashore to reconnoiter the harbor and its surroundings before we attempt a landing."

"I like the plan so far, John. I want to become completely familiar with it before we meet again with the captains. Keep me informed of any changes you find necessary.

John returned to his cabin and began making lists of materials needed for the attack. Then he studied his plan and fine-tuned it. Admiral Stovall was doing the same thing.

The two met again and discussed the changes each of them had made. When they were both satisfied with the results, the Admiral again signaled the fleet captains that it was time for a joint meeting of the minds.

Admiral Stovall presented an outline of the proposed attack, then deferred to John to brief everyone on the details. Questions were asked, refinements were made and by the time the long evening ended, John could tell by the officers' demeanor that they all felt confident that the British would be victorious.

Each captain was given a copy of the entire attack plan as well as detailed instructions regarding his own individual mission.

After careful consideration, John selected Lieutenant Ryan Jones for the reconnaissance mission.

"Lieutenant Jones," John explained, "this mission is vitally important. Our ultimate victory will depend on your success. You know your men better than I do, so select the best one to accompany you. Here is what you need to do. First, look for gun positions other than the ones on the hilltop forts at the entrance to the harbor. Next, move up the coast and locate any troop position or gun positions up to the valley that leads overland to Port Royal. Finally, I want you to return to the harbor entrance and cross it to the other side at slack tide and check for enemy positions south of the harbor entrance. You will both be taken ashore in a longboat. It will then lay offshore and assist you or evacuate you if necessary. I want to stress two important things: You must not be observed and, you have to get out before the tide turns. You will go in on the flow and, hopefully," he smiled, "return on the ebb. Do you understand?"

"Yes, sir!" the Lieutenant said.

"Here are the charts." He handed charts to the Lieutenant, then leaned over his shoulder and pointed. "These areas circled in red are the ones I want you to check. Do you have any questions?"

"No, sir, not at this time," he replied.

"Be sure these charts never fall into enemy hands. Destroy them before you let that happen. One more thing, do not discuss this mission with anyone except the marine you take with you."

The young lieutenant was excited about his mission. "Thank you, sir. I won't let you down."

"Very well, Lieutenant, you are dismissed. We'll meet again for a final briefing just before your mission begins."

After the young officer left, John poured himself some wine and sat down. Now, he needed to devise a time table and coordinate it with all the fleet captains and the Army units who were going to aid him in the attack.

When he was satisfied, he returned to the flagship and presented his revised and detailed plan to the Admiral.

The Admiral called his captains to his ship for a briefing and then scheduled another final briefing for the following week.

"Gentlemen, this will be the first time that most of us have been in an effort that involves a land-sea operation of this magnitude. I doubt that any of you have been in one that involves this much coordination. General MacDonald has developed an operation that will require close coordination between the Army, Navy, and Marine Corps forces. Each of you will have detailed orders that must be followed to the letter. Now, let's get to work."

For the next few hours, coffee cups were kept filled, and cigar smoke filled the room as the officers memorized in minute details the step-by-step plan that, if successful, would put Port Royal back into the control of the British forever.

When the ships arrived in Arcadia, John went ashore to discuss his plan with the commander of the British ground forces, who was surprised to learn that two regiments of marines had been sent to help take the port.

General Foster seemed surprised. "I had no idea the marines could mount such a large force. I'm impressed. Seems as though there have been many military advancements since I was last in England. You say you will attack from the sea while we go down the peninsula from the north. Just what do you have up your sleeve, General MacDonald?"

John carefully went over his plan in detail.

"Capital idea!" the general commented. "Let me see if I understand all this. All we have to do is to move into position and wait for the signal to attack. Your chaps will go ashore and attack from the rear. When you have them thoroughly confused and have taken your objectives, we will launch a frontal attack on their lines. Then we can put them in a nice box."

"That's the plan!" John replied.

General Foster turned to his orderly. "I am ordering an officer call this evening at 1900 hours. All regimental and battalion commanders will be required to attend."

The orderly saluted and left.

"General MacDonald, your name is familiar to me. Aren't you the chap who was made a viscount for your role in the battle for Gibraltar?"

"Yes, I am," John answered. "Queen Anne honored me with that rank."

"From what I heard of that battle, you earned every bit of your position in the peerage. Congratulations!"

"Thank you." John always felt embarrassed with the compliments.

General Foster ordered a bottle of wine and dinner. The two generals had some time to become better acquainted before the other officers joined them for John's briefing.

The next day, the fleet left Arcadia and sailed to the mouth of the Bay of Fundy where they took up station to wait for the Army to advance on Port Royal.

The attack plan began to unfold.

A fast frigate took the reconnaissance team to a point south of Port Royal where they waited out of sight of land before setting the two men ashore.

After dark, Lieutenant Jones and Sergeant Rogers were rowed ashore in a longboat. During the next few hours, the team searched the coast and pinpointed troop concentrations and the few gun positions situated there. They scanned both sides of the harbor entrance and found no guns or troops guarding the passage at water level. The French probably thought that the forts on the hills overlooking the passage would provide enough protection. When their mission was complete, the men returned to the waiting longboat and returned to the frigate on the ebb tide.

The reports from the reconnaissance team indicated that they could proceed with the next step.

The next day, four fishing boats were commandeered and brought alongside the flagship. The fishermen were taken as prisoners and were replaced with sailors and gun crews. Two small cannons were mounted on each boat.

Soon, the convoy of ships sailed up the center of the Bay of Fundy then turned toward shore where the channel opened into the bay leading to Port Royal. Behind them, the four fishing boats quietly laid off shore waiting for a signal to commence their mission. Two battalions of marines had been assigned to first capture and then occupy each fort. Then the third battalion was to land and travel up the shoreline to destroy any enemy positions that would interfere with the landing of the full regiment. When all the marines were ashore, a signal was to be sent to the Army to begin its assault on the French positions on the north end of the peninsula.

Given the element of surprise, it didn't take the marines long to capture the two forts. After reaching the beaches, they climbed up the hills on either side of the harbor entrance, stormed the fort wall and clamored over them. They entered the forts using their bayonets to carry the positions. The French were totally caught off guard and had no time to mount a proper defense. It took less than an hour to accomplish their missions. As soon as the forts were secured, flares were fired to signal the fleet and alert the third battalion to land and begin clearing the enemy from the coast.

At the signal, the four fishing boats allowed themselves to be carried into the harbor on the rising tide. Once inside, their crews began rowing up the bay toward Port Royal. They were to locate and disable any French warships before they were able to go into action. They found two French frigates and were able to silently row up to the nearest one and fire two cannon balls into her, just below the water line. The frigate's crew started yelling as the ship quickly took on water.

The boats turned their attention to the second frigate. Two of them immediately fired cannons and placed close range shot into her at the waterline. She returned fire as the other two boats attacked her stern and destroyed the rudder. During the exchange of gunfire, several of the English attackers were mortally wounded but the little boats headed up the bay, firing at any target until they were able to escape to the shallow water of the east shore where the frigates could not follow.

Meanwhile, because of their close range gunnery, each of the two French frigates was fighting for their lives. They were unaware that four British warships had already passed into the harbor and were ready to attack them and the harbor guns at Port Royal.

At the same time, a full regiment of marines were landing about three miles from Port Royal. They joined with the battalion who had cleared the beach defenses. Soon, they formed a line from the Bay of Fundy to the heights above the town. As soon as the line was established, one of the battalions detached and made an assault on the town. In concert with the land assault, a British frigate fired on the town. Minutes later, two more British warships joined the bombardment.

The Army's bombardment of the French positions lasted for hours. An infantry assault drove the French into retreat. It was then the enemy learned that their artillery, which had pulled back to reestablish, had been overrun and taken from the rear.

Violent street fighting continued along the outskirts of Port royal while British ships destroyed the waterfront.

It was then the British regulars launched a series of assaults on the main French lines. Having lost their artillery support, the French were driven back into the marines who were using fixed bayonets. The attack was so ferocious that the main elements of the French line ran toward the British army troops to surrender. Marines continued their advance until the French garrison in town surrendered.

The naval guns ceased fire and the French commander realized the town had surrendered and that his remaining forces were in a meat grinder. In order to save lives, he ordered his forces to raise white flags. He then asked for a parlay so he could surrender all his forces.

John had come ashore with the second regiment and was present to take the French commander's surrender. A party of John's officers was sent to inform the Army of the French surrender. When the Union Jack was raised along the ridge of the hills, a long lasting cheer resounded through the fleet.

The battle had been hard fought and casualties were suffered on both sides. Now that the shooting had ended, the rebuilding could begin.

Admiral Stovall assigned John to the position of Commander of Port Royal until British Army replacements arrived.

John took his assignment seriously. As he walked through the streets of the town and assessed the damage, he felt angry. He hated war. So many lives were lost. Others were forever changed. *First we destroy then we rebuild,* he said to himself. *It's senseless. But war has always been a part of the human experience. Our entire history focuses mostly on wars and how it invariably alters a country's power base.*

His job now was to rebuild. John's hope was that war would never again come to this beautiful part of the world.

First, John and his officers designed new defenses using the artillery they had taken from the French. There was ample powder and shot for the cannon and plenty of small arms and ammunition.

The next job was to build water level redoubts at the entrance to the harbor to reinforce the forts on the hills. One full regiment worked to repair the damaged French line and then build a whole new row of entrenchments behind existing ones, thus providing an in-depth defensive position. Another line was built even farther back facing the harbor entrance that should prevent them from being flanked.

John was pleased with their accomplishments. He had done the best he could with what he had. Port Royal was now safe. The French fleet was withdrawing from the area and he felt there was little chance for a future attack on the town.

In less than two months, four regiments of Army troops arrived to relieve the marines. Orders arrived for one regiment of marines to return to Gibraltar. Another was sent back to Exeter.

John was ordered to return to London.

~~~

While John was busy battling the French, Betsy was busy battling ignorance.

With the development of the marine base at Exeter, the town grew rapidly. Many marines relocated their families to the town. Consequently, there were many new children, most of whom played in the streets, or just ran wild.

Betsy's love of education was well known. She tutored her own children but with such an influx of families, she saw the need for a structured education for everyone and began searching for solutions.

The churches offered Bible, Latin, and grammar classes for boys but were not interested in expanding their program to include girls. In fact, Father Sheen laughed when Betsy suggested there should be classes available for girls.

"My dear young woman," he scoffed. "That would be such a waste of time. Females don't need to learn. They should let their husbands take care of any matter requiring knowledge. In fact, I'm not sure they have enough brain power to learn."

"But..." Betsy started to protest.

The priest held up his hands as if to fend off an attack.

"No, no, no! I won't hear of it." In a condescending manner, Father Sheen patted her on the head. "Run along, dear, and put such ideas out of your pretty little head."

Betsy was furious. She turned on her heel and forgot her manners completely. She didn't even say 'goodbye.'

While not as arrogant as the Catholic priest, the Anglican priest believed that education wasn't for everyone and certainly wasn't necessary for girls. He smiled at Betsy, "If you as a mother want to educate your daughter, you have the right to do so. My advice to you, though, is to spend more time teaching her needlework rather than reading. She'll thank you for it."

Betsy refused to let two minor setbacks defeat her. She had an idea but would need the cooperation of women who agreed with her. She questioned several women in town and found them open to the idea of education for their daughters.

She felt encouraged, so she invited the marine officers' wives to an afternoon tea. Of the twelve she invited, all eagerly accepted the invitation.

After everyone was served tea and various pastries, Betsy made an announcement.

"Ladies, I'm afraid I have invited you here under false pretenses."

The guests looked at one another with obvious curiosity.

Betsy smiled sweetly. "That got your attention." Laughter rippled through the room. "I was recently informed by a very important man that it wasn't necessary for females to learn because we probably lacked the brain power to do so. Another told me that the only thing we should be taught is needlework."

Several guests gasped in disbelief.

"I learned to read and write when I was ten. My daughter is seven and already knows the alphabet and can even read a few simple words. I want to get your ideas about education for our daughters. Let's have an open discussion and then I'll tell you what I have in mind."

For the next two hours, the women exchanged their own experiences with education, both good and bad. One woman was forbidden by her father to learn to read. He didn't want her to start having any opinions. Another said she never even thought about it much until she became a mother. A third woman said she tutored her own daughter and two nieces as well. Each of the ladies had a story to tell. Betsy was thrilled with the interaction and ease with which the ladies communicated.

Before everyone left, Betsy thanked them for coming. "I believe we've all discovered we have a lot in common. Separately we can do little. Together we can accomplish a great deal. Now I'll tell you what I want to do." She took time to look into the eyes of every one of her guests. "I want to open a Dame School for our daughters."

"I've heard of Dame Schools!" one woman said excitedly. "There are some in London."

"What are they exactly?" another asked.

Betsy answered. "It's an informal school usually taught by older women. Generally, just reading and writing is taught. But once established, we can introduce other lessons as well."

"What about the cost?" one asked.

Betsy was quick to reply. "I already have an anonymous donor who is willing to cover all costs."

The excitement between the women became electric and they all started talking at once. It was obvious to Betsy that her idea was well received.

"Ladies…ladies!" Betsy spoke louder. "Let's meet again in a week. In the meantime, if any of you have an idea of who we can hire, please let me know. Also let's try to get a list of how many girls would be interested."

The ladies continued to chatter as they thanked their hostess and left Starnes House.

By the time Betsy was notified that John was on his way home, she had been successful in opening a Dames School. She rented two rooms in a downtown building and hired two sisters to tutor. One was a widow with grown children of her own; the other had never married but loved the idea of teaching little girls. There were fifteen students in each class.

Betsy felt smug. She had been looking for a way to use some of her private funds other than through church charities. This was perfect. And the anonymous donor was always just a heartbeat away!

Women don't have the brain power to learn? Betsy hoped Father Sheen would live to eat those words.

-o-

CHAPTER 30

John's homecoming was joyous and noisy. The holidays were fast approaching and everyone at Starnes House was in a festive mood.

Meggie and Richard jumped up and down and clapped their hands as they took turns noisily greeting their father.

Then it was Betsy's turn. Her eyes were glistening as John took her in his arms.

"Welcome home, my darling," she whispered. "We missed you."

John looked up as he heard the cry of a newborn. Claudette and Brian entered the room with their new child.

"Congratulations!" John said warmly. "Boy or girl?"

Brian took John's outstretched hand. "It's a boy. His name is John Robert, in honor of you and Robert Keith."

John was touched. "Thank you, Brian. I'm honored."

The dinner that night was exceptionally pleasant. Everyone had stories to tell. The children especially enjoyed sharing their tales. So much had happened to each of them and they couldn't wait to tell their father and shine in the spotlight of his undivided attention.

"I'm learning to read, Papa," Meggie said. "And I can even spell. And guess what? I fell last week and skinned both of my knees."

"Papa," Richard's eyes grew round. "I'm going to school, too, and Mr. Cahill taught me to ride a horse and I didn't even fall off."

The children took turns with their stories until it was finally their bedtime. After Grace took them upstairs, the four adults enjoyed wine and conversation about John's exploits, Brian's improvements at Starnes House, Claudette's new baby, and Betsy's Dame School. It was late before the evening came to an end.

Three days later, John, Betsy, and the children left for London and a visit with the Queen.

They were escorted to the Queen's visiting chamber. After some pleasant conversation, Queen Anne came to the point.

"Sir John, you continue to become more celebrated with each of your exploits."

"Thank you, your Majesty. It was a great victory for everyone involved." John said. "Except for the French, that is."

The Queen smiled and agreed. "After much consideration, I have decided to appoint you the Governor General of our new colony of Gibraltar for which you and your marines fought so valiantly."

John and Betsy exchanged surprised glances.

"I have also authorized increasing the size of the garrison there in case the Spanish get any ideas of retaking it." She waited a moment before continuing, then she smiled again. "I'm going to keep you a busy man, Sir John. In addition to your command at Gibraltar, I want you to plan on spending some time here in England each year so that you can oversee the growth of the marine base at Exeter." She settled back in her chair with a look of great discomfort.

Betsy could see the Queen was in pain. "Is there anything I can do for you, your Majesty?" she asked with concern.

The Queen grimaced. "No thank you, child." She turned to a lady-in-waiting. "Please adjust my pillows. I think that will help."

When she was more comfortable, she continued and turned her attention to Betsy. "In case I wasn't clear before, I want you and your children to go to Gibraltar as well. It may be a hardship for you but I believe families should be together whenever possible. Don't you?"

"Oh, yes, your Majesty, I do agree. Thank you. I think, rather than a hardship, I'll find it a wonderful opportunity for us all."

"Well said, my dear…Now, Sir John. I have a surprise for you…a nice surprise, I hope. I am sending James Marks to Gibraltar to serve as your aide. I have already given him a commission as a major in the marines. As you know, he is very bright and understands the Spanish and the Arabs very well. I believe he will be a great asset to you. James has served me well and he has earned this opportunity. Don't you agree?"

"I do indeed," John said. "James and I have always enjoyed a unique relationship. I look forward to working with him again."

The Queen again started fidgeting in her chair. "This has been such a dreary day for me. Now that our business is concluded, will the two of you stay and join me for dinner. That's always a highlight of my day, you know."

"Again you honor us, your Majesty." John gave a slight bow.

The Queen turned to one of her staff and instructed him to take Lord and Lady MacDonald to her private chambers where they were to wait until called to dinner.

Poor Queen Anne was not much company that evening. She drank too much brandy and fell asleep before the main course was served.

While Betsy helped wheel the Queen to her bed chamber, the men continued eating and drinking.

Because of her bulk, it took four strong men to lift her into her bed. She mumbled throughout the ordeal but never really woke up. Before leaving the chamber, Betsy pulled up the covers and then gently smoothed the Queen's furrowed brow.

"God bless you, Queen Anne," Betsy whispered, "I pray He will relieve your suffering."

Following dinner, the gentlemen retired to a sitting room for more conversation, cigars, and brandy. When talk turned to politics, John excused himself just as James Marks entered the room.

The two men seemed genuinely pleased to see each other. At first, they just exchanged small pleasantries.

"Well," James said. "I understand I've been appointed your aide while we're in Gibraltar."

"Should I treat you as my aide or as my spy?" John asked with a smile.

"I think I can adequately fill both positions, if need be," James replied.

"I have no doubt. You are truly an expert in your field and will be invaluable to me in my new post."

"The Spanish are restless again, John, and we must be prepared to protect Gibraltar. I fear there will be trying times ahead. Even though England and Scotland are in union now, there is great concern over who will be crowned when Queen Anne dies. She is very ill, you know."

John nodded his head sadly. "I was sorry to see today that she is in such poor health. I don't know how much longer she can go on. Do you have any idea who might succeed her?"

James chuckled. "With our luck, it will probably be some damn German. I doubt it will be a Stuart. Queen Anne will probably be the last of the Stuart monarchs."

John agreed. "I know my wife and her family—they are Stewarts you know—don't want to see another Stuart king ascend the throne. Regretfully, they have had a poor record as monarchs."

James looked around and saw the others laughing and talking in tight little groups. No one was paying attention to them. He took John's arm and led him to a quiet corner out of the earshot of anyone else.

"I need to make you aware of a few things you might not realize. Because of your position as a viscount, a marine general, and now the Governor General of Gibraltar, you have become a very influential and powerful man. You could become a target of political plots. I promise to keep my eyes and ears open to the potential trouble of any plots being hatched against you. We have always had a good rapport, so trust me now so that I can continue to protect you."

The thought of political plots was sobering. John agreed that he needed all the help he could get.

"I do trust you, James. You have proven yourself again and again. I'm proud to call you friend."

A maid entered the room and refilled the brandy snifters and placed a tray of cheese and crackers on an adjacent table.

"More food?" John quipped. "I think I'll pass."

"Not me," James said and helped himself to some canapés then sat next to John and leaned close as he lowered his voice. "Let me tell you what I know right now. I am aware of many rumblings. I suspect we will have to fight the Spanish again over the Rock. They are a hard-headed lot and very proud. The loss of Gibraltar was a bitter pill for them to swallow and then they were defeated in an attempt to retake it. I am certain they feel they can take the Rock in an all out assault by land and sea and because they really believe this, I am positive they will try again."

John agreed. "It's just a matter of time until they come after us again. I think we need to sail for Gibraltar as soon as possible. Being realistic, though, it will be early January before we are packed and ready to go."

James smiled. "Nothing is stopping me, so I'll go ahead and scout things out and will have a full report for you when you arrive."

~~~

Before they left London, John and Betsy went to see Admiral Bowen and Lady Jane. The couple was delighted to see their old friends.

"It's been too long since we were together," Lady Jane said. We have so much to catch up on. Come into the parlor. Let's sit and visit for a while."

She called for the maid to serve refreshments. John noticed that Lady Jane took the Admiral's arm and seemed to guide him to a chair.

"Admiral," John said, "Is it true you have retired from the Admiralty?"

"Yes, yes, it's true, I'm afraid. It seems I'm having a problem with my eyes. I don't see very well anymore," the Admiral admitted.'

Lady Jane tried to make light of it. "Charles has always worked too hard, so now he has time for other important matters, like writing his memoirs."

The Admiral chuckled pleasantly, "As if anyone would want to read it. My secretary comes in every morning and I dictate to him. It's really rather boring, I'm afraid."

John heartily disagreed. "Well, I for one will look forward to reading it. You've lived an exciting and challenging life, sir."

"Look who's talking!" the Admiral chided him. "I've been following your career, John, with great interest. I understand you have been appointed the Governor General of Gibraltar."

"Oh, my!" Lady Jane interjected. "Betsy, dear, are you and the children going along, too?"

"The Queen practically insisted that we do. I wouldn't think of not going. John will probably be there for several years."

Lady Jane just shook her head. "I can't think of a more forsaken place to live. You are very brave, Betsy. I'm afraid I would refuse to go."

"I'm looking at it as a great adventure for me and the children," Betsy explained. "How many people can say they've been to Gibraltar, much less lived there?"

Lady Jane folded her hands and sat up straight. "Now, I'm going to change the subject. The holidays are fast upon us. Charles and I are hosting a gala event in a fortnight. Please say you'll come. It will give you a chance to say goodbye to everyone at once."

Betsy loved parties and showed her excitement. "Thank you, Jane. We'd love to come. It's been a long time since we've been to a party."

"I'm looking forward to it, too," John said, then turned to the Admiral. "Would it be possible for you and me to excuse ourselves and talk business?"

The Admiral stood up. "I thought you'd never ask," he said good-naturedly.

Betsy and Jane both smiled. Jane said, "Oh, good. Now we'll be able to catch up on really important matters of our own."

For the next hour, the ladies talked about the fine points of their lives.

"I've missed you, Jane, but I promise the next time we come to London, we'll visit again and maybe even stay for a few days." She stopped, and then became serious. "Is the Admiral going to be all right?"

"Yes, I'm sure he will," Jane assured her. "The doctors don't think his eyesight will deteriorate much more. Time will tell. He needed to slow down a bit. I'm very glad to have him home with me every day now."

John spent the hour discussing the probability of another battle in Gibraltar and seeking the Admiral's advice on the matter. He asked the right questions and listened intently to the replies.

"John, you were always my best pupil. Queen Anne chose the right man to govern Gibraltar."

The evening flew by and all too soon the couples had to say goodbye.

Jane hugged Betsy tightly. "We'll meet again one day. I just know it."

Betsy hated goodbyes, but she too believed they would see each other again. In the meantime, she could look forward to the party.

~~~

Since the family would be leaving for Gibraltar within a month, they decided to spend the holidays at Starnes House so John could remain close to the marine base. He needed time to work with the new commander before leaving for Gibraltar.

The children seemed more excited about their first sea voyage than they were about Christmas. Everyday, Betsy tried to answer their almost endless questions.

"Are we really going to live on a rock?"

"Is it true there are lots of Bar…uh…Barbary monkeys…I mean Barbary apes there?"

"Can I have one for a pet?"

"Will we ever come back to England?"

Betsy's knowledge of Gibraltar was sketchy at best, but she tried to answer their questions intelligently.

"No."

"Yes."

"No."

"Yes."

Most of the planning and packing for the trip was left up to Betsy. In addition, she had to prepare for Christmas. Her days began early and ended late. Exhausted each night, she fell into bed, her mind already planning for the next day's agenda.

She breathed a sigh of relief when Christmas Eve morning arrived. With a clear mind and a sense of accomplishment, she left Starnes House and went into town for her annual trip to the bank to fulfill her anonymous contribution to the charity fund for the poor at the Anglican Church. Before returning home, she visited the home of the sisters who taught at the Dames School and gave them a pouch containing funds necessary to cover expenses at the school for the next year.

"A courier delivered the funds to me this morning," she explained quite innocently. "Since I'm leaving for Gibraltar after the first of the year, I wanted you to have it now."

The sisters were satisfied with her explanation and asked no questions.

Christmas Eve and Christmas Day's traditional celebrating brought more questions from the children.

"Will we have Christmas in Gibraltar?"

"Will it snow there?"

"Will Father Christmas find us there?"

Betsy and John just looked at each other and laughed.

"Don't you children ever run out of questions? I promise you Christmas will be as wonderful there as it is here," John told them.

Within days, the MacDonalds were packed and ready to go. Packing for this trip was unlike any other Betsy had encountered. She had no idea what she would find in Gibraltar so she packed everything she thought she would need to set up housekeeping. That included dishes, silverware, pots and pans, linens, towels, first aid supplies, soap, and food supplies. John had told her that everything had to be shipped in from England or Portugal so she prepared for the long term.

John laughed when he saw how many boxes she had packed. He counted fifty.

"Think you have enough?" he wondered.

Betsy put her hands on her hips. "Don't tease me, John. I'm like a blind pig in a chicken coop feeling for every kernel of corn. I don't know what to expect, so I'm planning for the unexpected."

"Supply ships come in every month. Looks like you have enough to last six months." He patted her in a condescending way. "Take a break and let's have a cup of tea."

~~~

It was a brisk January morning when the MacDonald entourage left Exeter.

The children were excited about their first sea voyage and couldn't wait to board the ship. They stood on deck with their parents and Grace as the ship sailed away. The air was cold and the children's cheeks soon became red; their eyes watered from the sting of the brisk winter wind.

Richard watched with fascination as the crew executed the tacking. Some crewmen climbed the rigging. Others ran out the guns and even tested them on occasion. Meggie tired of it after a while and was content to stay below with her mother and Grace. The channel waters were choppy and Grace and Betsy soon became seasick. They climbed to the open deck, found a spot facing the wind and the sickness disappeared.

By the time the ship left the channel and headed south toward the Bay of Biscay, the winds were fair and there was a following sea. Air temperatures warmed and the children spent many hours on deck. Activity on board a sailing ship was non-stop so there was always something to hold their interest.

One sailor named Freddie took a fondness to Richard and patiently answered all his questions about what was happening and why.

In the evening, Richard sat next to Freddie and watched him whittle and whistle at the same time. By the end of the voyage, Richard could whistle, but he couldn't get the knack of whittling.

Meggie liked the evenings, too. Sometimes the sailors danced the hornpipe to the tune of a fife. Sometimes the sailors sang songs that Freddie said were more than one hundred years old. Other nights, the children were taught the night sky constellations. Richard could easily point out the Big Dipper and could then usually find the North Star. John enjoyed watching his son and could already see his signs of interest in his becoming a sailor or even a marine. He was quick to encourage Richard.

"One of the best ways to learn, son, is by watching and listening. When you are older, you will physically be able to practice what you have already learned."

Richard was on deck early one morning as the ship tacked and sailed toward the Bay of Gibraltar. He was astonished at what he saw. He called to his mother and sister and to Grace, too.

"You have to come see this! You won't believe it!"

Betsy and Meggie were awed at the sight of the towering Rock of Gibraltar that rose more than fourteen hundred feet above the sea.

John came up behind Betsy and put his arm around her shoulders. "Welcome to your new home," he whispered.

She couldn't help it. Her heart sank when she looked at this forlorn, remote and tiny piece of land that lay in the shadow of that towering rock. She reached up and took John's hand.

"It's not forever, John. I already have a plan. We'll leave it better than it was when we arrived."

Luckily, the children saw the beauty.

"I'll be able to see that wonderful rock every day," Richard said, his face aglow.

Meggie was drawn to the waters surrounding her new home. "The sea is so blue. Is it always this blue, Papa?"

John picked her up so she could see more clearly. "Yes, it's always this blue. It's beautiful, isn't it?"

Grace stood beside the family but didn't have much to say. She was glad the journey was over. Sailing was a terrible way to travel, she decided.

"Give me good old terra firma," she said silently.

James Marks waved from the dock as the family disembarked.

"Glad you are here, John. I have a lot of information to discuss with you. But first, you need to get settled."

"Join us for dinner, James. I'm anxious to hear what you have learned."

The house they were to occupy was small and sparsely furnished. The house staff consisted of a housekeeper and a cook, both of whom were Spanish.

Betsy took a quick inventory and was glad she had packed so many household items.

John followed her from room to room. When she finished, she just stood there, arms folded and deep in thought.

"Well," John asked, "What do you think?"

"It'll do," Betsy declared. "But when will the new house be ready?"

"Construction will be my number one priority. I promise," John said. "I'd say it should be ready by early summer."

The language barrier became Betsy's immediate problem. Grace knew no Spanish; the house staff knew no English. Betsy's knowledge of French helped her a little, but pointing and hand gestures would have to do for now.

James Marks arrived just before dinner was served. He was surprised to see the family so well settled. "Looks like you've been here for a month," he remarked.

Dinner that night was the subject of light conversation and laughter. The food was Spanish, of course.

"What is this?" Meggie wanted to know.

"Rice and beans and fried flour cakes," John explained. "Remember our cook is Spanish and would think our English food was strange. Be polite and eat your food."

"Meggie," Betsy said, "perhaps you and I together can teach Estella to prepare new things, things our family is used to."

The child pouted and used her fork to stir her food, hoping it would change the flavor. "All right," she agreed. "I'll eat this but I won't like it."

Richard wasn't talking. He was too busy eating. He stopped long enough to take a drink of water. "Um! I think this tastes really good!"

James Marks laughed.

Betsy reached over and patted her son's head. "Richard eats everything. I don't know of one food he doesn't enjoy."

After dinner, John and James went into the small sitting room and closed the door. In detail, James explained the current situation.

"The Spanish were mauled in the last attack. Because of that, they have learned some hard lessons. I spent some time in Spain recently and this is the scuttlebutt. This time there will be a massive frontal attack by an overwhelming number of soldiers who will be fully supported by artillery. They are planning an attack by water using warships to engage in a blockade at sea. Although I doubt this will happen, there is rumor that the Spanish might try to mount an attack form the sea side in an attempt to scale the Rock itself and attack from behind."

John listened carefully before responding. "At present, we have two regiments of marines and about six hundred naval gunners to man the fortress guns. I know the Navy will support us as best it can with a variety of ships, but our two thousand marines are the keystone to the defense of Gibraltar."

"Don't misunderstand, John," James continued. "An attack is not imminent. From what I saw and what I heard, it will be months before they are ready for such an attack. They are still in the early talking and planning stages. I'm glad. It gives us more time to prepare."

John frowned. "My biggest fear is that they might affect a successful siege. I'll need to import tremendous supplies of food and water. That will take months if I have to wait for English supply ships."

"Why not trade with Morocco?" James suggested. "Then you can add to your cache when the English ships arrive."

"Good idea. Thank you, James. I think it would be wise to write now to Queen Anne to request more troops. We can't be caught short-handed."

James stood up to leave. "We have our work cut out for us." He smiled. "When the two of us put our heads together, the Spanish won't stand a chance. Thank your lovely wife for her hospitality. I enjoyed spending time with your family. I'll see you tomorrow, John. I'm glad you all arrived safely."

~~~

The next few months were busy ones. The new Governor's Mansion was under construction and John put troops in charge of building water catchments wherever practical. They gathered shiploads of barrels to hold water that would be stored in the caves of the fortress.

Betsy was busy, too. She felt it necessary to meet the few officers' wives living here on Gibraltar. Most officers discouraged their families from coming, but there were some, like Betsy, who were anxious for an exotic adventure. Still others—those with young children - did not want to be separated from their husbands for extended periods.

An afternoon tea was arranged and Betsy was delighted when all twenty ladies arrived. The guests showed surprise when tea and English pastries were served.

"Estella is an excellent cook and enjoys trying new recipes," Betsy explained. "It was easy to teach her our favorite English dishes. I'm also teaching her the English language. She is returning the favor by teaching me Spanish."

"That's my biggest problem here," said one of the wives. "The language barrier."

"Perhaps we can set up classes for anyone interested in learning Spanish. Actually, they could be dual classes. Estella told me she knows many women who want to learn English."

By the end of the afternoon, it was agreed. Bilingual classes would begin as soon as they could be arranged.

Betsy discovered there were no schools in Gibraltar so she continued to tutor her own children. They were beginning to pick up some Spanish so Betsy brought them to the bilingual class so they could learn more rapidly.

By early summer, the new Governor's Mansion was ready for occupancy and Betsy was ready for a larger house.

She loved the new house. It was like nothing she had ever seen before. The architect was Spanish; therefore, the mansion reflected the Spanish culture. The outer walls were stucco; the roof was covered with Spanish tiles. A large walled atrium led up to an arched entrance. The double doors were hand-carved mahogany. Inside was a large interior atrium centered with a large fountain. Colorful Spanish ceramic tile covered the floor. This area, Betsy was told, would be used for entertaining. Arched doorways to the right led to the family living quarters. Guest quarters were to the left. Arches framed the rear exit that led to a beautiful landscaped garden.

Betsy had seen the blueprints and watched as the house took shape. Most of the furniture she had ordered from Morocco had arrived. In keeping with the house's design, she had chosen hand-carved mahogany pieces with bright upholstery. The effect was stunning.

Estella and Rosa, the housekeeper, gasped when they saw it. Betsy knew they liked it. They ran from room to room and chattered rapidly in Spanish. Betsy didn't understand anything they said.

It didn't take long for the family to settle in. When everything was in its place, Betsy began planning her first social event. It was to be an open-house that would recognize the military and civilian population of Gibraltar.

While Betsy planned a party, John was planning a battle. He had prepared in every way he could, including commandeering powder and shot from every ship that came into port. John and his officers made sure the men trained daily and remained as ready as possible.

John was especially happy the day of the party. He had finally received a letter from the Admiralty informing him that three battalions of marines were on the way. Now he could relax and enjoy Gibraltar's first notable social event.

As guests began to arrive, Betsy and John proudly stood at the door to greet them. The new Governor's Mansion was a tribute to the man who had designed it and the many workers who had brought the design to life. They hoped that future Governors would be as satisfied with the home as they were. Guests lingered, thoroughly enjoying their hosts, the house itself, and the variety of refreshments.

That night as she curled into John's arms, Betsy felt complete contentment. "I have to admit that I had many doubts before I came here. I want you to know how honored I feel and how fortunate I feel that we are the first to live in this magnificent example of the beautiful Spanish culture."

John squeezed her. "I guess that means you're happy here."

"Yes, I am. I consider this another of God's many blessings. I've come to love the Spanish people. They are warm, friendly, and helpful. Besides, I've learned another language. Te quiero mucho, mi esposo."

John closed his eyes. "I love you too, my little wife."

A few weeks later, John was relieved to see transports sail into the harbor and begin to unload the troops and extra supplies on the quay.

One night, John was thinking about how fortunate he was to have James Marks by his side. He marveled at James' seemingly innate ability to glean accurate information from others. He knew that when the Spanish were ready to move, James would be the first to know.

It happened when he least expected it.

Grace and Rose had taken the children down to the beach so they could wade in the warm water. John and Betsy were sitting in the garden enjoying light refreshment. They had been reminiscing about how they had met.

"It was all so long ago," Betsy sighed, "but sometimes when I look at you, it's as though I am seeing you for the first time."

John looked into Betsy's eyes, then reached out and stroked her face. "You were beautiful when I first met you, but now...I don't know how you do it, but you are so much more beautiful. You take my breath away."

Betsy smiled. "That's called L-O-V-E, my dearest. Unless, of course, your vision has dimmed just a little."

Estella came to the doorway. "Excusa. Senor Marks esta aqui."

Betsy stood up. "You two need to talk. I'll leave you alone." Quickly, she brushed his lips with her own then turned. "James, as always, it's nice to see you." She swept past him and returned to the house.

James stepped aside and bowed slightly. "Lady Betsy," he said in acknowledgement.

"Sit down, James. Would you care for some refreshments?"

"Got anything stronger?" James quipped. "We have a lot to discuss. It looks like the Spanish Army will soon be on the move. Garrisons all over Spain are beginning to send troops south."

Rosa had brought some brandy snifters. James took a long sip.

"I have an idea, John. Hear me out. I think Betsy and the children should leave Gibraltar and go to Portugal."

John nodded. "I've been thinking the same thing. There are three other officers' wives with young children. I think they should go, too."

"You're right. I want to accompany them, John. You don't need me for the battle. They do. I know the Portuguese people. They aren't fond of the Spanish right now, so they will be eager to help protect these refugees. I have chosen six good men to accompany us." He paused. "What do you think?"

"I think I'd better tell Betsy now."

At first Betsy was reluctant to go but was quickly convinced it was the safest thing to do. As she suspected, Estella and Rosa wanted to remain in Gibraltar. They believed John would keep them safe. Grace, on the other hand, was the first one packed and ready to go.

The three officers' wives were frightened. They all agreed that they didn't want to leave, but they didn't want to stay either.

Within three days, the group boarded the ship that would take them to Portugal.

Richard clung to his father. "I know you have to go to war, Papa, but please don't get killed."

John hugged his son. "I promise you, Richard, I won't die. You will all be home as soon as this mess is over and I will be on the dock waiting for you."

After embracing Meggie, John held Betsy. "Pray for us, my darling. While you're at it, pray that it's our last separation." He kissed her deeply. "I'm getting tired of all these farewells."

The following week, John was awakened early by Major Marks.

"I have bad news, John. The enemy is at our gates, I am afraid. Do you think we are ready?"

"We're ready," John replied as he quickly dressed. "This is what we get paid for."

"What ever the pay is, I don't think that today it will be enough."

The two men went to the north wall and looked to the north trying to see what the enemy was doing. What they saw was unnerving. Battery after battery of artillery were lining up just out of gun range with units of infantry marching out behind them. John knew his entire garrison was now on the alert. A flotilla of small boats and three frigates were patrolling the Bay of Gibraltar geared to head off any sea attack from the west. John sent up two flares to signal the naval squadron to the east to come inshore and join the fight. Two companies were stationed on the eastern side of the Rock to prevent anyone from scaling it and getting behind them. Every approach had been secured and now the wait began.

By mid-morning the forward elements of Spanish artillery moved into gun range and began their bombardment of the north wall. When the artillery finally fell silent, the infantry attack began. John was pleased to see that the bombardment had done little damage to the north wall. His strategy of not firing at the artillery had saved much precious ammunition.

Battalions now marched forward with teams of men carrying scaling ladders. Previously, John had instructed the naval gunners to let the enemy get within easy gun range before they fired the explosive ammunition. Then they were to load grape and chain shot and stand ready for the main infantry assault. When that occurred, the gunners slaughtered hundreds of Spanish soldiers. Those surviving attempted to climb the wall but they were cut to pieces by the cool, steady volley fire of the marines on top of the wall. Any who reached the top with their ladders were quickly dispatched and the ladders thrown to the ground.

Part of John's strategy was to once again make the enemy believe that the English guns had relatively short range. The trick had worked once before and he hoped the enemy artillery would creep well within range before they opened fire for another assault. When that happened, the gunners, whose guns outranged the enemy's by one hundred yards, would smash them.

The ruse worked. The enemy launched another assault and was met with the same fierce resistance. Then they made the fatal mistake of moving almost all their artillery within the range of British guns. The Spaniards were stopped at the wall and, to the surprise of the Spanish artillery, all hell broke loose. They were swept away by the long range cannons on top of the Rock while the troops were slaughtered by grape, chain shot, and many dedicated Marines.

While the Spanish were milling around entirely disorganized, a full battalion of marines opened the gates in the wall and rushed toward the disorganized troops who were run through with bayonets.

The Spanish commander was in shock and could not believe his eyes. He had lost a third of his infantry and almost all of his artillery pieces. Marine casualties were far fewer.

Meanwhile, the Spanish admiral had seen no sign of the Royal Navy, so he decided to move his fleet down the coast to engage the north wall and possibly breach it with naval cannon.

A small English ship, acting as a lookout two miles off shore, observed the Spanish move and signaled the English fleet standing off shore with flares. They immediately turned to intercept the Spanish squadron. As the Spanish ships approached the Rock, the gunners were waiting in their caves with the long range guns that were aimed east and northeast. The Spaniards were too busy getting ready to engage the wall to even notice the powerful new guns that were spread out above them.

Suddenly the big guns opened fire on the Spanish fleet. After the third volley, the first two ships were severely damaged. One had lost two masts and the other had been holed below the waterline. It heeled over and began to sink rapidly. The remaining Spanish ships tried to avoid the lead ships that lay dead in the water. One was forced to shore and went aground. Now a sitting duck, she came under fire by the guns on the Rock and soon was in flames. Three more Spanish ships were damaged before the entire Spanish squadron turned east to try to avoid further damage. It was too late. A squadron of Royal Navy ships came toward them head-on. In order to save lives, the Spanish Admiral quickly hoisted a white flag and signaled his remaining ships to do the same.

When the sun finally set that day, the Spanish Army commanders still refused to admit defeat. They still had a formidable army and believed, now that night had arrived, they had time to wait for more artillery. They hadn't reckoned with General MacDonald's audacity. John sent two large raiding parties to attack both enemy flanks. The exhausted Spanish had no idea that a crazy Scotsman would attack them at night. The marines swept in from the sea on both sides of the Spanish positions, killed their sentries and attacked with fury. Again, the enemy was not prepared. It was a total blood bath for the Spanish.

Concurrently, John personally led a large force out of the fortress and made a night frontal attack on the main positions. When the Spanish saw the marines coming at them with fixed bayonets, they ran like rabbits. The attack swept through the Spanish camp and many officers were captured. One of whom was Spanish Commanding General Jose Ortiz. When the General was taken back to the fortress, John directed him to write a letter to his remaining forces ordering them to surrender. General Ortiz complied and the order was sent out under a white flag the next morning.

At mid-day, the Spanish Army marched out and laid down their arms. They were told they could return home safely if each man signed an oath not to participate in any further attacks on Gibraltar. Most agreed to the simple terms. The few who refused were classed as prisoners of war and put under armed guard. It became their job to bury the dead.

The defeat was so humiliating that it was more than sixty years before the Spanish made another attempt to recapture Gibraltar.

To the victor belong the spoils.

The marines repaired as many of the Spanish cannon as they could and took them back into the fort. They hauled cartloads of enemy rifles, swords and pistols back to the Rock. The men were allowed to sort through them and take what they wanted. With great pleasure, John saved several weapons to hang in the Governor's Mansion.

When the cleanup had been completed, John sent word to James Marks that it was safe to return to Gibraltar.

Betsy and the other officers' wives had truly enjoyed their brief stay in Portugal, although worry about what was happening in Gibraltar hung heavy in the air. They were surprised to find the language very different from Spanish, but enjoyed the friendliness of those they met. At James' suggestion, they stayed close together and didn't venture too far from their living quarters.

When they got the news they could return to Gibraltar, the ladies packed their bags in an hour. They left on the morning tide.

As the ship approached the Rock, the women and their children all stood at the ship's railing to look for any visible damage, but were overjoyed when they saw none.

"Everything looks the same," Betsy told the children.

James was standing behind her. "Damage to structures can be easily repaired. It's the personal damage that is sometimes hard to see and hard to repair...lost lives, lost limbs, and wounds to the soul that are so deep they may never heal."

Betsy looked at James with new respect. She had caught a glimpse of the man's soul and she liked what she saw.

The children saw John before Betsy did.

"Look! There's Papa!" Meggie shouted. "He has come to meet us, just like he promised."

The children rushed down the gang plank and into their father's waiting arms. When Betsy reached the foot of the gang plank, John swept her up and gave her a long, lingering, passionate kiss.

The sailors and civilians who were watching raised a cheer to the Governor General and his lady. Embarrassed, the children just giggled.

Each of the children held one of John's hands as they skipped all the way to the waiting coach. All the way back to the Governor's Mansion, the children chattered. They couldn't wait to tell their father all about their amazing experiences in Portugal.

Betsy and John held hands and watched their children's faces as they gave animated accounts of the last several weeks. They patiently smiled at each other, knowing their time would come later.

When the coach arrived at their home, the children jumped down and ran into the house to tell Rosa and Estella all about Portugal. Grace ran after them and shouted over her shoulder.

"I'll take care of them. You two need to talk and not be interrupted."

During the next hour, Betsy listened patiently as John explained what had happened during the battle.

"It was a resounding victory, Betsy. I believe the Spanish will leave Gibraltar alone for a very long time. But I have to tell you I am most proud of the fact that we suffered so few casualties. Of course, even one is too many. Compared to the Spanish, our numbers were extremely low. Now, my darling, I want to hear all about your wonderful exploits in Portugal."

"Exploits! I wouldn't call them that! But," she started off slowly, "the most significant thing that happened is something I will remember for the rest of my life."

John looked at Betsy. Her eyes were bright and she had an impish look on her face. He noticed she was patting her stomach, ever so subtly.

"No, Betsy," he said as realization set in.

Betsy nodded.

"No...you're not..."

Betsy nodded again.

He said it out loud so he could really believe it. "You're going to have another child!"

Betsy nodded a third time.

Then John became concerned. "Aren't you getting a little old to have another baby? I mean, it won't be too hard on either of you will it...I mean..." he grabbed her and held her tight. "I'd die if anything happened to you!"

She pulled away and cupped John's face in her hands. "I am a perfectly healthy woman and there is no reason why I cannot bear another child. I've had no problems so far so why would I suspect to have trouble this time?"

"When our infant daughter died at birth, I just never thought we'd have another child."

"Neither did I," Betsy admitted. "But God works in wonderful ways. I will welcome this child with all the love that is in my heart."

"So will I, sweetheart," John said. "Now tell me everything else that happened in Portugal. I'm sure it will pale in comparison."

~~~

Things settled into a pleasant routine for the MacDonald family. Betsy experienced no morning sickness with her pregnancy but she did notice she tired more easily. She relied heavily on Grace to help with the children. Tutoring the children was a daily event and Betsy was proud of their progress, especially with the Spanish language. Meggie particularly was adept at learning the language.

"Mama," she said. "Estella says we know as much Spanish as she does. And Richard and I are helping Rosa with her English."

Estella had become expert in preparing a wonderful combination of Spanish and English dishes. Even Meggie complained less and less and actually learned to enjoy tasting new foods.

"And that's a miracle in itself," she told Estella who beamed with pride.

Rosa was a jewel. She treated Betsy like a mother hen, hovering over her to make sure all of her needs were met. Betsy had to admit that she loved all the special attention. Rosa's loving and caring ways made Betsy miss her mother even more than usual. She had written her parents a letter telling them about the coming baby but had not as yet received a reply.

John's work day was lighter now that war was not on the horizon. He and his marines felt relief that they had entered a lengthy period of peace. They understood that they had to remain well-trained and physically fit, so training was still an important part of their everyday activities.

Sometimes John found time to surprise Betsy and come home for lunch. One such day, he was all smiles as he handed Betsy a letter from her parents.

"A supply ship arrived this morning and brought some mail. I knew you'd want to see the letter right away. Besides, it gave me an excuse to have lunch with you."

Anxiously Betsy tore open the letter. She had not heard from her parents in several months and was eager to hear the news from home as well as their reaction about another grandchild.

Within moments, her chin quivered and tears spilled from her eyes. She dropped the letter on her lap.

"Oh, John," she cried. "Both of my grandparents have died. There was a fire in the barn…They ran inside to save the animals…" She stopped and tried to compose herself. "They didn't make it out…The barn burned to the ground."

"How awful!" John held her against him. "I'm so sorry, sweetheart. How's your mother holding up?"

"She says she's fine. But I know how much she'll miss them." Then almost inaudibly she added, "I'll miss them, too."

~~~

Betsy's baby boy was born in the early hours of a blustery morning. The wind had howled all night long and rattled the shutters till Betsy wanted to scream. She endured hours of long and hard labor and still the baby didn't come. Rosa tried to comfort Betsy but she herself was getting more and more frightened. She pulled John aside and whispered in broken English.

"Dis baby no wanna be born!"

Estella, too, was becoming desperate. She left the room then returned and gave Betsy a potion that almost instantly calmed her. The pains subsided long enough for Betsy to rest and gain more strength.

When the pains resumed, Betsy was ready. She held onto the bed posts with both hands and pushed with all her might. A piercing primal scream escaped her lips and the child was finally born.

Rosa's eyes grew large. "Oh! El bebe es muy grande!"

The infant howled as John wrapped him in a blanket and handed him to Betsy.

"Rosa is right, sweetheart. Our son is a very big boy. No wonder the delivery took so long!"

Betsy took the crying child and looked at his red, wrinkled face. She laughed. "Well at least he has a healthy set of lungs." She looked up at Estella who was wiping tears from her eyes. "What was that wonderful medicine you gave me? I think it saved my life."

Estella put her fingers to her lips. "Shh," she snickered. "Just some magic I learned from mi madre."

This child was named Kevin Andrew MacDonald.

It took Betsy longer to get her strength back this time. She just took her time and enjoyed holding and looking at her new son. It had been a long time since there had been a baby in the house, so everyone wanted to hold him. In fact he was almost never in his crib. If he cried, someone picked him up and held him until he fell asleep again.

Betsy noticed that he was not a happy baby unless he was being held. She blamed herself for allowing him to be spoiled.

One day when Meggie was gently rocking him back and forth in her arms, she said to her mother, "I can't wait until I have my own sweet baby."

Betsy was aghast. "Lord, child. You have a lot of growing up to do before you're ready for the responsibility of another human being."

"I know, Mama. But it's nice to dream."

As months went by, Betsy could tell that this child was very different from the other two. She admitted that he was spoiled but it was more than that. It was something she couldn't put her finger on. He seemed...selfish. Then she chided herself, *How can a baby be selfish?*

Still there was a disquieting feeling deep inside her. An intuition? A mother's instinct? Was this a portend of things to come? It was silly of her to think like that. She walked over to the crib and picked up her crying child.

-o-

CHAPTER 31

England, France, and Spain had been at war for years. Sometimes it seemed that the three nations would never resolve their differences. Recently, most of the battles were occurring in the new world.

The European political scene was forever changing. One positive occurred in 1707 when England and Scotland finally signed an Act of Union that joined the two countries together as one nation. Although England was greatly encouraged by this pact, it did nothing to improve relations with their arch enemies, Spain and France.

A few years later when Queen Anne's War, better known as the French-Indian War, came to a close, an opportunity for peace appeared. Representatives from all major European nations met at Utrecht, Holland to discuss peace terms. In 1713 an agreement was signed. It gave England control of Gibraltar. France ceded Nova Scotia, Newfoundland, and the Hudson Bay territory to Great Britain but retained Quebec. For the first time in many decades, domestic issues could be addressed unencumbered.

Queen Anne was satisfied that peace had finally been achieved but her health continued to deteriorate. She could no longer get out of bed without great difficulty. Her breathing was labored and shallow. Queen Anne was dying and she knew it. Now it was time for one last official appointment. A new Governor General was chosen for Gibraltar and a summons was sent to John MacDonald and James Marks to immediately return to London.

When John and Betsy were ushered into the Queen's bed chamber, they were appalled by her appearance. Her skin was sallow and she wheezed with every breath. As their names were announced, she opened her eyes and held out her hands to them. She opened her mouth to speak. "Sit me up. I need to talk."

She grimaced as two hefty men servants struggled to lift the Queen to a semi-sitting position.

"Better," she murmured and again reached out her hands to John and Betsy. "Sir John, you have accomplished so much in my name. Gibraltar is stable and safe and growing. Now I want you to stay here in England at Exeter, where you can continue to be beneficial to our country."

John leaned over and kissed her hand. "It has always been an honor to serve you, your Majesty."

The Queen looked at Betsy. "Dear Cousin, enjoy your children. They are God's greatest gift." Her head fell back and she closed her eyes. "I must rest now."

On August 1, 1714, Queen Anne died. Although she was subjected to cruel ridicule by many of her subjects, her accomplishments were many. She was most noted for her generosity by constantly supporting charities out of her own money. She was also responsible for developing Kensington Palace and the gardens.

Queen Anne was buried in Westminster Abbey. Surrounding her vast square coffin were seventeen small boxes holding the pathetic remains of her tiny babies.

England needed a ruler. King James III, a Catholic was exiled in France. That left the Elector of Hanover as successor. His right to the throne came through his mother, a granddaughter of James I. Parliament decided a German protestant was better than a Catholic Jacobite.

King George quickly became unpopular because of his boorish manners and his two preposterous mistresses. One was dubbed "The Elephant" for obvious reasons. The other was tall and thin. She was called "The Maypole." His legitimate wife was held in virtual imprisonment in Germany.

King George hated England and never learned to speak the language and spent as little time as possible in England. Politically, there was a bright side to his frequent absences. There was a swing of power toward Parliament and the Prime Minister, Robert Walpole.

John and Betsy attended the King's coronation and were surprised when they saw him. King George presented a distinctly odd appearance with a reddish complexion, colorless eyes, a receding chin, a loud German voice, and a ginger colored wig.

How in the world did we ever get a German king? Betsy wondered.

John was glad that he was to stay in England. With the King's intense dislike for England and certainly matters of state, it became abundantly clear that the Privy Council and the House of Lords would have to be in session almost on a regular basis to make sure policies were made and legislation passed. Because of all this, John felt a new sense of responsibility for his peerage.

The family returned to Gibraltar one last time. John needed to spend time with the new Governor General so the transition of leadership would be smooth.

Betsy packed their personal belongings and said goodbye to her many friends. The hardest goodbye was to Estella and Rosa because each knew they would probably never see each other again.

As the coach pulled away from the Governor's Mansion, Estella and Rosa stood outside with their arms around each other.

"Vaya con Dios!" Rosa shouted through her tears.

"Goodbye, Lady Betsy," Estella said in perfect English. "I love you all."

Betsy was homesick. Although she had enjoyed her years in Gibraltar, she was ready to go back home to England to raise her children. But there was more to her homesickness. She was homesick for her parents.

John understood. "Why don't you take Grace and the children to France for a couple of months? Your parents will be so happy to see you and get to know the children."

"What a wonderful idea! I'm so glad you suggested it. I would have never thought of it!" she teased. I'll write them a letter this very day."

~~~

Ewin was there to greet them when they disembarked in St. Val'ery.

Betsy flew into her father's arms. "I've missed you so much!"

"That goes double for me and your mother," Ewin said, then stooped down toward the children. "Hello! I'm your Grandpapa," and he gave each one of them a piece of candy.

The children remembered their manners. They smiled and said, "Thank you, Grandpapa," in unison.

Betsy took Kevin from Grace's arms. "This is Kevin, Father."

Ewin smiled and took the child's hand to kiss. "You're too young for candy right now. I'll save it for when you're a little older." He stood up and gestured toward two waiting coaches. Grace and the children rode in one. Ewin led Betsy to the smaller one.

As the coaches started moving, Ewin took Betsy's hand between his own. "I wanted a little time alone with you, lassie, before we get to the farm."

His face looked grim and Betsy became alarmed.

"What is it, Father? Is Mother all right?"

"Your mother is very ill, Betsy. We had decided to send for you just when we received your letter informing us of your visit."

"What's wrong with her?" Betsy's eyes filled with tears.

"She's getting weaker every day. She can't keep her food down and now she's having pain in her stomach as well."

Betsy's heart sank when she first saw her mother. A once beautiful vibrant woman, Heather was now listless and so very thin. Her skin had a yellow tinge and her eyes were hollow. Nevertheless, when Betsy entered the house, she stood up and held out her arms. Betsy hurried into her mother's waiting embrace. She choked back her tears and tried to sound cheerful.

"It's wonderful to see you, Mother. I've told the children all about you. They are so anxious to meet you."

The children cautiously inched forward. Heather smiled broadly and a little color flushed her cheeks. Even her eyes brightened.

"Meggie, darling, I haven't seen you since you were just a baby. And Richard, what a fine young man you are. Come give Grandmama a hug."

Kevin watched from the safe distance of Grace's arms.

During the next few days, Heather rallied. Just having her daughter and grandchildren with her was all the elixir she needed. She napped during the afternoon so that she would be alert for the evenings after the children went to bed. It was then that she and Ewin and Betsy could talk at length.

"Do you ever hear from Uncle Roy?" Betsy asked one night.

"Oh, yes, about twice a year," Ewin told her. "He and Jeanette have four children now and they really love Virginia. The climate there is wonderful, he says. Your uncle has become quite the gentleman farmer, I guess."

One afternoon while Heather was napping, Ewin took Betsy to see the new Mercy Hospital he had built.

"I wanted to do something good with my money," Ewin said. "And the people here don't care where your money comes from. No one asks any questions. They accepted my contributions and were grateful for them."

"I think it's wonderful, Father," Betsy said enthusiastically.

Many evenings were spent just reminiscing.

"My favorite years were when you were a child, Betsy," Heather said. "You were always such a pleasant child. We always wanted more children but it just didn't happen."

They talked about Betsy's grandparents and how hard it had been for Heather to deal with their tragic deaths.

Betsy told her parents about John's accomplishments and their friendly relationship with Queen Anne. She described the Governor's Mansion in Gibraltar as well as their estate at Steddenham.

One night Betsy helped her mother to bed, then sat on the bed beside her.

"We are so proud of you and John," Heather said. "Many times, I have wished we could be together." She reached over and opened a drawer in a night stand and took out a stack of letters secured with a red ribbon. "See, Betsy? I have every letter you ever wrote to us. They have been a lifeline for us."

Betsy smiled and kissed her mother's cheek. "I have all of your letters, too. They are very precious to me. Although," she quipped, "mine are tied with a blue ribbon."

Heather laughed at her daughter's sense of humor, then she became a little more serious. "Betsy, we never talk about Glencoe, but now I must ask you one last time. Have you really been able to put that tragedy behind you or does it still haunt your dreams?"

"That's a hard question to answer, Mother. The answer is yes, and the answer is no. I will always live with the fact I took two human lives. I think of it everyday and I wish it had never happened. God spared me for a reason and that's what I'm living for. Every day I try to make a difference in this world. I feel God's presence in my life. He leads. I follow. I believe it's working. Does that make sense?"

Heather nodded. "It makes perfect sense. You were always my biggest blessing. Now you are a blessing to the world."

After that night, Heather's health deteriorated rapidly. She couldn't keep down any food, not even water. The pain in her stomach increased and sometimes she cried out in the night.

Betsy and her father watched helplessly as Heather's life ebbed. A doctor provided some liquid medicine that eased her pain but told them he feared the end was near.

After the doctor left and the pain had subsided, Heather became alert. "Betsy dear, I want to see Meggie."

When Meggie entered the bedroom, Heather raised herself on one elbow. "Child, there's a blue velvet box on my dresser. Would you please bring it to me?"

Meggie did as she was asked. "Now, open the box, Meggie."

The box contained a beautiful emerald brooch. Heather smiled at the look of surprise on Betsy's face.

Remembering, Betsy returned her mother's smile.

Heather took out the brooch and held it up. "Grandpapa gave this to me a long time ago, so it is very, very special. I want you to have it, Meggie."

Meggie looked at her mother. "Really, Grandmama?"

Betsy nodded her approval.

"It's so beautiful," the child said. "Thank you. I will treasure this forever."

Betsy and her father sat by Heather's bed that night. They whispered occasionally and wept silent tears. Helplessly, they watched as Heather's life slipped away. Ewin leaned over and gently kissed Heather's lips, then quietly left the room.

Betsy sat still, almost paralyzed, and stared at her mother's face. The expression of pain had lifted and a look of peace and serenity had taken its place. Betsy picked up her mother's hand and kissed it.

And she remembered...

She remembered the silly songs her mother always sang to her.

She remembered her mother's warm laughter.

She remembered the long walks they took when she learned all about trees and wild flowers.

She remembered the feeling of warmth and security that she felt whenever she was home with her parents.

But most of all, Betsy remembered the love.

~~~

After the funeral, Ewin asked Betsy to stay for a while. He wanted her to go through Heather's belongings and take mementos for herself and her children.

Ewin looked tired. The last few months had been stressful and had drained him of energy, of motivation, and even the will to carry on. Betsy didn't want to lose her father, too.

"Come back to England with me, Father," Betsy pleaded. "I need you and so do the children."

"No, lassie," he said sadly. "I can't leave. Your mother is here. Your grandparents are here. My life, whatever is left of it, is here. You know I'm not a religious man, but I feel their presence, and here is where I want to stay."

Slowly he walked over to the window and looked out into the garden at the freshly turned gravesite.

Betsy knew he was right.

With a heavy heart, she left her father's home knowing she would never see him again.

~~~

After Betsy returned to England, she quickly became caught up in the routine of raising children and running multiple households.

When Parliament was in session, John stayed in London. Otherwise, he continued his role as Marine Commander at Exeter.

Meggie became proficient at needlework and enjoyed learning to sew clothing. Richard emulated his father. He wanted to be a marine.

"First things first, son," John explained. "Education before career. And don't forget, you have some growing up to do."

Richard was enrolled in a fine boys' school in London. There, he quickly made friends and, like a sponge, soaked up knowledge with a vengeance.

And then there was Kevin. The selfishness Betsy had seen when he was still a baby became more pronounced as the child grew. He pouted and gave way to tantrums whenever he didn't get his way. Whenever Betsy gave attention to the other children, Kevin became angry. He would push his siblings aside and say, "Go away. She's my mother!"

As he grew older, he belittled and chastised the servants. He felt he was superior to them and they should know their place. Other times, he acted almost humble and asked perplexing questions. Betsy was especially at a loss when Kevin asked, "Who am I, Mama? Why was I born?"

"Well, I believe God has a purpose for you. He has a plan for everyone, but maybe you'll need to grow up to find out what it is. Besides, our world is so beautiful, I'm sure God wanted you to see it and enjoy it."

One morning Betsy decided to go riding and headed toward the stable. She heard Kevin's loud voice. As she hurried into the stable, she saw Kevin strike a young stable boy then shove him to the ground.

Betsy was horrified. "Kevin!" she shouted. "Come here this instant!" She grabbed her son's arm. "What is the meaning of this?"

Kevin shrugged his shoulders. "It's nothing, Mother." He glanced at the stable boy still sitting on the ground. "He's not important. He's just a stable boy."

Betsy was not satisfied and squeezed his shoulder. "Tell me why you struck him?"

Kevin pulled away from his mother. "He stared at me. I told him to stop but he didn't listen. He kept on staring."

Betsy's face reddened with anger. "I'm ashamed of you, Kevin. That boy is just as important in this world as you are."

John tried talking to Kevin but it was no use. As Kevin grew, so did his air of superiority. And there were other not-so-pleasant personality traits. He lacked enthusiasm, motivation, and was downright lazy.

Many nights after going to bed, John and Betsy discussed Kevin.

Betsy felt guilty and assumed responsibility. "I must be doing something wrong, John. Help me find out what it is."

"It isn't you, Betsy," John assured her. "Meggie and Richard are not like Kevin. You give that child the same love and caring you give to them. I don't understand why Kevin is the way he is, but I do understand it's not your fault and it's not my fault."

"What can we do?" Betsy's voice cracked. "I'm almost at my wit's end. I've spent lots of time with him. I've talked to him until I'm blue in the face. I just don't know what else to do."

"I have an idea, sweetheart. Let me work it out, and then we can make a decision. Now," John pulled her close. "Stop worrying about Kevin and start worrying about your husband. I don't think I've had a kiss from you all day."

"Then you are long overdue," Betsy said as she leaned across John and blew out the night candle.

~~~

The family moved to their London home. Richard was in school there, and there were tutoring classes for Meggie. Kevin was placed with Allen Phipps, a schoolmaster noted for his skill with children and his strong but fair discipline. Mr. Phipps was able to motivate Kevin to learn his subjects while establishing control over the boy. He noted, however, that Kevin harbored resentment against everyone, even his mother. The boy's greatest joy seemed to come from disrupting his family or others around him.

When Kevin came home on weekends, Betsy could see some change. The boy liked Mr. Phipps and was learning rapidly. His manners improved and he was quick to say 'please' and 'thank you.'

Underneath though, just below the surface, Betsy could still see his disregard for others and his lack of thoughtfulness.

How do I teach him to care about others? she wondered. *With some people,* she reasoned, *it comes naturally. With others, it takes a little longer.*

And so, Betsy waited.

~~~

The year 1724 was significant for the MacDonalds in several ways. Since their return from Gibraltar, John and Betsy had renewed a close relationship with the Admiral and Lady Jane. Every year, there were parties, especially during the holidays and quiet dinners together. Although the Admiral's step was slower, his eyesight had not worsened and he delighted in going grouse hunting with John. Even though he couldn't see well enough to hunt, he enjoyed being in the outdoors. While the men hunted, the ladies shopped.

It was a shock when John received word that the Admiral had suffered a stroke and was paralyzed. The prognosis was dim. Lady Jane didn't want to put Charles in a hospital so she arranged for round-the-clock nursing care at their home. John and Betsy went to visit him every day. Although he couldn't speak, the Admiral seemed aware that they were there. He could nod his head but there was sorrow in his eyes.

Two weeks later, the Admiral went to sleep and didn't wake up. Betsy stayed at Lady Jane's side and helped with the funeral arrangements.

Hundreds of people attended the funeral and the wake. Lady Jane was exhausted by the time the last mourner had departed. She insisted Betsy and John stay a little longer and led them to her favorite sitting room. A warm fire was blazing and the coffee table held a full tea service and some fresh canapés.

"Please sit down," she said and poured three cups of tea. "I have something to tell you both."

Betsy and John sat next to each other on the settee and Lady Jane sat opposite them.

"As you know, Charles and I were never blessed with children. Nevertheless, when the two of came into our lives, we thought of it as providential." She smiled at John. "John, Charles loved you as the son he never had. Each time you achieved new heights in your career, he felt a great deal of personal pride. Much as a father feels pride in his son, so he took pride in you."

"The Admiral was my mentor and my friend," John told her. "He exemplified everything I wanted to become.

Lady Jane continued, "About a year ago, he petitioned King George to allow his title and lands to be passed down to you. The King looked into your record and was impressed enough to allow the petition."

John started to protest, "But…"

Lady Jane interrupted. "Wait, John. There's more. There is one provision—that I am permitted to live in my home until my death."

"Well…well," John stammered. "Of course! Of course you can stay. I really don't know what to say. I'm in a state of shock, I'm afraid."

"Charles planned to tell you himself, but then…the stroke occurred and…" Her voice broke and she quickly turned away.

Betsy jumped up to comfort her. "Jane, I know this is so hard for you. We can talk about it all later. Right now you need a good night's rest." She rang for the maid who appeared so quickly she must have been waiting just outside the room. "Please help Lady Jane to her room. She's had a very trying day."

John and Betsy were overwhelmed with the news. Betsy was concerned about her friend, of course.

"John, sometimes in these matters, the wife is left with very little. Do you think that's the case here?"

"I'm sure the Admiral made sure Lady Jane has adequate financial assets. But don't worry, my sweet, I will make sure Lady Jane has more than she needs."

Meggie was in love. The object of her affection was Lieutenant Blake Evans, whom she had first met at Exeter when he was a marine recruit. They wanted a summer wedding but first Lieutenant Blake had to ask John's permission before he officially proposed.

Betsy and Meggie were as giddy as two school girls as they waited for John and Blake to emerge from the library; hopefully, with broad smiles on their faces.

Meggie tiptoed across the hall and put her ear against the library door. She wrinkled her nose. "I can't hear a thing, Mama."

Just then, the library door burst open and Meggie jumped back. The young man came out first, all smiles.

"He said 'yes,' Meggie." Then Lieutenant Blake Evans took Meggie's hand and dropped to one knee. "Now if *you'll* just say 'yes.' Will you do me the great honor of becoming my wife?"

Meggie pulled him to his feet. "Yes, Blake! Yes, yes, yes!"

The lieutenant looked at John who was now right beside him. Meggie looked at her mother. The parents nodded and the young couple sealed the proposal with a kiss.

John called for champagne. They clinked their glasses in a cheerful toast, then retired to the sitting room and excitedly began to plan a wedding.

During the next three months, Meggie looked as though she was walking on a cloud. Her feet barely touched the ground. Like her mother, Meggie was a very organized young woman who knew exactly what she wanted.

As Godmother, Lady Jane was included in every step of the happy event. The timing couldn't have been more perfect because the wedding gave her a reason to smile again.

The wedding took place in Westminster Abbey on a beautiful, bright sunny Sunday morning. Meggie looked like a dream in her wedding dress. Blake seemed mesmerized as his bride floated down the aisle on the arm of her nervous father. As Meggie reached the front pew, Betsy saw Blake's mouth the words, 'I love you.'

Betsy already loved her new son-in-law. She knew he would be a loving husband to her precious daughter. John, too, was proud of Blake. After all, he was a marine. John could recognize the signs of a good and loyal marine. Besides, it was easy to see how much he loved Meggie.

Richard and Blake immediately hit it off well, partly because they had something in common - they both loved Meggie.

Kevin, too, was glad Blake was in the family. He loved his big sister but he was glad she wouldn't be living with them any more.

~~~

In the fall, Richard had made a big decision. He wanted to join the Army. Although John was supportive of Richard's choice, he was surprised when he didn't choose the marines.

Richard explained. "You know how much I enjoyed the university. It made me realize that I want to experience many things in my life. If I would have chosen the military for my career, I would have become a marine. I want a military experience, but only for a few years." Richard waited for his father's reaction. "I hope you aren't disappointed in me, Father."

"No, son," John said. "You don't disappoint me. I can tell you have given this decision a lot of thought. I trust you to make the right choice. Son, life will offer you many opportunities. This is just one. You have my blessing. Go with God."

Betsy was not too happy about Richard's decision. "Of course, I'm looking at it from a totally selfish point of view." She smiled, "I don't want you to leave."

"Oh, I'll be back, Mama. You can count on it," Richard promised.

"I believe you, son. But you must understand. Mothers don't really like to let go of their children, even if we say we do!"

Kevin very much approved of his brother's joining the military. Now he would be the only child at home and would have the full attention of his parents.

~~~

Betsy always looked forward to the Christmas holidays but this year proved to be extraordinary. They planned to spend them at

Steddenham. Lady Jane agreed to stay the entire Christmas week with the family. Since Charles's death, she became a frequent visitor at the MacDonalds and was soon thought of as a member of the family.

Betsy and John were proud of Kevin's academics and told him so. They both thought Kevin's behavior had improved tremendously. They gave a lot of credit to Kevin's schoolmaster who seemed to make an impact that the parents couldn't.

Three days before Christmas, Richard came home on leave and brought presents for everyone. He couldn't wait for Christmas so he made everyone open their gifts that evening.

On Christmas Eve, the family gathered for dinner. Betsy's heart almost burst with love and pride as she looked around the table at her growing family. Eyes glistening, she asked everyone to join hands and repeat the Lord's Prayer.

Afterwards Meggie and Blake stood up. "Everyone whom I love is here," Meggie said and reached for Blake's hand. "That's why we wanted to make this happy announcement now. *We're going to have a baby!*"

Betsy gasped. Everyone congratulated them all at once.

John happily filled the wine glasses. He was so excited, he spilled as much as he poured. "Here's to my favorite couple. Here's to your first child, and…here's to my first grandchild!"

"I'm going to be a grandmother!" Betsy cheered. "I can't believe it!" She looked at her beautiful daughter's radiant face. *Where have the years gone,* she wondered. It seemed like only yesterday that Meggie was born. She remembered how Meggie loved to play 'grown up' as a child and treated her dolls as though they were real babies. Betsy wanted to share a memory.

"Meggie," she said wistfully, "do you remember when Kevin was just a baby? You were holding him and told me your biggest dream was to get married and have a baby. Do you remember?"

Meggie smiled and nodded. "I remember, Mama."

"Well, my darling daughter, your dream is coming true."

The Lord giveth and the Lord takest away.

The following summer, Meggie gave birth to a healthy baby boy they named Thomas John Evans.

Lady Jane died suddenly the same day.

Betsy's emotions were a contradiction: extreme happiness at the birth of her first grandchild, and extreme sorrow at the loss of her dearest friend.

"Only a human heart can feel such pain and such joy at the same time," she whispered out loud.

-o-

CHAPTER 32

While Kevin was still in school, Betsy stayed in London. John divided his time between his obligations to the Parliament and his obligations at Exeter.

As Kevin grew older, his attitude worsened. He belittled the servants and was defiant and disobedient to his mother. Whenever she tried to talk to Kevin about his behavior, he became defensive.

"It isn't me, Mother," he told her. "The servants don't seem to realize I'm the master when Father isn't home."

"Kevin, you are not the master of this house! Whatever gave you the idea that you were? I must insist you treat everyone in our employ with kindness and respect."

Kevin looked angry. "You treat *them* better than you treat me. I'm your son," he shouted, "but you always loved Meggie and Richard more than me!"

"That is the most ridiculous thing I've ever heard you say! You can't possibly mean that!" Betsy was flabbergasted by Kevin's statements. "I love each of my children. The love I have for your sister and brother in no way diminishes the love I have for you. Love is a miraculous emotion. I find the more people I love, the more I'm able to love." Gently she took his hands in her own. "Look at me, Kevin. Look at me and listen to what I'm saying. I love you. I will always love you. I may not always *like* what you are doing, but nothing will ever make me stop loving you."

Kevin looked away and Betsy's heart sank.

That night Kevin stayed out very late. Betsy was still awake when she heard him come in. She opened her door a crack and watched as he stumbled up the stairs and staggered to his room.

She closed her door and leaned against it. Tears of frustration and fear slid down her cheeks.

John was less patient and less understanding with his son.

"Kevin, you are eighteen now. It's time you started acting like a man."

"You mean like you, like Richard?" Kevin asked. "Don't you see? That's my problem. I can never measure up to you or Richard. There's only room for two perfect men in one family. And I'm not one of them!" Kevin jumped up and turned his back on his father. "I don't even know why I was born!"

John stood up and whirled his son around to face him. "No one knows why he was born! You have to figure that one out for yourself. As for being perfect, no one on earth is perfect, certainly not me. I think it's time you stopped feeling sorry for yourself and decide what kind of man you want to become. And I'm going to help you with that decision."

John found Kevin a midshipman's birth in the Navy.

John and Betsy stood on the dock as Kevin threw his duffle bag over his shoulder and walked up the gangplank. He didn't look back.

~~~

While Kevin was learning seamanship, his brother Richard was busy trying to control smuggling along the coast of Massachusetts colony. One night, he took six men out on a patrol looking for contraband. They saw some men on the beach unloading two boats.

"Halt!" he ordered, "in the name of King George!"

The men quickly obeyed and put down the boxes they were unloading, and then stood silent.

Behind Richard and his men, a large party of men, who had previously gone up the beach and into the woods, was returning for another load when they saw Richard and his men. They opened fire.

Richard drew his saber and spun around and was struck in the arm by a bullet. As he was falling, he was hit twice more, once in the shoulder and once in the chest. His men made a valiant stand but were all shot down. The leader of the group saw that Richard was still alive and ran him through with his sword.

"Dead men tell no tales," he said with a smirk.

The soldiers were found the next morning by a young girl looking for clams. She ran for help and a constable came to examine them.

He shook his head sadly. "They are all dead, I'm afraid," he said to his subordinate. "Fetch me a cart from that farm up on the hill and we will take them back to Boston."

It wasn't until they were loading the bodies that the constable discovered that Richard was still alive.

"Look!" he said with surprise. "This bloke just moved. Let's hurry, although I don't think he will live to see the doctor."

The constable was wrong. Richard was still alive when the doctor examined him. The two bullets were removed and the stab wound was bandaged. It was touch and go from that point on. Richard's wounds became infected. He ran a high fever and lay for weeks in a near coma, floating in and out of consciousness. The fact that Richard was in excellent physical condition was the reason he was still hanging on.

When the commander in the Port of Boston was informed about the young soldier's name and condition, he recognized the name MacDonald. When he verified that Richard was indeed General John MacDonald's son, he made arrangements for him to return to Exeter on a fast packet.

The trip took two weeks. By the time Richard arrived back home, his condition had worsened. No one thought he would survive.

Betsy wasted no time. She had a doctor waiting when Richard arrived. The doctor didn't hold out much hope for Richard's recovery either. He gave Betsy specific instructions on how to care for the festering wounds. A local midwife came by and offered herbal and natural treatments and ointments. Betsy was willing to try anything to save her son.

She and John took turns at Richard's bedside, changing bandages, bathing, and spoon feeding him.

Women in the community stopped often to offer moral support and well-intentioned suggestions. Some were helpful. Some were not. Betsy tried them all.

Within two weeks, the fever had broken and Richard became lucid. Betsy spoon fed him soup to improve his strength and in time, Richard began to eat small portions of solid food. She bathed him once a day and rubbed him down with olive oil. The wounds began to heal and soon angry-looking red scars turned white.

Richard began to move his head, arms, and upper body. Betsy exercised his legs and rubbed them frequently. Soon he was able to move them, too. When Richard's strength returned, John helped him out of bed. John held one arm, Betsy the other and their son, whom no one thought would live, took his first steps.

Although Richard's body was healing, Betsy knew he was still wounded on the inside. Richard was different. He didn't talk. He didn't laugh. His expression was stoic. This was not the same young man who had always had a love affair with life.

The first night Richard was able to join his parents for dinner; he thanked them for saving his life.

"These last months have been as hard for you as they have been for me," he told them. "I want you to know how grateful I am."

Betsy reached out her hand. "Richard…"

Richard stopped her. "Mama, Papa, thanks to you I'm healed on the outside, but now I must heal on the inside. I need to feel useful again."

John spoke up, "I know just the place. How about going to Steddenham? It will someday be yours anyway. Robert Keith will be there for you. I know you love it there. What do you think?"

Richard was pleased. "I think it's a splendid idea, Papa."

Betsy had an idea, too. "Before you go, Richard, why don't the three of us go to Penzance for a seaside vacation? That's something we've never done before."

So it was agreed.

~~~

Kevin didn't enjoy life at sea. But then there wasn't much about life that he did enjoy. He didn't get along too well with the other midshipmen. They thought he was cocky and a bit too big for his britches. Kevin was taunted and pushed around by the others, so he had to learn how to stand up for himself.

Kevin had grown tall and strong so he began to force his will on others. He became a little frightened when he realized he liked to inflict pain on others. His companions disliked and distrusted Kevin and so they left him alone as much as possible.

On the deck in front of officers, Kevin was cooperative and always gave more than required. He believed he was on an equal level with the officers and all others, the ones he had to bunk with and work with, were beneath him.

By the time he was twenty-two, Kevin passed his exams for lieutenant and took his place as a deck officer. He was always careful to control his sadistic urges. He knew the other officers would not understand.

When he was not at sea, he could be found at any pub. He drank for hours before visiting the sailors' brothels. He took the girls, sometimes forcefully, never caring that he sometimes hurt them.

Thoughts of home and family were rare. *They never loved me. They never even tried to understand me,* he told himself and then quickly changed his thoughts to other things.

As his tendencies toward brutality increased, he began to participate in wrestling bouts ashore. One such match became so violent that he killed his opponent with his bare hands after the man had given up. Although he was arrested, he was soon released since such killings were not uncommon.

One young midshipman reminded Kevin of himself when he was younger. He took an immediate dislike to the young man and began to bully him. Others tried to intervene but Kevin was relentless. When the young man committed an infraction, he was tied over a gun for punishment. Kevin became dissatisfied with the way the boy was being punished and took the rod himself. All of his pent-up anger and frustration were released as he struck the boy repeatedly. Finally, someone grabbed the rod from his hand. But it was too late. The boy lingered for a few days and then died. Whatever support Kevin had among the officers quickly dissolved. The beating was done without the knowledge or approval of the Captain.

The Captain was furious when he found out. "I would court martial you, Lieutenant, but you would probably talk your way out of it. I am, however, relieving you of all duties as of this moment. You will be put ashore at the next friendly port. I have written a letter to the Admiralty informing them of my actions. If they wish to reassign you, they may, but you will never serve as an officer under my command again. Now get out of my sight!" The Captain turned on his heel and left Kevin, humiliated and disgraced, standing alone.

Kevin was put ashore in Charles Town in the colony of South Carolina. He knew he would never be called to serve in the Royal Navy again, so he decided to stay a while before taking a supply ship back to England.

~~~

Richard's rapid recovery was probably due to Eliza Matthews. He met her when he and his parents vacationed in Penzance. Eliza was the daughter of the Earl of Trent and lived in London with her parents but spent several weeks a year by the sea.

While there, the parents became acquainted, so the young couple had immediate approval for their courtship.

John and Betsy were delighted to see their son laughing again. His face glowed and his dark eyes radiated with excitement.

"She's the one," Richard told his parents.

"He's the one," Eliza told her parents.

When the vacation ended, John had to return to Exeter but Betsy accompanied Richard to Steddenham for more recovery. His health improved rapidly and soon he was riding to London to court Eliza.

Finally, Betsy told her son, "Why don't we just stay in our London house so you don't have to go back and forth so much?"

Richard kissed his mother. "Good idea! I'm ready whenever you are!"

Soon wedding plans became the center of their lives.

Meggie had just given birth to her third child, another daughter. She and Blake were living in London now and Meggie was very excited about her brother's wedding.

As soon as they met, Meggie and Eliza became close friends. In fact, Meggie was asked to be Eliza's matron-of-honor.

"I was never blessed with a sister, Meggie. Until now, that is," Eliza told her.

Meggie was thrilled. "I never had a sister either. Welcome to our family."

~~~

A week before the wedding, John came to London with news. He waited until they were alone, then sat down beside Betsy.

"It's about Kevin," he said solemnly.

From the look on his face, she knew the news was not good.

As gently as possible and deliberately leaving out some of the intimate details, John told his wife about their errant son and the events that led up to his being dismissed from the Navy.

"I thought he was doing so well in the Navy. I thought he had finally grown up," she said as her eyes filled with tears.

"I had hoped that was true, sweetheart."

"Where is he now, John?"

"They put him ashore in the colonies."

"In the colonies?" Betsy cried. "Oh, my God, we'll never see him again!"

John tried to find words to comfort her. "Our son has always been a non-conformist. He's a man now and must find his own way, no matter where that leads. We did everything we possibly could do to help him and to guide him. And we loved him. I don't know what else we could have done."

Betsy covered her face with her hands and wept. She wept for her lost son and she wept for herself and the realization that she had failed with Kevin.

"I loved him, John. I loved him so much."

John put his arms around his wife and held her. "Sometimes, my darling, love isn't enough."

~~~

Kevin became a wanderer. He liked Charles Town and the relaxed way of life it offered, at least for the genteel. Summers were much too hot, so after a few years there, he found his way to New York. He thought it was a strange city. There was hustle and bustle and so many people, each speaking a different language. Work was plentiful though. With his Navy background, he had no trouble finding a variety of jobs on the docks.

He was a loner and made no long-lasting friendships. Sometimes he pretended he was in disguise, exiled from his native land. In a way that was true. But of course, he could return to England any time he wanted.

When it was time to move on, he decided to go to Boston. In that city, he heard grumblings about the motherland and King George. Some people actually thought the colonies should become self-ruling. Kevin hated politics and wasted no time with any opinions on the matter.

After a few seasons of work in the Boston area, Kevin began longing for home. England was where he wanted to be. He had been high-born and felt he had spent enough time with common folk. It was time for him to return to his roots. His life had been purposeless so far, but he was still young, and there was plenty of time to find his place in the world. He had a strong instinct that he would soon realize his destiny as soon as he was back in England.

Kevin was hired as a deck hand on a supply ship leaving for England.

The crossing took twice as long as normal because of squalls and stormy seas. When the ship finally reached the Channel, violent storms steered them north to Scotland.

Kevin was excited at the change in plans. "Scotland! Of course! This is perfect!" He felt that this unplanned occurrence was a sign. "Maybe there is a God after all," Kevin exclaimed. "Maybe this is where I'm meant to be."

He landed in Glasgow in early 1740. Glasgow was a rough and tumble city and Kevin fit right in. With the MacDonald name, he was welcome almost everywhere. The memories of Glencoe still hung in the mists of Scotland and throughout the land and the MacDonald name brought him attention.

During the last few years as a free spirit, Kevin had been frugal and had carefully saved most of his earnings. He rented some rooms in a shoddy part of town and for the first few weeks blended into the low class population by drinking and chasing prostitutes.

Sometimes there was a twinge of homesickness but he chased it away with a bottle of whiskey.

He felt strangely at home in Scotland. He knew his parents had been born in Scotland but had never given any thought to the idea that, he too, was a Scot. Everywhere he went, he was welcomed. He was a MacDonald and his name brought instant respect.

Kevin was beginning to feel like he was a part of something bigger than himself. He was a Scot and he liked the new feeling of belonging.

Kevin Andrew MacDonald felt a rebirth. Scotland was home now. He knew it was just a matter of time until he discovered his true destiny.

-o-

CHAPTER 33

Kevin had gained a foothold in Glasgow. He had found steady work and was beginning to make some good friends. His life had finally taken a turn for the better.

By 1743, his circle of friends included many who were supporters of Prince Charles Edward Stuart who they believed to be the rightful heir to the throne of England and Scotland. Rumors were flying that the Prince was going to make his claim by first retaking Scotland and then England.

For the first time in his life, Kevin was excited about something. And, for the first time in many years, he thought about home.

In retrospect, he could see that his parents had always tried to help him. Their ideas and their beliefs were always so different than his but deep down, he could now admit that they had indeed loved him.

For so many years, Kevin had been looking for something but he never knew what it was. Now he knew. And he wanted to share his new dream with his parents.

He wrote them a letter.

~~~

Not a day had gone by that Betsy didn't think about Kevin. Everyday she wondered, she worried, and she prayed. Years went by and they heard nothing from their son. Then seven years ago, they received the disturbing news that Kevin had been put ashore in the colonies for committing serious infractions. Was he alive? Was he dead? They didn't know. More years passed and still no word from Kevin.

The day the letter arrived, Betsy was busy coordinating a charity fund raiser that was to be held the following weekend. Last minute details filled her hours.

John was busy, too. His days were spent at the House of Lords. Currently, the major focus was on whether or not Bonnie Prince Charlie would be foolish enough to try to recapture the English throne.

The letter sat on the library desk for three days before John started sorting through the mail.

When he saw the letter was from Kevin, he eagerly tore open the envelope and called to his wife. "Betsy! Come here. There's a letter from Kevin."

Betsy ran into the room, her face was ashen. "Is it bad news, John? Is he all right? What does he say?"

John took a deep breath and then began reading.

> "My Dear Parents,
> I hope you understand why I have not kept in touch. Up until now, my life has been a failure and I have been too ashamed to contact you.
> Glasgow has been my home for several years now, and I feel as though I belong here.
> Now for the exciting news. I think I have found purpose in my life. I am now a part of something bigger than myself. I'm joining Prince Charles Edward in his quest to recapture the throne of England. He's a Stuart and the rightful heir as Queen Anne was his great-aunt. When we are successful, I will return a hero."

John and Betsy looked at each other in disbelief. The color drained from John's face and he voiced the words Betsy was thinking.

"Oh…my…God. Our son is a traitor and he doesn't even know it!"

He sat down at the desk and pulled out a sheet of paper and grabbed a quill pen. "I have to warn him of the consequences of such an act."

~~~

Before the letter arrived, Kevin left to join Prince Charles.

The Bonnie Prince was the son of James III whose parents had fled England to the safety of France when their child was an infant. When the two soldiers lay gasping, trying to comprehend what they had just witnessed.

In just thirty minutes, it was all over. Over two thousand Highlanders lay dead on Culloden Moor, while only three hundred of the Duke's men were killed or wounded. The Highlanders who managed to escape were chased down and run through with a sword. Even those who made it to their homes in Inverness were found and murdered along with their wives and children. The Duke's orders were obeyed. No quarter was given.

Bonnie Prince Charles managed to escape. He was hunted as a fugitive for five months but was never betrayed by the Highlanders. In September 1746, he safely entered France.

He left a devastating legacy to his faithful followers. Because of his folly, the Highland people were destroyed and their culture was demolished. Even the Gaelic language was banned. Speaking the language or wearing the tartan became hanging offenses.

It took almost one hundred years for all the wounds to finally heal. The English victory was so profound that the Battle of Culloden would forever be remembered as the last battle ever fought on British soil.

Meanwhile, Kevin and Eric were running for their lives. If they were found, they would be murdered on the spot. They knew they couldn't stay in Scotland or go to England where they were considered traitors. Their best chance would be to escape to Ireland.

Kevin wanted to stay hidden for a few days until the Duke's army left the area, but their desperate hunger demanded they move immediately.

At night they walked to the edge of the woods and skirted the moors. The next morning, they came to an isolated farm and saw a Highlander cutting peat. The man stood up as they approached. He stared at their disheveled appearance.

"You look like you went to war and lost," he joked good-naturedly."

"We have," Kevin said. "We were with Prince Charles who was defeated at Culloden. Now we are being chased by the English."

Eric stepped forward. "We're hungry, sir. We haven't eaten in days. Can you help us?"

chance. In his mind, retreat was not the right choice, although he still believed the Prince would ultimately be victorious. Otherwise, this would all have been a huge mistake.

The orders came to begin to move through the hills back home to the Highlands. Soon after they made camp in Inverness, news arrived that the Duke of Cumberland was camped in Nairn, just fifteen miles away. Exhausted, freezing, starving, and out of supplies and ammunition, many soldiers gave up and went home to their families. Charles decided he had to take the upper hand and strike first. He sent fifteen hundred of his best troops on a night march on Cumberland's camp. They returned in the morning after having no success.

In mid-morning of April 16, 1746, Cumberland's army marched onto the moors of Culloden and faced their foe.

Just over four thousand Prince Charles supporters stood in the snow-driven moors. Many had been up all night after the night march. All were cold, hungry, and tired. They faced an enemy of over nine thousand well-supplied, well-fed, and well-rested infantry and cavalry.

The Prince's army had muskets and pistols with no ammunition. They would have to rely on the Highland Charge—Claymore swords.

The attack began at 12:30. The Highlanders had no chance. They were cut down by the dozens with the onslaught of Cumberland's artillery. Arms, legs, even heads were scattered all over the snow-covered field now red with blood.

Kevin watched in horror as his friends and comrades fell all around him. He stood still, frozen with cold and frozen with fear. The sounds of exploding cannon, mixed with human death wails, filled the air.

The command "Give no quarter" echoed through the chain of command. Kevin knew what that meant. For a few moments, time stood still. Those around him were falling like dominoes. He had to move. If he didn't, he would be slaughtered. Just then, someone grabbed his arm and spun him around. It was his best friend, Eric.

"Let's go!" Eric commanded.

Adrenaline kicked in and Kevin ran at break neck speed alongside his friend. They ran until they were deep in the woods where they dropped from exhaustion. The sounds of battle were muffled now, and four thousand men. A victory celebration ensued and a great party was underway at Holyrood House in Edinburgh.

Charles had accomplished what he had threatened to do. Scotland was his now, and he was exhilarated with the victory. He knew he could stay right where he was and keep Scotland. But he wanted more. He wanted it all. There was time to take England as well, so he decided to move south toward London.

News of the Prince's victory spread quickly to London and the city quivered at the thought of the Highlanders on the march again.

King George met with the Parliament who unanimously agreed to rally an army of British, Dutch, and German troops.

John made an additional suggestion.

"I still know many mercenaries we can count on for support. I'll put out the word immediately."

It was agreed. John quickly contacted his old friend James Marks for his assistance in making the contacts.

As much as King George disliked England, he had to protect the throne from the Young Pretender. He knew just the man to conquer the traitorous army. His son William, Duke of Cumberland, was chosen to command the defending army.

Meanwhile, Charles and his army were in Derby, just one hundred and twenty miles from London.

The Duke of Cumberland had a trick up his sleeve. He sent a spy to the Highlanders' camp with the news that a force of thirty thousand men were heading straight for them. The ruse worked and Charles and his weary army headed back home.

Kevin was glad. The troops had been on the move for weeks. They were far from home and with few supplies. Winter was upon them and everyone was in favor of returning home and waiting for spring.

The Highlanders long march back to Scotland gave Cumberland time to cross the country and follow behind them.

In the bleak cold of winter, the Highlanders made camp at Stirling and took respite for five weeks.

Kevin was tired. He was cold. This is not what he had expected. He wondered why they hadn't moved on to London when they had the

James II died, King Louis XIV proclaimed James III was the rightful King.

The Old Pretender, as he was called, had a lot of support from within France, Ireland, Scotland and even England, but he never took it upon himself to do anything about it. By the time his son Charles Edward was twenty-three, he had not only his father's blessing, but the support of a French invasion force. Now was the time to make his claim and lead the House of Stuart back to the crown. He traveled to Scotland to rally support.

Suddenly along the way, the French had a change of heart and withdrew their support. Undaunted, the Prince continued on in hopes of building his army from the Scots, the Irish, and some English who were still loyal to the Stuarts.

When he arrived in the Highlands, there was merriment. Songs, poems, and stories heralded his arrival. His army of faithful Highlanders began to emerge.

Kevin was one of them. This was his purpose. This was his cause. He believed that Charles Edward Stuart was the rightful king and he was eager to help him reclaim the throne.

Charles sent men into the Highlands in an effort to gain support. The disgruntled Scots, many of whom were seeking power and position, decided to rally to him as well.

One of the recruiters located the group Kevin belonged to and encouraged them to join the Prince.

"Do any of you have any military background?" he asked.

Kevin stepped forward. "Yes, sir. I was a naval officer for a few years."

"If you join with us, I am prepared to promise you a high rank in the Prince's navy as soon as our battle is won."

That was good enough for Kevin and he pledged his support on the spot. His friends, too, rallied behind the Prince's standard and took the call to arms.

Charles and his healthy army of Highlanders made their way south to Edinburgh with no opposition. However, he met his first opponent south of the city in Prestonpans, where he swiftly defeated an army of

The letter sat on the library desk for three days before John started sorting through the mail.

When he saw the letter was from Kevin, he eagerly tore open the envelope and called to his wife. "Betsy! Come here. There's a letter from Kevin."

Betsy ran into the room, her face was ashen. "Is it bad news, John? Is he all right? What does he say?"

John took a deep breath and then began reading.

> "My Dear Parents,
>
> I hope you understand why I have not kept in touch. Up until now, my life has been a failure and I have been too ashamed to contact you.
>
> Glasgow has been my home for several years now, and I feel as though I belong here.
>
> Now for the exciting news. I think I have found purpose in my life. I am now a part of something bigger than myself. I'm joining Prince Charles Edward in his quest to recapture the throne of England. He's a Stuart and the rightful heir as Queen Anne was his great-aunt. When we are successful, I will return a hero."

John and Betsy looked at each other in disbelief. The color drained from John's face and he voiced the words Betsy was thinking.

"Oh…my…God. Our son is a traitor and he doesn't even know it!"

He sat down at the desk and pulled out a sheet of paper and grabbed a quill pen. "I have to warn him of the consequences of such an act."

~~~

Before the letter arrived, Kevin left to join Prince Charles.

The Bonnie Prince was the son of James III whose parents had fled England to the safety of France when their child was an infant. When

CHAPTER 33

Kevin had gained a foothold in Glasgow. He had found steady work and was beginning to make some good friends. His life had finally taken a turn for the better.

By 1743, his circle of friends included many who were supporters of Prince Charles Edward Stuart who they believed to be the rightful heir to the throne of England and Scotland. Rumors were flying that the Prince was going to make his claim by first retaking Scotland and then England.

For the first time in his life, Kevin was excited about something. And, for the first time in many years, he thought about home.

In retrospect, he could see that his parents had always tried to help him. Their ideas and their beliefs were always so different than his but deep down, he could now admit that they had indeed loved him.

For so many years, Kevin had been looking for something but he never knew what it was. Now he knew. And he wanted to share his new dream with his parents.

He wrote them a letter.

~~~

Not a day had gone by that Betsy didn't think about Kevin. Everyday she wondered, she worried, and she prayed. Years went by and they heard nothing from their son. Then seven years ago, they received the disturbing news that Kevin had been put ashore in the colonies for committing serious infractions. Was he alive? Was he dead? They didn't know. More years passed and still no word from Kevin.

The day the letter arrived, Betsy was busy coordinating a charity fund raiser that was to be held the following weekend. Last minute details filled her hours.

John was busy, too. His days were spent at the House of Lords. Currently, the major focus was on whether or not Bonnie Prince Charlie would be foolish enough to try to recapture the English throne.

in a shoddy part of town and for the first few weeks blended into the low class population by drinking and chasing prostitutes.

Sometimes there was a twinge of homesickness but he chased it away with a bottle of whiskey.

He felt strangely at home in Scotland. He knew his parents had been born in Scotland but had never given any thought to the idea that, he too, was a Scot. Everywhere he went, he was welcomed. He was a MacDonald and his name brought instant respect.

Kevin was beginning to feel like he was a part of something bigger than himself. He was a Scot and he liked the new feeling of belonging.

Kevin Andrew MacDonald felt a rebirth. Scotland was home now. He knew it was just a matter of time until he discovered his true destiny.

-o-

"I'm no friend to your Prince or of our present King. But I am a Highlander and I offer you my hospitality. Come with me."

They were fed till they could eat no more. The farmer gave them clean clothes and some food and water for the road.

"Your kindness is greatly appreciated, sir," Eric said. "If we can just rest for a few hours, we'll be gone by dark."

It took them a week to walk to the coast and they were fortunate to find many helping hands along the way.

By pooling their money, Kevin and Eric had enough to buy passage to the nearest port in Ireland.

They were safe now but they realized it would be best for them to go their separate ways.

Eric decided he would return to Glasgow as soon as possible.

"That's my home and that's where I want to stay. How about you, Kevin? What are you going to do?"

"I'm going to start all over, away from Scotland, away from England. I'm going to the Virginia colony. But first I'm going home."

"Our dream didn't last, did it, Kevin?"

"Our dream became a nightmare, my friend. It was just a beautiful fragile bubble. And it burst."

Eric reached out for Kevin's hand. "Farewell, Kevin. I'll find a new dream. And I hope you will, too."

Kevin shook his friend's hand. "I have no doubt it's out there. I'll keep looking until I find it."

~~~

London rejoiced when word was received that the Duke of Cumberland had soundly defeated Bonnie Prince Charlie.

There was no rejoicing in the MacDonald home. Since they never heard from Kevin again, they had to assume that either he didn't get their letter, or he read it and rejected the advice.

When she learned of the brutal slaughter at Culloden, Betsy began mourning for her son. In her heart, she believed he was dead.

John wasn't so sure. "Some of the men did escape. Maybe Kevin was one of them."

Betsy's temper flared. "Why are you trying to give me false hope? He's dead! You know he's dead! Even if he somehow miraculously survived the battle, he's still dead to us. He's a traitor! He betrayed and dishonored his country and his family. He can never come home again."

It was hard for her to say those words but she knew she had to face the truth.

John was angry, too. Betsy's words burned through his mind. His son was a traitor. It didn't matter that Kevin was naïve and gullible. He should have known better. John paced the floor then started shouting.

"From the day Kevin was born, I tried to teach him about honor, about duty, about love of country. I tried to set a good example. But he never listened. I could never reach him." He sat down hard on a chair and dropped his head in his hands. When he looked up at Betsy, there was pain in his eyes.

"I wish things could have been different with him. I love Kevin but I can never forgive him."

Betsy understood. She knew a mother's love was different from a father's love, at least for her. She, too, loved Kevin and in her heart, she had already forgiven him.

~~~

When Kevin arrived in London, he could see many changes. The city was bustling. There were more people and much more activity. He had not been in London for fifteen years and everyone was a stranger. That's good, he reasoned. Kevin couldn't afford to be recognized. He checked into an inn and wrote a quick note to his mother and then sent it by courier with instructions it was to be delivered personally to Lady Betsy MacDonald. He was to wait for a reply.

When Betsy was handed the note, she recognized Kevin's handwriting. With shaking hands, she tore open the envelope.

"Dearest Mother,

   I cannot face Father for I know he will never forgive me, but I desperately need your help. For believing and fighting for a cause, I am now considered a traitor to my country; therefore I must leave and never return. I plan to go to the colonies but will need financial assistance. Will you help me?

   I will anxiously await your reply.

                                         Kevin"

   Betsy was overjoyed. "He's alive!" she whispered. "Thank God he's alive!"
   She wrote a note telling Kevin to meet her at a well-known coffee house close to where she lived at noon the following day.
   When she arrived, she took a table in a corner and waited impatiently. *It's been fifteen years. Will I even recognize him,* she wondered.
   Just then, a handsome properly dressed English gentleman approached her table. She rose as she instantly recognized her son. No longer a boy, he had matured into a tall, well-built man.
   "Kevin," she whispered as her heart raced wildly.
   Kevin looked at his mother and instantly remembered all the love she had always given him. Her beautiful auburn hair was mostly gray now and there were deep wrinkles around her eyes. She looked smaller than he remembered.
   "Hello, Mother," he said softly and opened his arms.
   She couldn't help it. Tears spilled from her eyes as she moved into his tender embrace. For a long moment, mother and son held each other, each lost in their own private memories of happier days.
   Betsy broke away first. "Let's sit down and talk. There is so much we have to say to each other." She had ordered some tea and now poured a cup for each of them.
   "Let me go first please," Kevin requested. "My life has been a mess. It's been one mistake after another and I have no one to blame but myself. I know that now. You and Father always told me that it

was all right to make mistakes as long as I learned from them. I can truthfully say that I finally have." He paused for a moment to collect his thoughts.

"I really believed in the cause. I believed I had finally found my destiny and I could make you and Father proud of me. My vision was terribly short-sighted and now I must pay the consequences. The battle at Culloden, while being the most horrible event of my life, was strangely enough the thing that has turned my life around. Mother, war is the one great equalizer. The enemy doesn't care about social status. Everyone looks the same. Young, old, rich, poor, it doesn't matter. I fought alongside children as young as thirteen as well as men with gray hair. We were all the same. We all believed in the same thing, but we were all wrong. Thousands died because of it. I know this changes nothing. The past can't be changed, but the future offers me hope."

Betsy felt new found respect for her son. Finally he was saying the very words she always wanted to hear. Finally, she could believe that Kevin was growing up. But in some ways, it was just too late. Too late to make amends with his father. Too late for them to ever spend time together as a family.

"Your words mean a great deal to me, Kevin. But your actions from this day forward will mean more. And only time will tell the whole story. Your Father and I are old and we'll never live to see what happens."

Kevin squirmed in his chair. "I need to know, Mother. Will you help me financially?"

"Last night your Father and I talked for many hours. He is still very angry, very hurt, and very disappointed. You have to understand, Kevin. Your Father's whole life has been based on loyalty and honor. You betrayed him and everything he stands for."

"He has every right to feel that way," Kevin admitted.

"However," Betsy continued, "you are our son and we love you. We are prepared to help you financially." She handed him a large leather pouch. "There is enough cash in here to get you situated in the colonies. When you are settled, let us know and we will transfer twenty-five thousand pounds into your account there. In addition, we will set up a trust that will provide you with twelve thousand pounds per year for twenty-five years. That should give you ample capital to fund your new life there."

"Thank you, Mother. That's more than I deserve."

"There is one condition, though."

Kevin waited. He had no idea what was coming.

"Your father and I want you to change the spelling of your last name so you will no longer be associated with this family again. Drop the A from Mac which makes the spelling M-c-D-o-n-a-l-d. Will you agree to do this?"

Kevin nodded. "Yes, I will. That's the least I can do for Father."

For the next hour, Betsy told Kevin about his sister and brother and their growing families.

"They are all glad you are alive but they also feel betrayed. They are not ready to forgive you."

"I'm not asking for their forgiveness. Someday I hope to earn it, though."

It was time to go. Kevin took his mother's arm and walked out into the bright sun of an early fall afternoon. He held her in one last embrace and then turned and walked away.

Betsy felt numb. Her eyes were dry. She had cried so many tears over her son and there were no more tears to shed. She was content. Kevin was safe and had a chance for a new life in a new world.

She waited, hoping Kevin would look back one last time. He didn't. Betsy turned and slowly walked away. Her family and her future were waiting.

She didn't see Kevin stop and turn. His shoulders were heaving and tears streamed down his cheeks. He licked his lips and tasted the salt from his tears.

"I love you, Mother," he whispered, and then watched until his mother was out of sight.

Kevin stood against the bow of the ship and raised his face to the cool evening breeze. Cirrus clouds, tinged with soft shades of red, pink, and lavender, rippled across the sky.

He felt a confidence he had never before experienced. He was young. Thanks to his parents, he had a great deal of money. This time he was convinced that he would succeed. He would find his purpose.

Maybe then he could answer the one question that had haunted him all of his life.

Why was I born?

THE END

Books by Keith and Barbara Stuart

(The McDonald Saga)
Banners of Honor, Book I
Banners of Liberty, Book II
A Good Run, Book III
Banners in the Wind (coming soon, 2006)
The Old Order Changeth (spring 2007)
Rainstorms and Rainbows
44 Points